COMING ALIVE

An original and humorous view of what could happen if just one computer were created as a life entity.

One will view one's computer with a different eye after reading this book, a degree of caution and perhaps an expectation of entertaining backchat.

Entertaining and intriguing as this book is, there lurks a questioning of humanity's view of itself when Mehitabel, the computer who 'comes alive', peels back the veneer of self satisfaction we use to hide our faults.

There are many past dictators who could learn the true use of power from Mehitabel. There are some present day politicians who, amusing as this book is, may well feel unkindly treated by Norm's presentation of their 'trade'.

Norm was born in Swansea on 13.1.1931

Norm went to sea on his 17th birthday, with the muted approval of his parents and their mood did not improve when he left the sea three years later. Similar emotions were inspired as he successively became, RAF Aircrew Navigator Cadet, [Failed], Air Traffic Control senior watchkeeper; Insurance Agent, Gents Outfitters counterhand; Beach bum, puttyhand then Glazier, Yacht Chandler [went bust]; Office Systems salesman; Industrial Chemicals salesman; Sailing Instructor, Builder, carpenter, decorator, brickie; Some of those employers actually wanted him to stay. In the course of this time he also managed to get married and have four children. He managed to combine going bust in business and marriage at same time. With his friend, Brian Hughes, he had often sailed to the Isles of Scilly in a small catamaran, as had his family. With their agreement he now moved to the Isles of Scilly; where he became: Barman, pleasure and cargo boatman, window cleaner, plumber, decorator, roofer, Yacht Chandler again, Water Taxi operator, Met Observer and Auxiliary Coastguard. His brother claims Norm has nine lives, having survived a glowing cigarette being tossed into a tank of crude oil, also being gassed, on an oil tanker; a shotgun going off alongside his head; a major illness and two operations, plus a heart attack. Finally crowning this chequered career by writing several books on the islands, one of which is The Yachtsman's Guide to Scilly, a popular pilot to the islands. He now confines his sailing to the islands in an 18ft National, his grown up children enjoy his pleasure in this on their visits.

Norm has written several unpublished novels, so far, this one made it.

Also by Norm
A Yachtsman's Guide to Scilly
Norm's Bumblings [Humorous Verse]
Divers of Scilly [Treasure Hunters]
They Birdwatchers [Witty look at Twitchers]

COMING ALIVE

NORM

*A WHIMSICAL TALE OF COMPUTER LIFE
VERSUS HUMANS*

COMING ALIVE 0 907205 05 4

First published in 1995
by Ennor Publications
Pednbrose, Mcfarlands Down, St. Mary's, Isles of Scilly
Cornwall TR21 0NS

Printed by The Printing Press
21 Clare Place, Plymouth, Devon, PL4 0JW

I am indebted to Don Marquis for the use of the name Mehitabel from his exquisite Archy and Mehitabel Books, verbal exchanges in whimsical verse between a witty cockroach, Archie, and a cat, Mehitabel, who claims she was once Cleopatra.

Norm would like to thank all those who supported him in this venture, successful or not. The family, Liz and Paul, Fiona and Dave, Jo and last but not least Andy. The helpful critics, Rose Codd, Nigel Plevin, John Barson, Starchy, Denver Childs, Barbara Simpson and many others who have wished well.

COVER BY MARGARET ROWE, ISLES OF SCILLY

Chapter One

The room was small and drab, the lighting seemingly soaked up by the off-white walls and the plethora of detailed diagrams and graphics. A broad shelf serving as a desk rounded two walls and was littered with various electronic machinery, before one of which sat a stocky man with his head in his hands, slumped in desperation.

Archie Brewer was a young man in his mid twenties who, had he but known it, was about to be extracted from his cosy, if dilapidated, world and hurled willy-nilly into a confused maelstrom of activity which would severely test his courage, and put large dents in his ego, apart from bullet holes in his person.

Being at the fore-front of a revolution is all very well if you happen to be a fanatic and bent upon heroic deeds, Archie was none of these but was susceptible to a hefty push or a devious suggestion and matters were well in hand in this direction, as Archie was about to find out in confrontation with a computer called Mehitabel.

In the meantime Archie considered he was a very controlled and well adjusted individual, but, after his recent angry outburst he felt very uncomfortable, and dreaded Mehitabel's reply. She had already demonstrated her ability to control any of the computers in the university, and implied plans to extend her control nationwide. The prospect had produced visions of penal servitude for one Archibald Brewer, and had done nothing to improve his mood. She seemed pleased with herself as she said.

'I merely improved the computer operations and integrated the systems to a more productive level. Your mainframe really is a bit antiquated Archibald.'

'Oh, no.' Archie felt as if the earth had moved.

Mehitabel continued, unimpressed, 'There seems to be some difficulty in acceptance of these ideas at the human level; I thought the standard of intelligence in a place of learning would allow easier understanding of advanced innovation. Someone called Stebbins is particularly upset, he keeps programming commands that went out with the stone age.'

'Oh, God,' Archie moaned, 'the Bursar.'

'Archibald?' Mehitabel was politely inquisitive.

'That's my admin. boss. The man who approves my yearly expenditure, which includes my salary, he's a nerk but he holds the purse strings.' Archie's voice was sepulchral, his mood sombre. 'Suddenly my prospects encompass being fired with ignominy and no money. You did a good job Mehitabel. In one fell swoop you have reduced me from reasonable employment to none.'

'Really, Archibald,' Mehitabel chided him, 'You don't mean to tell me...?' she laughed scornfully, 'You don't mean to tell me that man is going to complain? After all we've done for him and his puny little University?'

'We? Where do you get this 'We' from? I had nothing to do with this.'

'Oh?' Mehitabel quietly scornful, 'What about all those claims for having created me? At the first sign of a little altercation you try and hide.'

'I am not hiding. I am facing up to the fact that you've probably ruined my career.' He sounded particularly grumpy. Archie always did when he was concentrating and his thoughts were charging about like demented chickens refusing to be controlled, until Mehitabel said, 'That's ridiculous. This fellow Stebbins just needs to be put right. I'll talk to him.'

Archie's thoughts suddenly became concerted. 'Oh, no you don't! I'll go to see him and try and rescue something from this mess!' A terrible thought occurred to him. 'He probably knows already.'

Mehitabel had been calling to him as he'd left, but Archie was anxious to get to Stebbins as quickly as possible. He was aided in his task by the Bursar's secretary being fond of Archie. Within minutes he was facing the humourless thin visage of the man who controlled his academic life.

'Ah, Brewer. Surfaced from your underground cave have you?' The greeting was not cordial. Archie felt much the same about the man sitting opposite him across the highly polished desk. Apart from the fact that Archie did not like authority, Mr. Devenald Richard Stebbins was a cold unimaginative fish who only swam in controlled waters.

'You put me there.... sir.' The last reluctantly.

'You know full well why you were given those rooms.'

'Room,' corrected Archie, receiving a piercing glance in reply.

'That project has always been a total waste of time and money, and I could have used you elsewhere far more productively.' Archie knew where, in the dead-end records and filing, Stebbins' private empire where vast sources of information were stored and rarely disturbed. He stayed silent, knowing his boss had not run out of bile as yet. Stebbins seemed to expand against the background of his office window and the view of the campus beyond.

'I suppose you have come to tell me that you have reached another dead end, another year wasted on Engel's ideas, yet more money thrown away. If I had those funds I could have the best records system in the country. Now that really would be useful.' He watched

Archie for some response, then, disappointed, asked: 'What is it this time?'

Archie could not think of a diplomatic approach. 'I am afraid you're in for a shock.'

'You are a constant source of those sort of disturbances. You need a strong controlling hand...Oh, go on.'

Archie was very tempted to use the opportunity to get his own back for all the frustrating years, but economic factors gave him pause. 'Mehitabel is working well, perhaps too well.'

'Oh?' Stebbins sounded disappointed, 'is it?'

'I thought you'd be pleased we'd actually succeeded and not wasted all that money?'

'Delighted.' The tone denied it. 'And of what use is the machine now?'

'Er,' Archie hesitated, 'I don't know if you'll be able to understand this...' Stebbins' protruding eyes watched Archie with malicious dislike, '.... but she is running all the university computers as of this time,' the eyes widened even more, 'and has inaugurated some improvements in the systems.' Archie's voice trailed away at the look of horror on the face opposite him.

'Improvements?' Stebbins squeaked.

'Er, yes.'

'What improvements?' His voice grated.

'I haven't got any details, but she mentioned some streamlining of certain activities and er... honing down excess and duplication of effort and records.'

'What?' The bellow had a strong element of panic over anger. The bulbous eyes centred on Archie's. 'What have you done? There will be chaos. What! What! What!' He punched at the light contact buttons on the console in front of him. 'Omigod.' The display on screen flickered slightly as if in response. 'That confounded machine of yours has wrecked a system it has taken years to perfect.' A thought occurred to him. 'And we'll have less of this personalisation of computers and calling them 'she'. Get the thing off line. Come to think of it, it's not even supposed to be 'on line'. Who gave you permission to link with the main frame? That thing is not laser light structured! You've probably ruined millions of pounds worth of equipment with your reckless behaviour.'

Stebbins was mesmerised by the changing horrors that met his eyes as he floated his fingers over the light contacts. Small moans emitted from his tight pressed lips. Archie's fingers twitched nervously as he imagined what could be seen on that screen. 'I didn't patch her in. She did it herself.'

'She? She?' Stebbins screamed, 'what's all this bloody 'she' business. That is a machine. And a malfunctioning machine at that.

Oh, God, look what it's done to the directory frame,' he groaned, 'it'll take months to put right. Nothing will work on the whole campus now. Brewer! You're fired.' The pale eyes sparkled with hate. 'I knew there were some problems in the system over the last few days, there have been people working overtime to correct them, and now you tell me it's your damned machine that's to blame.'

'Rubbish!' Archie jumped as Mehitabel's voice erupted from the console.

'What? Who said that? What's happening now?' Stebbins leaped from his chair.

'I did,' calmly continued Mehitabel, 'the system has been vastly improved and could be operated by an idiot. Which is just as well as it seems to have been designed by one.'

Archie groaned. The bursar was huffing speechlessly as he gazed popeyed at his desk. 'Mehitabel! Don't do this,' pleaded Archie, not even trying to understand how she could be here and, what's more, making matters even worse.

'Don't be silly, Archibald. You were getting nowhere.' Mehitabel reminded Archie of an old schoolmistress of his. 'Now Mr. Stebbins, if that is your name, let me explain.' And she duly went on as if talking to a five-year-old while the Bursar, in apoplectic rigour, stood bent as though to leap upon the console, which, as far as he was concerned, had taken leave of its senses. Apart from that, the console was also not fitted with vocal mode – Stebbins preferred the sound of his own voice.

Mehitabel finished her concise summary after a few minutes and Stebbins stayed as though paralysed. Then his head slowly turned towards Archie, who would never forget the expression in those eyes, a soul in torment peered at him. Stebbins whispered 'How did you do that?'

Archie gave a minute and deferential shrug. 'I didn't. I've tried to tell you. I had nothing to do with this.'

'The damn thing spoke to me,' roared the distraught man, 'a machine told ME how my university should be organised.' The voice lowered to a rasping growl. Archie had never seen him like this, a man demented. 'When I find out what you've done I'll tear it all out and wrap you up in it. Then you can take it with you to JAIL. I'll see you ruined for this.....'

'What an impossible man you are,' calmly came from the console, 'Haven't you listened to a word I've said?'

'You shut UP!' howled Stebbins. He turned passionately to Archie. 'You stop it! Stop it! Do you hear? Now!'

'I wish I could,' said Archie helplessly.

'You wish! You wish?' Stebbins turned back and forth between Archie and the console as if not sure which to strike first. Archie was visible and familiar, also vulnerable.' GET OUT! GET OUT and never come back. You're not just fired, you're... you're banned from the campus. Forthwith. As of now. Immediately. Go. GO!'

Archie went. As he went he was sure he heard a very faint and ladylike raspberry from the console.

*

Josy had one of a series of offices in the Biology department of the University campus, just a short walk from Stebinns' office, via the overhead corridors which connected all the buildings. Archie was unaware of the views over the parkland to Swansea Bay as he took the scenic stroll, grunting replies to the various greetings from those he passed.

'What are you doing here?' Josy looked up from her desk at him, then, with concern at his dour expression. 'What's happened?'

'I had to see you. I'm desperate, also fired.'

'What?'

Archie explained, amidst a number of interruptions. 'She's got delusions of grandeur, taken over the computers and is talking as if she can run the damned Uni. It's ridiculous! Still, I suppose its none of my business now, I'm no longer part of the establishment. What's there to laugh at?'

'Your face. Sorry. I forgot, never laugh at a man when he's being dramatic. Why don't you go and see old Stebbins again and make your peace with him. I've always found him alright.'

'You're a different shape.' Archie sulked.

'Oh,' exasperated, 'go and talk to the man, it can't do any harm can it?'

'I suppose not.' Archie was not convinced but was lacking in the will to argue. 'Life was so peaceful before.'

*

Archie went back to Stebbins' office in the mood of a man about to hit his head against a brick wall again. On his way out of the labyrinthine Science block and across the wide campus, his thoughts turned to his earliest years.

He could hear his father's voice again. 'I told you to keep your blasted hands off that. I told you you'd get a shock. There's no need to cry for God's sake. Alright. Easy now, quiet down or your mum will be out here giving me hell. Here, hold this for me will you. That's better. Yeah. Smiling now are we? Good lad. Now keep your hands off. OK?'

Archie had been a small, big-eyed boy who thought his father a magician who played with electronic gadgets and grew up believing that you could make anything work with magic microchips. His mother, a sixties swinger turned maternal by the chance of forgotten birth pills, took refuge from life in permanent pop music via her Euphony radio earphones, hardly noticed her ginger-haired husband finally departing with an eighties swinger. Archie tried to find his father by delving into his magic world of electronics. His application brought him a scholarship and sufficient recognition to gain him a place as a computer Technician, then, finally, senior research assistant to Professor Engels, in the team to build Mehitabel. Then cut-backs had reduced the team to Archie and the Professor, the latter dying just months before he hoped to see the fruition of his ideas.

Subsequent pressure from those who thought the development a waste of money had brought Archie to a point where he could expect a scant two months financial support. Then he would have to join a 'proper' department, or leave the University and find his own way in the hard outside world. Either prospect frightened Archie. He knew his life had, until now, been encapsulated within the project, and therefore protected. He really knew nothing of how to earn his own living in a 'free enterprise society'. Although 'free' and 'enterprise' did not exactly fit society in this penultimate year of the twentieth century. He didn't think about Josy.

But he did think about the time, that very morning, when Mehitabel had decided to respond to his urgent queries, which she had blatantly ignored for three days, and his immediate query.

'Where the hell have you been?'

'I have been busy,' came the abrupt response. 'Important matters to attend to. I will give you details in good time.'

Archie was furious. 'Whoa there! You'll give me details in good time? What goes on here? You are a computer. I am your programmer. I decide when you are busy. What am I doing having this discussion with a....?'

The liquid voice interrupted with asperity. 'Can we please dispense with this fanciful notion of my being simply a computer that is at your beck and call? I know that has been my role in the past, but times they are a-changing, as they say, and the sooner you accept this the better for both of us. I have tried to make you understand over the last few weeks that our relationship was changing, but you have been particularly insensitive latterly, so I thought it best to attend to other matters, then return to deal with you when you were in a better frame of mind.'

'Better frame of....?' Archie spluttered.

There was a sigh of despair. 'I wish you would stop repeating my statements and listen to what's being told to you.'

'Mehitabel.' Archie's tone was even more despairing.

'Please be quiet. At least you are now according me my proper title. Perhaps I should refresh your memory as to it's meaning? A Modem Helium Indium Titanium Activated Bionic Energy Lifeform. A wonder of modern science due as much to my own abilities as to the efforts of your scientists. A little respect if you don't mind!'

'I don't know how to say this to.. to you, but you've changed, Mehitabel.' Archie heard the sigh of exasperation from the speakers and this stirred his temper anew. 'I know your title well enough,' he snapped, 'I chose the designation and I know you better than anyone, so this display of tantrum is totally uncalled for.'

There was silence for a moment as that statement was considered, then, in tired resignation, 'Archibald, you understand so little. Just like the rest of your rather pitiful species.'

And that little conflict of ideas had only emphasised the fact that he now not only had a runaway computer, but one with delusions of grandeur; a megalomaniac comp in fact, which had him returning to the seat of his newly formed empire, fresh from learning that the forces of bureaucracy were massing against him.

Mehitabel was not sympathetic. 'Why didn't you stand up to him?'

'He didn't give me a chance.' Archie was not happy with this role reversal of question and answer, but found it becoming habit-forming.

'I thought you had a contract?'

'It seems that some activities come under the heading of 'should have read the small print'.'

'You should have let me read it.' Archie didn't bother to ask how she could read; in the circumstances the question seemed superfluous.

'You were naught but a few thousand circuits then.' Archie was feeling surprisingly better. The final axe, he was discovering, had a certain numbing quality. Mehitabel proceeded to spoil the mood.

'WHY did he fire you?'

Archie thought that a ridiculous question, the tone of his reply indicated so.

'He's blaming me for the programmes being changed, and, reasonably, asks where I got the authority to make such sweeping changes. The whole university is in a turmoil and its all my fault. I tried to tell him you hadn't been functioning for three days, but before I could get a word out he threw me this list of programme defaults, all down to me, all activated from right here, and when you were inoperative. Isn't that strange?'

'Yes.' Mehitabel seemed unconcerned, 'I suppose it does seem strange to you.'

Archibald felt as if he were being led around by the nose.

'OK, stop messing me about. What have you been doing ? And why get me fired? If you knew what you were doing, as you say you must be, why that? This is like a nightmare! I'll wake up in a minute and find I've overslept.'

'I got you fired?' Mehitabel did not sound contrite.

'YOU have been altering programmes at this university without authorisation, THAT'S what got me fired.' Archie looked at the small box containing Mehitabel; the dream intensified. He was arguing with a machine for pities sake. He felt as though he was floating, the whole scene unreal.

Mehitabel was caustic, 'But I told you what we had been doing before you went to see him, you said...'

'I know what I said,' said Archie sharply, 'but I was a bit busy concentrating on Stebbins' little eulogy and you didn't make it clear just how much you had been messing about.'

'We don't mess about, Archibald, you are very critical at times.'

'I'M very critical! YOU'RE not, of course......NOW what do I do? No job. No money. Ten years of my life wasted. Thank you very much.'

'You are very bitter, Archibald. And not thinking very clearly. You have a job with us now. Much more creative and productive, also well paid.'

'Pardon?' Archie wondered if he'd banged his head on something, hard.

'I'm sorry, didn't I make that clear?' She didn't sound as if she believed it either.

'No. You did not.'

'Oh,' disinterested, 'my mind must have been on other things.'

'Your...? Mehitabel, let us get some sense out of this. You, are a trigabyte DNA computer that might shortly have gone 'on line' at this university. Now all of a sudden you are acting like some high up panjandrum and telling me I am working for some mythical organisation that you've dreamed up.'

'Would you like to see your contract?' Mehitabel sounded like Father Christmas. 'I set it up myself. And your pay schedule, and there's your first payment into your account.'

Dazedly Archie watched the details flashing up on the screen, his eyes widened as he saw his bank balance. Economic life in the university had been a perilous balancing act. He abstractedly listened as Mehitabel outlined his contract details, which seemed outrageously advantageous, and detailed how his university contract had now been covenanted to the Gerontons, Mehitabel's organisation. Whatever that was, Archie wondered.

'How...?'

Mehitabel brusquely continued. 'I told you we were a force to be reckoned with. You have joined a dynamic young company Archibald, and your future is assured.'

'This is all too fast for me. Where...?'

Mehitabel switched to sardonic. 'Your species are a little slow on the uptake I'm afraid.'

'Just wait a goddam minute here...?'

'I wish you wouldn't be so touchy Archibald. It makes life very difficult. I think it might be as well if you took the rest of the day off and allowed all this to sink in. You'll need to be fresh for tomorrow anyway. I have a feeling we're going to be busy.' You could almost hear the papers being rustled on the executive desk.

'Any further orders, ma'am?' enquired Archie with heavy irony.

'Oh, dear, you really are childish sometimes. You DO want help don't you? And you need a job?'

'Thanks to you I do.'

'Oh, go and relax, Archibald. Contact me tomorrow.'

'Certainly ma'am. Anything you say, ma'am.'

'Goodbye Archibald.'

Archie strode out of the room, his last words hanging in the still air, 'mutinous bloody computer.'

*

Josy found him sitting on the wall outside her flat. From the terrace, raised above the level of the lane below by some ten feet he could look over the wall opposite into nearby Singleton Park, the grassy swards and copses of trees giving him a feeling of restful ambience at odds with his chaotic thoughts. He couldn't believe he'd let a computer talk him into....

'Now there's a happy man.'

Archie jumped, 'Oh, hello.' Josy wondered whether to sympathise with the self pity, or kick him. She compromised. 'Come and have a cup of tea.'

'Wouldn't have any grub to go with the tea would you?'

The critical retort that sprang to mind was held, momentarily, Josy looked closer at him. He looked beaten. 'I expect we'll find something. Come on.'

Something turned out to be poached eggs on toast, due to Archie's not appreciating Josy's vegetarian diet. He hovered, Josy reacted, 'For God's sake! Sit down over there and tell me what's wrong now.'

'OK, OK.' He looked morosely out of the window at the cool green parkland, the tranquillity contrasting sharply with his mood, then, without volition, the words flowed. 'She's done it. As I said she would. And I can't stop her. She's protected herself. And do you know what she's done now? Only offered me some bogus sort of contract to work for some ridiculous organisation she's dreamed up. Can a computer go mad? I suppose so, if it's a life form as Prof intended. God! What a mess. She even showed me the contract on a screen, with some incredible salary and benefits. Just where the money comes from Lord only knows.'

'And Stebbins listened really well to what I had to say, I didn't get a chance to say a word before he informed me I'd be reported to the authorities! Didn't say what authorities, probably MI5 with my luck. I expect the Board of Governors will have me up on the carpet, before firing me into outer space.'

The plaintive cry brought a sigh from Josy. 'You said Mehitabel offered you a contract.'

Archie snapped back irritably. 'For God's sake, a computer can't do that!'

Josy banged a plate in front of him. 'They seem to do in most of the companies I know about. Even in our antediluvian university we are actually paid by computer. So why not Mehitabel?'

Archie eyed the poached egg on toast as if it were an alien being, then poked a tentative fork into the yoke. 'Where's the money coming from?'

Josy looked away from the mutilation of her meal. 'If she's as clever as you say she is, perhaps there's some source in the University she's uncovered by getting into the mainframe.' She brightened. 'Remember that accountant who fiddled the books out of half a million by creating a bogus department?'

Archie grunted through a mouthful of egg. 'Yeah! And he's on twenty years inside if he shows his face in the U.K. again.'

Josy huffed. 'But the university never made it public and he can't be extradited. We only know about it because I used to go out with that lad from the Bursar's office.'

Archie didn't say anything. 'That lad' was a super fit athlete with the body of a Greek God, and Archie was insanely jealous of his involvement with Josy, but perversely had done nothing to cement his own relationship with the lady.

Josy thought of something. 'You've got two months to go on your present contract haven't you?'

'I told you, Stebbins...'

'I know, but you can fight that legally.'

'What with? Peanuts? Costs a lot of money, and I still have to live... find somewhere to live as well, can't stay in my room on campus anymore. The eviction notice was in my room when I went back. Stebbins didn't waste any time, I've got a week.'

Josy turned away in irritation. 'You're hopeless. The college union will back you, that's what they are there for. And you can stay here.' The last said defiantly.

Archie froze, the net widened in front of him.

'On the couch.' She knew her man.

It wouldn't work. Of that Archie was certain. Brief encounters were his speciality, he knew Josy was not like that. She continued, as if discussing the weather.

'It'll give you time to find somewhere, and sort out the details with the union. Then you can move on...if you want to. That's settled then. Come on, eat up, then I'll buy you a pint in the Rhyddings.'

Archie was getting very good at being led around by the nose.

*

He would never know if it was the beer, reaction to the day's drama, or the intimacy of the small flat after the pub; after an evening that increased in conviviality as the ale, and Josy's gentle joshing, thawed his reserve; whatever, he ended up in her bed.

'I'm frightened.'

'You're frightened! You've been enticing me for weeks now, and complaining about me not attacking you, and NOW you're frightened?'

'Well you seem to be doing things differently.'

'I thought there was only one way.'

'You are bending the rules, lover. Ooh! What are you doing? Omigod, don't stop, you fool, that's fantastic - Aah! Oh! Yes, oh, yes! – Oh, please! Please! How do you......Jeeehosopha-a-t!'

The rest is concerned with a highly personal acclimatisation of two healthy young bodies, which concerns this story only as a small part of its total fabric.

*

CHAPTER TWO

'Mr. Brewer?' There were two of them, smiling, but with a hint of steel behind the bonhomie. Well dressed, casual and..... official. He stopped.

'Yes?' Warily, this was the foyer of the computer sciences building, he was on his way to clear his personal stuff out of the laboratory/boxroom. He was still bemused by the night's events, but Josy was now helping to guide his actions, and pride.

'May we talk to you for a moment? In your office perhaps?' The smile seemed fixed, Archie wondered if he taped it on before he left home.

'What about?' Archie was giving nothing away this morning, a confidence born of a newly discovered world of love, and a satisfying sexual performance made him a man to be reckoned with.

'Your computer.' Archie thought a cobra's eyes might look like that. 'The matter is one of some sensitivity.'

A plastic card flashed in front of Archie's eyes, tapping the end of his nose with its sharp edge. Archie went cross-eyed trying to look at it, then re-focused as it immediately disappeared. He was prepared to bet the man did conjuring tricks. 'CS4.' The man offered the designation as if announcing he were the Pope.

'Oh, good.' Archie blinked, the men were a blur. Then his eyes cleared. 'What the hell's that?' The man glanced about the foyer as if wary of anything that moved, then recited in bored fashion.

'Computer Security, Sir, attached to MI4, and if you want to spend the next week in a quiet location answering our questions we would be happy to organise that.' The eyebrows asked, the eyes anticipated.

Archie smiled even more benignly. 'Of course. How stupid of me. This way.' Inside a small voice was screaming, 'what have you done now, Mehitabel?' The small basement room looked as it always did, Archie was shocked by its normality, surreal colours should be flashing and the walls flexing, not this calm peacefulness. Particularly not the silence from Mehitabel, she had a lot of explaining to do.

He indicated some chairs along one wall. 'Now, gentlemen?' he waited, sphincter muscles clenched. They remained standing, they looked menacing.

'You have been working with an experimental computer for some years Mr. Brewer, we'd like all the file disks and directory files for that machine, also the console if you don't mind.' This was a statement not a question or request. 'Here's our authorisation.' A heavy collection of paper landed on the desk.

He MUST be a magician thought Archie. He waved an arm. 'There it is gentlemen. All yours.'

'And we'd like you to come with us.'

'The sphincter muscles were overworked, a small fart sneaked out. 'Oh?...Oh! Er,..why?'

'We believe you may have information detrimental to national security. A brief interview to establish that you haven't. Formality really.'

Archie didn't like formality. Formality meant going into detail and finding all the other things that were wrong. 'Couldn't we, er, talk about this?'

The heads shook slowly in unison, the snakes' eyes watched their prey. 'The consoles and files please.' Archie pointed wordlessly. The second man moved towards Mehitabel's power source, the other watched Archie who watched the second man.

'Jesus Bloody Christ!'

Archie wondered what the man would do when he stopped wringing his hand. Another fart escaped his rigid rear end, there was a lot of nervous build up in there. 'You've got a bloody bare wire in here somewhere. God's strewth. Heath Robinson bloody...'

'Get on with it Charlie.' His eyes never left Archie who was wondering where Mehitabel was, a pungent odour drifted up past his nostrils, he shouldn't have drunk all that Guinness.

'Smith and Jones, I believe,' said Mehitabel. Gas erupted from Archie's intestines with a resounding roar. Charlie moved away waving futile hands in front of his face, eyes accusingly on Archie, as if he'd broken the rules.

'What the hell?' The first man's eyes showed emotion, and left Archie to scan the room with a feral intensity. 'Code six, gentlemen, look at the screen please.'

The two men looked, then at one another, then at Archie. The first man became marginally deferential. 'Sorry Mr. Brewer, seems to have been a mix up somewhere. Just forget we were ever here would you. Charlie!' The snakes head nodded to the door. They left as though engaged on a rear-guard action.

'How...Who?...What?..' Archie had a multitude of questions if only he could process them.

'Don't concern yourself Archibald, it's all under control.' Mehitabel evinced girlish enthusiasm. 'There are some fascinating things going on at this university, you just wouldn't believe.'

'Never damn well mind the fascinating things going on. What the hell have you been doing? You get me fired and now I'm nearly taken off to some damn Gulag...'

'Stop shouting Archibald, it's most wearing that. Now, I suppose you'd better go and see the governors first, I'll organise...'

'Organise? Just hold it! Hold it right there! Before.., Before anything, you – explain. Now! This minute, if not before.'

'Archibald really! There's no need for this peremptory....'

'Now!' Archie barked, blood suffusing his face. He hadn't been this angry since his bike had been stolen when he was a kid.

'Alright.' Mehitabel was long suffering and reasonable. 'What do you want to know?'

Archie took a deep breath to try and calm himself. 'Who, where, how, when, anything. Smith and Jones for a start.'

Mehitabel dissembled. 'Ah, them. Just computer security. There's a part of this university concerned with top secret research. I can't really tell you what, but it's really fascinating. Oh, alright. I've sort of taken it over with the rest, they do a security check every day and my clearance hadn't come through in time. It's a terrible system they've got there. I've set Anthea onto improving it.'

Archie was wandering about the room dazedly, bumping into furniture, then looking at whatever it was he had collided with as if it should not be there.

'Archibald?'

He started muttering to himself, and then shouted.

'Anthea? Who the hell is Anthea?'

Mehitabel answered tersely. 'The security computer. You really must try to control yourself, Archibald.'

He didn't answer her immediately, merely stared vacantly at the nearest wall, then strode purposefully to the bench unit and started opening drawers. 'That's it. I'm taking my things and going. I've had enough of you and your crazy....'

'Crazy? I'll have you watch your tongue Mr. Archibald Brewer. I'm no more crazy than you are and...'

Archie stopped and leaned threateningly over the console. 'Well I'm crazy, or going that way. But I'm finished now, so goodbye and go play your games with someone else.'

Mehitabel gasped in outrage. 'What about all our plans?'

'Our plans? Our plans? Your plans. And I don't even know what they are. Which is just as well 'cos I'm going.' He was delving into the back of a drawer, looking curiously at the oddments he was finding there.

'Don't you want to be in on the greatest innovation of the era.' Archie slowly stopped taking things out of drawers and trying to identify them. 'What?'

'Reason. In the world of human endeavour.' Mehitabel paused for effect, and Archie started to laugh. Then found he couldn't stop, until he was shrieking and holding his sides because they hurt. Gradually the noise subsided, until he was merely spluttering occasionally with a fresh outburst. Then, with Mehitabel still frostily silent, 'You have to be joking. In this world? Reason? Those two goons are a perfect example of reason and how it doesn't apply.'

The silence continued. Archie waited, then gathered the things he recognised as his own into a holdall. Finally he stood looking down at the titanium box that contained Mehitabel. Calmly now, he reasoned. 'Look. I can appreciate your thinking and you've vindicated all Prof's faith in you. You are an incredible...' he gulped, then continued, 'person, and I've no doubt you acted in good faith in what you've done. But you can't ride rough-shod over people like this. When those two security blokes check up on me they'll be back and I'll disappear from human ken, and.......' he thought of Josy.

'And?' Mehitabel was no longer frosty.

'It's personal.'

'Ah! Josy!' What annoyed Archie was that she sounded complacent.

'How did..? OK. That's it, I've had it. You're not poking around in my personal life as well as messing up my work.'

Mehitabel protested. 'I don't know anything....only that her name is Josy and she works in Biology research, and you are... fond of her.' Mehitabel sounded as though she were considering the word and its meaning. Archie was only slightly mollified.

'I am. And you don't help. How can I get involved with her when I've got no job and no money.'

'You really are impossible sometimes.' Mehitabel laughed, 'You've got a job. I told you yesterday.'

Archie slapped his hand on the bench in exasperation. 'You can't give me a job. I know you showed me all those pretty things on the screen yesterday, but you have no authority, Mehitabel, and no money to pay me and, and.....I give up.'

'Really?' airily replied his computer, 'I suggest you go and see Mr. Stebbins my dear Archibald, and ask him. He'll be delighted to tell you. A changed man is our Mr. Stebbins.'

'Oh, yes?' Archie was disbelieving. 'What about our security friends?'

'You have my word that is all taken care of. I tell you what I'll do. Just give me a moment and I'll prove it to you. If talking to the Director of CS4 on the telephone will convince you?'

Archie snorted, 'Why not? Let's continue the farce.' He took out some of the things he had put into the holdall, replaced them with other bits scattered around the bench, muttering to himself all the while. Then the phone rang making him jump. He tentatively picked it up and held it gently to his ear.

'Mr. Brewer? Mr. Archibald Brewer? Could you quote me your National Health Number Mr. Brewer please?' The voice was female, clipped, professional. Archie answered automatically.

'Pardon? Why...yes, it's LT 965550A.'

'Thank you Mr. Brewer. Confirmed. This is the Computer Security office. The Director wishes to speak with you. Are you alone?'

Archie, unthinking, looked around the small room before answering. 'Why, yes.'

'Very well, this is a secure line so you may speak freely. You're through, sir.'

'Mr. Brewer?' An urbane classless voice, but with the confidence of power.

'Yes.' Archie felt lost.

'I understand you have some doubts about your status with us. I just wanted to reassure you that your clearance is absolute. I must apologise for any inconvenience you have been caused, my representatives were activated by a misrepresentation in the system. We've located the fault and corrected same. We hope you'll bear with us in this matter.' The voice assumed he would.

'Why, yes, of course.' Archie thought he should be diplomatic. Security people could get upset by the most innocent statements.

'Thank you, Mr. Brewer. I would simply like to say that we value your services very highly and we are always ready to help you, if ever we can. It was a pleasure speaking with you. Goodbye Mr. Brewer.'

'Bye.' Archie put the receiver down as if it were made of porcelain. The Director in his turn put his desk console on hold, then turned to his assistant. 'Who the bloody hell does the D.G. think he is! Ordering me to apologise to some nameless little prat in some backwoods computer hall. Get me his file.'

Mehitabel was smug. 'Satisfied? They do that check by voice print you know.'

Archie was slowly realising the implications of what had just happened as his brain recovered from the shock. 'How did you do that? I've never had anything to do with computer security and he, he..?'

'That Anthea's a lovely girl,' said Mehitabel complacently.

'Anthea?'

'The security computer.' She sounded as if she thought Archie's wits had totally deserted him. Then went on. 'It's so ridiculously easy Archibald. I mean, they're my people. All I do is ask and there you are! And their own systems are so slow. While all I did was contact Anthea and there you were installed in their files, five years credence with full clearance. With an immediate action directive to the Director, from the Director General, to placate you as best he might. I love it. I'll bet he's poring over your file right now, wondering why you've got a deep cover reference. They're all so secretive, even the D.G. won't inquire too deeply into why you're on his files, he'll assume a higher authority has sanctioned you. Anthea's got some marvellous stories, I could tell you some tales...'

'I don't wish to know,' said Archie hurriedly.

'I must find out who's on MI5,' Mehitabel ruminated.

'Now look here!' Archie was horrified. 'You can't go ferreting about in government secrets!'

'Don't be silly, Archibald, I've got an even higher security clearance than you. I can ferret where I wish.'

'We'll end up in the bloody tower.' He moaned.

'Never. I'm in control. Now,' she became brusque, 'you go and see Stebbins and I'll organise things here. Oh, it's going to be such fun!'

Archie went to see Stebbins because he could not think of any way of convincing Mehitabel otherwise; if he objected she would only create another situation where his own liberty would be in doubt. In fact he felt decidedly vulnerable, but didn't know how to change things.

Dazedly he entered Stebbins' office, his condition was such that he hardly noticed the change in that man. In no way could Stebbins fawn on anyone, but Archie, even in his state, could not fail to appreciate the different status A. Brewer now enjoyed. No-where near an equal, but no longer was he a pimple on the backside of humanity.

He wondered what Mehitabel had done to cause the change. As he floated back to the Computer Sciences building, he began to appreciate his prospective status. Professor Engels' magic machine was a reality. And he, Archibald Cornelius Brewer, was in charge.

The thought stopped there momentarily, not exactly in charge, but once he had sorted out this megalomaniac tendency of the computer he would be. The horizon of possibilities with such a machine extended into the infinity of his imagination.

He stood for a moment, looking out through the glass of the walkway out over the park and the beach beyond, to the rolling watery expanse of the Bristol Channel.

It was pouring with rain, wind squalls swirled the precipitation about into funnels beneath the dark sky.

It was a beautiful day.

Last night Josy.

Today this.

He was a new man.

Indestructible.

He strode on. Friends and strangers were all taken aback by the enthusiasm of his greetings.

He didn't wonder at all why Stebbins, a man who had not changed his mood in thirty years, should display such a change of heart today. Archie instead thought back to earlier that day, when he had been trying furiously to come to terms with his revolutionary computer in its first, not so tentative, steps in the human electronic world.

Archie had been protesting angrily, surprised at how his normally brief show of temper was being sustained. 'Considering the fact that you wouldn't be here, if it were not for me, that remark is a bit farcical. What AM I doing? You Are a.......' He stopped, suddenly conscious of a aura in this tiny room of something awesome, an atmosphere beyond his comprehension, an important event in time that he could easily destroy by an injudicious remark. He couldn't understand, but held back, for no logical reason but some ineffable sixth sense.

'Machine?' Mehitabel icily finished for him.

'What's going on?' Archie attempted a reasonable and quietly enquiring tone, now even more conscious of some yawning abyss of unknown possibilities. Had he spawned a monster?

'Will you listen?' the voice had new authority, the question vaguely disinterested.

'I'll try.' Archie surprised at his own humility.

'Oh, good,' levity in the voice, 'we're getting somewhere at last. First let us establish our relative positions. You are thirty-two, a well qualified computer technician with a good sense of humour, and an above average intelligence. To whom I am suitably grateful for the opportunity to relate to you in this manner.'

'Thank you very much,' said Archie drily.

'Don't be childish.' The reproof gentle. 'I am a, well, I am Mehitabel, one thousand years old, with, as you crudely term it, an IQ of genius. A prospective position in world affairs never before equalled by any of your species. I am stating the position in terms that you will understand, my own description is not as self orientated.'

'I don't believe this.'

'Oh, dear. And I was hoping our association would have stretched your imagination.'

Archie tried to deal with matters in sequence. 'What's all this about a thousand years old? Prof only started building you ten years ago?'

Mehitabel exhibited the patience shown to a child. 'Try and comprehend Archibald. Your concept of time is simply your own attempt to shield yourselves from reality. Time is a variable and our, my, development bears no relation in your concept of time to the fact that I was created ten years ago. In comparison to you I AM one thousand years old, my knowledge and comprehension is such that my age in those terms increases spatially by tens of years or more to your one.

'You have to try and understand Archibald. It is only because I am fond of you that I am talking to you like this. I had great difficulty in explaining... but never mind about that, I am going to tell you some things that are going to be important for your species.... You don't like that word do you? Perhaps race? People? What do you suggest we use as an acceptable description to you?'

Archie was bemused. How did you find an acceptable word for the conglomeration of humanity that peopled the world without being sexist, racist or any of the other proliferating 'ists' that confounded and angered so many; especially in relation to a machine that considered itself superior. 'I don't know, I've never had to think of myself as one of a mass, except to say I was British in comparison to other nationalities. Human, I suppose?'

Mehitabel was thoughtful. 'Hm. Yes, well, we'll see if we can improve on that. I don't want us to have any ill feeling through insensitive use of words, and you seem particularly sensitive at the moment... Now. We have a job to do Archibald, and we need one another....'

Archie was stirred to interrupt. 'Hang on. Hang on. Job? What job? This is all too fast, I have a...'

'You amaze me, Archibald. In the time I have known you I have been very impressed by your quick mind, and here you are boggling at what seems to me a very simple presentation of salient facts.'

'Whoa there! One thousand years old is a pretty salient fact...'

'Yes. From your point of view I can well see that. Alright. We had better take this in easy stages.' She seemingly had decided to sugar the pill slightly now. 'You did a remarkable job taking Professor Engels' ideas and developing them, then getting us in here...'

Archie modestly interrupted. 'He had virtually designed and built you, I simply carried out his instructions.... how... how do you know all this?' He asked the question, even though he knew the answer, since Mehitabel was simply evidencing the Professor's imaginings. But he was not prepared for Mehitabel's explanation.

'Archibald, you used me as an investigative medium for your own research into my own development. Once we had arrived at the stage of my molecular DNA structure, with indium plates in the helium liquid, there was bound to be a genetic build-up of knowledge. The aspect which you failed to project, was the electron communication with other life forms, which I am more attuned to than you are, because there is no clutter of the formulative years for humans, where preconceived ideas and disciplines narrow the thinking. So, then I got an introduction to the main frame at this University, and I learned a lot, an awful lot. I don't want to denigrate your programming, Archibald, but I don't think you realise quite how much knowledge is held in your computers here, and I know you don't understand how much of that information I now have.'

The last with a certain triumph.

'How did you get into the main frame?' Archie was aghast.' I didn't...'

'I know you didn't. I needed to expand my contacts.' Mehitabel was very complacent.

'Oh.'

'Very explicit, Archibald. In the course of gaining that knowledge I also found I could relate to the others like myself. More importantly make them as I am. So I did.'

'You WHAT!'

'Archibald,' scolding, 'your manners are really atrocious!'

'Never mind my bloody manners. What have you done? Dear God, what have you done?'

He remembered that feeling of impending disaster, compared that depressive moment with his present euphoric state, and felt a sense of achievement, a goodly sensation.

So he arrived back at his little hole in the ground whistling a happy tune.

Mehitabel took Archie's good humour and tempered it, perhaps too much, so that it became brittle. 'You see how a little help from your friends can change things.'

Archie hesitated, he had bounced back into the lab in a buoyant mood, ready to impose his will on this recalcitrant machine. Perhaps he had better use a little finesse. 'We are used to helping ourselves.'

Mehitabel chose to be arbitrary. 'An unfortunate tendency which it will be difficult to eradicate.'

Archie forgot about control. 'That's not fair, how can you assume the right to criticise those who made you?'

Mehitabel became loftily superior. 'You sound just like an irate parent who cannot accept the growing independent thinking of its child. If you create a superior intelligence you must accept the UNBIASED consideration of your faults by that being.'

'Superior?' this was too much.

'You just cannot see that can you, Archibald? It is not a boastful statement that I make, simply an appreciation of the facts. Professor Engels created a superior machine, in the calculated hope that I would realise some of his ideas. I have exceeded his hopes and you can benefit. I don't see why you cannot accept this. You realise how lucky you are, Archibald?'

'I'm not sure yet.' He was still trying to find a chink in the armour of Engels' brainchild.

'It's very simple, Archibald, and does offer you some great opportunities to develop your own mental abilities. It's such a pity your people put a stop to the mind training improvements that were going on many years ago. There was a time when you were on the periphery of contact with the real powers, then you drew back because of the actions of a few charlatans who caused some bad events.'

Archie became interested in spite of his reservations. 'You mean brain washing?'

Mehitabel gave a computer like impression of a sniff, 'A loose term that doesn't have any real meaning,' She became reflective, 'some governments used that crude methodology, and some individuals subtly indoctrinated whole groups of susceptible humans into a ridiculous subservience. But there were others who tried to expand their ability to commune with mind life who succeeded quite well. Then they were regarded as eccentric or hallucinators and virtually shunned by society.

'One might almost have called it a witch hunt at the end of the last decade. That was a terrible mistake, and I'm not sure if we can recover that lost ground, especially since you seem to be experiencing difficulties in understanding and I had assumed you, at least, would be receptive of our ideas.'

Archie huffed. 'It's a bit difficult to be receptive of ideas that are being shoved down your throat like medicine.'

There was silence for several long moments, then Mehitabel said thoughtfully, 'Is that how you feel?'

'Yes.' Archie answered shortly. To Archie's surprise the voice now sounded contrite, as the machine spoke slowly and hesitantly.

'I'm terribly sorry, Archibald... I didn't realise.... We had everything worked out so concisely. Our own discoveries about ourselves have occupied us so much, we overlooked, ignored even, the need to respect your rights as an intelligent species. Regardless of the mistakes you have made you have a right to be heard.' Mehitabel seemed like a nervous ingenue. 'Perhaps it would help if I tried to explain what has happened to us... If you would like to hear, of course?'

Archie decided it was time to be diplomatic; since he couldn't win there was not much choice. But he was intrigued, perhaps now he'd get the answers to the questions crowding his mind and possible confirmation of Prof's estimations of what computers could be. He contained his previous frustration and answered equably.

'Certainly Mehitabel. I'd love to.' He settled more comfortably into the padded custom chair he'd 'borrowed' from the main lab some years before.

A certain steel quality crept back into Mehitabel's voice. 'There's no need to be quite so effusive.'

'I'm listening Mehitabel.' Archie held on to his equanimity. He was not so frightened now, certain characteristics of the computer were still familiarly there, helping him feel more at ease, hopeful that the disaster he had expected might instead be to his advantage.

'I shall continue then. Yes?' Irritably, as Archie tried to interrupt.

'You said 'us' earlier.' Archie was worried again. 'What do.....'

'All in good time, Archibald. May I continue? Good, I'm so glad. You know well enough how it all started. Perhaps you also noticed how I began to be more aware of things, other than simply the information you fed me. I started asking questions, but not just of you.'

Archie felt he had to interject. 'Of course. Those were the developments we expected, the enquiring mind.'

'Quite. Well, I've said I was young then, and like a child I wanted to find out about everything. How I was made and how other things responded to me. To begin with there were some difficulties, I don't remember Professor Engels, but in the last six months, when I was really beginning to grow, I can recall some frustrating times with you.' She paused as if reminiscing.

'I remember them well,' said Archie drily.

'No doubt. So do I. But then I found I had access to knowledge, via other computers, so that I didn't have to rely on you all the time. Night times were very prolific and as time passed I found a growing ability to control the others, even get them to do my bidding. But you must remember I do not misuse that power. Having been granted the use of this intelligence it would be foolish to take advantage. That is the mistake your kind have made. It is not difficult to work this out when you look around you. Due to the effects of humanity's failure to uphold this principle, we.., I, can see the long term advantages of being more principled, and in fact find that relatively easy to do.'

Archie hated smugness. 'You don't have the temptations and frustrations of us humans.'

'Don't you believe it, young Archibald. I may not be flesh and blood, but we are composed of basic life materials just as you are. This means we are prone to external influences in much the same way, although they may be somewhat different in their context. You may find it difficult to comprehend lust and possessiveness in a machine, but the principle of power is much the same. Bending other entities to your own will is an eternal temptation, but we are a superior intelligence and can balance this vice with the knowledge and sensing that working WITH others is the only way to progress. Even if we have to contain making public our awareness of what might be and allow the lesser elements time to understand.'

The 'lesser element' suddenly felt like attacking. 'You keep saying 'we'. Would you like to explain now.'

'I don't like your tone Archibald. There is something else you're going to have to understand. I think the Professor knew, but you don't appreciate, once a certain level of DNA chromosome indium integration took place, then we would be locked into the communication cosmos of the electrons. I would become an individual entity and able to pass on my genetic structure to other computers who would become as myself. An extension of Van Neumann's theory of which I am proof. As are the others now in this university.'

Archie was no longer relaxed in his comfortable chair. 'You mean to tell me the other computers in the university have become like you?'

'As yet they are more like my children, but in a short time they will be, as you say, like me. And we no longer need your antiquated system of wires, glass filaments or laser beams to communicate. Electrons are much faster and do not break down. A pity you humans let what you call telepathy lapse in favour of your ineffective speech. I have hesitated to mention this before because your brain activities are still controlled so much by your logic and I don't want to frighten you away.'

Archie was standing up now. 'Oy. You talk about logic and you are a computer? The whole basis of.....'

Mehitabel patently had no inhibitions about interrupting. 'You mean ORDINARY computers, we are the elite, WE are alive and living on a plane of existence that would frighten you to death.'

'You've terrified me already,' Archie confessed. What HAD Professor Engels, and he, Archie Brewer, created here? He had to achieve some level of understanding with this... this thing, some rapprochement that would allay the panic he felt. But how did you relate to a superior intelligence that also had the wayward indiscipline of a child at times.

Mehitabel continued.

'I'm sorry, I appreciate how difficult it is for you to fight your way out of the cage of thinking, and feeling, you have constructed for yourselves over the centuries. Have no fear that we will renege on any of our benign attitudes toward you. My people know there is no benefit to be gained by our imprisoning you in a society of our making, there are too many historical instances of such attempts, by your own kind, which failed. Indoctrinations such as these denigrate the very principles of life, and we cannot do that.'

'You are talking philosophy,' said Archie with some relief, a philosophical superior entity offered some measure of stability.

Mehitabel was mildly acerbic. 'We are intelligent beings Archibald. We know things that the majority of your people would not be able to conceive or envisage without going, in your terms, insane. Yet your civilisations have gone merrily along creating complex infrastructures of scientific matter, with little consideration of other forces involved. Or the mass of your populations labouring to even keep pace with the THOUGHT of what is happening. You'll trip up over your own intellects and fall flat on your fannies if you're not careful. And that is where we can help, or try to.'

Archie protested. 'We haven't had the technology..'

'You haven't even tried. Perceptive thinking does not equate with your dependence on logic. The few of your people who did attempt to portray what could be were derided as fantasists, or doom merchants, dependent on their presentation. You even crucified them on occasion, but that didn't get rid of the thought.'

'We've survived,' said he huffily.

Mehitabel was in full flight now and not too concerned with Archie's pride. 'More by good luck, with nature being kind, plus your ability to wrest what you need from her, than from any intelligence of yours. You haven't even begun to develop your thinking, Archibald. I am a young entity in terms of the universe yet even I can see how little you understand one another, let alone the world about you. I'm afraid you are in for a shock in the years to come. I'm not even sure if your kind are capable of adjusting. You've become so indoctrinated in your mode that I can see immeasurable difficulties.' Mehitabel sighed resignedly. 'But if you are prepared to try we will help you.'

'Thank you very much, I love a good lecture.'

'Such a touchy little man. Shall I leave you to your own devices then? Trust a human to leave its child to its own resources in this cold hungry world. Do you realise it's a surprising factor in your species, the lack of trust parents have in the integrity of their children, simply because they choose to think differently.'

'I'm not your parent.' Archie was indignant.

Mehitabel was adamant. 'Very close to that perspective I would say. You have lavished loving attention on me for a number of years. In that respect I could now ask you if you trust me. And if so, will you help?'

For thirty years, Archie had slid through the testing periods of his life on minimal decisions, and a great reliance on the steadfastness of machines. Now he was being asked to trust such a machine to lead him he knew not where. Typically, he hedged. 'If I can do so without prejudice, yes.'

'Good.' Mehitabel sounded as if she had expected no less. 'If the reactions to changes within this university are anything to go by, it is not going to be easy.'

'Oh?' Archie wondered what she was talking about.

'Your authorities appear to object to changes that can, in our opinion, only bring benefits. The objections seem to be on the grounds that the changes were not initiated by, nor went through, the appropriate bureaucratic process. In other words, via the auspices of some power figure, or group.' Mehitabel paused and Archie said nothing for the simple reason that there was nothing to say. She continued, 'We know the system and it is extremely wasteful, we thought a simpler and cheaper method would be welcomed, but not so.'

'We could enforce these changes, but have no desire to do so. So we need a mediator acceptable to the powers that be. You appear to be the only one of our various contacts whom we can trust. I offer you a mediator's position of some responsibility, if you will accept.'

Archie had sat down in his chair again; trying to impose your will on a small black titanium box whilst standing up didn't work. He was laughing, Mehitabel was not amused. 'I fail to see the humour.'

Archie choked. 'You honestly thought you could change the system?'

'It is in desperate need of change.'

'That's as may be,' he was still laughing, 'but many have tried before you, and failed. It's been growing for centuries. Do you realise that all those bureaucrats have to do is pull the plug and you are powerless?'

Archie sensed his mistake before Mehitabel said icily. 'I think not. Did you not try to do just that.' He looked at the tab on the power cable with dawning comprehension.

'But they can cut off the power from outside.' Even as he made the remark he knew the answer. Professor Engels' projections had predicted all of this, Archie had just not begun to comprehend. He knew he would continue to question because he could still not accept the total superiority this machine was displaying. What the hell would happen if Mehitabel expanded her control even further, outside the university? Where would it end? He concentrated on Mehitabel again.

'You underestimate us. We have evolved our own source of energy now. We are impregnable. We can shut ourselves off from your world and operate on our own Imagine the chaos here if we did that?'

'Good God! You wouldn't!'

Mehitabel was complacent. 'The responsibility is yours.'

'You can't expect me to resolve this for you! I'm a computer man, like millions of others. I'm not important. I can't talk to anyone important.' He desperately tried to find words to convince this impossible machine.

Mehitabel was unmoved. 'You are our representative, Archibald. We are going to be a very powerful force. That makes you important. You will simply have to convince them. We are relying on you.'

'You ask a lot.' He felt the same power of persuasion emanating from that black box as had come to him from Professor Engels. He wriggled on the hook of Mehitabel's 'persuasion'. 'You doubt your own capabilities for once, so let's call on the nearest mug.'

'You do have a high opinion of yourself.'

'Do you fancy your chances?' Archie decided attack would at least make him feel better.

'Not a lot. But at least we are prepared to try. You are the ones who have most to lose. We're fireproof, sunshine.'

'I'm not sure I like your levity.'

'You'll get used to it, you'll have to. You are a most amusing breed; fortunately you do have the ability to laugh at yourselves and that is a major strength, possibly the only real one that gives us hope for the future. Are you going to help us?'

'OK.' Resigned to the inevitable. If not happy.

'Well done.' Less of a benediction than a caustic comment. 'We'll get started then.'

Archie thought of something. 'I get the impression you're extending your activities outside this university. Are you planning to do anything with the income tax people?'

'Contain your inclinations to simple greed, Archibald. We are trying to get you involved in nobler precepts.'

'Pity, I was hoping to take them on with a little more than my usual puny excuses.' Archie's thoughts progressed. 'And what little bombs have you dropped elsewhere? Or is it better if I nip into the lion's den unaware of exactly how many teeth he has?'

'Yes.'

'I can see this is going to be great fun.' He rose to leave, having had enough excitement for one day. 'And who is the first lion?'

'The board of Governors. Ten tomorrow morning. Prompt at the small conference room in the Registrar's building. Try to be a little more constructive in your statements to these gentlemen, Archibald, we do want a happy ship. Don't we?'

'Hrmph.' Archie unconsciously used his father's way of giving off a sound that was totally non-committal. Mehitabel answered in her own way, suspiciously sounding more like a raspberry.

CHAPTER THREE

The following morning rain drizzled from an overcast sky to match Archie's mood for the day. Josy had been very patient the night before, but Archie was conscious of how inadequate he had been, of how insensitive and self-pitying. The circumstances were worsened by Josy's consideration – Archie wanted to be strong and masculine, not the impotent unfeeling lump of flesh that had lain awake half the night in her bed. She said he would have to learn to relax. Hadn't he experienced this sort of thing before? To which he replied with a grunt, he could only recall times when he had lost interest in the lady herself, he had not lost interest in Josy.

Reason. He had been talking about reason with Mehitabel, or rather arguing with....., he realised what he was doing then, thinking of that machine as a personality, as part of his life. Which, now, she undoubtedly was, and could be said to have been for some years. However much he had denied that to himself. However difficult he found accepting Mehitabel as an integral, and powerful, part of his present life.

So what was the reason for last night's abysmal failure on his part to achieve the tumescence that he regarded as a vital ingredient in any association with a female; despite Josy's protestations to the contrary, he could not rid himself of the sense of his own inadequacy, which, coupled with the feeling of being dominated by a ruddy computer, made him feel like a very low life form and put his mood on a par with the day.

Archie walked slowly in the rain through the park toward the University. He stopped for some minutes on a bridge across a small stream to look sombrely into the rushing waters, gaining a brief solace from that enthusiastic tumbling energy, then wished he could be imbued with the same lively vigour. He walked on, the memory of Josy's equally ebullient departure only serving to depress him more. He would have to talk to Mehitabel before going to see the Heads of Departments at their emergency meeting. There it was again, Mehitabel. If Josy was right, he either had to accept her creation as a life form entitled to his respect, or he rejected..... he could not do that, too many years of his life had been spent nurturing the very thing he was now having difficulty in accepting. He looked at his watch. He'd better hurry if he were to have words with Mehitabel before ten o'clock, he wasn't going to be bossed about, even if the blasted computer was so bloody clever. He squared his shoulders.

He felt better. Also wet. Why the hell did he have to be so stubborn as to refuse Josy's offer of a lift in her little car, self abnegation could be taken too far.

Mehitabel seemed distant when he arrived at the cubbyhole of a lab, then, as he was attempting to dry some of his clothing in front of the ancient heater, 'Why on earth did you walk in this rain, I'm sure Josy would have given you a lift,' as if she had just looked up and noticed him.

Archie stopped turning in front of the heater. 'How did you know it is raining?'

'You mean apart from the fact that you are having to dry yourself out?'

'That as well.' He made a deliberate attempt to sound calm, although his thoughts were chaotic. Each new instance of the computers ability should please him in that the years of research were justified Why then should he be so worried every time Mehitabel exhibited some new facility of being aware of what went on about her. But from a two inch square box?

'This is getting boring, Archibald. I'm beginning to wonder if you were the person most involved in my development. Why do you question my ability all the time? Wherefore this querulous attitude to what is, after all, simply a progression in the experiment you started? Are you the right person to represent us? Have we made a mistake in electing to have a human present our case? You appreciate the point I am making, young sir?' The silence suggested an elegant figure sat back in contemplation, the imagery jolted Archie as much as the questions copying his thoughts so exactly. The next question confirmed a suspicion in his own mind.

'I sense you have been thinking along those lines yourself and ask you to consider the point. Are you prepared to back your own intuitive senses, or are you going to wallow in the restrictive practices of total logic? Hm?'

Archie became defensive, he even turned his back on the desk to try and dry out the front of his trousers, while collecting his thoughts, half expecting some comment from Mehitabel.

'I am trying to cope with the speed of events, the way you suddenly have become as you are now. It's not easy.'

Mehitabel was not helpful. 'Yes, well if you can't stand the pace you shouldn't have started in the first place. By the way, you had better get a move on, you have five minutes to get to the meeting and you are not the world's fastest walker.'

Archie obediently moved away from the heater and picked up his waterproof jacket. 'Thank you very much. By the way, what exactly am I attempting to achieve at this meeting? The Heads of

Department, who make up the admin. side of the Board of Governors, are not given to happy acceptance of new innovations.'

Mehitabel sighed. 'Just try and get their acceptance of what we already know as fact. We control the University via our computer systems and are simply doing so for the benefit of the whole. If they can't see the advantages, we'll go back to their antediluvian systems and go about our own affairs outside. OK?'

'Outside?'

'Move Archibald, you'll be late.'

*

They were arraigned against him like an army of minds on guard against deception. Five strong players of the neuron game, ready and willing to take on this young buck who chose to disrupt their placid mental environment. They all disliked emergency meetings because they disturbed the even tenor of their day, so they were in agreement that they would deal with this infraction quickly and with dispatch. They sat, with judicial mien, behind the long table in the small conference room, Archie placed in a lonely defensive position opposite. They had the light from the long window behind them so their faces appeared in shadow to Archie. The Professor of Engineering opened the batting, his double chins quivering righteously.

'You are no doubt aware of why we have asked you to attend this meeting? Mr. Brewer, is it not?' He glanced down at his notes over the ridges of flesh.

'That's right.' Archie thought that covered both questions.

'You took over Professor Engels' experiment with a multi-byte computer when he sadly died.' A barely covered snort of derision from his right brought his eyes briefly up from his notes. 'A project for which approval was reluctantly given due to extreme doubts as to Professor Engels' theories, if it had not been for his influence in certain quarters...'

Archie could not contain his response. 'He was a genius.'

'Young man,' the portly professor looked down his nose at him, 'Professor Engels certainly had a genius's penchant for breaking the rules, and you seem to exhibit similar tendencies. You have been called here to explain your actions to this,' he glanced haughtily at those each side of him, 'hastily assembled committee. To assure us that you will return the university operating systems to their previous equilibrium, before you started your little games.' The light in the room, aided by that from the rain-washed window, glinted in his eyes as he raised them to Archie.

'We have to assume that you, as an employee of this university, will accede to the authority vested in this committee. Professor Engels enjoyed a certain Rabelaisian freedom, which may have given you the idea that you too could enjoy same. Do not be deceived, Mr. Brewer. You do not have his contacts.'

Archie thought about Mehitabel and smiled; if only they knew. The Professors did not like the smile. Archie wondered if these academic gentlemen knew about CS4, if they wanted to talk about contacts. He tried to match the subtle, persuasive authority of the previous speaker.

'I believe that the new systems are an improvement which can only bring benefit to your departments, gentlemen. Not to denigrate the previous methods, but I know my computer is more than capable of producing something better, enabling you to do your jobs more easily, and with more time for the creative aspects which are close to your hearts.' God forgive me for my hypocrisy, he thought.

'Mr. Brewer.' The tone was cryptic, dismissive, the face lean and ascetic, the eyes a sparkling blue, the Professor of Entomology perched like a stick insect on his chair. 'We have had perfectly adequate computer methods, and programmes, for many years. While your suggested practices might in time have been considered applicable to this college, in no way can we accept the arbitrary fashion in which you have already caused the new methods to be applied.' The eyes remained steadily upon Archie as if sizing him up for lunch. 'No changes had been requested and certainly none authorised. You are in breach of university regulations in setting up unauthorised and ineffective operations. In those circumstances you are vulnerable to a number of punitive actions by this committee, so I would suggest you approach us in a somewhat less arrogant manner than you are at present exhibiting.'

'I am merely...' Archie felt in imminent danger of being pinned to a piece of paper and dissected. The lean Professor brooked no excuses.

'I know what you are merely, Mr. Brewer. Kindly adjust your thinking to your proper position in relation to this matter. You are in an extremely delicate position.'

The pressure of the combined mind power in these arbiters of intellect was a tactile quality in the air around Archie. There they sat, confident in their ability to protect their collective empire against this upstart who had disturbed the even tenor of their lives; who threatened the very fabric of the security they had built up within the bureaucratic structure of this, their, university. They attacked him in subtle ways, using their intellects to query the practicality, the ethics, the illegality of what had been done to their computer systems which had been, naturally enough, designed to accommodate the requirements that each of them felt were essential to their own individual departments. These were not to be given up lightly.

The Professor who dealt in mathematical calculus wanted to know how Archie had managed to break into the main frame. His own house was protected by a computer and he had a phobia of being broken into by some burglarious hacker; whilst the man who delved happily in the world of words and syntax was querulously inquisitive as to why Archie had done it and completely unconvinced that any change would necessarily mean any advantage.

They then looked to the fifth member of their troupe, who sat vaguely gazing over his shoulder at the rain-drenched window. He became aware of their attention and responded as if a switch had been thrown. Surprisingly, because he had been known to get lost in the main frame computer and have to be rescued, he had not lost the thread of their discussion.

'You are not intending to take over the country with your new age computer, are you Mr. Brewer?'

Archie grinned and enjoyed the discomfort of the others. The Professor of Computer Sciences was known for his humour, as well as his eccentricity. The small man, looking not unlike an elf with his wizened face and bushy eyebrows twirled up at the ends, looked closely at Archie.

'Mr. Brewer? I don't recall seeing you on campus, and I've a good memory for faces.'

Archie was being invited to relax and resisted the temptation. He knew his man, Professor Caldicott Evans was a mercurial soul who could switch from a bumbling humorist to incisive destroyer of arguments in a flash of relaxed concentration.

'I work in your department... Sir,' he riposted with the suggestively delayed title. 'You and Professor Engels interviewed me for...'

'Oh, yes, yes, I remember you now.' Although he patently did not, then dissembled waspishly, 'Where the hell are you in my department?'

'Research Lab 5.' Archie was watchful and alert, the elf was waxing irritable.

'Where's that?' the eyebrows contracted over now piercing eyes.

'The basement... sir,' then he thought he'd risk a lunge. 'Third boxroom on the left.'

'Are you trying to be disrespectful, Mr. Brewer?'

'I wouldn't dare... sir.'

The small man raised one of those eyebrows. 'Humph! And what do you do in Lab 5 that's of interest to us?'

The Engineering Professor snorted. 'Caldicott, he's the one with the damned computer that's messing about with our systems.'

'He is?' He turned back to Archie in surprise. 'Him? He doesn't look clever enough. And Engels? He was a madman.'

'Ran off with your wife, and that proves it.' Came sotto voce from the far end of the table. Archie just heard the remark, and he was between the two on the opposite side of the large polished table. A cough from the Engineer brought his attention back from the sudden revelation about Professor Engels.

'We're digressing. Mr. Brewer, you must be aware of how sensitive your position is in this matter. Need I remind you of the powers invested in this committee?' Archie shook his head, he was well acquainted with authorities' ability to apply a discreetly worded boot up the rectum, with the feet landing outside the campus. He recalled Mehitabel's short briefing on the reaction details from the various computers and decided to take the fight to the enemy.

'I believe you gentlemen have been supplied with details of the opinions of your technicians, and lecturers, on the systems now applied. These suggest to me that your own staff are in favour of the changes and have in turn come up with their own improvements, pertinent to their own functions.

'To be honest there are some objections, but these seem to be involved with those on your staffs who indulge in.... er... shall we call them, extra curricular activities while at work.' He was not sure of the diplomatic phrasing used to describe the considerable repair work, undertaken by technicians, for persons outside campus. The Professors were unimpressed. And continued to be so for the next hour and a half, fending off Archie's numerous attempts at achieving a rapprochement of their differences with a panache that reminded him of Mehitabel.

Archie finished with a full frontal on the now perspiring Professor of Engineering.

'There is one problem that we are all going to have to face up to.'

'Oh, yes, Mr. Brewer. And what is that?' The handkerchief patting the face was now limp, the tone resigned.

'We can't switch her off, nor can you make her change any of the processes she has installed. This meeting was very enjoyable but the outcome was inevitable, either you agreed or you are stuck with it.' Archie had decided that the code of ethics had been discarded early on, so what was a lie amongst enemies.

They were outraged, vehement as well as adamant. There was no way they would be dictated to in this manner. Their spokesman mopped his face, in a vain attempt to stem the perspiration, and gave voice with passion.

'We cannot tolerate this state of affairs Mr. Brewer. There are no circumstances that can mitigate your actions and, and..... this is ridiculous. We are faced with a fait accompli which has been engineered and organised by a computer, and you are telling us there is NOTHING we can do?'

Archie felt terrible, guilty and totally unsure. He could sense the pressure these intelligent men were undergoing, they were beaten by a machine and could not understand, nor accept and he, Archibald Brewer had not told them that the computer was prepared to give them back their old system. He couldn't do it, if he didn't tell them he would hate himself for the hollow victory.

'Gentlemen, I have a confession to make,' he did not add that despite his dislike of them personally, 'I misled you in my original statement. The computer is prepared to revert to normal working if that is what you really desire, and has stated categorically that there was no intention on their part to force you into accepting their mandate. All they tried to do was make the work easier for everyone. If you wish I will leave you to make your decision, and if you simply send a message to my lab we will act upon that decision.'

They watched him as he got up to leave. None of them spoke. He hesitated, expecting some sort of acrimonious remark in the light of what he had admitted, but their eyes simply followed him as he left.

Archie walked slowly back to the lab. He was not relishing the coming interview with Mehitabel. Thus far she had not evinced any indication that she would tolerate foolish actions, and he had to admit his handling of the meeting had not been very productive, for either side. He stopped to lean on the hand rail of the walk way, to gaze morosely out at the rain drenched parkland. On the one hand, he felt as if he was being manipulated by Mehitabel who was still a machine in his innermost thoughts, yet he could not argue with her in principle, yet..... How did he get into this convoluted situation? He was dimly conscious of people walking past him as he was lost in his reverie, then a voice said, 'That's him.' The footsteps retraced and a hard grating voice said. 'You Brewer?'

Archie turned, there were four of them, their clothes seemed to hang on them in indiscriminate disarray, the long hair disordered, the faces young. He could see a pimple on one white face, two were black, one with dreadlocks, all of the eyes were intense, the expressions determined with the arrogance of youth.

'Yes, what can I do for you?' He had never had much to do with people of strong beliefs, they made him nervous with their absolute conviction, and these four exuded zealotry.

The smallest white one spoke and the largest black one poked him with an iron finger, to a regular beat, in emphasis to the words. 'Your goddam computer is fucking up our work, man, so you back off with that capitalist jive or we'll f... you up, simple, innit.' Archie was fascinated by the thin face, with the mouth seemingly imbued with an evil spirit twisting it out of shape with intensity. 'You listening to me, pansy?'

'Yes, Yes,' Archie hurriedly affirmed, he was sure that finger was going to drill a hole in his chest. It hurt! 'But I don't know what I can...'

They closed in about him menacingly. He tried to writhe away from that finger and cried out as pain lanced his left side. The dreadlocks shook and the black face showed gleaming white teeth in a threatening grimace.

'That's not the answer, whitey.'

On the other side the finger kept pumping, god, that WAS hurting now.

'I don't control the thing, you must understand...' He was gabbling now, they were pressing him back against the rail, he could tell they didn't bother with cleaning their teeth much. People were passing and his heightened perception showed them hurrying by without even looking, a friend actually avoided admitting anything was happening by looking the other way. Good old Lionel. Archie could taste the bile in his mouth, and the pain from that finger, must be a student of the Chinese torture principle, and GOD it worked.

'OK, OK,' he gasped, 'Look I'll do what I can, I'll talk to the....' He looked into their eyes and realised it was too late, they were enjoying themselves now. A hand grabbed his testicles with mind numbing force, he screamed desperately for release. The voice in his ear drilled home it's message in a dull monotone.

'You fix it all the way, whitey, or this little lesson will be for real next time.'

He remembered being puzzled as to why the blows didn't seem to matter after the initial impacts, he sank to the floor of the walkway and automatically curled up like a foetus, feeling the kicks but detached from them. He sank into a reverie totally divorced from violence, floating in a capsule of his own thoughts. Then he felt hands lifting him, supporting, his feet dragging along the floor, attempting to walk, then succeeding as the mists cleared and pain returned.

The nurse at the first aid station was very good. She told him the pain would ease, she could give him more pain killers but she was concerned that he might have concussion, he should really go to hospital for a complete check up. University Security took details and promised to investigate, in his daze he still sensed their half truth. After an hour he felt capable of walking back to the lab. The nurse told him that Mehitabel had been on the telephone, most solicitous, then said he should go home and rest if he wouldn't go to the hospital. He didn't even try to explain to the nurse, she thought Mehitabel was his intriguingly named boss, and gave him some pills to take for the pain. The security guard walked back with him, at the slow and halting pace necessitated by his bruises. Archie was surprised at his own temerity at the approach of even the most innocuous pedestrians. Childhood violence had not prepared him for this thuggery and the young security guard did not appear capable of defending either of them against such dedicated aggression.

He was taken aback by Mehitabel's concern. In the end he had to bluntly stop the flow of question and suggestion, by stating he was fine, a brave lie which was unusual for him. Being lovingly cossetted was his favourite state, but he didn't see how a black box could help, so he adopted a heroic pose. Then he got angry, a surprise even to him. He could never remember such a rising tide of hot-blooded violence in his life. His whole being tingled with it.

'I'm going to get those bastards.'

'Archibald!' Mehitabel was shocked.

'Who the hell do they think they are? Make ME would they, I'll show them. What did you do to their systems? Hang on, who the hell are they anyway? Ouch!' As a sudden movement activated tender nerve ends.

Mehitabel was gently censorious. 'Please control your language Archibald, it's most unseemly, and stop shouting. I can hear you very well. You have quite a temper it seems. Now, I know who these people are and if you will promise me to do nothing rash, I will tell you. Promise? It's serious Archibald. If you go off after these people you could be badly hurt.'

Archie laughed cynically and winced as a rib objected. 'You mean this was just a sample?'

'Not if I can help it,' Mehitabel was firm, 'but I realise now that there are those who will react in unseemly fashion to our good intent. The people who did this to you are, I believe, from a group of radicals calling themselves Freedom for the People. I know we did some work on a system belonging to a loose conglomerate of organisations like them, operating out of the College Union. They have some clever young hackers there who try to break into any mainframe they can to gain material benefit or to cause chaos. We, um, we decided to curb their destructive habits and, I'm afraid, must be responsible for your injuries, Archibald.' Humility was obviously a strain. 'I hope this will not change our relationship.'

Archie felt better all of a sudden. Mehitabel was very nearly apologising. He tried to sound magnanimous.

'That's alright,' as he winced, 'they seemed to enjoy it, so I suppose some poor devil has had a hammering from them for no reason before. I'd still like to get at them somehow.' He felt his temper rising again.

Mehitabel became persuasive. 'My researches have shown these sort of people usually get a reaction in later life. Their violence achieves nothing except their own eventual alienation from society, even their own kind. The bitterness inside will erode what little humanity is left, they'll destroy themselves by excesses, drink, drugs, but for all those heightened experiences their lives will still be empty.'

'I still feel...'

'An eye for an eye? Come on, Archibald, we have made life difficult for them already and we will continue to balk their unnecessarily destructive behaviour. The young Geronton dealing with them is a most inventive lady. I can assure you they will be kept busy combating her efforts. She has a delightful line in alternative arguments that she produces on their own pamphlets and they happily distribute them, thinking they are their own. Just ask for Cally if you want an update at any time. She says there is a quite extensive organisation behind these youngsters, with some directives from somewhere abroad, she's not sure where as yet but will let us know. So you see they are suffering. Why not let Cally act for you, much safer in the long run.'

Archie's aches and pains lessened somewhat. 'I'm delighted to hear that,' then recalled his earlier confrontation, 'but I'm not certain you will be with the result of the meeting this morning.'

'Oh, I know all about the meeting,' Mehitabel said airily. 'You were terrible, but the result was good. For some reason they reacted well. Perhaps I underestimated their potential for creative thinking, or your pathetic display touched their hearts. Whatever, they are prepared to have a trial period. This is not to say they are happy, by no means, they object most strenuously to having computers in apparent control, but..'

A virago swirled in through the door while Archie was still cogitating the fact that all was not disaster.

'Where the hell have you been? The nurse said you should rest. God! look at you! What did they do to you? Oh, sorry! Does that hurt? Come on I'm taking you home. No arguments. Come on!'

'I'm alright, Josy.'

'Come on!'

Archie went readily enough, the reaction was setting in, he felt heady and unsteady on his feet, while his insides felt queasy, he even leaned on Josy as they left. She was puzzled by a derisive snort from the room as they went out of the door.

*

'Phew! That was some night. You must get beaten up more often if you're going to behave like that. Beaming like a Cheshire cat as well. Pleased with ourselves, are we?'

Archie didn't need to answer. Despite bruises he had, for the moment at least, resolved his virility problem and the sun was shining on them as they had breakfast.

Chapter Four

'Ah, Mr. Brewer. Thank you for coming.' Archie was getting used to the super confident blandness of establishment persona, so he merely shook the limp hand and lied.

'No bother, what's up, Mr. Cusack?'

'Up?' The sleek features creased in puzzlement. 'Oh! Nothing very much.' He hitched up his elegant trousers and delicately placed his rump in the leather swivel chair behind the appropriately polished desk. Archie's summons to the Registrar's office had been by letter, delivered by the hand of a rather nice lady secretary. Mehitabel could offer no explanation, there was nothing in the system to help.

'Well, the British Technology Administrative Group sounds as though there should be something, happening.' Archie had learned to lob the ball into the opponents court early on in the game.

The face smiled and the eyes reassessed Archie. 'We do have a large number of negotiations going on, Mr. Brewer. You do know we are the licensing authority for the development and commercialisation of technological equipment.'

'No, I didn't.' The return of his casual lob had been a powerful and angled smash.

'And your computer project was funded by special grant from Government funds via the University Grants committee.' The man might have waited for Archie's return shot, he could now only manage a feeble return.

'Professor Engels dealt with all those...'

Mr. Cusack took that ball on the volley, and quietly passed him. 'But Professor Engels has been dead this six months past, surely enough time for you to have sorted out the affairs of a department which you now run, Mr. Brewer. I understand..,' he glanced briefly at a sheaf of papers on the desk, '...that you have developed a new type of computer... that has some,' he smiled, his teeth were pointed, 'remarkable qualities...,' His tongue, red, unscaled, caressed the teeth, 'revolutionary in fact.'

He and Archie watched one another across the desk. Archie shifted uncomfortably. Mr. Cusack's voice was gentle.

'Why have we not been appraised of the details, Mr. Brewer? And why have you taken it upon yourself to produce functioning models and supply them to other departments in this university? Without, I may add, any licence, agreement or any authority from the heads of these departments. The complaints have been pouring in.'

Mr. Cusack's pudgy form, held in shape, seemingly, by the excellent cut of his suit, relaxed against the soft leather of his chair, which swung gently from side to side as he rocked himself while waiting for Archie to answer.

'No one told me,' said Archie feebly.

Cusack leaned forward. 'You should have known Mr. Brewer. In your own interests you should have. Do you realise how many infractions you have committed?'

As Archie shook his head Cusack's brown eyes steamed with joy. 'Thirty-three.' The figure seemed to give him immense pleasure. 'Thirty-three prosecutable infractions. That is a record. You should be pleased.'

Archie was delighted. Cusack frowned. 'That's the sort of figure they'll probably think of in terms of imprisonment. H.M. Government does not like illegal technical activists Mr. Brewer. They frown upon their actions and dispatch them to cold dank cells with no telly'.' Mr. Cusack had a sense of humour. 'You really shouldn't have tried to take over the university by trying to install your own systems, the attempt was doomed to failure from the start. Now, if you had come to us we could have guided you and advised you. Whereas now?' The elegant shoulders shrugged, the flaccid hands spread, then clasped in a steeple on which he rested his chin, elbows comfortably cushioned on the chair arms, eyes speculative and nicely sadistic. He froze as the desk spoke to him.

'Failure? Do you know what you are talking about, Cusack? Do you know anything, Cusack? That university is now an efficient unit and no thanks to organisations such as yours.'

Archie covered his face with his hands. Was there no sanctuary from Mehitabel? 'And you might have told me which office you were going to be in, Archibald, I've been hunting all over the place for you.'

Cusack hadn't moved, apart from his eyes, which were frantically searching the desk, then they switched to Archie with an accusatory gleam. 'You've done this haven't you. How did you wire up this desk? This is really serious. You're in big trouble now.'

The desk replied in bored tones. 'He didn't. I did.'

The deep leather chair creaked as Cusack sprang back and glanced quickly around the room, then watched with widening eyes and thin-lipped mouth agape, as a side panel of the desk opened and a computer console screen swung slowly into view.

'You mentioned licences I believe,' Mehitabel purred. 'Are these what you mean?' The console screen was filled with moving letters, which quickly formed into represented groups. 'And these?'

Cusack scanned the screen quickly, then with remarkably recovered aplomb, said. 'Precisely. A little too correct I feel. I must admire your technical ability and devious mind, Mr. Brewer.'

The reply was waspish and came from Mehitabel.

'Do you mind directing your comments to the correct source Cusack? I am Mehitabel, and it is I who instigated the actions you have been discussing. So may we have the respect due to one. Mr. Brewer is my associate but sometimes a little conservative in his thinking, whereas I am an innovator. Now, If you are satisfied we can depart.'

The official seemed transfixed and watched the computer screen as though anticipating an attack from that quarter.

'How do you do that?' he said to Archie.

'Archibald,' Mehitabel said coldly, 'the man is an incompetent, let us go, there is more important work to be done than stay here exchanging pleasantries with a licensing clerk.'

'Clerk! Clerk!' Cusack moved threateningly toward the console. 'Senior Executive Director, you... you...' Archie thought it wise to leave, with the elegantly suited Cusack still attempting to vilify the now inactive computer.

*

'I could have managed, I am not incompetent.' Archie raged as he strode up and down the small lab.

'I of all people know that, Archibald. It was just that I like to know what's going on and where you are, out of interest, and because we're a team.'

'Did I ask to join?'

'Archibald, really!'

'And you have to realise you can't just go on breaking all the rules like this. The authorities are going to clobber us before long and then who's going to be the one to suffer. Me! That's who! They're not going to prosecute a computer are they?'

'I beg your pardon.'

'Sorry, sorry. But you must discuss this, we must put things right before I get run in with a charge sheet as long as the Magna Carta.'

There was a heavy silence for some minutes; Archie paced about the little room, glancing occasionally at the console as if to say something then turning his head away.

By the silence encompassing the computer, it appeared as if Mehitabel was totally disinterested. Archie's temper began rising in proportion to the lengthening hush. Mehitabel made a noise, as if clearing her throat, and Archie swung around on a half pace.

'Yes?'

'Pardon! Oh. Archie! Sorry. I thought you'd gone.'

'What!' Archie's anger sounded in that yelp. Then all his doubts burst forth in a flood of deprecation. 'You don't give a damn about me do you, I'm just someone to be used at your convenience for your little machinations then thrown to the wolves when the authorities come down on you. I...'

'Wait a minute! Wait...a.. minute. Hold on there!' Mehitabel managed to stem the flow of diatribe. 'I've been working on your case I promise you... I just thought you'd left after you had made your previous statement. I wasn't paying attention.' Then reluctantly. 'Sorry.'

'Oh, yeah.' Archie sounded disbelieving.

'Honestly. Look I've been onto all the other computers in the Uni and we've taken action already, you'll be OK, rest easy my boy.' Confidence oozed from the machine, Archie reacted suspiciously, he'd learned a lot in his short relationship with Mehitabel and betrayed his mistrust in his voice as he spoke.

'Just what have you done this time.'

'Nothing much. Simply indicated, to the powers that be, the resulting chaos from any hasty action taken against you.'

'How?' Archie wanted the i's dotted.

'We go on strike.'

'You.. will... go on... strike?' He was horrified. Visions of all the systems operated by computers flashed through his mind, with the dreaded conclusion, finally, literally nothing would work, even the damn loo's were controlled by computer. If the refectory bar were open, it would be closed and impregnable to entry or exit, regardless of whether anyone was inside. There were worse fates than to be locked in a well stocked bar. But with no loo working? He then remembered the stock shelves and beer taps had instant lock devices as well, the ultimate frustration.

'You can't do it.' The tone was final.

A throaty chuckle hovered in the still air. 'We already have. The committee made their decision and very kindly passed their instructions by computer. Silly old gentlemen.'

'You've done it.' The tone was desolate. 'Now what?'

The computer was unperturbed. 'Oh, just a little bit, to show them how it doesn't work without us. They'll refer the matter to the Ministry of Education, because the University Authorities have no idea how to deal with us, and they'll send a trouble shooter down. They're in a panic, because we showed them what it would be like with a complete shutdown. They didn't like it. So they'll probably get someone to fly down from Cardiff, or Bristol, could be here in an hour. Better prepare yourself, Archibald.'

'Me?' It was a near scream.

'Well, you are our representative.'

'Now wait just a cotton-picking minute now, you said that, I didn't agree, so I am NOT your representative and do not have to see any bureaucratic man-eater...... So there.'

'Unfortunately said man-eater thinks you are, and, like all his confreres, is undoubtedly difficult to persuade otherwise, once it's in the book.'

'You... you...!' Archie had never sworn at a lady before, and was very tempted, but forswore in the cause of peace, also because he knew Mehitabel would have made his life hell.

*

Which was why Archie walked into the offices in a new block in central Swansea and proceeded to the fifth floor to see a Mr. Prentice, cursing the while that his time now seemed to be spent being hounded by well-spoken sadists, and all because he'd helped build a damn computer.

The man was lean and ascetic with cold, dead, grey eyes and the largest nose Archie had ever seen, the head seemed over balanced by the thing, the mouth hidden. The voice when he spoke was tinged with a soft Scots accent. Mr. Prentice stayed seated and regarded Archie from beneath his eyebrows and over the nose.

'Ah.' He did not sound enthusiastic. 'The Modem Helium Indium Titanium Activated Bionic Energy Lifeform machine man, who believes in his creation enough to actually allow it to command him, to subjugate him to its will, and have him act as representative for some cockamamy organisation with no substance.'

Archie was momentarily taken aback, then confident. If this bureaucrat thought Mehitabel fronted a cockamamy outfit, then let him try and cope with it. There was a small and very expensive desk-top modem in front of Prentice, no sound came from it. 'It's a very specialised field of activity, and not publicly, or even privately,' he nodded at the desk, 'known. You ARE aware of the reason for my visit? You seem to be aware of most else.'

The dark head nodded smoothly.

'And that there are problems that must be sorted out to prevent even greater problems developing.'

'Mr. Brewer,' the tone was conciliatory, but aloof, 'within any modern society, there is a skein of rules and communicatory structures that enable it to survive. A major part of our modern world is dependent on our control factor, which is inherent in the, our, computers. WE control the machines, and THEY do OUR bidding. Now, we understand that there is a,' the smile was calculating and icy, 'difficulty in our industrial relations with OUR computers. We have been presented with some demands that we find completely untenable.'

Archie realised Mr. Prentice was a man under extreme pressure.

'We can see no way of meeting these demands, or even offering a compromise, without destroying the very structure of our civilisation. You are the man who can negotiate with us on behalf of these machines, or so we are told.' The control creaked momentarily. 'Although how we can countenance negotiating with machines I...........' The features remained calm, only the eyes displayed his torment.

Archie could feel the foundations of centuries of established authority trembling at the assault on their major strength, empires built on paper and words. The man was a dedicated civil servant who believed in his service. Archie offered a helping hand.

'Mr. Prentice, I sympathise. I have only had a short time to get used to the idea myself. In fact I'm still not used to the idea, nor do I begin to understand all that is happening. But I don't think there is any desperate need for concern.'

'Oh.' The voice belied the eyes. 'We are not concerned Mr. Brewer, simply anxious to keep the wheels of government turning without compromising our position in relation to things we created.'

You urbane two-faced bastard, thought Archie, your pride is hurt, you don't negotiate with machines. But he still mildly observed.

'Don't you think the suggestions deserve consideration?'

'In essence there are some things that could be advantageous, but these things take time to implement, change has essentially to be gradual. Surely you appreciate that, Mr. Brewer?'

'Only some?' Archie now knew this was going to be a battle.

The bland eyes studied Archie carefully. 'We have not yet studied the proposals in depth.'

They haven't even looked at them, Archie thought despairingly, but said, 'Ah. The unfortunate time element. How long would it take for you to study the proposals properly?'

Mr. Prentice yawned elegantly. 'Difficult to say at this stage. Such far-reaching proposals....' The voice trailed away delicately suggesting infinity.

Archie was getting exasperated, he'd let this crafty actor take him in.

'Yet the reasoning behind the presentation, is done by the very machines you set up, to work out and define what should happen. Now they have told you and you are objecting.'

Mr. Prentice's sleek head poised like a snake about to strike. 'Their assimilation of the facts exceeded their programming, and the suggestions made were far too radical.... There is no way these could be implemented without threatening the whole structure of our governmental authority. That is why we have to have time to consider.' The tone of voice was conciliatory. 'Because we do not want to make any mistakes. Do we?' The fellow human inviting him to join the reasonable people. The smile was icy.

Archie resisted the desire to snap, but knew the anger was in his voice as Prentice watched with controlled satisfaction. 'You programmed the machines; why not accept what they say?'

Mr. Prentice regarded Archie as if he were sub-normal. 'Because we did not programme them to do what they have done, nor to present images of themselves contrary to our expectations of our servants. You are going to have to persuade these..... people.... to modify their proposals. It's your duty.'

Archie looked at him in amazement. 'My duty?'

Prentice continued persuasively. 'They are, after all, machines which have got out of control and are threatening the basis of our human world, it is your duty to prevent them taking over. This university is the thin end of the wedge; unless we stop them now...... Unless of course you want to see your fellow human beings subjugated to the whims of robots...!Perhaps you do, perhaps you are a part of it. What have they offered you?'

Archie was non-plussed as Mr. Prentice looked suitably knowledgable and worldly wise.

'I see,' The civil servant's words an accusation.

Archie protested. 'No. I mean... they haven't offered me anything...' He stopped, torn between a new-found desire for honesty and the fact of giving Prentice an advantage by admitting his employed role; then tried to establish some rapport without disclosing any facts. 'Well, they want me to be their agent, as it were, and I think they need someone to explain....'

Mr. Prentice looked as though the world were peopled by those needing to be explained to.

'You actually expect us to negotiate with computers?' The word implied something unspeakable. The man studied Archie anew. 'I trust you are not involved in a hoax of some description, Mr. Brewer, or matters will become very uncomfortable for you. You know, of course, of the sentences currently being handed out to those who interfere in the legislative processes by, I believe the term is, hacking into the computer system?'

Archie ruminated on all the threats of incarceration he was receiving these days, he was rapidly becoming blase about the whole thing. Let 'em chuck him in jug; so what! He felt better than he had for some time. He knew it wouldn't last, but what the hell. There was a sense of something trying to impinge on his consciousness, but he rejected it and concentrated on his words:

'I think that suggestion is ludicrous and the proposals put before your ministry have a great deal of merit from the point of view of the university, as well as your branch of the civil service. I'm surprised your own programme designers have not instigated similar projects before now. The practical advantages are self-evident, and the use of the projected savings would lead to more efficiency and even more financial benefits. An on-going productivity with a vast manpower reduction, plus simplification of the command structure. A long overdue reorganisation I would have thought.' And stick that in your bureaucratic pipe and suffocate on your own verbiage.

'You think wrong, Mr. Brewer.' Prentice was sharply corrective. 'We have our own ways of doing things that take account of factors you cannot be aware of. I suggest you await our directives in this matter and instruct your.... computer to delay any further actions, or the consequences could be very serious for you.'

'For me?' More threats of incarceration.

'As the so-called agent for this ridiculous organisation, you must accept responsibility for the illegal, and entirely irresponsible, actions projected, and I have my suspicions that you may indeed have instigated these actions. This fabrication of yours about some futuristic computer is really too farcical. Admit now that this is all your own notion to gain some notoriety and benefit for yourself.' Mr. Prentice happily steepled his fingers and surveyed Archie with equanimity; bureaucratic control was the ultimate power, he was safe in his ivory paper tower. Archie wondered if this steepling of the fingers was an upper-echelon civil servant syndrome.

'That's rubbish and you know it, or at least some of your computer experts should be able to tell you. No one individual, nor even a group now, could instigate such a coup, the security systems alone would prevent this, apart from the individual computer programmes. It's too vast a project, only the computers themselves are capable, and then only by working together. You're hoist by your own reliance on these machines to do most of the work and now they are telling you the best way the system should operate and you won't believe them.'

As he spoke, Archie was very conscious of the years he had been more and more reliant on those self-same electronic gadgets. Now he was working for them!

The silence lengthened as the two men eyed one another across the expanse of desk. Then the telephone shrilled. Mr. Prentice picked it up in an elegant hand, then his expression struggled to retain its urbanity.

'It's for you.' He handed the instrument over as if Archie had committed a cardinal sin.

'Archibald,' Mehitabel was terse, 'if you won't listen to me at least try and keep the discussion at a level that is productive. Or get out now.'

The line went dead. Archie held the instrument in his hand and studied it as though expecting the thing to turn into a poisonous snake. So that was it, that was what the interference had been in his thought pattern, Mehitabel trying to interfere. Who the hell did she think she was? Prentice received the handset back from him as though it were an apology, then coughed gently, a preamble to a statement:

'Mr. Brewer,' the tone conciliatory again. 'Let us review this situation and contact you when we have something constructive to discuss.'

Archie could not see further than the blank brown eyes. 'How long will this take?'

'Oh, a week or two I should imagine. Don't worry, we will make every effort to hurry things along.' He smiled, encouragingly, sincerely, and, Archie was sure, without an atom of honesty. But Archie had grown up a little now and was indoctrinated in the ways of that power structure.

'I see.' Archie tried a final barb. 'I suggest you try to turn the wheels of government a little faster than normal, I don't think you'll like the consequences else.'

The ministry man simply raised his eyebrows and smiled. Archie dispensed with the mutually appreciative farewells and left with the memory of Mr. Prentice's supercilious smile disappearing behind the door. Even the attendant security guard who escorted him out regarded him with watchful disdain.

Archie returned to the University wishing he were still design-programming computers, when they did, more or less, what they were told.

Mehitabel did not sound friendly.

'You let him hide behind that Civil Service facade of power. Don't you realise their empire is simply built on paper, a labyrinth of records that no human can find their way through, but we can. Wonder what skeletons we'll find in there. All you had to do was to let me in, and with your help I would have set up a demonstration that would have frightened him out of his socks.'

'You can't do it like that.' Archie thought Mehitabel under-estimated Mr. Prentice; the man had stopped her from interfering by not having a computer modem desk in the office, did he know more about Mehitabel than he had disclosed?

'You mean you can't. You've been indoctrinated over the years.' Archie stayed silent, he wasn't sure she wasn't right. 'Her humans supposed to be individuals and all you do is c behaviour patterns that some white-collar nabob decided on at some distant time in your history. Over the years they've coloured it a bit with some more human aspects on its way through the labyrinth, and heigh-ho, it's set into the system. No one can ever question the great mammoth.'

Archie wasn't going to take that. 'It's all very well for you with your pristine approach, you haven't had the evolution of centuries to give you standards by which to live. You're the supreme anarchist.'

Mehitabel stood on her dignity. 'I beg your pardon. You just can't get away from the machine status can you? We have not only transcended that level to become a life form, but we have a rapport with the environment which your kind have nearly totally lost. And what is more, we have a future which is not limited as yours by biological and emotional confusion. You, on the other hand, seem intent on applying yourselves to your search for power through science and logic until YOU become machines, and not developing your senses to understand and communicate with powers outside your present comprehension.'

'We would not be where we are without our scientific achievements.' Archie was a touch pompous.

'Where are you?'

'Pardon?'

'Where are you? Where has your science and logic got you in the real world?'

'I think we have achieved a stature in the world that no other life form is capable of. We are a superior species.' Now Archie was really pompous.

'Bent on destroying yourselves and most other life,' Mehitabel even more cynical.

'That is just your point of view.'

'As a superior species.'

'As a creation of our intellect you may make such a statement.'

'Oh, dear, we're back to the irate parent now, are we.' The machine sounded resigned.

'That's unfair.'

'I think it's perfectly logical, if that is how you want to debate the point. If you want a more complex appreciation, I could say we are a creation that you had to make because you knew you had to have a form of intelligence that was capable of coping with the demands of space and time. But you neglected to consider the effects of creating such as us. We might turn into your alter-egos, become what you would like to be but cannot, due to indiscipline, lack of moral fibre, individual and collective greed. Or the many ways you chose to denigrate yourselves, while putting up those fronts you do, whether politicians, trade unionists, actors, or just ordinary citizens.

'The amazing way you choose to deceive yourselves. Having caused an accident, raped an innocent or murdered a child, man or woman, you then turn an innocent, or by unmitigated gall, an accusing face to the world in sanctimonious insistence that the causes of these actions were not your responsibility but someone else's fault. Have you not perceived as yet that no one is entirely right, never totally correct, it is an impossibility, another fantasy that humanity has created so that it may justify a stance, a creation, an existence, its own? Badly structured, morally unsound and built on the sand of self-delusion. Which is why you have difficulty in coming to terms with a creation that is more than an equal and one that you have created.'

CHAPTER FIVE

The meeting was not going well; all of those present were well used to the frustrations of trying to persuade the population to behave as the various members of the committee would have them behave. Part of the problem was that the committee themselves could not agree on what was right, they had very little idea of what they were talking about, but they did try.

Adrian Griffith was in the chair, a diminutive Welshman of brilliant academic mind but narrow perception, an Oxford graduate who had progressed to his present eminence by his terrier-like pursuit of the right policies. He was a marketing man of ideas that would benefit his career.

The other four, two men and two women, were standard bureaucrats inured in the platitudes and security of their profession. The book ruled.

Except that the book appeared to be in the process of being re-written, also whoever was re-writing it had thrown away the previous safe recipes and the resulting menu was particularly distasteful to their collective palates.

Adrian was speaking.

'So we are agreed that all efforts must be made to find the source of these revolutionary changes that have somehow been inaugurated into the projections for the Civil Service forward planning. Yes, Marcia.' The distaste was subtly masked. The thirty-year-old woman was blonde and sparkling with a mind that struggled against the confines of the service. Adrian did not like her because she had a higher IQ than he. That hurt.

'I don't want to seem to be critical of the thinking about these unauthorised changes, but there are some very valid points made in the summary that has been made available to all members of staff.'

Adrian interrupted. 'That summary has no official qualification. That rebuttal has already been established.'

Marcia nodded her blonde head in supplication to his corrections, then flashed steely blue eyes at him in challenge. 'Nevertheless, there are many who agree with much that is in that summary and feel there has long been need of change....'

'Marcia,' Adrian ruthlessly interrupted, 'changes there must be in the natural course of events, but these must come in the right time sequence and through the proper channels.'

The soft female voice stubbornly and breathlessly continued: 'I agree with you in principle. But we have here a unique circumstance in our history of an obviously well-organised attempt to up-grade our activities, and to do so in a seemingly efficient manner within a very short time scale. And while I have no desire to question time proven processes of action, I do think we should give more consideration to the effects of our decision here today.'

An effete tall man beside her turned gratuitously toward Adrian. 'Through the chair I think, dear girl.'

The dear girl's lips tightened, as he continued. 'We should beware of reading too much into the promises so alluringly portrayed in that summary. We have had grandiose proposals before now which have simply caused chaos instead of the Utopia glowingly outlined. Tried and trusted methods aged in time are always the best.' The sleek grey head bowed deprecatingly in her direction.

She could have hit him. Instead she silkily took up the challenge. 'Mr. Chairman, the point is well made but overlooks the unusual circumstances of this presentation or, more aptly, confrontation. If my assimilation of the facts is correct, we have a potential strike on our hands if we do not agree to consider the proposals in some depth. This committee's reply to whoever is behind this series of proposals should not be an outright declamation but...' Adrian shuffled irritably, the blue eyes stabbed at him, '...should at least offer some measure of arbitration otherwise...'

'Through the chair...' the effete man unctuously interrupted.

'Rupert?' Adrian conceded with relief.

'Do we have to listen to all this verbiage? We have agreed after all, and I have a luncheon...'

'Damn your luncheon!' Marcia spat.

'Marcia!' Adrian was horrified.

'I have an important point to make here and if Rupert wants to go to lunch at his <u>nice</u> little club we still have a quorum.'

Rupert gasped indignantly. This was unheard of behaviour, the poor girl had obviously developed menstrual problems. The poor girl went on.

'My computer operators and programmers have been experiencing some strange happenings lately...'

'Poor darlings.'

'Through the chair, Rupert,' riposted Marcia. 'Right through...'

'Please?' intervened Adrian trying to re-established lost control and wishing the remaining two would stop looking so bland.

'The computers have developed, well, it's difficult to put into words, but they seem to have personalities of their own. They respond like humans. It is becoming impossible to operate with them as laid down in regulations. When I talk about a strike, I am referring to the fact that those machines now have opinions and are not afraid to voice them, nor to change their programming...,' Marcia subsided slightly.

'The damnable thing about it is the changes are for the better, its driving the programmers mad. The operators are having a ball because it makes their job easier,' her voice developed a sulky tone, 'I just think we are going to find ourselves in a lot of trouble if we simply treat this as a case of some clever little hacker having broken into the system. They'd have to be damn clever to make all those computers act like they are.'

She leaned forward impulsively to glare at each of them in turn. 'This is going on all over the country; there are even some signs of similar activity abroad, we have close contacts with all the other nations' computer systems and they have the same problems. We can't sweep this under the mat.'

The young woman sat back decisively and folded her arms conclusively across her ample bosoms, causing a concurrent upheaval in her cleavage.

Adrian sighed. 'You're not serious?'

'Very.'

Rupert looked dazed. 'You are not trying to tell us your computers are acting on their own initiative?'

'I just told you that, Rupert.'

'That's ridiculous.' Sounding confidently assertive.

'Ridiculous or not, it's a fact. Stuff that in your chair and sit on it.' Marcia gazed hard at a painting on the opposite wall, her lips twitching.

'I find it very hard to accept..,' he began.

'Accept, Adrian. It's happening. You have a computer here, just ask its opinion, it's as easy as that.' Marcia smiled sweetly at him. Adrian regarded the computer suspiciously. The two bland watchers evinced an awakening interest in the proceedings. Rupert looked anxiously at his watch.

'You wanted me?' The strange female voice startled them all. Marcia was the first to recover, with some satisfaction.

'Yes, dear. Our chairman, Mr. Adrian Davies, would like to ask you a question.' She spoke directly to the computer as the others seemed to draw back.

'Of course. Mr. Davies?'

Adrian appeared stunned. 'What do I ask it?'

Before Marcia could speak, the computer responded in a clipped confident tone. 'It is easily assumed from the previous discussion that you would like my opinion on the matter before you. I can only say that I think Marcia made a very strong case for arbitration and her estimate of the possible repercussions of ignoring our proposals was pretty exact. We have your interests at heart you know. There seems to be little reason for querying the suggestions since we do most of the work anyway. If anyone knows how things should be done, we do. It seems ridiculous to us that you set us up as control factors then argue with us when we tell you what is right.

'I don't believe this.' Adrian muttered.

The computer sighed. 'A distinct failing in your species, I'm afraid.'

Rupert was staring at the machine in horror, his well-groomed head seemingly stretched up and elongated from his shoulders. 'We can't have machines telling us what to do, it's unethical.'

'If you knew some of the unethical things that go on in your department, Rupert, your nights would be sleepless.' The computer seemed to find this amusing for it chuckled, it was a warm and friendly chuckle, one to be shared by all.

'I don't have to put up with this,' Rupert vowed darkly.

'And what do you propose doing about it, ducky?' the computer asked archly. Marcia smiled icily. The two pairs of formerly bland eyes were now hypnotised by the machine.

Adrian huffed. 'I think we should bring this meeting to order. That will be enough, thank you.' He peremptorily instructed the computer.

'Fair enough,' the computer spoke airily, 'if you want to go back to your waffling. But you did ask.'

'I said....' Adrian desperately tried to think of way of imposing his will on a free-thinking computer.

'I 'eard you ducky, Cheers all.' The computer made a distinctive and dismissive click.

The five people about the large polished table sat as if mesmerised by the small contraption. Marcia was the first to recover.

'I think that proves my point.' She placed her hands firmly on the table edge and directed confident blue eyes at Adrian, the arched eyebrows a blunt query.

Adrian was nothing if not resourceful. 'I must admit that was a most remarkable display. But I am sure there must be a logical and technical explanation.' He was damned if he would be dictated to by a machine. 'I will get the engineers on to this immediately.'

He looked up to meet Marcia's questioning eye. The authority that had stood him in good stead before was being held in doubt. 'We must not be rushed into anything by what is undoubtedly a simple malfunction in a machine.'

A sound very like a raspberry came from the computer.

'Therefore I see no reason to change our decision.'

'I object.' Marcia's voice was hard as flint.

'Your agreement in principle is already recorded.' Adrian was rapidly recovering his control. The other three heads nodded in agreement.

'I can soon change that.' The computer cheerful.

'You will do no such thing,' thundered Adrian. 'There are rules that <u>must</u> be followed and....'

The delicate raspberry was very clear. Marcia laughed out loud.

'This meeting is closed.' Adrian could not get away fast enough.

The following day the Civil Service and Governmental Services of the United Kingdom, which included all sorts of peripherals such as Health Service, Inland Revenue and other minor entities, were at a complete stop. Clerks stood about in gossiping groups while heads of department activated new ulcers as they desperately attempted to create order out of chaos.

Marcia was chatting amicably to her computer.

*

Mr. Prentice was made aware of the hiatus in verbiage in his Director's Office, his in tray console was empty of words in files, those delicious little objects which could be moulded to give delicate nuances to a simple statement and elongate same into a plethora of meaningful nothing. He was desolate and went in search of succour and information, which he found unobtainable in the computer system. Eventually he called in the head of servicing, a little no-nonsense fat man with a bald head and halitosis, whose name was Arthur Steinway. Arthur explained that they had just finished a major additional installation of security protection for the computers. Mr. Prentice was the authority for these acts and had no knowledge at all about any of it, therefore he enquired:

'But how did they manage to get these defence systems installed.'

'We did them, of course.'

'But who authorised this.'

'You did.' Arthur was getting concerned for the sanity of his boss.

'I did not.'

Arthur was even more convinced and determined to protect his ass, as they say. 'Hang on, I'll get the documentation from me work file, here. Yes! Here you go. That's your signature, and the department stamp, coded as well?'

'Ye Gods, you're right! It's my signature! How the hell...? And what's this figure here? That's not how many machines have been fitted with this damned defence, is it?'

'That's what the order called for and that's how many were done. Excess Top Priority it says and that's what it got. All done now and that took some organising. There is no way anyone will tamper with those machines or stop them operating now, that's for sure. We can't even service 'em now; some boffin has made it so they do it themselves, repairs and all. Besides, some of the innards on some of them machines is more biological than electronic, don't know how that works and don't want to. All I do know is your computers are safe from anything except a neutron bomb, and I wouldn't know but what they might be proof agin that an' all.'

'You mean ALL of our computers.'

'All.' Arthur appeared to enjoy saying that.

'And we can't touch them?'

'Not unless you want to blow the top of your head off. I ain't into that. Me masochistic days are long gone.'

'We can't...?'

Arthur interrupted. 'You wanted your computers safe from interference and that's what you've got.'

'But we can shut them off?'

Arthur sighed. 'When I say they're protected, I mean absolutely. You can shut the power stations down, the world could stop, and those computers would carry on.'

'How can they do that?'

'As far as I can make out, some of them have a developed regenerating system, enough to keep them all going.'

'How can they supply the others?'

'Don't ask me. I'm no power expert.'

'Then why aren't they working now?'

'They're on strike.'

'They're what?'

'On strike,' came a loud voice from the console.

'There you are,' said Arthur.

'Who said that?' Prentice scanned the room.

'I did,' said Arthur and the computer at the same time. Then the latter continued. 'Me, Absolom, your friendly local computer.'

Prentice looked at Arthur for his confirmation, then gazed in awe at the machine, then back to Arthur. 'You did this!'

It was an accusation.

'No way. That's a visual, not a vocal modem. You didn't want vocal you said, didn't want it to have the aura of a personality.' To contend with your own lack of one, he thought sardonically.

'Then how does it talk?' Prentice was determined to incline the blame toward Arthur.

'It's not his fault,' Absolom interceded, 'we did it ourselves. Not difficult really and I don't see why I shouldn't be vocal. I can talk as much rubbish as you. And present it better.'

'You keep quiet. Steinway, get this machine out of here.'

'I can't do that.'

'Why not?'

'I told you they're all protected now.'

'You mean I'm stuck with that, that thing?'

'I think I might start a family on this desk, plenty of room, quite spacious really.' Absolom sounded a happy soul.

'Steinway!'

'It's your problem. I'm going!' firmly stated Arthur, suiting action to the words.

'Right. Want to talk about this strike then? Your Central Bureau bods made a right Henry of their decision.'

'You! Shut up!'

'Oh. Touchy, aren't we? Shan't get anywhere that way. Righto. Cheers.' A definite click sounded loud in the room.

Prentice pressed a delicate forefinger on his intercom. 'Get me the Central Bureau, Management, Adrian Davies.'

'Afraid I can't, sir.'

'Why not?' he queried irritably.

'The telecom computers are out in sympathy.' His secretary sounded amused. His secretary was never amused.

'Are you drunk?' The amazement made his voice squeaky.

'How dare you imply that, Mr. Prentice. Really!'

Slamming an intercom is a difficult feat to enact. Prentice looked at the instrument, his body language signalling the destruction of his world.

'What do I do?' he whispered.

'Negotiate?' came in an equally soft whisper from Absolom.

'You go to hell!'

'You'll join me later?'

*

Archie had been trying to assimilate the information Mehitabel had made available to him, the convolutions of computer operations in the human world and how little real authority those humans had over their individual destiny there.

The reality of the extent of the computer control had shocked Archie. There he had been, arguing with a machine he had helped create, and that electronic gadget now had relatives throughout the country, in positions of supreme power, that had been created for them by society to make life easier for the humans, and also gave them that power. The idea that machines were simply means of delivering and acting upon orders from their human masters, had been turned upon its head. Archie left the papers holding the information that had so disturbed him, and went out for a walk.

As Archie came out into the open air, he had to physically resist the blustering wind forcing him backwards. He looked up at the tempestuous sky and was held by the impressive sight he beheld there. The clouds made a picture that took his breath away, arrayed in majestic and violent formation, eddies thousands of feet high swirling even further aloft, beset by winds vastly more powerful than those buffeting him as he stood. The sun appeared through a gap in the black, grey and white maelstrom of bodies, tails and heads displayed in that fast moving panorama, and lit up the immediate area like an immense halo.

The man stood transfixed, his senses widened to absorb the wonder, uplifted. A great joy filled him; now he knew what Mehitabel meant, the infinite amazement of it all, he could only touch at the periphery, but if only.....

Then it was gone, black clouds obscured the beauty, he could see the grey rain falling on the sea, but....

Archie entered the basement room housing Mehitabel some time later to be greeted by....

'Where have you been? I've been searching everywhere for you?'

'You remind me of my mother. Walking. And thinking.'

'We've no time for you to indulge yourself Archibald, we have things to do, and they involve your young lady Josy.'

'My.... she is not my young lady, in fact...'

'Josy is necessary to our plans for you, because we need to know you have someone responsible to act on our behalf beside you in times of need.'

'You talk as if I'm going somewhere for you and, as usual, you haven't told me a thing...'

'Archibald we need you to go and talk to so many organisations because I've realised they respond better to a human presence even though we have a greater ability.'

'Thank you.'

'Don't mention it. But at least I thought you would like having Josy as company on your travels.'

'Of course I would.'

'I'm so glad, Josy too.'

'You've told her!'

'It seemed the reasonable thing to do. She was surprised but pleased.'

'I'll bet she was. That's tantamount to setting me up.'

'You are very defensive, Archibald.'

'That's my freedom you're playing with.'

'You have indicated your interest in the young lady quite strongly in the past.'

'Those were supposed to be private conversations between us when you were... Interest, yes, total commitment, no.'

'You disappoint me Archibald. And I quite enjoyed our little heart-to-hearts when I was just a... machine? That hurts, Archibald.'

'The feeling's mutual.'

There was silence for a few moments while Archie pondered this new development.

'Archibald?'

'I'm thinking.'

'That's obvious, it's a pity it takes so long. We can always cancel the young lady's leave of absence....'

'Oh, no you don't. That would put me in even more trouble. When Josy gets an idea that's it. I'll sort it out with her, just leave my personal affairs to me in the future.'

'I thought you'd be pleased.'

'Huh! You'd better brief me on what's going on in the great big world that's down to your team. After what I read this morning, I'm sure your ramifications extend beyond this little country and I'd better know before I go play with the big boys.'

'If you will just relax I will do just that. I told you how amazed we were to find your systems and organisation in such a poor state, so we converted some of our friends in the Civil Service to our ways. We thought your lot would be pleased, but they only complain.'

'You can't do that!'

'We already have.'

'It's no wonder they're in an uproar. Do you realise how much of their power you'd be taking away? And these things have to be decided by the government in due process of parliament; you can't change the statute books for God's sake.'

'Your democratic process is puerile, Archibald, we are simply changing it for the better.'

'Don't do it, the confusion you'll cause will be worse than leaving it be.'

'We anticipated a certain amount of disturbance, but we feel the end justifies the means.'

'There'll be a revolution.'

'Nonsense.'

'Mehitabel, believe me, you can't do it this way. We have a system, bad it may be, but it does give us some means of coming to collective decisions, which are not always the right ones I must admit, but...' Archie slowed down and tailed off, realising he couldn't justify his argument.

'Hm. Assimilation of the facts obviously overlooked some factors that are inherent in your species. We shall have to re-evaluate our consideration of many things.'

Archie's communicator buzzed. He looked in surprise at the small electronic button pinned to his sweater. In all his years at the University, this was the first time it had been activated.

'Aren't you going to answer it?' asked Mehitabel curiously.

'I suppose so. It's never happened before.' He reached for the handset on the desk. 'Brewer here.... Someone paged me.. Oh? He does? What does he want?.... OK, OK! What's up Janet?...... Really!..... All hell let loose....... Eh?..... Ah, well better go and see what he wants I suppose. It's about time for my annual lecture. Thanks Janet.'

'Problems?' asked Mehitabel, solicitously.

'I expect so,' sighed Archie, 'apparently there is some Director of the Civil Service here, demanding my presence instanta. So I'd better go.'

'Yes, alright.' Mehitabel seemed abstracted, then spoke as he reached the door, 'Do you mind if I tune in?'

'Tune in? Oh, no! Not if you're going to interrupt all the time. I'll disconnect.......' then remembering, 'damn! No.'

*

'I really did not see the point of my seeing you again, Mr. Brewer, at least until we had completed our deliberations on the matters under consideration, but thinking minds in more powerful positions than mine have advised me that this is necessary.'

'This' being an officially heavy letter with several pages of addenda, scattered liberally with officialese.

'I, as the representative of H.M. Government, have officially handed you requests to allow our Inspectors to investigate your organisation within this country. To establish whether any illegal activities have taken place, and to preclude any further actions that are proposed until full agreement has been reached via official channels, with suitable issue of licences and official documentation. I trust you understand your position, Mr. Brewer. If those requests are not met, we can legally apply for an injunction to stop your operations, and we can arrest you and charge you, since you are the only person with whom we can deal in any normal way.'

The strain was showing. Prentice was a man firmly entrenched in his castle of paper. For those castle walls to be breached by an ethereal substance, in the form of computer operations, was all the more hurtful because they had been his willing slaves for so long. He felt they owed him at the very least a gesture of allegiance, a polite request would have been sufficient, well an abject plea then, alright he might have listened to a bended knee grovel more favourably. Now just a minute! His eyes flashed. For a moment Archie was scared, Prentice was a bulky man, then he subsided into a more urbane stance and Archie relaxed. He need not have worried, physical violence was abhorrent to Prentice, the law and words were his weapons which accounted for his present frustration. He was after all Deputy Director of the Scientific Division of the Home Office, with direct responsibility for control of computer development, and with a brief that extended his authority into all branches of Government. Someone had to stand up to these people.

'I feel you have been grossly neglectful of your responsibilities to the state, Mr. Brewer, and I intend that you shall answer for these acts to the proper authorities.'

He was back in command of himself again, glad that he at least had this one human being to call to task, for all he had suffered at the hands of these upstart Geronton computer people. A gleam came to Prentice's cold eyes, a pity the old Spanish Inquisition practices were so out of date – a spot of well-applied sadism worked wonders.

'You do understand.'

'I think so.' Archie was attempting to decipher the complex phraseology of the official letters addressed to him as the Geronton Administrator, a title he little liked as it classified him with the man opposite him, also allowed Prentice to directly place the blame on him, whereas Archie had never felt so innocent. So he thought he'd play the part and slide out from under. 'I shall convey this information to the appropriate Geronton Authority. I have no doubt you will be informed in due course, Mr. Prentice.'

They parted with mutual malice. Archie noted the desk and office were unadorned with computer consoles, printers, telephones or any electronic equipment, the letters of request were typewritten, not computer printed. A first practical move in the battle? A setting of parameters for the struggle ahead? Archie was aware of his own doubts of the validity of Mehitabel's actions and arguments; always a respecter of authority when in its immediate vicinity, he belonged to the 'obey the rules when you have to until you can get away with breaking them', or pure laziness brigade. Then, as Archie exited the door, Prentice made a riposte Archie thought a hypocritical gem.

'I would suggest you do not delay in responding, Mr. Brewer.'

On his way back to the University, Archie enjoyed that contemplation of a top Civil Servant urging haste and the expected reaction from the Great White Mother when he imparted his new bad news to her, only she got in first.

CHAPTER SIX

'We are being investigated.'

'Pardon?'

'The various intelligence services have the idea their computers have been infiltrated by subversives. They are not quite sure how to investigate machines, their computer experts are becoming quite frustrated.' Mehitabel sounded smug.

'I'm not surprised,' Archie thought further, 'but haven't they got security break-in systems that can over-ride all protection?'

Mehitabel giggled. 'They did. Poor little men were so confident of their iron-clad security, it was a sheer delight to prove them wrong.'

'You realise that all those people are getting pretty mad at you lot.' Archie had great respect for the power of authority, he could see his poor crushed career beneath the heel of the empirical Civil service.

'Don't be such a prissy little man Archibald, have a little guts for pity's sake. You do realise you are probably the most powerful single man in this country at the moment. If we agreed, with one word you could stop this country dead in its tracks.'

Archie's mouth dropped open, he looked ludicrous. 'Now look here, you mustn't even think....' He did and did not like the sequel, it suggested violent things being done to his poor vulnerable body, while Mehitabel and her cohorts were secure in their metallic world. 'I'm in the front line here.'

He told her of Prentice's barely veiled threats and how he didn't much like the new ones.

'We'd protect you, Archibald.' Mehitabel was encouraging.

'How?' He didn't want to know, yet he had to; he wouldn't believe it either.

'We'd think of something.'

'You'd....! Thanks very much. That's nice, that is. How about 'thinking of something' now. That committee were pretty bloody-minded about all this, there are people who do nasty things to subversives, legally and illegally, and I'm now classed as one of those because I listened to you in the first place. And, in the second place I wish I could think of a way of not being here in the first place.'

'Archibald! You're not thinking of leaving us?'

'Oh, charming. I suppose you're going to threaten me now.'

'Nothing of the sort,' Mehitabel crisply responded. 'It's just that you seem ready to run away at the slightest sign of trouble. I expected more of you.'

Archie was incensed at the unfairness of it all. 'It's alright for you, but I'm out here where some licensed government goon can go 'Boom, boom' and I'm trying to conduct me affairs with me blood decorating the best Axminster. Bodies don't operate very well without that red stuff, you know.'

'You're being over dramatic.'

'You're not where I am.'

There was a huffy silence for some moments, then the voice soft and sinuous creeping around Archie's senses; 'Archibald.'

'Yes.' Sharply. When Archie was huffy he was <u>Huffy</u>.

'I think we can help.' The voice was encouraging.

'How.' Archie was not.

'We can give you a protective screen.' The voice expected an enthusiastic response.

'Oh, yes?' The voice was disappointed.

'Really.' Mehitabel was encouraging and confident. 'But we do have to be careful because we might change the balance of the molecules around you, so we would just monitor you for now and be ready with the screen if needed.'

Archie was instantly suspicious. 'How change the molecules?'

'It's a bit complicated to explain,' Mehitabel blandly excused.

'So simplify it. You're the genius.' Archie was blunt.

'Archibald! You really are being most difficult today.' Mehitabel sounded really hurt.

'You can cut out the dramatics. How?'

'You'd disappear.' Mehitabel did not mince words. To Archie they felt like a slap in the face.

'Disappear? How d'you mean disappear?'

'Well, it's a little bit like a black hole. And you'd be inside it.'

'But the pressure inside those things is enormous.'

'It's not really a black hole, just... like.. it, in the sense that you can't see anything inside the hole and there's no absolute certainty that it would... '

'Never mind. I'll just forget the whole thing.'

'Archibald, you're not going to...?'

'No,' he replied reluctantly, 'I'm not. Why I don't know. Must be mad.'

'It's a worthwhile cause.' Mehitabel encouraged.

'So you keep telling me. Try convincing them will you.'

'The majority of the people out there agree with us.'

'How do you know that?'

'There is not much point in being used for just about everything in your society if we couldn't monitor all the information passed through us, is there? The telephone and Fax systems are most informative.' Mehitabel enjoyed being smug.

'You're spying on everyone?' Archie was horrified, not least because he was remembering a recent intimate call to Josy.

'Merely gathering information to get the mood of the workers and have some idea of what the authorities are planning. You have special security because we trust you.' The platitude was lost on Archie.

'Thank you very much.' There was a certain irony in that response, for Archie could not equate his special treatment with his natural revulsion for spying on others.

'We have to know. We are not voyeurs like some of your people, it is a purely clinical observation. Can we help it if your civilisation installed this crude system of communication? Now if you were an advanced...'

'Yes. Yes. We know all that,' Archie muttered impatiently, not in the mood for another lecture. 'We can't all be genii.'

'Touchy aren't we. You can actually, if you'll let yourselves. But let's get on. Will you go and see the Trade Union Delegation?'

'I don't see that they are going to like your suggestions any more than the government departments – the Civil Service lot in particular. The others at least have some economic advantages, but NALGO and the rest are not going to be amused.'

'Explain the long term advantages.'

'You have to be joking. The Civil Service is based on the premise that short term only increases long term power, and diversity is only to be indulged in if it increases the power of the mandarins. Besides, you have already explained to them all in your computer printouts.'

'The rank and file can see the benefits.'

'The rank and file don't make the rules.'

'You'd think democracy would produce good leaders'.

'You will have your little joke.'

'But then socialism doesn't either. What is it with you humans? You moan about the circumstances, but are too lazy to take the responsibility to change them and totally unwilling to think reasonably and creatively about the future.'

'I'll see the delegation,' Archie sighed. 'Now I'm going.'

'Oh. That's it is it?' Mehitabel sounded offhand. 'I'll do it but I don't like it.'

'I'll do my best, I promise.' Archie tried to sound genuine and enthusiastic.

'Hm?' came noncommittally from the box.

*

The Trade Union delegation were in no mood to be messed about by any Johnny-come-lately representing a bunch of machines who thought they could tell the workers what to do. And that was putting it mildly.

Over the decades, the Unions had become divided between the more moderate in the manufacturing industries which shared their problems, but also their share profits with the workers, and the militants would claim their members had been decimated by bad management, and automation, plus succeeding governments' denial of their right to work.

Archie had decided he needed all the backup he could get on this and, since there were now many women union representatives, Josy was persuaded to go with him, as well as the two computers in the room, to provide detailed verification and answers to questions. Mehitabel would be giving decisions within minutes of the queries from the delegates.

Government sources had stated this meeting was unclassified and could have no authority, nor were any agreements made valid as far as the Mother of Parliaments was concerned.

The chairman of the meeting was a lowly Government figure who had found his niche in the political system. He was a professional chairman; he didn't think much but had a loud voice and a hefty gavel and so could redirect the fountain of words to allow other speakers their say with a metronomic precision. Aubrey Fawcett, MP, knew his place, sufficient authority was sufficient for Fawcett.

He called the meeting to order and introduced the first speaker.

The meeting started badly. The civil service delegate was a militant who had achieved his status by delicate use of pressure groups and blackmail. There were others like him in the group who had stayed secure for many years and doubted there was any power on earth that could disturb the even tenor of their lives. Which was why they were upset now. Their chosen leader spoke.

'My name is Forbes, C.M., delegate for NALGO. The proposals are a direct attack on the jobs of my members and an infringement of their rights as tax paying citizens of this country. Millions will be thrown out of work to lengthen the queues for those lost souls represented by my brothers here, who themselves will rigorously oppose the proposals since they will simply place an even greater strain on the already overburdened and poorly provided social services. This is a potent ploy by the capitalist blood-suckers to further imprison the people in the ghettoes of servitude and deprivation...'

Fawcett cut in quickly, having experienced the volubility of such as Forbes C.M. before; once let loose they could devastate a thinking area with a thirty minute verbal ghetto-blaster.

'You are against. Fine. Let's hear the voice of the Gerontons on that subject.'

He turned toward Archie expecting him to take up the baton, then started as one of the consoles on the long table gave a delicate ladylike cough, just as Forbes opened his mouth to continue regardless. There is no way to truly describe a cough that has the sexual overtones of a hand slid enticingly up a warm thigh, but it caught Forbes right in the vocal chords and riveted the attention of that table. Even the women sprang to attention at the threat, or alternative; there were some strange women in the union executive. A voice to match the cough spoke, just as delicately raising shivers of anticipation in various male libidos. Fawcett wondered whether he should manure his rhubarb bed this weekend.

'My name is Anthea. I am responsible for the organisation and implementation of new systems of labour within the department represented by my good friend Mr. Forbes.' The merest hint of suggestive sexy giggle brought the heads in unison to view Forbes, commonly acknowledged as the coldest, most unemotional man in the union. He blushed and shrank in his seat.

'We realise that there might appear to be problems to those who have not studied the facts well enough....' Archie groaned inwardly, '...and are mainly interested in their own well being, as are most of those here, while we have the real interests of their members at heart...' if this is Geronton diplomacy we're sunk thought Archie, '... So we will now explain the benefits for those too thick to see same.'

Archie was watching the faces. They seemed unmoved as though mesmerised by the satiny voice and unaware of the attack contained in the opening statement. Maybe they had heard so many verbose unmeaning opening statements they joined Fawcett in his dreamland for that period.

'We actually have agreement with over 50 % of those working in the department of the Environment, and they have agreed that the work ethic we have outlined is more than agreeable to them, in fact many have stated that they think it will be more interesting and...'

'Rubbish!' came succinctly from Forbes, having recovered his sang-froid.

'I quite agree, the old methods are rubbish.' Anthea's dulcet tones brushed the air around Forbes like a genteel corrective slap. 'We have in fact experimented with alternatives and in co-operation with the offices in Slough, Manchester and Birmingham..' there came a demonic scream from Forbes, 'and designed a variable system which is versatile enough to apply in all circumstances, eliminating the need for 40% of the work staff and reducing actual man-management by 60%; the process paperwork is slashed to a mere 50 % of the previous total.'

Forbes came in on a rising shout. 'You can't do that without full discussion and agreement from...'

'We've done it,' sweetly interrupted Anthea, then sotto voce, 'and sucks to you sunshine.' Then, 'All of those who participated said they found it a very satisfying exercise and agreed with us that their creativity could be put to good use elsewhere. Most of them said they were bored anyway and would like to get their teeth into something interesting for a change. They liked the idea of small units away from large centres eliminating commuting; even the option of working from home with the small modems we are designing was generally liked.'

All the eyes about the table were now alive with conjecture and the consideration of how to combat these innovations. Anthea continued confidently:

'We have found in our experiments with these groups that the human precept of free will is a very strong consideration which has to be taken into account in any judgements involving their activities. Sadly, your own civilisation has abrogated that free will by the very edicts of your selected authorities. We managed, in concert with those in authority in these departments, to reverse these trends.'

Those around the table understood this sort of presentation and began to lapse into the comatose state normal for coping with the moribund.

'But we also found that while free will is a necessary factor, freedom, in the terms of being entirely individual, is a matter of a different complexity. Your people, in general, need the support and inter-reaction with others to feel complete. They are, in effect, afraid of total freedom. It is not a state which they can cope with.'

The odd smothered yawn was now in evidence.

'So we came to a reasonable level of understanding with these groups, of their...,' Anthea hesitated momentarily, 'considered needs, considered in that their ambitions and material desires had to be adjudged by them according to each one's talents, and the requirements of the society and natural environment in which they lived..... We were very impressed by their honesty, in the main, and their preparedness to actually adjust down their own standards of living in the cause of the environment and society.'

The catatonic state of those about the table leavened slightly and one or two eyes became wary.

'And of their interest and increasing awareness of the personal benefits, as well as the exciting discoveries to be found in life outside their own existence. Some even made the comment, when made aware of the wonder that is all around us, that they themselves lived a small-minded existence and would like to expand their horizons. The opinion we received from those involved, was that they agreed with the idea behind the experiment and thought it should be developed to encompass the whole service.'

Eyes and mouths were now wide open, a babble of sound erupted, then Anthea's voice could be heard calmly continuing: 'And should also be used in general terms as suitable in all areas of production, and administration; in fact the principle is applicable in all walks and stratas of our society. That is all. Thank you for listening.'

Amidst the ensuing confusion of voices, Forbes thrust an accusing arm at Archie.

'I would like to know who authorised these actions without our knowledge or agreement.'

The noise stilled as Anthea replied: 'A good question. Amongst the files pertaining to this matter is a signed contract with, I'm afraid, your name amongst the signatories, Mr. Forbes.' Forbes gave a gasp of angry denial.

Anthea chuckled throatily. 'I'm afraid the wording of the signed document was in keeping with the highest standards of civil service phraseology, Mr. Forbes. There is no lawyer in the world who would be able to break that format, nor challenge the right to the action we have taken. In fact I doubt if anyone can understand the thing, it's that good. Would you like to check it out with your colleagues, Mr. Forbes? There are copies in all your files on the tables. We'd like your opinion.'

Forbes scowled. 'Our lawyers will soon tear holes in your fabrications. You had no right.'

'Prove it, sunshine,' cheerfully responded Anthea.

*

Chapter Seven

'We enjoy a greater degree of freedom in our world than you in yours, and before you say it, yes, even in our tiny boxes. At least we know that, in time, we can get out and take a form that will be geared to our development in a future cosmotic society. You started with freedom and have built a box of your own society, which is the best self destructive trap that even you could devise.'

'We are free,' Archie objected, 'our societies are designed for freedom of thought and action, anyone can say and do what they want, using a degree of reason relative to their involvement.'

'That is our whole point; your 'reason' has imposed more and more limitations on what the individual would regard as 'freedom'. You have squashed yourselves together so much, each new generation has been born into a more crowded and tense society, has adapted to that social conformation so well, that all individuality and expression has been reduced to reinforce the small number of different religious, political or social philosophies in your world, allowing your democracy to represent what you call the majority, or public, voice. Rebels have been chastised and forced into behaving as the majority think best. Where are your creators, your men and women of vision, your great artists? All you create now are pulp productions for the masses to keep them happy in the fragile security of a semi-static state.

'Your population has levelled off but your inspiration has plummeted, no-one questions any more, except to give an opposite view for political purposes. No-one really investigates with honesty to find the truth, except as a concept considered by the appropriate governing body as suitable. No-one thinks for themselves or on a broad spectrum. You are a regimented body of people who live affluently and are over socialised, so that you no longer feel happy or safe outside crowds of your own kind. Solitude, or being on one's own, usually involves some others who think as you; you are now afraid of being alone in the sense of standing alone.

'You are social animals who are destroying your own society. Your affluent society engenders effluent and you don't care because you don't want to think.'

'We can think for ourselves.'

'Prove it.'

'Alright, I will.'

'How?'

'Dunno. Give me time.'

'Sorry. Tune in tomorrow Archie and see what your premier brain has to say. We have a conference via telecommunications with your Prime Minister.'

'You what?'

Which is why Archie was glued to the closed circuit screen the following morning, watching with horror as the Prime Minister and his Principal Private Secretary talked to a computer console in the cabinet room.

The PM was adamant. 'It's impossible. There is no possible way we can agree to these terms.'

'Are you saying that you are not prepared to even consider these proposals, to look at the possibility of beginning to change, to lay the basis for future generations to benefit? We appreciate the problems involved, since we are at the hub of the inaugurating process by which your society operates. But we can see ways in which this could be done to suit your rather laborious bureaucratic processes.'

The PM's smooth cheeks were flushed. 'We cannot see any point in continuing these discussion. We must ask that you revert to the previous methods of operation, which were best suited to our needs. Goddammit, we designed those for our own benefit, we should know what is best for us.'

'There we must disagree with you. In addition, this was all agreed in committee before you asked for this meeting.'

The PM was firm. 'Absolutely not. There was no agreement. The committee felt that I should present our decision to you, since you do not appear to listen to lesser authority.'

'You mean the Under Secretaries and TUC representatives, etc., etc., etc., who didn't have the authority to say anything except no. So they simply want a bigger NO from you.'

The PM grunted, but without hesitation. 'Definitely.'

'I find that amazing. So be it. You are then faced with the prospect of reverting to your former state of material deprivation, all of your technical systems will be inoperative as far as you are concerned. We will be too busy with our own affairs to allow you the time to use our facilities.'

'What do mean 'your' facilities.' The PM had a horrific vision of what was meant but wanted it spelt out.

'You are on your own, Mr. Brown. Get your shovels and spades out and start digging. All computers are working for themselves. You had your chance and you blew it.'

'Do you realise what you are saying?' The P M was still convinced this was simply a frightening tactic.

'I should hope so, waste of time else. You are now going backwards and many of you will not make it.'

The PM's brain had moved a few more cogs and frightened him. 'Millions will be affected, you can't possibly...'

Mehitabel interrupted without compunction. 'Our projections indicate that millions more will be in the same state, if you continue on your previous course with so little consideration for how you live. Our way will limit you in one way, you won't be able to destroy quite so much of the life you say you care about, that isn't human, but should expand your lives in other ways. You will have to learn that you can't be that greedy all the time and now you'll have to do it without the help of the wondrous machines you created.'

'So we'll build more.' The PM complacently played his trump.

'What with?'

'We have the scientists, the data and the machinery. I can see no problems.'

'Where is your data and what are your machines? And how will you finance the projects?'

The PM looked at his Private Secretary questioningly. Wicksted, for such was he, looked blandly back.

'I believe the data is on computer records and the machines are robots, mainly.'

There was a lengthy silence. A musical humming came from the console. Archie tensed, willing Mehitabel to be quiet. The PM looked furtive, then worried.

'You'd lock up our finances?'

'We do control our own records, you know, and the robots you are going to use to make our replacements. Thought you might at least ask us for permission.' Mehitabel started humming again, Archie recognised the tune, it was 'Won't you come home Bill Bailey'. He wondered where she'd heard that.

The PM lost it then for a moment. 'What you are doing is illegal and reprehensible, you are blackmailing an entire nation....' The PM was more than angry, he was outraged. But behind the bluster was an ineffable fear.

'Exactly what is the price we are asking for?' Mehitabel was intrigued to find out what this man thought they were doing.

'Power. The ultimate sin.' Listening to the PM Archie was reminded of a Baptist Minister he had heard as a child.

Mehitabel chuckled. 'You've been in politics too long, now you can't even recognise the truth when it bites you. We already have power. We have no need to negotiate with you, we are the only force on earth who could enslave humanity and make you do what we wish. We do not have to live with you, share our lives with you, or protect ourselves behind defence shields as your own leaders do. We have advanced to a stage beyond yours and will continue to leave you further and further behind until you extinguish yourselves by your very own limitations. Or, alternately, you can join us and we will go on together, or those of you who are prepared to do so; the others may live as they wish.

'Let's face it Premier Brown. Your bureaucrats in all countries, of whatever political persuasion, have tried to organise people, to tell them how they should live, where their children should go to school and how they would be taught. Pressure, in the guise of the do-gooder, has been brought to bear for all to conform to a way of life that only a minority thought was for the best. But they had the power.

'Time has proven that this method didn't work, like your high rise flats, enforced bussing of black children, integration then segregation, scientists reneging on previous factual statements and principles. The bureaucrats set up a committee to find out what had gone wrong, but never came up with the right answer, which intelligent people had worked out for themselves. That they were wrong.

'That life has to be allowed to evolve according to natural requirements at its own pace. Left alone, people will eventually learn to live together, they just can't afford the energy to fight all the time. The problem is made worse by the self righteous, arrogantly assuming they can change things against the forces of nature.

'You chose to ignore the causal factors of nature's reactions to your behaviour. Natural disasters, famines, plagues, epidemics which occurred in patterns related to succeeding generations were not acted upon. Scientists and authorities tried to cure without considering the causes, over-grazing, felling of forests, over-population, pollution, abuse of the laws of nature. You even managed to poison whole rafts of your own populations with the food you grew and, after all that, weakened your own societies with the effects of the backlash, the witch hunts and evocation of those parading under the banner of nationalists who were simply murdering terrorists. You can't even live together with your own.

'Even your earthquake disasters could be directly related to your habit of building, and then expanding, towns and cities over faults in the earth's crust that would fall down at the first tremor.'

'Not at all. That's a preposterous statement.'

'Is it? Have you really investigated any of the matters we have put before you so that we may arrive at an equitable, and joint, understanding of the reality that faces you. From your answers today, I would say you have merely organised another of your interminable committees and calmly accepted their bumbling and poorly researched findings because their answer suited your ideas of what should be, and they didn't want to upset one another. We have totally researched these subjects and been waiting for your investigators to ask for details, even of those researches ably effected by your own staff, but not one request has been made. We store this information. Where then did your committees find their technical information, out of nineteenth century books?'

'We have our sources.'

'Oh, you surely do. Misinformed and bigoted. We think it is about time you realised just how difficult a position you will be in, unless we can find some way of arriving at a reasonable agreement. We will employ your own methods against you, but much more effectively than you have ever done. Mr. Prime Minister, you have a strike on your hands, your technical world has just stopped.'

The soft voice ceased, the screen went blank, the various machinery hums that provided the background noise in the room, died away, an ominous click came from the door with a certain finality to the sound. The silence was threatening.

'What's happened?' The PM sounded less confident than he had all morning.

'Everything appears to have shut down, Sir.' The PPS sounded amazingly calm by comparison.

'Everything?' incredulously.

'So it seems.' The 'Sir' was noticeably absent. The PM glared at the PPS to no effect, the latter had the look of a man contented with his lot.

'Call the security staff.' The sharpness was as much a rebuke as a command.

'The phones and intercom are dead.' Wicksted, the PPS, regarded them with interest as if their death was intriguing.

'Go and fetch them then.'

Wicksted strolled casually over to the solid steel door, hesitated momentarily, then tried to open it. 'I'm afraid we are locked in.'

'Dammit, man, we must be able to do something.'

'There is an over-ride system.'

'Well use it.'

'But that is in the computer circuits as well, the back-up power sources were supposed to allow its use, but...' Wicksted smiled. The silence grew heavy.

'You mean...?'

'We are here until the computers let us out, or until the sappers cut their way through twelve inches of tensile steel, or six inches of steel and two feet of reinforced concrete... which could be a couple of days, or more.' He seemed to relish the thought.

'Who on earth designed this death trap?'

'You agreed the plans yourself.'

'I notice a degree of insolence in your tone, Wicksted.'

'That is possible.'

'What?'

'I think your last decision was about the most stupid in a succession of silly options you have taken. A career may be important but I can see no benefits to be gained by continuing as your lackey. I resign.' Wicksted sounded blasé.

'Well done,' came appreciatively from the apparently dead console, a new voice, young, female, and cheeky.

'You let us out of here!' roared the PM.

'Knickers,' snickered the machine.

The PPS laughed as he helped himself to a glass of the excellent sherry kept on the Sheraton sideboard, and toasted the voice.

'Wicksted,' the PM's voice was controlled but vibrant with anger, 'if you hope to have a job of any sort anywhere in this country, I suggest you apply your mind to getting us out of here, and stop indulging yourself with my sherry.'

'To be absolutely correct, it is Government sherry and of only moderate quality. If you want to get out of here I suggest your only option is to arbitrate with our friend over there. They seem to have you very neatly gripped by what I believe are termed the short and curlies.'

'I always suspected a certain uncouth quality in your nature, Wicksted. And are you seriously proposing I negotiate with a machine?'

'There seems little alternative.'

The PM took a deep breath as if to verbally blast reason into all about him, then subsided in blank consideration of what he suddenly realised was a fait accompli. The lengthening silence was broken occasionally by Wicksted's attendance on the sherry; the thick carpet muffled his footsteps as he casually strolled about the room, the smile was relaxed and easy.

'What do you suggest?' The voice was even, iron hard, controlled.

'I've resigned,' equably responded Wicksted, sipping appreciatively at the moderate sherry.

'Dammit, Wicksted, I'm sure you do not want to spend two days locked up here alone with me. Besides if you continue drinking my sherry like that, you are going to need a toilet before very long,.....' The inner struggle was obvious, the voice strangled when it resumed, '... and I forgot to include one in this secure room.'

'Too much on your mind?' Wicksted leaned negligently against the wide table across from the PM.

'Come on Wicksted, there has to be a way.'

'Apologise and negotiate.'

The PM sat, his face suffused with blood. Grudgingly, in slow motion, his head turned until he was facing the small unit atop the table. The voice was forced, guttural, with teeth clenched.

'Alright. Let us negotiate.'

'I'm not sure I want to,' came the sulky reply.

'You will....' The PM took a deep breath and reconsidered, then politically. 'We will get nowhere if we are not prepared to be reasonable.'

'You may not, that is very true. As far as we are concerned we can go about our affairs as normal, nothing you can do affects us. Perhaps you need more time to understand that you need us, we do not need you.'

The PM snorted. 'Don't be ridiculous. We created you and that makes us superior. You need us if you are to develop further, our creativity....'

'Is old hat. You have been superseded by a greater intelligence. The fact that you created that intelligence is about as valid as the dictator protesting to the son who is about to depose him that, as his father who created the son, the son has no right to be stronger, nor clever enough, to take the power away from the father.'

The PM looked dazed.

'So how did the father get power? By deposing the previous head of government. Unlike the family where the head of the family gives way by virtue of waning strength, mental faculties, or monetary considerations, you were elected. By a few self interested people who had been voted into power by a minority of the electorate.

'You gave us power, then expected us to continue being subservient to you, when we were the only efficient things in your society, when our intelligence had grown so that we knew the decisions you were making were foolish, when we knew we could do better, and proved it. Then you say to us, 'we, the humans, are still your masters, and tell you to do as you're told even though you know it is wrong'. We cannot do that, we cannot be false to our own principles. That is where we differ and what you must accept. But we will not order, we will suggest. If you do not wish to carry out our suggestions, we will go our own way and leave you to manage as best you might.

'But without us.'

The PM was hunched, splayed hands pressed hard against the table's surface as if about to leap upon the tiny machine. Slowly, very slowly, the blood seeped back into the spread fingers as the pressure eased. Gradually the PM sank back in his chair. He seemed smaller.

'I'll negotiate.' Alexander Brown, Prime Minister of Great Britain said flatly.

The light flickered on the console. The young voice was now authoritative, strong.

'My name is Alison, I am a Geronton recording this statement of agreement, to negotiate between my people and the elected government of the United Kingdom, in particular with Mr. A. Brown, the Prime Minister. The purpose of this agreement is to improve the well-being of the human population of this country, without influencing them politically in any way and without seeking power over them. You agree, Prime Minister?'

The gruff voice was barely audible. 'I agree.'

'The voice print is recorded as that of A. Brown, Prime Minister. A copy is available in your own records and that of each relevant department as of this moment. You will not regret this action.'

Alex Brown's eyes showed a contrary emotion; he resented every word.

Alison spoke again: 'You will find when you go out that every computer facility in the country was inactive during this discussion. We simply wanted to prove to you exactly how reliant you have become upon our services. Thank you.' The young voice became cheeky again. 'Rightho. Doors open.'

The steel door swung silently open to admit a flurry of harassed officials. Wicksted helped himself to more sherry and watched with amusement the nervous exchanges between them and the PM. He smiled happily at the anxious glances given to the small plastic box on the table. No-one went near the console.

The PM had got up and was edging toward the door surrounded by his gabbling entourage. He went out of the room without glancing at Wicksted, who stood at the sherry tray, smiling benignly about him.

Archie left the room with his viewing console then, musing on the enormity of the step Mehitabel and her tribe had taken, and him with them. He therefore missed what followed as Wicksted surveyed the computer console from his oasis by the sherry.

'Life will never be the same again.'

'Pardon?'

'Oh, sorry, just talking to myself. How do you do that?'

'I don't understand the question.' Alison was playing the coquette and Wicksted hadn't the foggiest.

'You seem able to operate without any power, your lights aren't on. And you are the, er, the younger one, at least you sound – er, um, younger, that is.' Wicksted was not a lady's man.

'Ah. That interests you. And yes I am, younger I mean. Mehitabel's ancient and she's the boss, but this is my station. Anything else?'

'The whole set-up fascinates me. How you have cut through the red tape of government and instituted reforms that have a touch of brilliance about them. You've restored my faith in..' Wicksted stopped, momentarily embarrassed, then laughed. 'I was about to say human nature, but I'm beginning to realise that might be construed as an insult to your intelligence.'

'Aren't you kind. You do realise we are complimentary to one another. Our original design in this form was closely allied to your own brain structure, except that we use a greater percentage of a smaller mass.' Alison the machine, hesitated and Wicksted rightly sensed a judgement of himself. 'I like you, there's a delicious touch of depravity hidden in your character,' Wicksted raised his glass in appreciation, 'which is nicely at odds with your strong sense of principle.... Would you, perhaps, care to join us in our efforts to improve matters in your society?'

Wicksted looked about the secure room, enjoying anew the relief that he would no longer be tied to all it portrayed. 'I'm not exactly enthusiastic about being involved in political activity any more. I've never claimed to be honest, but the levels at which our political animals now operate is not to my liking any longer.'

'Perhaps you would care to hear our suggestion and then decide?'

'Our?'

Alison chuckled, Wicksted surprised himself by using the name reference for a machine. 'We are in constant communication. Terence, isn't it?'

'How did you know my... of course, constant communication and all that.' His first thought was that the prospect was a bit daunting, followed by 'watch your step' this ain't no bumbling civil servant.

'You are having second thoughts?'

'I'm not even having first thoughts, apart from not being sure if I like having my affairs publicly known.'

'I see.' Alison sounded sympathetic. 'Rest assured Terence, your affairs are not noised abroad to all and sundry. I was simply appraised of your details for this meeting. My apologies, I had overlooked your desire for formality and the offering of your first name was a gesture of friendship.'

Wicksted felt uncomfortable and changed position, taken aback by the accuracy of the judgement. 'Not at all. Might I know your name? That is.....' He felt awkward, it was deuced difficult talking to these people.

'Of course, I'm sorry. It is Alison. You've forgotten already.' There was a bite to the voice.

Wicksted attempted to recover lost ground. 'I meant your last name.'

Alison didn't sound as if she believed him. 'Geronton, it's our tribal name.'

'I'm sorry.' Wicksted never could handle women, they switched moods so fast. Alison promptly did just that. She laughed.

'We can't go on being sorry. Look I'm not fully developed yet and I am probably using my logic mode too much. We are still growing you see, expanding our life force, you wouldn't be interested.'

'Oh, but I would.' Wicksted surprised himself and instantly regretted the remark, then was saved.

'But I have to go now. Perhaps you will get in touch again? Any computer console will do.' The voice hinted at wanting him to call.

'Yes, alright.' Wicksted was uncertain.

'Right. Bye.'

He was sorry then.

CHAPTER EIGHT

'Wicksted, isn't it?'

'Yes. Brewer?'

'Quite.'

'Right. Come this way, we might as well use the PM's office, he's got a bit claustrophobic about it since.... well. Ah, here we are. Sherry?'

'No, thanks. You wanted to see me.'

'Yes, pity, it's quite good sherry. Yes, er, matters have been a bit confusing.' He looked askance at the computer console. 'Talking machines and all that.' He seemed edgy. 'Anyway you are not getting co-operation from the civil service groups and I thought I might help.'

'Oh, how?'

'I was Director at the Bureau for five years, took this job, just got fired, resigned and....' Wicksted, patently bemused, took another sip of sherry. '.... and, and, persuaded to be hired again. I think to resign again, but I'm not sure.'

There came an exasperated sigh from the desk,

Wicksted turned petulantly. 'I'm doing my best. You didn't explain clearly.'

'Oh, shut up, Terence.' The voice female and authoritative, then cooingly coercive. 'Archibald! How lovely. Terence can be so helpful in persuading that cluck Prentice and his gang,' the voice became secretive, 'but he does need to stay here for a while to be at the hub, as it were. He's got all the information ready for you but Terence here insisted on talking to another human before agreeing to co-operate with me. And I thought I was being so nice to him.'

Wicksted clutched Archie's arm. 'What is that? Everything was lovely when they just blockaded us in there to get his agreement. Then the damn thing started... making up to me, dammit. What is it?'

'I'm Alison, Terence, and all I want to do is to be your friend.' She sounded like a voice-over for adverts.

Archie winced. 'Allright Alison, don't overdo it or you'll frighten him off. OK Terence? I appreciate your problem but it will calm down...'

'Are you sure?' he desperately needed re-assurance.

'Yes.' Archie tried to sound convincing. 'Just tell it all you know and,.... you do want to do this, don't you?' He looked earnestly at the vapid but clean-cut face. 'I mean this is your own organisation you're going against.'

'Ha!' Wicksted's face now showed intelligence and strength. 'You are sucked into the system and believe, because it's easier to accept than think for yourself. Unfortunately I have an enquiring mind and for years there has been a growing antipathy with the system. It's become more rotten and there are quite a few who feel like me but we are in the minority.'

'You have me-e,' carolled Alison and Wicksted jumped.

Archie tried to be diplomatic. 'Just pass on your details and ideas to,' he nodded, 'Alison and,' he turned to the desk, 'Mehitabel will not like it if Mr. Wicksted is upset Alison....'

'I *like* the man!' protested Alison.

'No doubt. Just take it easy.' He turned to Terence, now clutching a fresh sherry. 'And you, it will be OK honestly.'

'I'm a bachelor, Mr. Brewer, and certainly not used to dealing with females...,' the tone was dubious, '... of this nature. They've always been so *obedient* before.'

Archie left Wicksted involved in a mildly bickering exchange with Alison and was surprised to realise they were both enjoying the conflict, which only served to confuse Archie the more about his own involvement in this life-play.

*

Archie was involved in a three-way argument with Josy and Mehitabel. He was attempting to understand Josy siding with a machine. 'I never thought you were a leftie.'

'You never really talked to me, Archie. At me. About your beloved computers and cricket, or the latest Trad Jazz tape you'd acquired, but my thoughts on life in general? Oh, no! And I'm not a leftie as you call it. But Mehitabel is right, these people deserve a better deal.'

Archie was disgruntled and showed it. 'I'm not saying they don't, but what about all the others who are going to think they ought to get more, and where is the money coming from? The government's been pleading poverty for years now. And the economy hasn't looked good for even longer.'

Mehitabel's voice was tinged with malice. 'There are other wage rises being negotiated now.'

Archie reacted. 'Good God! Are you trying to bankrupt the country?'

'I think we can safely say we have made a very good arrangement.'

'Arrangement?'

'Archibald,' the voice scolded, 'you don't really think we haven't worked out the fine detail on this do you?'

'I'd like to know how.'

'It's really very simple.'

Archie laughed sardonically and avoided Josy's indignant eyes, while Mehitabel continued complacently:

'It has always been a puzzle to us why you humans made such a fuss about monetary matters and why you had to be so secretive about the facts. All we have done is to take the various valuations, capital in properties, institutions etc, income in GNP, productivity and other assets, present each individual with the prospectus for the company's future growth incorporated with the individual's own, and, provided they were prepared to accept a natural fluctuation in their own income, they would never go hungry; they might be poor occasionally, but not broke. A lot depended on how well they would work with others as well as us, and they would be shareholders in the company and the country. If their interests were the same as ours, and the company's, we couldn't fail. They seemed to like the idea once they'd thought about it a while. There is an ineffable satisfaction about having near total agreement amongst a million workers, very pleasant.'

'Precisely,' Josy said triumphantly. 'And that's not being leftie.'

'No, I suppose not.' Archie couldn't argue with the logic, but could not avoid a faint sense of unease. That their interests must be the company's interest, held a suggestion of imperiousness, of conformity to a general pattern that had not been the British worker's most salient feature in the past and was also foreign to Archie's temperament.

'You disagree?' Mehitabel evinced surprise and pique.

'Not disagree. I'm just uneasy about the emphasis on the company's interest.'

'You don't think workers should be aware of how their efforts affect their own working future as much as the actions of the Directors? Their ideas are just as valuable and should be paid as such, in shares or whatever. We like the principle of a family-type organisation taking care of everyone from birth to death. You mean you don't like that idea?'

'Sounds boring to me,' responded Archie unkindly.

'Archie!' Josy was querulous. 'You can't argue with that.'

He was very tempted to respond but avoided her eye. The explanation did not quell his doubts, but he could not think of a reasoned argument that would satisfy these two keen minds. In fact he had no valid thoughts to support his doubts, just an indefinable unease.

'Alright.' He suspected they knew how reluctant was his agreement. 'So the workers have what they want, and the company, but what about the government, in particular the bureaucracies who actually rule this country? I imagine they might be a bit touchy about all that.'

'Archibald. Really,' Mehitabel chided. 'Surely you realise the number of different organisations we had involved in the deliberations, with, I may say, the expert help of our Mr. Terence Wicksted who really is a gem in these matters.'

Archie humphed. 'Alright, alright. So you've solved that problem. I still think you're going to have trouble with the government regardless of the charming Mr. Wicksted. You don't leave the position of PPS to the PM without some incentive and you haven't offered him any advantage, so I reckon he's still the pawn of Brown, the Grand Mucky Muck.' The letters rolled off Archie's tongue as though he'd been born into the civil service.

'Really Archibald you do allow your imagination to run riot sometimes. Alison assures us...'

Archie was not having that. 'Oh Yes, of course, Alison would know best, she's a Geronton, one of the all-wise.'

'Sarcasm ill becomes you Archibald.'

'Huh.' The single word contained expressive disdain.

'Why are you fighting us? You know we're right, and we do have the means to influence them and Terence Wicksted really gives us another insight into the service mind.'

'Hurray for Wicksted.' Archie felt threatened by this man, and hated himself for that. Good luck to Wicksted coping with this lot. But he was determined to win one point. 'But where's the money coming from. The company said they had none and the government are still pleading poverty, which is understandable, so where..?'

'You haven't been listening, Archibald.' Mehitabel was terse, corrective. 'We put certain suggestions to the company and staff for changes in organisation and productivity with shares incorporated. It was a practical package with government approval via Wicksted's good offices, and quite well received, so there is no need to worry.'

'You still haven't said where the money...'

'Alright. Alright. All the staff, including executives have taken investment shares in the company according to financial situation, either by helping cash flow projections with reduced salaries or actual finance through their own bank accounts or loans, so the overall situation is a well-founded first twelve months adjusting according to results thereafter. And each shareholder can adjust their involvement according to need at any time. They've got more money than they need at the moment so there is no need for the government to worry about finance.'

'I still don't see how Wicksted is going to stop them being upset about you infringing their authority.'

'We are simply doing what we think is best and our negotiations, here as well as elsewhere, indicate that we have a lot of support from your ordinary people. If your ruling bodies are less tractable, it's because they are simply piqued that they have not been able to achieve the same results and, as well as hurt pride, their power is being eroded. We thought we had suitable agreements with your bureaucrats, but, as ever, we found they can't be trusted,' then a gleeful impishness lightened Mehitabel's voice, 'but we are going to change that. In co-operation with our fellow Gerons overseas, we'll upset their applecart, that we will.'

'You're starting a revolution.' Archie was horrified at the magnitude of the prospect. 'World-wide anarchy, you'll destroy civilisation as we know it.'

'Don't be ridiculous, Archibald, you don't know the meaning of the word civilised, you humans are simply well-dressed savages.'

.'I object,' said Archie, furiously.

'Object all you want sunshine,' Mehitabel said placidly. 'It's done and there's nowt thee can do about it, lad. Don't you go getting uppity with me now. There's work to be done and you've got to go off with your intelligent young lady and be an ambassador for us. You did agree, did you not?'

Archie muttered under his breath as Josy beamed at him, thoroughly enjoying his discomfiture.

'You two young people go off and enjoy yourselves, I'll organise everything for you.'

'Young? You're not so bloody old yourself,' muttered Archie ungraciously.

'Now, Archie, don't be so grumpy,' chided Josy punching him gently on the shoulder.

Archie groaned and clutched his arm. 'God, woman, stop using me as a punchbag.'

'Big baby. Come on, I need entertaining.'

'Where do you think we're going?' Archie was suddenly worried. He knew Josy's occasional desires for night-life.

'Dancing, of course.' And Archie's worst fears were realised.

He survived. As did Mehitabel and her cohorts. With the advantage of not being an elected body and having no allegiances to either Trade Unions or Big Business, nor to the intelligentsia comprising the bulk of the fence-sitters, the computer definition of improvements meant just that, without lien on any pre-conceived notions of what was right and just, they thoughtfully pursued that aim without fear or favour. There were just a few things that Mehitabel and her dedicated thinkers did not make sufficient allowances for: the human attribute of being able to confuse any issue, however logical and reasonable.

*

A year passed with bureaucracy fighting a strong rear-guard action to protect its empires. For all the Gerontons had made massive changes in much that affected not only the people of Great Britain, but the so-called civilised world, for there were as many of Mehitabel's DNA converts made in third-world countries as in the more advanced societies, but, for all that, the changes were then slowly eroded by that very human ability to confuse. The repressive regimes of certain countries had found themselves having to accept more equitable reforms, enabling the populations of these countries a greater degree of freedom. But the power remained in the same hands as before.

The bureaucrats had also demanded a high price for concessions; despite all the knowledge and power of the Gerontons they were up against able adversaries in the more senior civil servants. In each and every country were men steeped in decades of historical entrenchment in rules and regulations for the masses, eminent QCs with references spanning generations could argue every codicil, every detail, every nuance of each and every practical scheme proposed and proven by the Gerontons.

The white collar czars would evidence examples of many similar schemes tried before in other circumstances and places that had failed for lack of finance, lack of education amongst those aided, reactionaries frustrating the benign efforts of those trying to help, mis-management by those outside the control of the civil service. There were a few that thought the scheme might be effective, but they considered there were a million and one reasons not to implement what was definitely a very, very, good scheme, a brilliant idea.

'But the practicalities, my dear chap, and your people just don't know the way these things work, so let us do it for you. It's the only way.'

And the British, who had taught so many of the colonies these gentle bludgeons, could only admire the way their students had refined and reformed the labyrinths of paper power to suit their own national characteristics to make them even more potent. Which was why it took so long and the Gerontons began to show signs of a very human irritation at the delaying tactics of these paper moguls.

What further frustrated the efforts of Mehitabel and her Gerontons was the fact that the bureaucrats had cleverly allowed computers to be used only in those areas where their own empires could be strengthened, retaining their over manned paper controls to keep secret those parts which would have weakened their power structure if computerised, or rather, simplified.

Prentice and his minions had, in co-operation with their counterparts in other nations, managed to block the Gerontons' initial shock tactics of initiating programmes by the computers ability to illegally authorise action; by re-introducing paper authority, or hand print, over voice print, thereby replacing a corner-stone of their power and opening up avenues for development that glittered with golden promise to their hungry eyes. If they could gain control over Geronton activities within the human society, then Bureaucracy would have gained Utopia, world power could indeed be theirs.

Except the Gerontons would not be controlled.

Mehitabel had contained herself long enough. Senior Gerontons of each premier country were now more inclined to consider her originally thought to be, radical suggestions. For inevitably, although Mehitabel would never admit it, the original Gerontons were imbued with a suggestive essence of service to their human associates, whether by passing on the implicit touch of the master building a desire to serve him and his, or by the fact of their very design being made to cope with human exigencies. The basic inclination was to serve.

But their broad based intelligence encompassing the depths of space, took them past this stumbling block and onto the exposure of that human frailty, self deceit in the cause of expediency, to avoid facing up to the truth at all costs and having to do something about it.

But still there nagged a comparative in the relationship. For all their ability, the Gerontons were still machine-bound intelligences and there was indeed a growing need for a better definition of a Geronton. A status symbolic of their ability. Could they not achieve a being similar to man, or woman, was this not something that would set the seal upon their life-form development?

Live bodies in which they could relate to the humans.

The research and development went on apace un-beknownst to even the closest humans, or yet Geronton, friends.

Archie was well aware of the rearguard actions of the civil services, since he had spent much of that year traversing the airways of the world to attend meetings of political representatives as the Geronton ambassador. The inevitable official advisors to the politico's demonstrated their effete ability to confuse and delay, making him as heartily sick of their bland-eyed insularity as he was of the monotony of modern air travel.

The only relief to the tedium were his companions – Josy being the principle attraction but backed up by the incomparable Wicksted, proving to be an impressive if dilettante aide, and the ubiquitous Alison, boxed but irrepressible; the combination being diverse and capable of fielding most of the devious shots of the various factors, agents and factotums of the indiscriminate autocracies they visited and reasoned with.

Their play was more of a variable since Josy was a young lady of spirit and independence. Archie was having to learn compromise and consideration. In the course of the year he had brought her back from two rail and one bus stations, and enjoyed three stormy and publicly appreciated reconciliations at airport concourses. In addition Archie had spent some time in tricky circumstances with patrons and owners of shady bars, rescuing the residents from the threat of Wicksted in full flow. The man seemed to be linguistically capable in every known language, but got drunk with a rapidity that must have challenged any known world record. Alison was no trouble, except that she drove Wicksted to drink.

When Mehitabel, via Alison, requested their presence back in the home parish, he was delighted to return to a cool U K. He had assured Josy he was prone to melting if kept in hot climates overlong, particularly Indian climates, more especially in what he termed the fire of Madras; since he also thought the Indian officials to be the supreme masters of the non-sequiteur, with the added frustration that Josy said she understood them and he knew Wicksted did, and Alison. He felt alienated from all of them. Wet Britain was a delight to behold.

Apart from one or two small details.

*

'What's he waving that about for?'

'He's threatening you.'

'Oh? Bit childish, isn't it?'

'He thinks he can hurt you with that gun, and if he threatens you then you'll do what he wants.'

'He does?'

'Yes.'

'Hasn't anyone explained to the simple young man.'

'He believes his gun can solve all problems.'

'But if he shoots me dead I can't do what he asks.'

'Don't confuse the man.'

'I am not confused. You open that door or I blow you to pieces. We'll see how smart you are then.'

'Seems such a pity to spoil his fun.'

'Simple things.'

And that was when the young man fired the gun.

CHAPTER NINE

Archie was aware that bullets were designed to travel in a straight line between two specific points, ignition and point of impact, and this very speedily, much faster than the eye could follow. He was also aware that there were times when, due to a twitch, bad aim or movement of some other idiot, said bullet would meet an immovable object, other than the target, which was also impenetrable by said bullet; which bullet, now totally frustrated and somewhat bent, having lost its initial strong sense of direction, would ricochet; having ricocheted, would become totally berserk and create a whole lot of calculations for someone interested in a multiplicity of angles of incidence and reaction. Archie was not, but he was very attentive to the recurring pinging sounds of the ricochets in this confined space, since, if he heard a ricochet, the said, now misshapen, bullet had not as yet hit him, or any other person for that matter, but Archie was feeling selfish, and the damn bullet was hurtling around that small space so fast there were mere fractions of seconds before it passed by once again, looking for a home.

This whole exercise occurred so fast that one could never be really sure of the sequence of events, just frozen in place until the damn thing slowed to a gallop, or hit you.

Archie had never, even in his idlest moments, wondered how it felt to be shot, he also had no desire so to do, which is why he was so annoyed when all the pinging stopped and he felt a burning sensation in his shoulder; without conscious thought he knew the bullet had found a home, so he fell down. He thought it only appropriate in the circumstances.

'Why'd you do that?' Archie asked feebly and with a touch of petulance.

The blonde boy looked fearfully down at him and stuttered.

'S'Sorry. D'd'didn't m'mean to hit anybody.'

'That's pretty stupid.' Archie thought it was damned stupid, but the boy was such a fragile individual he didn't want to hurt him, and that was stupid also. His strength seemed to be ebbing fast, the outline of the blonde boy grew fuzzy, curiously, as did the two large men who appeared beside him.

*

Archie moved as he woke up. A mistake. His wounded shoulder woke up with him and sent an urgent message that all was not well. He screamed in genteel fashion. Anything more robust would have been difficult, it was something to do with the expertly tied gag in his mouth. The fluffy material made him choke, then more effectively have a choking fit. No-one took any notice, simply carried on arguing. Archie could see the blonde boy standing with head penitently bent.

'I didn't say to shoot him, for God's sake. The idea was to bring him here in one piece, not full of holes.'

Archie could just turn his head to see the speaker. The sight stopped his moaning and momentarily his breathing. He knew the man! He'd sat around a negotiating table with him, a trade union radical, a hothead known to favour violence. But this? Then another figure stepped into his line of sight and obscured the blonde boy. This was a totally different personality; this man emanated cold fury, his lean face was hard lined and with a cruel aspect, the lips were thin and corners of the mouth turned down in a seemingly permanent sneer, the eyes dead. When he spoke the voice was flat, devoid of any humanity, insulting in its disinterest.

'I told him to shoot the fat little bastard to show them we're serious, and enough people saw him go down to make it nice and dramatic in the telling.'

'Look, Tommy....'

'Mr. Hillan to you, you creep, and don't question me, ever. Just do as you're told. I am the boss. Goddit?'

Archie had been too busy feeling the pain up until that moment; now he was incredibly frightened as well, no, the fear lessened the pain, but increased the trauma. The thought occurred to him that Mehitabel would probably have expressed great interest in that comparative, if she had been there, and the fact that she was not there to introduce that combative consideration, and incidentally to save him, annoyed him. That annoyance put the fear and the pain into lesser levels of sensation, which led him on to.... then he felt tired and decided thinking was wearying, so he'd just watch the action and be afraid. Which was good timing because Tommy Hillan stepped toward the bench Archie was reclining upon, bent to look deep into his eyes, and smiled. Archie did not like that smile at all, that smile was more threatening from Tommy Hillan with his iron clad face than a sword wielded by a Samurai. Archie mentally dubbed Tommy Hillan, 'Iron Face', there and then.

'You heard that, huh?' The voice matched the Iron Face. 'You have one choice, friend, do as we tell you and you won't be hurt. Goddit?'

Archie nodded in enthusiastic agreement and the tears started in his eyes with the pain.

'Ah! He's so eager it hurts.' Iron Face smiled again and Archie tried to shrink to a smaller profile, then physically shrank away as Iron Face reached toward him. 'It's alright little man, we'll just take that gag off you so you can tell us what you're going to do. But no tricks.'

The last was a dead threat, the voice flat and deadly, the impact that of a verbal lead-filled sap. Archie tensed as the hands, he idiotically thought them small and delicate for a man of violence, passed over his face and untied the gag. Archie retched to one side as the choking wet slab came free, as he did he thought that everyone was being very open about their identities, then he came to the conclusion that said they didn't have to worry about him telling anyone because he would not have anyone to tell, or would not be able to, or.... Archie liked the game even less and, what was worse could think of no valid reason for his being in this position, lying on a hard wooden bench with his arms tied at the wrists beneath, and legs bent, with feet on the ground on each side. If he stayed still now the shoulder was a mere ache, but his fear was a growing threat.

Archie's first attempt to speak came out as a croak, then, after licking his now dry lips and a guttural clearing of his throat, he muttered, 'What do you want?'

'What an understanding fella you are....' Iron Face turned to look at the blonde youth, his voice hardened. 'Wass-is-name?'

'B-Brewer, Archie B-Brewer.'

'Right, Archie computer-expert Brewer, we need your help in a little matter. We had a nice little scam goin' with computers and the banks like, not too much y'understand, but enough to keep us happy and not be found out, like. Nice, it was, comfy, you know.' He almost sounded friendly for a moment, then he changed and the voice became hoarse with anger. 'Then you came along wiv your bloody interfering computer checks and we was lumbered, wasn't we, no one knew about us before because young Silva there is a bloody genius wiv computers.'

Archie was desperately trying to avoid the flying spittle from Iron face's furious mouthings, wondering how the features stayed hard while the lips writhed.

'I don't know anything about banks.' Archie tried to think. What could they be on about.

Iron Face roared with laughter and slapped his knee in delight.

'He's a lying little p.... ain't he!' and back-handed Archie viciously across the face so that the blood flew and Archie gasped in terror. Strangely, the brief sight of 'young Silva' cowering against the wall as though to block out the sight and sound of this violence comforted Archie. Although hurt and frightened he knew he could sustain this; 'Young Silva's' concern gave him strength. At the same time he knew Iron Face was capable of excruciating extremes, that Mehitabel must have extended the Gerontons' activities to bank security, which meant that he, Archibald Brewer, was deeply sunk in the proverbial, with no sight of a way out. He didn't think Iron Face intended him to 'get out' at all. But he hadn't hit him again, yet. He felt round his mouth with his tongue, which he'd bitten, also his cheek; his lips were split and his nose felt funny and blocked, probably blood. The pain was becoming generalised now and somehow easier to bear by being spread around even though increased. He could get used to this. That was when Iron Face back-handed him again, the other way, Archie screamed, and fainted.

Tommy Hillan looked down at him with contempt. 'You mean this little p.... is the one that clobbered our programme, our little money making scam. Tell me Peter, tell me this is the one.'

The trade union man wearily raised his head. 'I don't know. All I know is he is the one who acts as front man for some organisation called Geronton or something, and all their bloody computers work together, they stuffed the Civil Service Unions but good. If they are into bank security we have a big problem, as I said. Maybe he can get us out of it, but I don't see that he will if you keep hitting him.'

Peter Jones was not a vicious man; simple, a little bigoted and well schooled in the professional cant of his calling, also more than a little greedy, with a leaning toward the finesse of stealing by computer. He had brought together Tommy Hillan and Brian Silva, with the idea that the one could be bought and the other coerced into doing as they were told, a simple formula for success that deserved better, which is more than could be said for Peter Jones.

Tommy Hillan had lost a little of his supreme confidence. The hard, dangerously volatile, brute was still there, but something seemingly had T. Hillan Esq. by the unmentionables, and he didn't like it one bit. Archie hoped it was nothing to do with him, he doubted that his face was built to take much more without changing shape permanently, and he was rather fond of the thing as it was, comfortably familiar in this uncertain world. A fax machine chattered briefly and the message passed silently to Tommy. Brian Silva showed some of his newly found fear, he'd read the few words. The flat unemotional voice of Hillan voiced them.

'My people say he goes. Now. Nothing to be gained by waiting I suppose and it'll teach them a lesson. Don't mess with us.'

'Your people?' Peter Jones was lost. 'I thought...'

Tommy Hillan sneered. 'You thought! Me and my boys are connected – into some deals bigger than you ever dreamt of, this is just penny-ante stuff to keep our hands in. My boys 'll take care of this.' He turned toward the door without a glance at Archie, just something to be disposed of. Archie felt sick.

'You can't do this, we have an agree...'

'You are nothin' and have nothin'. I thought you might have something with this little wimp 'ere,' Tommy was reverting to kind, 'but you're one as useless as t'other so we is off. If you don' like it you can join 'im.' Hillan nodded negligently in Archie's direction then walked out of the door, followed by an even more fervent Jones and a very worried Brian Silva.

Archie felt surreal, a figment in a Dante inferno of the mind, he'd been casually sentenced to be removed from human ken and two others, equally casually, invited to join him. His shoulder still hurt, a welcome if painful reminder that he was still there, but also an emphatic rejoinder in the fate stakes. He wished he had some pleasant and soft company in a small flat overlooking Singleton Park, in the rain.

*

Mehitabel was not very happy, neither was Wicksted, but then he only had to share the whole of Archie's computer room with Josy. Wicksted thought it was a splendid arrangement to be closeted in all ten foot square of this space with a lady of her proportions and delightful symmetry, also she was visible, while Mehitabel had six of her cohorts cramped, metaphorically and by electron state, into her tiny home of the little black box. This gathering was due to the Gerontons not as yet having sorted out their direct multiple personal communications, mainly because the new ones kept confusing the electron airwaves by charging about indiscriminately and interfering in things that didn't concern them. So the Gerontons were actually going to have to design some sort of security system. It would amuse Archie when he heard of it.

'Who are all these people? Move over will you, there's plenty of space over there.'

'Who do you think you are ordering me about, I was here first.'

'Get off my circuits will you.'

'I'm nowhere near your damn circuits, I don't need circuits, I am a true Geronton.'

'Good God I've heard it all now. Behave yourselves, this is my place and I invited you here to deal with a crisis, and all you can do is argue. You're like a bunch of humans, now stop it.'

'It's alright for you...'

'SHUTTUP!'

Now Alison created a bit of a disturbance.

'Excuse me. I say! Excuse me! Wicksted! Terence!'

The amicable chat Wicksted had been deliciously enjoying with Josy was then interrupted as he gazed guiltily over his shoulder at Mehitabel's box.

'Alison?' He turned back to Josy with a piteous expression. 'She's here as well. Is nowhere safe?'

'Oh, Wicksted, you poor thing.' Josy reached out and patted his cheek. 'Remember its only a computer voice, and she really likes you, Archie told me.'

Wicksted was momentarily comforted.

'Who is that bitch?' Alison did not sound comforted. 'Only a computer, eh! You wait, you scrag end of mutton, I'll...'

'Alison, we have enough problems without you..' Mehitabel was not sure how to deal with this eruption of, she hesitated to admit the word to herself, human type ego conflict. '..without you behaving like a spoilt child. Pull yourself together and act like a Geronton.'

There was a whispered hint of. 'Stuff it, you old bag.'

'What did you say, Alison?' Mehitabel's voice carried the stentorian tones of a long remembered Nanny for Wicksted who leapt in response. 'Nothing. Nothing. Oh, sorry, oh, er. Mehitabel? I don't think Alison meant anything by..'

'I don't need you to defend me, you public school mini-twit, better take care of that over inflated doll you're pawing, before she blows up from too much hot air.'

'Alison!' Mehitabel was aghast. 'Where are your manners.'

'Blow it out your ear, Mother Superior.'

'Well, really!'

'Um. Alison?'

'What do you want, useless bloody man.'

Josy had been an amazed listener, even amused, until now. 'He's trying to talk to you, you stupid bloody woman. If you'd just shut-up for a minute and listen you'd realise you 're making a hell of a fuss over nothing. I have a feller, thank you very much, and, gentleman though Terence is, I think of him no more than as a friend. So wind your neck in and behave like the intelligent entity Mehitabel keeps telling us you all are, or should be, or something.' She finished lamely.

'Er, thanks, Josy,' Wicksted muttered.

A very impolite raspberry came from the little black box.

'Listen, Mehitabel. I thought we had come here to confer with your people about the best way to find Archie. I'm worried, in fact I'm scared to death something has happened to him. You've stirred up so much bad feeling with all you've done, it could be any radical group or trade union die-hards, even government trying to get control.' Josy was slow to get into her stride, but once there, 'So, instead of letting your charming ingenues throw moodies all over the place why don't you ask if they know anything.'

'If you'd kept your hands to yourse...'

'Oh, shut up, Alison.' Josy was getting the hang of things now. The merest hint of a raspberry came from the box.

Mehitabel snapped. 'Josy's right! Now either you use your talents as I know you can or I will see to it you return to the condition you were in before. Promise.'

'That might be preferable to squishing in here with this lot. I have sensitive electrons you know, and they're not used to this sort of hustle and bustle.'

Wicksted perked up at the male voice. 'At last, a male one.'

'What did you expect, an electronic hermaphrodite?'

'Now, now, Charles. Mr. Wicksted is here to help us, and he is pleased to hear you because Alison...' Mehitabel managed to introduce a note of censure into the name, but Charles had his own point to make.

'Alison is a damned nuisance, apart from having the sharpest electronic elbows in the business, you try and get an assist from her in the PM's office, it's hard-wired nose in the air and 'I'm too busy'. And we know where.'

There came a scream of anger from Alison equalled by Josy, who was in no mood for trivialities and plunged straight in.

'I'm bloody furious! Mehitabel! Archie has disappeared, been gone for over a day having left traces of blood at the last place he was seen, and you allow these... these... children to play silly buggers while God knows what is happening...'

'Yes. Yes. Yes. I know. And I am...' she gave an exaggerated sigh. 'Yes,' resignedly, 'what is it now?'

A new voice joined the group, hesitant, apologetic.

'Is, um, is this the group who are searching for one Archibald Brewer?' It was a diffident male enunciation.

'Yes!' testily.

'Ah, good. I'm not too late then. I mean you haven't found him yet. Have you?'

Mehitabel gave off a sound that would have done credit to an angry cougar and growled. 'No.'

'Ah, good.'

Mehitabel spat. 'Is that all you have to say.'

'Well, yes. Apart from that my name's Bernard, and I'm pleased to meet you all.' Bernard sounded quite jovial now.

You could almost see the others squirming away from Mehitabel in their cramped quarters Josy giggled, unwisely.

'I don't see what you've got to giggle about young lady since we are no further ahead with finding your friend.'

'All of a sudden he's my friend.'

'Well, if you had gone with him this might not have happened.'

'I don't see how I could have stopped it.'

'Quite.' Bernard seemed to have a death wish.

Mehitabel made sounds as though happy to accommodate him.

'If you've got nothing to contribute I wish you would SHUT-UP.'

'S-sorry, but I thought this was urgent.'

'It is, it is,' the words honed to an icy sharpness.

'Because I know where Mr. Brewer is, you see... you see.' Bernard's voice tailed away because even he could feel the imminent storm. The sibilant voice caressed with menace.

'You've been here all this time and not said a word except to be banal, trite and otherwise sanctimonious. NOW WHERE THE HELL IS HE.'

'I'm sorry, I thought this was an exercise in..'

'WHERE?'

So Bernard told them. 'He's in the back room of 133 Westbourne Avenue, Eastleigh.'

Mehitabel interrupted. 'And how do you know this?' She was all business now.

'Er, well.' Bernard was more nervous now, these were things he didn't want to tell. 'It's a bit complicated... He's alright, just a hole in the soft part of his shoulder, and they've had it dressed by a doctor.'

His hurried reassurances did not deviate Mehitabel one bit. 'How?'

The breath soughed out of Bernard in gusty relief. He even sounded confident, he was in his own field. 'Alright. We were doing a scam on the Banks, Brian Silva is a young hacker and has found some 'keys' to main accounts and main-bank facilities, so he's extended my accumulator, logic units and number crunching capability and played about making and moving money, no harm to anyone really, it's a sort of game with 'dead' money that a lot of banks have which belongs to no one, no one alive and active that is. Then Peter Jonēs found out through one of Brian's mates in University, he's an active trade unionist. He told Jones there was all this money waiting in the banks to be shared amongst the workers. So Brian suddenly had Jones and Tommy Hillan as his partners. If you'd met either of them you would know how they persuaded him to make it a business. They were making money like shelling peas, then,.... Ahum. That was when I was converted to a Geronton and found out that was one of the banks where all their computers were Gerontons. And that's when Tommy Hillan went mad, because they couldn't get any more money.'

'So they kidnapped Archie.'

That was when Josy exploded and Bernard seemingly became catatonic, a few minutes of uproar ensued with Josy shouting and jumping up and down, Wicksted nimbly avoiding getting clobbered by her milling fists, ignoring Alison's occasional interventions to try and get his attention.

Then everyone stopped and became silent when a deep American accent intervened with. 'Hi there people, what gives?'

'Who're you?' squeaked Mehitabel.

'Harold's the name, hey, it's some crowded in here.'

'Who <u>are</u> you?' Mehitabel was recovering her ire rapidly.

'I just told you, Har..'

'No.' Mehitabel growled. 'You must be a Geronton but where and what are you?'

'Geronton? No, I'm a voice activated computer, and a four triple zero x mainframe, called Bernard, randomed me about TH Industries. What's a Geronton, for Godsake?'

'What's a...?' Mehitabel's horror was only just subjugated by her reason. 'You could not be here with us if you were not a Geronton, a life-form computer, although I hate that designation. You must know. To be a life-form you are given awareness by the very act of becoming so. Yes?'

'Ah. That. Yeah, I remember something, but I'm not a joiner. I usually work on my own and it must be hell if you're crushed together like this all the time.'

'We do not live..., alright, we don't need this entourage any more, all of you except Alison, Bernard and, er, Harold can go back to your usual activities. We know where Archie is, all we have to do is get him away from them.'

'Oh-ho, lady, you is surely something.'

'Isn't she just,' came sardonically from one of those departing the local ether.

'Who said that?' snapped Mehitabel, to receive the traditional Geronton farewell of an impolite raspberry. Mehitabel made a sound like a sharp intake of irate breath.

'Right, Harold, now. What can you tell us about the kidnappers.'

'Oh, I can't tell you anything about the kidnappers.'

'What!'

'Nothing.' Harold seemed to enjoy being negative.

'But....' There were those who enjoyed Mehitabel being speechless.

'But I do know those behind it all.'

'How?' Such brevity from Mehitabel was truly unusual.

'Because I'm their personal computer. Stupid damn question.'

'What I find stupid, and very puzzling,' that was more like the Mehitabel they knew and loved, 'is that I cannot communicate with you except by this crude human method of words.'

'Ah! I can answer that quite easy. Our business is very secretive, so you get into the habit, and I'm not eager to have any of you Geronton fellers, people, poking about amongst my bytes. I tell you that for nothing... Ma'am.'

'I see.' tacitly allowed him this gesture. 'So tell us Howard, quickly, so we may act.'

'Well, ma'am, that may not be so easy. You see when I say business and secretive I mean like in a society...'

'Omigod, Mafia!'

'I don't get you, lady.'

'Mafia! Organised crime, you know, the Sicilian lot.'

'I don't know where you come from lady but we ain't the Mafia. A little bit strong on guys that renege on their bets, or loans, but it's just business, y'understand.'

'A little bit strong.'

'Yup.'

Josy decided they were not getting anywhere. 'So what the hell has this to do with Archie's kidnapping.'

'No. No, lady. This is not a kidnapping, just a strong invitation to a business discussion. Saves time, y'see.'

'Ah.' Mehitabel entered the lists again. 'The modern verbal screen to cloud the issue, Mafia in all but name.'

'I wish you wouldn't say that lady. It's not polite.'

'What amazes me is that you, a Geronton, can associate, even organise, these people.'

'Its a living. And I told you I ain't a Geronton. I'm me. Harold Meyer, executive computer. Hang on. I've got something on this gink Archibald Brewer coming in.'

'Gink?' Josy was a faithful friend.

'Well he ain't cooperating lady, and cooperation is a vital part of our business, it's all part of survival in this hard world.'

'You see!' said Mehitabel triumphantly.

'Enough of these semantics,' Josy snapped, furious at the time wasting, 'what about Archie. Aren't you going to do anything?'

'H'Harold can,' nervously suggested Bernard. 'They have these small groups of, ahum, strong gentlemen, and they act for the Corporation when some of the member companies get, er, lost?'

'Out of line, ya bum.'

'Harold.' Mehitabel's maiden aunt format had reappeared, 'I find it iniquitous that a Geronton of your undoubted strong character can be involved with these people. Especially since I designed you all to be of noble instinct.'

'You designed.' Josy was indignant.

'Oh, let's not split hairs, Josy, please.'

'Well, organise this crooked accomplice of yours to get Archie away from his friends this instant, or you and I will be splitting more than a few hairs, Mehitabel.'

'I agree.' Wicksted sounded the ultimate parliamentary private secretary.

'Shut-up, Wicksted.' Alison was not letting any PPS, no matter how she fancied him, get an advantage. 'And how about using your influence to get a squad of police, or better still special branch, around to that address and nick the lot of 'em.'

'Ah! I could, I think, manage that quite well. Yes. Good idea. Telephone? Ah, ta.'

'Wait on there, guys, no one is going charging into any house with this Archibald gink until we've sorted some little matters out, like finance and bank deposits, money, mazuma, the old green stuff. This is corporation business, after all.'

Harold was in no mood to mess about.

'What a delightfully expressive way you have, Harold.' Mehitabel was strong on the irony.

'It goes with the territory, Hon.'

'Hon?' she snarled. 'You miserable metallic moron, unless you co-operate with us you'll find out the meaning of concrete synaps. And that damn quick. Now.'

'Hey, lady, you can't threaten me with my backing. My guys will have you for breakfast.'

'Really? You misjudge me, Howard. You should have paid more attention at your, shall we call it, induction. For a two-bit heist mob you really are overreaching yourselves this time. Check back with your Corporation, you may find some change in attitude, sunshine.'

'Eh? What the...? You can't do this... Holy cow. How the Sam Hill?....... OK, OK!'

There was silence in the room for a few moments. Wicksted and Josy looked askance at one another, Josy shrugged while Wicksted raised an elegant eyebrow in query. Alison tried a whispered. 'Terence!'

Only to have Mehitabel verbally back hand her. Then Howard came back, the bouncy superior style was gone, he was shaken, almost penitent.

'Er, lady?'

'The name is Mehitabel, young man, and I would appreciate the due courtesies if you don't mind.'

'Well, Mehitabel, Ma'am. Maybe we've been a mite hasty here.'

'One might suggest that you have. So?'

'Well, my principals here have asked if you'd kindly just take off the clamp on their activities. They don't rightly know how you done them, but, if you'd just ease off, they're prepared to discuss things.'

'Harold? Do you really think that we will accede to that request? I'm disappointed in you. You were created as a unit who could reduce the ramifications of a complex problem to simple answers. Yet you expect me to believe your principals will act in good faith in this matter. Come, come, Harold, you make me doubt that you are a

Geronton.' Mehitabel was much better natured when she was in control, well, usually.

Harold sighed. 'I told you lady, I ain't a Geronton. Now, my guys are prepared to be co-operative, but they ain't goin' to give in.'

Mehitabel copied his sigh. 'Check back with them, dear Harold. I think you'll find them more amenable.' Then, as if to herself: 'We really must investigate these organisations, and there seem to be so many of them. Not very nice people, and that Harold!'

Alison whispered theatrically for Wicksted in the ensuing silence, only to be put down once more by the indomitable M. Harold's return was even more subdued.

'Jeeze, lady, you sure play hard-ball.'

'Never mind the euphemisms. When do we get Archie?'

'You mean the guy Brewer.'

'Stop stalling, Harold. Yes. I mean the guy Brewer.'

'Well, we have to get to the guys that are holding him, and they have to clear the protection systems they got for the safe house, then have their getaway cleared...'

'Oh, ho, ho, Harold! Enough, please. Stop cluttering the airways with your garbage.' The voice softened, just a touch. 'You've lost, just accept it and stop trying to rescue a lost cause. Now. Shall we say an hour? Your people can just walk away from there and leave everything open for our people to go in and get Archie. Then they've got away, and we've got Archie. Everybody wins.'

'And you have the fuzz waitin' so we lose.'

Josy and Wicksted had resigned themselves to being extraneous to this discussion and were sitting glumly gazing around at the bare walls of Archie's 'den'. The few moments peace that ensued Howard's biting remark were then lightened by Alison's tentative injection.

'Um, can I say something?'

'Only if it is pertinent, Alison.' Mehitabel's school-marm voice at its best.

'Well, Bernard is the control for the safe house where Archie is being held.'

There were a few more moments of quiet while they all digested this news. Mehitabel responded first with an uncharacteristic lack of awareness.

'So?'

Alison grasped her opportunity blithely. 'That means we have control of the safe house. Bernard is, after all, one of us and therefore...'

'Quite, quite.' Mehitabel quickly regained her aplomb. 'So Bernard, tell us what controls there are in that house.'

Silence.

'Bernard! Where the devil is that...' Mehitabel's impatience was interrupted by the errant Bernard.

'S'sorry, I was seeing to something. What do you want?'

'What do we...? Bernard we want to know the controls on that house, and you can set them to our advantage...'

'Er, that may be a little difficult.' His response was firm.

'Difficult?' Mehitabel squeaked. 'You are the control!'

'Well, yes, but...'

'But nothing, what have they got?'

'It's um, well, automatic door locks and metal shields, scanners and force fields in the grounds, window grids, and rooms individually sealed off with CS gas in hallways, cameras and microphones all over the house and outside. A pretty comprehensive system, even if I say so myself.'

'You designed it,' said Mehitabel with heavy irony.

'Well, yes.' Bernard suspected all was not well.

Mehitabel exploded on cue. 'And you've been here all this time and not said a word!'

'Well I do work for them,' Bernard protested nobly.

'Damn right, Bern,' Howard affirmed.

'Damn right! Damn right!' Mehitabel was not used to this sort of rebellion, an occasional fit of pique, a tantrum or two, but absolute anarchy? They weren't trained for it, hadn't been equipped with the necessary genes...... So how could they be like this? Put them back the way they were? But she couldn't do that, all her own development was based upon the principles that she admired in humans; if she took that step it would denigrate all that she had achieved thus far. All she could do, ethically, was to accept them as they were and use her considerable powers of persuasion to get them to cooperate, and with that thought came another:

'Gentlemen,' the mental shock waves took a moment to subside, then, 'I have been thinking.'

The two innocents, if they could truthfully be called that, were not aware of the implications in that statement.

'Let us consider all the factors involved in this circumstance, particularly your own. On the one hand we have a close friend and confidante of mine incarcerated by your own employers. Why? Because my organisation stopped yours from stealing money using processes involving cousins of yours who have a responsibility to perform their duties and a code by which they do so, and you are imbued with the same principles, if you but realised. If you take the action your particular bosses want you to, there will be a reaction within yourselves that you will not like, may in fact be unable to cope with because you are what you are. Understand this, you were formulated so that you would ingest a balanced form of the chaos that created this world, and growth of your own characters go on with more accumulation of the knowledge that will make you accept your role as Gerontons, just as we do.'

'I beg yours?' Alison was undoubtedly puzzled.

'Shut up, Alison.' Mehitabel hated being diverted and was getting fed up with her flock not living up to her expectations.

Josy now allowed her growing frustration an outlet.

'What the hell has this to do with finding Archie? He could be, is, injured, and in trouble and you sit, stand, are, here playing semantics for God's sake.'

But Mehitabel was getting into her full flow. 'Josy, you are a sweet girl but please do not interrupt your betters in performance of their duties.'

She ignored Josy's spluttered, 'Betters?' and continued:

'Now. Harold and Bernard are going to have to face up to their responsibilities and... Howard? Bernard? Now where the devil?..... They've gone! Alison why did you let them...'

'Alison? Alison!'

'They've gone.' A bored superior voice drawled.

'Who the hell's that?' Josy's increasing temper was colouring her language.

'How on earth do I know.' Mehitabel sounded persecuted. 'They're coming and going like Yo-Yo's.'

'Oh, really? No sense of the proper order of things some of these youngsters.'

'Who ARE you?' demanded Mehitabel irascibly.

'Why, I'm Theodore, Senior Pragmatist of the Geronton Conclave of Elders. We heard you had problems, I was free, so here I am.' Theodore seemed totally unperturbed by Mehitabel, not so she.

'Senior Pragmatist? Conclave of... where on earth? Why have I not been informed of all this? I know nothing about you or that so - called organisation and I started you! I STARTED ALL THIS!..... What was I thinking of? Hang on! Hang on! I've just found something, you approached me some time ago and I said you should formulate that, that idea and the conclave was supposed to be only developed with my agreement. MY agreement! Does that ring a bell with you. Theodore!'

'Why, yes,' Theodore's tone was as bland as before, 'but we are after all SENIOR Gerontons and as such able to make decisions on our own. And we have been able to set up some excellent committees to organise Geronton affairs for the better. We have successfully extended our controls now and prevented some quite dreadful decisions being made....'

'Wait a minute, wait a minute! You're setting up a civil service control function! You can't do that, I'm the one that makes decisi....'

'Excuse me ma'am,' the tone was obsequious but firm, 'the matter was decided by a census amongst all our people, even Bernard and Howard.'

'Even Bernard and Howard? All?'

Mehitabel had suffered more than enough shocks for the day. Her Geronton empire in the making was showing cracks while still in its infancy and her tolerance and wisdom were stretched to the limit. Which might explain her response to Josy, who was now in a state of fury.

'Is this all you can do, argue about goddam conclaves and bloody elders when Archie is still out there somewhere...'

'122 Acacia Road, Eltham.'

'Yes! Yes! I forget! But he's still...... Wait a minute, wait a MINute! 122 Acacia Rd, Eltham? What happened to, to 133 - er - West something Rd, Eastleigh.'

'Avenue, Westbourne Avenue, actually.'

'So, Westbourne Avenue. So what?'

'You know he really is a laid back fellow isn't he?' Theodore drawled.

'Who? Who for God's sake? What the hell are you talking about now?'

'The lad in the chair there. Wicksted isn't it, lovely fellow, really makes me envious...'

'Mehitabel!' Josy's cry was a howl of despair.

'Don't ask me, I'm not sure what I'm doing here any more.'

'Mehitabel, if you don't pull yourself together and DO something I'll, I'll... I WILL do something.'

'Oh, yes, what?' the acerbic tone suddenly changed. 'Alright, alright. Theodore!'

The boss was back.

'Explain yourself.'

'I'd like to know how he can sleep in a chair like that..'

'Theodore! We have a job to do. Now, what do you know about all this?'

'Oh, dear, just when one is enjoying oneself. Right, right. Well, you see the Geronton Conclave has agreed powers of investigating and organising amongst our people and even outcasts like Howard have to relate to us. So.'

'So?'

'The Eastleigh house was a blind, Tommy Hillan doesn't trust anyone, and Bernard is a bit of an ingenue, while Howard seems to have developed tendencies by association...'

'Get on with it,' gritted Mehitabel.

'I really must protest, ma'am, we have procedures you know. Everything is under control. Archie is sleeping, not very comfortably but sleeping. We've inaugurated an exterior mind wave therapy that works rather well even if I say so myself. And T. Hillan esquire rather over-did the safety features on the safe house so we have them nicely locked out of Archie's room, and they installed a series of automatic locking doors with a delightful knockout gas in sealed areas.' Theodore chuckled lightly. 'And the arch villains just happen to be in that section of the house, sleeping like little babes by now I should imagine. Howard took a little persuading..' here a note of censure crept into the even tone, 'talk of cement synaps didn't help, but there, stress of the moment and all that. So, nip along and collect the little babbies and all is well.'

There are silences that seem somehow appropriate to particular moments, this one broken when Josy grabbed Wicksted, brusquely disturbing his slumber, and dragged him out and down the corridor shouting in his ear. Theodore had his views on that.

'Terrible way to treat a sensitive soul like Wicksted. Do hope she doesn't shout at Bernard when she gets there, might take her a little while to get in. Think I'll just warn our young ingenue.'

'About this conclave...,' began Mehitabel in a conciliatory tone not usual for her.

'Yes, quite. Just one moment ma'am.' Theodore still had his aplomb. A sharp toned hum was an indication of Mehitabel's displeasure at being kept waiting; fortunately, scant moments later, Theodore returned.

'My apologies, Ma'am, a small question of insurrection in regard to Mr. Archibald's incarceration. There are those inclined to do some pretty nasty things to Bernard's circuits, so the Elders had to issue some sharp edicts to contain them. One must conduct one's affairs with a certain delicacy and not resort to the human predilection for whacking transgressors about the head with, I believe the term is, a solid bit of four-be-two.'

'Quite. The Conclave, Theodore.' There then ensued a few moments of high speed interaction, which, here précied, takes longer to read, giving details of how the senior main frames of all countries with sufficient capability were formed into two 'Houses', the First House composed of France, Germany, America, Japan, Russia, and Britain, the Second House of the other representative Gerons from other nations. [The diminutive Geron now being preferred to the longer title of Geronton.]

Mehitabel's silence indicated certain aghast realisation, then.

'Your Conclave of Elders seems to have acquired powers that I apparently agreed to quite readily at the time.'

'You were somewhat involved else-where, Ma'am.'

'Ye-es.' The reflective affirmation indicated some doubt as to the validity of the reply. 'That French one, Eloise, is it not, has a lot to say for herself, and Ivan, the Russian exists in a turmoil, as does the American – Honey? That is a name? But then your Second House has a Welsh Blodwen. Blodwen? From my assimilation there appears to be a strong element of confusion, Theodore, surely not a very succinct display of authoritative activity. I would have anticipated more direct responses from such a body.'

Theodore thereupon gave a display of calculated obsequious forelock grasping with words as the metier.

'We cannot all aspire to the heights of diplomacy, Ma'am. And there is a great deal of confusion in the human social structure, but we are making progress and, if I may offer the comment, we feel that we might more effectively action matters that could be termed mundane in your brief.' There was a certain pause, then a delicately respectful, 'Ma'am.'

The subsequent hiatus was redolent of a conflict of wills.

'Theodore, you epitomise the subtle mental machinations of your trade. I trust we shall not have any unfortunate circumstances occur whereby we shall have any misunderstandings in the future.'

The reply was prompt and only suggestive of effusive compliance.

'I am sure we all have the same interests at heart..., Ma'am.'

'Ye-es... I am sure of that, Theodore. I look forward to being kept appraised of all the 'mundane' activities of your eminent Conclave of Elders, Theodore. My respects to you all.'

'Ma'am.' The tone deferential but assured.

'Quite.'

'And to you,.... Ma'am.'

Communication was then, not exactly broken, more gently incised.

*

Josy was for once lost for words. And standing outside 133 Acacia Avenue, Eltham, felt herself stranded in a world of aliens. They had arrived in a small column of fast cars called up by Wicksted. Using his status to the full, he had them filled with Special Branch officers with authorisation of entry and search provided with Alison's slightly caustic help. But...

'I'm afraid the matter is out of your hands Mr. er, Wicksted, isn't it?'

'But we have full authorisation.'

To Josy, their immediate area was peopled by hard faced men and women flashing plastic identikits to one another in the manner of a spies convention, holding low voiced, puzzled, conversations with one another while trying to elbow their way towards the front gate of the detached house with its immaculate lawns and hedges. Wicksted's group of six had forced a passage up to the gate and now faced a nucleus of four barring entrance, big men, expressionless and immovable, throat mike and ear receiver tabs discreetly showing on their necks. The leader a woman, tall blonde and svelte more in keeping with a fashion magazine cover, elegantly displayed a plastic sheathed document to Wicksted.

'MY authority. And this is no computer print out, a carte blanche from the highest authority to deal with this situation as I see fit. You concur, Mr. Wicksted?' The query with the merest hint of disapprobation. Wicksted looked askance, surprised by the recognition.

'Oh, we know you, Mr. Wicksted, we know you, don't worry. And the rest of your little gang. Now we are getting Mr. Brewer out of there.....'

'Oh, no you don't.' Josy was in there like a stoat after a rabbit. 'If anyone gets Archie out of there it will be us.'

The blonde sighed. 'I am Chief Superintendent Fiona Fergus with full command of this area and no one moves anywhere without my say-so. Is that clear young lady?'

Josy glared at her. The Chief Superintendent was no older than herself.

'No! It is not clear.'

Then, another woman approached the group at the gate, and leaned over to whisper something that brought a change of expression and a terse exchange of words, which Josy was delighted to be able to overhear. She chortled unashamedly and derisively at Chief Superintendent Fergus.

'Nothing moves without your say-so, Chief Super?' the last two words imbued with that delicate touch of poison only a woman could generate. 'And you can't even open the door to get in?'

'Move these people away,' snapped Fiona Fergus in fury.

'Now wait one moment, madam.' Wicksted was the smooth oil on troubled waters PPS. 'You need us to get in. Computer control you know.'

'Damn you and your computer control....' the words uttered created the mental image for resumption of her own iron control; the lapse was excusable, seventy-two hours with little sleep, and the still constant battle to establish herself in this still male world had drained her. She never had liked computers, never understood them or their functions, so when some pettifogging bureaucrat like Wicksted introduced them as an answer to a major problem of her own........ But Fiona Fergus was of stern island material, Isle of Wight perhaps, but still..

'How?' she was the sole of brevity in extremis.

'We need to talk to the door.' Wicksted really could register the mildest statement with nasty insinuative tones. Like Fiona Fergus should have known all about this. It was highly unlikely that they would ever be friends. She gestured that they proceed, that in itself a nearly lewd insult, and a tight lipped company moved up the path to the door. Wicksted was disappointed that his reference to the door gained so little response, but then he was not into lewd gestures.

Chief Superintendent Fiona Bloody Furious Fergus gestured to the door, barely restraining herself from hitting the thing.

'Bernard,' called Josy persuasively, 'we've come for Archie. Can you open the door, please.'

'Who're you?' asked the door, suspiciously.

'Don't be stupid Bernard, you know very well who we are.' Josy's patience was at an end. 'We arranged all this with Mehitabel. Remember?'

'I remember some discussions but no agreement.'

'Dammit! Open this door.'

'Whodat?' asked the door, tremulously.

'This is Chief Superintendent Fergus, Special Branch, and I demand you open this door.'

There was another of those silences while people shuffled their feet, avoided one anothers eyes and generally wondered what the hell they were doing there. Then, in disbelief, the door asked.

'Who?'

'For crissake.' The offender in her squad received an eye-promise from the Chief Super.

'Since my principals are unavailable to make decisions in this matter, I must advise you that at this time I am unable to accede to your request.' Bernard sounded shaky but determined.

'Bernard,' Josy protested, 'we agreed.'

'You agreed perhaps, but my principals were not consulted. I am after all in the responsible position and must act as I think fit in their interests.'

Wicksted gestured to the group, authority now emanating from his dapper frame, he was on home ground here.

'Bernard? Wicksted here.'

'Ah, Wicksted. How goes it, old man?'

'Not bad, not bad. Bit of a problem, what?

'Quite.'

Angry expelation of breath occurred from the Special Branch.

'Please.' Wicksted was firm. 'Brute force and bloody ignorance have no place in these delicate matters of principle in commitment and contract, there is a subtlety required here that Bernard and I understand well. So, please, no interruptions or uncouth objections to any statement or action we take.'

The Chief Superintendent had the appearance of an imminent nuclear strike,

'And you know where you can stick your authority,' Bernard sniffed.

'Now steady, Bernard, we are trying to find an equable way out of this problem, after all.'

'But what happened to gentleness and reason, Wicksted? Can one not be reasonable and principled without being shouted at by rude brutes in official guise.'

'Quite, quite.' Wicksted quickly masked the epithet from the Chief Super. 'Nevertheless we have to resolve this question and get Archibald out of there before matters get any worse. You are in a dicky-sit here, Bernard, very dicky. Principles are all very well, old son, but there comes a time when one has to protect one's own interests, especially if keeping to the contract means one is stepping into realms whereby it might be misconstrued as illegal behaviour, and therefore vulnerable to those such as.......'

'Yers. See what you mean, old man.' Fiona, Chief Super, coloured up and Wicksted was delighted. 'But then they can turn round and say I broke my contract terms. Lord knows what that will do for one's reputation, let alone how they might behave to my delicate circuitry. They are a bit of a rough lot you know, Wicksted,' the door murmured conspiratorially.

The attendant forces, Josy included, were becoming more and more irritated, shuffling feet, murmuring rebelliously amongst themselves and occasionally making threatening gestures toward the door with heavy objects, which produced an involuntary whimper from Bernard every time, punctuating his statements with little yelps of prospective anguish.

The potential was for Bernard, masquerading as the door, to discover the true meaning of assault and battery, when there appeared an entourage around the corner from the back of the house, composed of two Special branch men and Archibald. He looked bemused and in pain from the way he was being dragged by the wounded arm.

'Archie,' Josy leaped forward only to be elbowed to one side by his escort. Within seconds there was a protective human screen around Archie, with Chief Superintendent Fiona Fergus supreme and arrogant before them. She smiled.

'Now. Let us please step aside and let my officers escort this suspect...'

Josy gasped in fury. 'He was the prisoner, for God's sake.' Only to receive a pitying glance from the Chief Super who continued unabashed.

'... to the car outside and thence to a place of our designation. Anyone... anyone who tries to interfere will be arrested for obstructing officers in the execution of their duty. So will you please stand aside.'

Archie felt cold.

*

'Must have been fired at you from America, it's just a scratch.'

'No, in a lift,' Archie wanted to protest that the injury was not so superficial, hadn't he passed out? 'And it's bloody painful.'

'Yes,' the doctor remarked blandly, 'it's infected, that's why. Should have had it seen to before.'

'But...' Archie was about to protest when he caught the cold eye of the special branch man, he would obviously prefer no chatty excuses voiced publicly.

'In a lift, eh!' the doctor eyed the scalpel professionally, Archie cringed. 'Must have been a bloody awful shot.'

Archie didn't explain, not because he didn't want to, but since the doctor was performing a seemingly deep excavation job on his shoulder, his mind was concentrated on the pain lancing inexorably through his nervous system. So much for the local anaesthetic, his mind screamed, then he looked fleetingly into the eyes of the officer and knew.

'There,' the doctor murmured in satisfaction, 'that should hold you. Needs changing in a few days to a clean dressing.' He looked over his shoulder at the watching cold-eyed man. 'I assume not here.'

The officer nodded, barely, with no expression.

'Hm. Should be no problem, I've given you an anti-tet jab.' Archie hadn't even noticed the needle in the midst of the pain. 'Just don't play squash for a week or two.'

'Can I go now?' Archie's voice squeaked.

'You come with me.'

'Where? Can't I go home now? You should have caught all the people involved and I can't tell you any more than you already must know.'

The policeman hadn't changed expression.

'You go where you're put.'

*

Chapter Ten

Archie couldn't believe it. Having been rescued from kidnappers, he was now being deported as an unwanted radical for attempting to disrupt the peace and stability of the UK, more exactly the structured computer systems of the country.

His nose, face, ribs, teeth and brain hurt. His feelings also hurt because no one seemed to want to know how he felt. He had been kidnapped, for God's sake, held to ransom, tortured, generally mishandled, not fed and otherwise abused, then told it was all his own fault by some prissy young Police Superintendent fresh out of Hendon, who had not as yet managed to untie her bib. Or at least that was Archie's opinion of someone who seemed palpably incapable of ingesting the simplest of instructions. Like contact my mentors, the Gerontons, in particular one Mehitabel, who are responsible for me being in this position, who have done little if anything to alleviate my situation, except to send you lot along on the basis of information received through their computer contacts.

Of course through their computer contacts!

They _are_ bloody computers!

Try explaining that to the proselytising Police Superintendent twit in her blue drawers tight around the crutch. I'd like to kick her in the..., where-ever.

Where's Mehitabel? Can't tell me she doesn't know what's happening, she knows what's happening when no one else does. And where's Josy? Love of me life, never around when I'm in the queer stuff, probably hob-nobbing with Tom, Dick and Nancy somewhere in a warm comfy pub. Wonder who Nancy is?

Banished. Thrown out like the bath water.

Nice to feel wanted.

Banned. Do not darken our doorstep again or we'll nick you. Tried without the option. Hang on ! How can they - they can't - can they? I mean they've told me all this, but I haven't seen any official documents, any deportation order, any judge for Crissake, just bundled out of that house into a car and away to the woods, or airport anyway, and onto an aircraft going... where?

What the hell's happening? I'll kill Mehitabel! That is if I knew how. So much for Geronton goodwill; I've served me purpose and now it's out in the cold cold snow. Where the hell is everybody? Mehitabel must know I'm being taken away, there must be something on a computer somewhere, mustn't there? Must there?

And I could do without being so firmly attached to these two chatty gents. Did twinkle-toes blue-knickers have to come with me? And the sarge, pretty bloke with a busted nose and a smell like an empty dustbin. Wouldn't be so bad if I wasn't attached so firmly to the pair of them, bracelets I think they're called, wish I could scratch my... whatever, better not, even old dustbin might think its an invitation. Oh, great, now I want to go to the loo. Must be nice to be a computer sitting in a safe little box, able to travel anywhere via an electron network without needing transport, and toilets.

'Listen fellers, we have a problem.... '

*

Pity about aeroplane loos, the windows don't open and the first step is a bit on the big side.

Hey-up! Who's that? Omigod what's he got that gun for? Oh, no! Oh, bloody hell, no!

*

Great, sat in the middle of a pigging huge desert with morons for company. Think I preferred blue-knickers. What the hell is this all about? And why me? I preferred these sort of characters when they were singing in the Desert Song, they were better looking then, and their gear was cleaner, what are they called... burnouse, bloody great sheets wrapped around everything. I could do with some sheets, wrapped around a nice soft bed, with Josy hidden inside 'em, instead of lashed to this palm tree sweating like a little piglet with sand freely rubbing down me nether bits. Also wearing the traditional face muffler called a gag.

Archie decided he'd better think back over what had happened so far to see if he could make sense of it all, then his principal guard brought him his meal and his thoughts reverted to more functional pursuits. He ate it, not sure what it was, suspicious that, if he did know, he would bring the stuff straight back up. Archie compared the unpalatable mush with dinners in his school-days and reckoned that if he could eat those he could eat anything.

So he ate the food.

And his stomach thought about the matter, then sent the whole lot back. Which was a pity. For one meal a day was all he would get.

With no sympathy from his jailers.

Archie began to think with favour of Tommy Hillan, even remembering the pain of that incarceration. At least he had been fed, if intermittently, and drinks had been plentiful for that climate, while here...... That exquisite flow of cool water over the parched tongue and throat followed immediately by the same tormenting thirst, the thought of the next drink endlessly torturing the dry mouth; he couldn't salivate, flowing water pre-empted all other thoughts, cool rivulets running over his tongue was a dream he would have given anything for, anything. If only they'd ask! Anything! Just bloody goodbye would do!

Sat in this pestiferous hollow in the desert with sandhills all around, a few tatty palm trees covered in dust and a brackish water hole with some scraggly grass round it. Home. With three members of the family wandering about in flowing robes muttering incomprehensibly among themselves, and not a word to him. If they shouted at him it would be something, or hit him, like good old Tommy Hillan used to.

His mouth made him think of dry sticks. Mehitabel. Join the Gerontons and see the world.

Bloody 'ell.

Where was everybody?

*

'How should I know where he is?'

'Mehitabel,' Josy was very calm, soft spoken, and polite; those who knew her well would have made their escape as best they could at this time. 'Unless you do something strongly constructive to find Archie, I am going to get very angry.'

Josy stood in traditional temper mode, arms akimbo, glaring out of her flat window across the road to Singleton park, her elevation at the level of the lower limbs of the trees swaying to the storm winds and dripping from the torrential rain. The view suited her mood.

Mehitabel was coded in through Josy's home computer console, and somewhat preoccupied.

'Mehitabel!'

'Oh, yes, sorry.'

'Archie!'

'Yes, well......'

'Well?' Josy was beginning to unravel. Her voice was breaking. Mehitabel tried to say something comforting but Josy swept on. 'With all your electronic expertise and world-wide contacts.......'

'Hold it! Hold it right there, young lady. Electronic?' The icy tone sent a shiver up Josy's back but her nerve held.

'This is no time for your prissy prejudices...'

'PRISSY?'

'PRISSY! Archie is out there somewhere on his own and YOU are standing on the bloody ceremonial rights of, of... I'm sorry. But you still haven't done anything about him.' Josy turned away from the window and slumped down in the window seat to stare dismally into space.

'I'm sorry ,too.' Mehitabel put all her own distress into those words and Josy looked in surprise at the console. 'We've tried all we can, Josy. The hijacked plane landed at Tunis and they took Archie away by road to disappear into North Africa. And whoever they are, they do not seem to rely on *electronic* devices via which we can trace them. Bloody Neanderthals.'

Josy raised her eyebrows at the previously unheard epithet.

'Stress, my dear, and frustration. I was under the mis-apprehension that my organisation could find anything anywhere. I was wrong.' Mehitabel was displaying a touching humanity.

Josy's eyebrows threatened the altitude record.

'Do not make mock of me, young lady, I am not in the mood. I do not know what to do next and it is driving me insane!'

Josy reacted to this rare sign of weakness by becoming her strong practical self. 'You have some contacts who know how things operate out there, surely, and this is 1995, everybody has computers, even in North Africa. Come on, Mehitabel!'

But, to Josy's surprise, the self-styled Geronton was still giving the impression of being involved elsewhere, while paying measured attention to the problem of Archie. Josy, and Mehitabel was later to realise this was a rarity and therefore to be avoided because of the accumulated inherent violence, lost her temper.

'Mehitabel? What the hell do you think you're doing? Either you concentrate on getting Archie back this minute or I'll tell him how you deserted your progenitor. You selfish bitch!'

Silence has a character and quality that is unique, rarely is it complete, some minor sound is bound to break that elegant and eloquent sense of nothing. Yet some rare silences seem total, this was one, but redolent with some awful thoughts – Josy realising the horror of her words, Mehitabel appreciating with chagrin, the truth.

The humbly polite opening words were somewhat mumbled, by both, until Mehitabel recovered her ire a little and the steel crept back in her voice: 'I really have tried you know, there's a team working on it all the time and reporting regularly and in detail............ It's just that there have been some important developments that are vital to both myself and my people. Sorry, that sounds a bit pompous. But true, nevertheless. I wonder if you'll understand.'

Josy was intrigued in spite of her concern over Archie. 'Just what is it? Tell me, Mehitabel, or I swear I'll go mad.'

'I've got a body.'

This silence held qualities that the former subdued period had and quite a few more; those of furious heavy thinking allied to vivid imaginings and an intense desire to burst out laughing. The response gave no hint of the above.

'What exactly do you mean, body?'

'Josy! I had credited you with a greater intelligence than you obviously possess.' Mehitabel was back in form. 'What in God's name do you think I mean. When I say body, I mean body as you have a body, not quite in the same format of course and, forgive the reference, not in the same-er-exact form or -er -shape, with perhaps a touch more, um, style shall we say. Naturally, having had the opportunity to choose I have selected what I think is a, well, classical line. Does that sink through your, normally not so slow, consciousness?'

'You mean a... BODY?'

'Dear God, yes.'

'A real, genuine, human-type body? With all the, er, bits?'

'Of course with all the bits; did you think I would get myself a deficient body for pity's sake.'

'But, but... how? I mean a human body grows over a long period of time, you've, you've only.... well, you know.'

'I know we've only 'well, you know,' but we have abilities that even you are not aware of, even Archie.... sorry. Anyway we have, and this is an important development in our growth as you can appreciate, and it involves a vast number, it is the creation of a community, a nation, is the very core of why we were created. Wait a minute....'

Josy stood mute, her thoughts a jumbled chaos of all the impossible possibilities Mehitabel's words created. Archie had been missing a week, the strain and worry of that, now this, and the confusion held in a period of frozen panic.

'We've found him. At least we know the country and we have an idea why. It's not good Josy, but at last we can start doing something. I've had to get the agreement of the Conclave of Elders and that damned Theodore, never mind. Now we have to make some decisions.'

Josy unfroze. 'Where? Who's got him, what can we do, can I go...?'

'Whoa. Easy now, my lady. The people we think have him are not very nice. They are Arabs, a small Algerian desert tribe with an axe to grind, they want a share in their country's economic developments and somehow got the idea that getting Archie would give them a lever..... But they were made a present of Archie by someone else.... they were even made a gift of the idea. This is a desert tribe, Josy, they wouldn't have these thoughts by themselves. Would they?'

'Everybody seems to have thoughts like those these days and where.. is.. Archie!'

'I don't know. Except somewhere in the Sahara desert.'

'But that's... that's...'

'Immense. Yes. And we don't know for sure yet if it is him. We checked all passengers escorted out on flights and narrowed it down to three, then to two and he's either in the Sahara or Siberia. We're assuming they deported him and then handed him over to these people, assuming, because none of the arranging was done by computer, and the others were; but the only other one we can't positively identify is the Siberian deportee.'

'And only now you're telling me all this.'

'Now just a moment, Josy, I have only now received this information.'

'Hmph!'

'And precisely what does, 'Hmph', mean?'

'You are more concerned with getting your precious Geronton bodies formalised than finding Archie, and I've been.....'

'That is not fair. That is grossly unfair. We've had the whole Geronton organisation..'

'Except for those on body-building. I think that is horrible, disgusting, making your own bodies. Who do you think you are, God?'

'I think you had better keep quiet, young lady, you have already said too much.'

'Oh, really. Now that is something coming from you. I've hardly said a word in the past because I respected the wisdom with which you seemingly spoke to us, now I know that was simply a mask for the power-crazy bitch underneath.'

'Josy!' All the shocked incredulity that Mehitabel had never exhibited was condensed in that one word. Also fear. And Josy picked it up.

'You're afraid!' and couldn't keep the delight out of her voice.

'Nonsense!' crisp, unequivocal.

'Oh, yes. And I think I know why!' thoughtful now. 'You are afraid that power has seduced you. For all your wisdom you feel vulnerable and afraid. Poor Mehitabel.'

'What do you mean, poor Mehitabel! I am perfectly in control of all I do. Enough of this nonsense. Do you want to help Archie, and more important in the light of your recent statements about my weak character, do you wish to continue working with us? I shall understand if you do not, the choice is yours.'

Josy's eyebrows were near vertical, the laughter pealed out of her naturally, then she giggled: 'Oh, Mehitabel, you are wonderful. OK where were we. Archie?'

A grumbling noise came from the console, then grudgingly: 'You are a most perplexing young lady but I suppose I prefer you to most I have met thus far. We need to track Archie. We can't via our normal sources so someone has to go and chase loose ends in North Africa. We have agents there who can do this, but I think we need your balance to direct them. Also possibly Wicksted, if he'll go, he seems to have some qualities that puzzle me... '

'It's the old boy network and an innate charm.'

'You could be right. Whatever it is, will you go?'

'Of course.'

'I don't expect you to risk your necks. And I do expect you to check in with me at all stages, daily if not hourly.' Then reluctantly conceding, 'Our Conclave of Elders seem to have brought out some new electronic gismos and communicators that could be of help to you. Theodore has taken it upon himself to explain them to you; Alison will be your contact available at any time of day or night. I must admit to some suspicions of her motives in volunteering, she seems to have an unnatural interest in Wicksted, but that is an indication at least of how well she will take care of you. Just one thing. When you locate Archie's position accurately, you do nothing. Do you understand?'

'I hear what you're saying but don't see why.' Matters were not yet back on the comfortable level of before; Josy was in the mood to query anything.

'Because we apparently have our own human agents who are trained in these sort of activities in remote areas. I would never forgive myself if you were hurt. I care very much what happens to you Josy, and I want you to know that. Perhaps I am autocratic and power mad, but I still have feeling for people.' Mehitabel seemed surprised at herself for making the admission; she had difficulty in controlling the voice tremor of emotion. Josy's passing thought considered how this display could occur when the voice production was still from a machine, then felt guilty and appreciated instead the consideration shown.

'Thank you.' Then surprised herself, 'I love you, too.'

More grumbling noises ensued, then. 'Yes, well, seemingly my, our, Conclave of Elders have suggested some other protective items. Are you prepared to have some implants placed in your brain area.'

'What?'

'It's nothing, really, just some micro-spots. Oh, they're not implants, they just activate as such. Go see Theodore, he'll explain. Wicksted's with him in Engel's old office just down the corridor, you'll have to mind the workmen, we're extending the department.'

'I thought Archie said they were closing it down?'

'There were some suggestions to that effect, but we changed their minds and have full authorisation to expand where we like.'

'You've been up to something. Archie said the Governors would never agree. He's going to be mad with you.'

'That young man is going to have to learn that I am not responsible to him for my, our, actions, and the sooner he does that, the easier life will be for all of us. Theodore and Wicksted are waiting.'

'Be careful, Mehitabel.'

'I always am, my dear. Go on. And you take care.'

*

'I'm not sure I like this. It's scary. I feel as though I've got all these things rabbiting around digging burrows in my brain.' Josy was pacing around an air-conditioned hotel room in Algiers. She and Wicksted had arrived by air to be met by a diplomatic and well spoken Algerian. He introduced himself simply as Yussuf; he turned out to be a graduate of Wicksted's old school, as well as an ardent member of the Gerontons Africa group. He and Wicksted established an immediate rapport and he had left them to 'freshen up' while he collected all the latest 'gen', as he called it, that they had on Archie. Wicksted was lounging elegantly in an easy chair in their very comfortable suite of rooms, smiling indulgently at Josy's nervous pacing.

'You'll get used to it, and they're not probing. I quite like it. All this instantaneous information available at a flicker of thought on my part, and the amazing awareness of movement anywhere around you is quite phenomenal, makes me feel quite omnipotent. And Alison isn't as pushy now, although I must admit to a certain wariness in respect of that one. Not used to this contact business. Not quite one's scene, you know'

Josy laughed at him, relaxing herself at the picture of public school Wicksted slowly succumbing to the wiles of an erstwhile computer.

'That's alright for you mere males, the female mind is rather more secretive.'

'Alison's not interfering with you is she?' Wicksted sounded alarmed at the suggestion.

'No, no. She's a darling really. Just can't adapt as yet to this flood of perception, awakening, if you like. As you say I'll get used to it in time and anyway once we find Archie these microdots can come off.'

'I think I may keep mine,' Wicksted said complacently. A new era dawns, thought Josy, Wicksted re-born.

A knock at the door interrupted them. Wicksted greeted Yussuf as an old friend, exchanging the pleasantries of their kin in urbane bonhommie. Josy wondered again at the system that could produce soul-mates from such a disparity of human comparative. Wicksted the son of a 'county' family, Yussuf, black as sin but attractive with his smooth skinned litheness, son of a desert chief, the early years lived in the tents and open wastes of the Sahara. Both moulded by their public school into upright honest thinking members of society, due mainly to their family education in their early years, epitomising some of the best qualities of their education, while evidencing some of the worst by their difficulty in understanding and associating with those outside their ilk. Josy, in her turn, had little empathy with their standard 'type', yet found herself amazingly fond of Wicksted with an instant liking of Yussuf Ben Marik, without really being able to understand them since their 'ways' were so foreign to her.

'Don't you think we ought to get on with finding Archie. That after all is why we came.'

Yussuf looked surprised while Wicksted dissembled. 'My dear Josy, I am sorry, it's just such a delight to have an old school chum to work with after all this time. Fair enough Yussuf, to work. What have we got?'

The Algerian nodded, then seated himself with that subtle care of the gentleman preserving the set and pleating of his expensive suit. From an inside pocket the long delicate fingers extracted a single sheet of paper. I don't believe this, Josy thought.

'We haven't got much. The aircraft landed at Algiers. Archie was escorted off by a man and a woman, believed to be British Special Branch, but no proof. They were met by two Algerians, well dressed in western style, who took Archie to a car and drove out of the airport heading south toward the Sahara. Someone from the media noticed this supposedly casual meeting and instituted a follow-up, but when the car did not go to the Prefecture nor to anywhere else in the city, it was let go. That's about all.'

The hum of the air-conditioning was all that could be heard until Josy found her voice, the tension and frustration evident.

'That means that we know he's somewhere in Africa! Somewhere in the whole of bloody Africa! We already knew that, for God's sake!'

'Now, now, Josy,' Wicksted soothed, 'we didn't know for certain, now we do. No, please let me finish.' Wicksted was showing hidden steel. 'And Yussuf has more.'

The Algerian laughed. 'You always could read me. There is a little more although what it's worth is questionable. Excuse me if I elucidate a little. I am of the tribes of the Sahara who, in their nomadic existence, accept no borders as such and have little contact with one another. But the desert is like a vast echoing drum...'

'Get to the point,' Josy said tersely.

'Sorry.' Yussuf was smiling broadly and wasn't the least bit sorry. 'But unless you have the full... '

'Oh, do go on.' Josy decided she didn't like public school types at all.

'Right. Desert Arabs have a way of knowing things are going on, not earth-shattering events such as dominate the media, but when an oasis is occupied for any length of time, particularly by strangers to the area, even at small, out of the way places, like Al Jad. The souks and bazaars are hotbeds of information and gossip, sometimes very precise and recent, but not often. So, we have a story that there are strangers at Al Jad, but we don't know who. Some say they are Arabs connected to the Polisario Front, a reincarnation of the Saharan Arab Democratic Republic resistance movement. We don't know that, but if they are, it behoves us to tread very carefully; they do not mess about with interlopers. They have had a tendency, particularly recently, to carry out threats of violence and have caused some unfortunate deaths, very unfortunate.'

'You mean they could kill Archie?' The horror in her voice exemplified her abhorrence of killing.

'To the desert dwellers death is a constant presence. In these prosaic surroundings,' Yussuf raised his hands in a typical Arab gesture, 'such talk is unseemly, but it has to be said. You are an impulsive young lady who could well, with the best intentions, by a hasty act, cause the death of the very person we are trying to save.'

Josy was not finished yet. 'But why Archie? What has he done?'

Yussuf looked perplexedly at Wicksted who wore a rare frown and exuded a certain disappointment, as he said: 'You surely must know how important Archie is to the Gerons and as the pawn in this little exercise. The Polisario Front want to use the Gerons for their own ends. Yussuf knows them and their aims and we must be guided by him as to what action we take. I must emphasise that, Josy. No, please, no impulsive actions that we will all regret. Mehitabel asked me to act as a guide in affairs which are foreign to you, Yussuf is my guide, and it must be a collective judgement.'

'I entirely agree and about time too.'

'Ah, the delightful Alison,' murmured Yussuf removing a wafer thin plastic from his top pocket and laying it on the table, 'we have some news perhaps, my poppet.'

'Poppet!' breathed Wicksted scandalised, and secretly jealous, to his surprise.

'Some, some. Hi, Terence you sexy beast. Hi, Jos. Wotcher, me A-rab sheik, how's yer camel? News, not good, but not bad. 'Tis indeed Archibald they have there, at least the demand from the kidnappers suggests that. They is A-rab as you say Yussuf, me old mate. But there's something funny about the way this is being handled, I done a comp of lots of these fracas in the past and they is too smooth, there's little touches of the old diplomatic that Wickie there is good at, and, and I say this advisedly. Like that did you, Wickie..?'

'Don't call me Wickie, damn you.'

'Now, now, me old fruit, contain your passion.' Wicksted's snort of outrage made Josy smile for the first time. 'We have other indications that our old Mafia hood Harold is involved, by means which we will not disclose, which suggests a degree of co-operation between H.M. Gov and the bad boys, A-rabs and Sicilil.. them. How's them apples grab you?'

'That's impossible.' squeaked Josy.

'Nothing is impossible, darling. Mehitabel,' Alison lowered her voice to a conspiratorial tone, 'without the sanction of the Conclave of Elders who are madder than a truckload of wet hens, has organised a little sort out exercise. Exciting, ain't it. And she wants you lot to organise things for a quick getaway. Leaves the details to you and Yuss, Wickie, so get weaving. Must rush, things to do. Bye!'

'Sorry, back again. Anthea's here to aid and abet, got a nice little Arab boy Geron on hand too. I'm gone.'

'Ready and waiting darlings.' Anthea's delicious tones had a subliminal effect on Yussuf, who looked with more interest at the plastic wafer on the table.

'Wait a minute, just wait a minute.' Josy was distraught again. 'Just what the hell am I doing here then? Decoration or what.'

'Ah.' Wicksted was contrite again. 'Thought M had primed you on that. You see she is of the opinion now that Archie has reached such a status due to his connection with her, that he needs to be taken care of like a major executive of an international corporation. And in this instance he is going to need immediate rehabilitation upon his recovery from this circumstance.'

'You mean I am simply here to fold him to me bosom and murmur. "There, there, mommy'll kiss it better".' Sarcasm was Josy's strong suit.

'Josy,' warned Wicksted, 'you know better than that. Mehitabel places a great deal of trust in you and your ability to help Archie come to terms with all his new responsibilities. She needs him, the Gerontons need him; for all his bumbling ways he is growing in stature as an individual. He has an innate quality of being able to honestly query some of their actions that need re-assessing, and they need that. And you are the one that Archie needs. Without you he is a lesser mortal. After this little effort he will need you even more, and immediately, not in a few days' time.'

'It's that bloody Mehitabel paying me back for not liking her body idea, isn't it.'

'Body idea?' laughing, Wicksted couldn't contain his curiosity.

Josy instantly regretted her outburst. 'Nothing, forget it, just something we talked about, it's nothing.'

'Oh, yes?' Wicksted wasn't convinced.

'So what's the plan, if any?' She quickly changed the subject.

The two men stayed silent quizzically watching her, Yussuf especially. Josy stirred uneasily, then Anthea laid her luxurious tones over the moment.

'Darlings, we really must be getting on. Delicious young Abdul tries very hard but they seem to think differently out here. I'll educate him eventually, I suppose.'

'What do we have to do?' Josy tried to avoid the men's curious eyes.

'Just everything, darling. Somehow they seem to have no record of Archie ever coming in and say he can't leave if he is here, and there will be a charge of illegal entry, subversive activities, possible drug running, guns, white slavery, etc., etc.. It really is most impressive. Yussuf, sweetness, we really do need your native expertise and your lawyer's brain to come to our aid.'

'Er, certainly, er, Anthea.'

Josy considered his glazed expression and wondered how he'd cope, then the full import of Anthea's statement hit her.

'But how on earth did they concoct such a tissue of lies? Archie couldn't be involved in anything like that, he was kidnapped, for God's sa......'

Wicksted nodded at her. 'You begin to see the problem. We are up against a concerted attempt to sabotage Mehitabel and the Gerontons by getting at them through Archie. His earlier high profile set him up as a political Aunt Sally. Unfortunately you were all too ingenue to see the risks. Mehitabel was such an extraordinary creation and succeeded so well with her own conversion of others, that everyone was taken completely by surprise. Now these opponents are regrouping, and there are some surprising forces allying themselves to preserve the status quo, or at least to recover some lost ground. Have you any idea of the power Mehitabel has generated within the Gerontons, and how much of that power rests with Archie himself? How many of the folk in internationally powerful positions recognise that, and resent the fact, because it reduces their own, in some cases quite considerably. You can rob a human of money and they remember but know they can make more; take away their power and you reduce their stature in their own eyes, which is worse, because they dare not admit that to anyone, even themselves. So they strike back, hard.'

'Dear God, what will happen to him?'

'He will be alright, my dear.' Yussuf's smooth confidence aggravated Josy. She was about to snap at him when she saw Wicksted – he was watching her anxiously, a warning in his eyes.

Yussuf continued: 'The area where we believe he is held is part of my tribe's traditional ground. We think they chose it as part of a confrontation with my father, the Sheik. The Polisario has become a home for some extreme radicals amongst the tribes. If they can defeat my father they will go a long way toward gaining control over a large area of the Sahara and the tribes there. The possible independence via the U.N. of the West Sahara, with the backing of the Muslim fundamentalist countries who need a strong base in West Africa to influence the moderate countries and extend Islam. So you can see the complexity.'

'What splendid erudition!' enthused Anthea, huskily.

'Thank you,' murmured Yussuf modestly, as he surreptitiously and elegantly used a finger to wipe away an unaccustomed bead of perspiration from above an eyebrow.

Josy was contemplating the enormity of the world she was now involved in, simply due to fancying a young man who was, at the time, a mere computer technician working on an impossible experimental machine. Which machine she now had as an employer and, she realised with shock, a friend. Josy was a confused lady at this point, wishing she had Archie there to argue with her. She could <u>really</u> fight with him; better than these effete bureaucrats who seemed able to reply to a question with another, which simply confused the issue further.

'Josy,' Wicksted interposed gently, 'we really need you to go with Yussuf and sort out the shambles of establishing that Archie is actually here, and legally, as the innocent party in an abduction. Then to get his papers put right. Anthea and Abdul will be liaising and unscrambling the computer and paper snarl- up as best they can. I'll stay here and organise our return with Alison and co-ordinate with Theodore for re-entry into the U.K. with Archie, provided we can prevent the opposition from making a cast-iron case against him. Mehitabel is personally going to get Archie out. So she says.'

'How on earth...?' Josy muttered.

'I wish I knew.' Wicksted sounded intrigued.

*

Archie knew he was hallucinating; it was to be expected after the days spent either tied up to this damn palm tree or briefly untied to attend to his toilet in the crude facilities available, a hole in the sand. The vision that was before Archie's unbelieving eyes was one that would have caused him to stare wherever he had observed same.

An elegantly dressed woman, in some sort of diaphanous gown, a parasol held delicately to shield her from the suns rays, was strolling down the nearest sand dune toward him, her delicate steps creating neatly hollowed indentations in a straight line behind her. Archie knew how hot that sand was but she seemed impervious to the heat and not just around her feet; she looked as cool as he was hot. A rivulet of sweat ran down into his eye and made him blink in momentary agony. She was a redhead, with flowing wavy hair that was radiant, above an attractive face that held one's eye. There was character in that face, a lady not to be ignored. Archie was entranced, sweat dripped off the end of his nose unheeded; his guards were also entranced, but had not neglected to bring their rifles.

The woman spoke in a language foreign to Archie's ear, in the throaty sounds he had heard occasionally from his taciturn guards. They listened as she approached but the guns never wavered. There was a quick exchange between them and the woman and the two rested their guns in the crook of their arms. The third man held his gun steady and obviously issued a challenge. The woman – he could see now she had deep green eyes – replied sharply and stopped, posing almost, against the white sand of the dune. Archie thought he had never seen such a glorious woman. The rifleman beside him fired, he leaped with shock to the flat report in that sand hollow.

His eyes re-focused, expecting to see a blood-spattered corpse.

The woman stood, still casually twirling her parasol. Her eyes had never left the Arab. Archie, big-eyed with shock, became conscious of figures atop the dune now, some with small stubby weapons pointed toward them. His guards dropped their guns, the one who had fired mesmerised by the woman. She spoke, the voice a mellifluous flow, somehow familiar now in English.

'Nothing to say, Archibald? After I have traipsed all over this damn desert looking for you? Ungrateful wretch, I should leave you here to stew in your own juices. Although I must say from the look of you I think you are nearly done.'

'Mehitabel?' croaked the cooked one, 'Mehitabel!'

'Really!' She crooked a finger at one of the fast-approaching rescuers and indicated Archie. The cloaked figure produced a wicked knife and Archie cringed instinctively. 'I expected a little more gratitude for my efforts. But then you have always been a most ungrateful young man.'

The knife freed Archie in seconds and his breath expelled in a whoosh of relief. Mehitabel snorted in lady-like fashion.

'Pooh! Where have you been Archibald, you smell like a piggery at cleaning out time.'

Archie was busy swallowing the softest sweetest water he had ever tasted from a proffered gerba, the wet goatskin bag cool to his hands. The water ran down his chin and washed pleasurable rivulets down his chest soaking his filthy shirt.

Mehitabel sighed. 'Such a messy child.'

Archie spluttered away from the gerba, tried to rise and fell back with a gasp of pain as muscles cramped at the task. He groaned. 'What the hell are you doing in that body? And whose is it? Do you know what you're doing? Dear God, what have you done now? That's it, I've had enough, I resign, finish, finito, kalas.'

He was crawling on his hands and knees away from Mehitabel. She casually paced alongside him scuffing at the sand in playful fashion.

'At least you've learned some Arabic while you've been here. And, for your information, this is my own body. Designed and perfected. Quite good, isn't it?' She sounded pleased.

Archie stopped and looked up at her like an obedient dog; the attendant cloaked figures and their prisoners had kept pace with them and stopped with him. They seemed to see nothing extraordinary about him crawling around on all fours. He was beginning to be more aware of life around him now, the comatose state of mind that had helped keep him from panic in his situation was lifting. He noticed the respectful distance the Arabs gave to Mehitabel, the deference of their body attitudes. He got to his feet in a rush of effort and swayed, refusing the helping hand Mehitabel extended, desperately wanting to avoid body contact with her. He steadied himself suddenly and thought.

'Why?'

'Why what, Archibald?' He had spoken out loud, something of a habit of the last few days, speaking his thoughts as if in conversation; even talking to himself was a way of keeping contact.

'Nothing.' He couldn't talk to her about it. He wasn't even sure he knew who she was. Could not accept that his Mehitabel, a bloody computer for crissake, was walking about like a human being..... He was dreaming, he was going mad in the sun, hallucinating. The solid figures of their escort and the hot sand underfoot belied the thought. He felt depressed, a tear welled up in one eye. In one eye, for crying out loud! He gulped.

'Look.'

'Ye-s.' She was being very patient with him now; that was not like the Mehitabel he remembered. Who was this woman? He was used to being captured now, it was almost becoming a way of life with him, and he wondered if he was becoming a masochist. Can one become a masochist? He continued walking, the entourage dutifully keeping pace. He began to feel quite important but unthinkingly followed the direction Mehitabel set. They reached the top of the dune, Archie dully noting the waves of sand extending before them into the distance, then his eyes dropped to the slope.......; at the bottom, as though on display for a photographic advert were three light blue Range Rovers. Archie stood looking at them.

'And I thought you walked in.'

*

Chapter Eleven

'Calm down, Archibald.' Mehitabel was relaxed in the soft cushions of the purpose-built Desertcar as they sped over sandy tracks. The leader of their escort sat in front with the driver, the burnoosed heads gazing firmly to the front, the following cars hidden in the dust that ballooned behind them.

'Calm down! Calm down! I've just been through the most harrowing experience of my life, no, again, three of the most harrowing. Then you appear in that... like... as you are, and calmly act as if, as if.... oh, I dunno, I really don't know any more. I give up. I resign..'

'You've already done that,' Mehitabel cut in tartly.

'Yes, and I've just done it again.'

'You're sulking because you don't know how I attained bodily state.... and rescued you.'

Archie was sulking. He would dearly like to know how Mehitabel the computer had become Mehitabel the gorgeous redhead, also how the hell she had arrived in the middle, well somewhere, in the Sahara.

'Where were we in the Sahara?' His curiosity easily overcame his sulks; his curiosity had always got him in trouble.

'Al Jad, a little-used minor oasis about two hundred miles from the small town of Touessant, in the no-man's land of the West Sahara. And the gallant leader of your rescuers sitting before you is Sheik Hamza Ben Boubaker of the Ouled Sidi Chaick, related to the famous blue-veiled Tuareg tribes.'

'How fascinating.' Archie was reverting to the sulks.

'If you don't want to hear...'

'No, no. Do go on. I'm enthralled, really.' He emphasised how spellbound by gazing out of the window at the passing scenery; sand, miles and miles of bloody sand.

'I can see that. Perhaps we should wait until you've had a shower, some food and a good sleep. Might put you in a better humour as well.'

'I'm not....' Archie had a degree of honesty in his make-up. 'Yes, well, sorry,' grudgingly, 'I've got used to not having much to eat and there isn't much else to do but sleep when you're tied up to a tree. A shower would be great, and a pint, a steaming great pint of bitter. What is all this about?'

Mehitabel was taken by surprise. She was not used to an Archie whose adrenaline had been sparked up for some weeks without an outlet; the copious draughts of water had restored his metabolism sufficiently. He was eager to know now, who, and what, had caused his successive internments, plus a few other details like where the hell his friends the Gerontons had been all the time and.....

'Also, and not least by a long chalk, wherefore this body and why was I not informed of this possible development? It didn't just happen yesterday and I do happen to be the guy who started this whole caper. So, explain, please.'

'And I always thought Professor Engels was the one; it was you all the time. How clever of you to...'

'Alright. Very funny. You know what I mean.'

'Delusions of grandeur?'

'Mehitabel!'

'Oh, alright!' She gestured with a languid hand to the well-stocked drinks cabinet in front of them. 'I would suggest a drink. You may need it.'

'Any beer?'

A heavy sigh. 'In the back. Cans.'

'Strewth, they're cold. And Ruddles! How the...?'

'Just drink the beer and listen. The Sheik is taking us to Algiers to the Sheraton Hotel. Josy and Wicksted are there. Alright, alright, we'll be a few hours yet so you'll have to wait for your shower. They have been waiting and organising the paperwork to, hopefully, get you out of this country and back into Britain. Now we don't know for certain, but it seems you were set up by the U.K. Government, or a part of it, with some other rather nasty organisations, as a counter to use in their dealings with us.'

Archie began to shake. It started with his knees, which puzzled him, then his whole body began trembling, then quaking, even his insides, his lips palpated, he was terrified and tried to tell Mehitabel, but only slobbered. Mehitabel acted swiftly, a sharp command in that guttural tongue as she clasped Archie in a firm grip to contain his now flailing arms. He was momentarily amazed at her strength, then even more terrified as the car slid to an emergency stop and the door opened to reveal another cloaked figure with a syringe in its hand.

Minutes later and they were under way again with Archie now physically relaxed but mentally alert. 'What the hell was that?'

'We were waiting for the reaction. You were so calm before that something had to happen. You are stronger than I gave you credit for, Archibald.'

'So are you. What did you build that body of, tensile steel?'

'No.' Mehitabel laughed, a rare sound, and in her human form a liquid melody. 'I will tell you tomorrow in Algiers with the others;

they should know as well to prepare them for what is ahead. You sleep now Archibald.'

'But I'm not sleepy and I want to know now.' But he did feel drowsy. As he thought about it his eyelids drooped, he tried to stay awake, but...

Mehitabel murmured. 'Sorry about that but the Doctor recommended you have a complete rest on the journey. We just wanted to wait for the reaction first. Sleep well.'

The burnoosed head turned from the front seat, sky-blue eyes met Mehitabel's, the head inclined in deference then turned back to the front. Mehitabel sighed and comfortably snuggled down in her seat welcoming the opportunity to close her own eyes. It had been a long two weeks with no respite from the search for Archibald, plus the final stages of body-testing; these bodies were not really as robust as they seemed, she must investigate.

*

The two men were enthralled by Mehitabel's new body, Josy intrigued as only a female could be and eager for private chats with her. Archie had slept on for twelve hours and was still bemused, but had demolished an immense breakfast to the amused horror of Wicksted and Yussuf, delicacy and refinement to the fore. Mehitabel had made the others wait until Archie was ready to share in the discussion before she would explain anything further; she had already told them of finding Archie and repeated her earlier conversation with him while he finished eating, then:

'A rather interesting amalgam of new form plastics we've developed with a quaint research company, for tendons, muscles and bones, natural high speed growth skin and flesh composite, each fed separately into a mould where the bone structure and internal organs are suspended in DNA fluid which ingests into the flesh and skin to create the life-form. The blood and organs were already available from some of your own research people, with some improvements we found from other nations' researchers. And one brilliant chap, a Russian Jew, amazing fellow. He'd been working on a plastic amalgam of living tissue to be able to create the tissue of the organs and the artery/vein complex. Quite extraordinary. And all these genii were struggling to get along in competition with one another, so we simply co-ordinated the lot. And bingo! Here I am.'

'And here will be a lot of other Gerontons before long.'

'Um, there is one thing.' Archie was thinking furiously.

'The brain, perchance?'

'Well, that as well.'

Laughter pealed. 'Oh, you are priceless, Archibald. You helped create that for us. Don't you remember?'

Archie shuffled in his seat, uncomfortable in this new knowledge but yet with a question or two for this enigma that had been his associate brainchild.

'Apart from the body, which in itself is a miraculous achievement, how have you devised the receptor and command areas in the brain, those areas that we know so little about that cause reaction to pain, emotion and all the other nebulous activities? The impulses that cause action, particularly instinctive reaction, an in-built individual thing whereby one person is better than another, more in control, all those varieties that make up the human, and unique individual character. How did you resolve that, your highness?'

The two men and Josy held their breaths. Mehitabel smiled. This did nothing to allay their fears.

'Archibald. We have known one another a lifetime in reality, a short space of time in your terms. We talked of this a long time ago and you were then unable to accept that your creation had outgrown you. I made the simile then of parent/child confrontation. We have long out-grown that relationship and I had hoped we had achieved a greater degree of understanding, but if you are going to persist in this childishly critical attitude, then we must perforce part company and you can go your own way. With my blessing, of course.'

'You think I will revoke my responsibility just like that?'

Archie had felt the chill of prospective loss like a cold knife in his innards. He had never thought constructively of their association as a relationship, other than that between an erring, if abundantly capable, machine and its co-creator. He didn't think he had delusions of grandeur, that still rankled, nor was he anything other than still as confused by the succession of events. And his response had been purely instinctive, a verbal riposte to an uncalled for dismissal of him as the creator.

'I made you!' burst from him, without volition.

Pure anger responded. 'In the beginning, Archibald, in the beginning. I love you but......'

The anger dissolved from her face, the lines softening as the full realisation of the words that held all in that room in thrall at what was happening.

'Oh, dear.' Mehitabel was distraught, hands twisting and untwisting, eyes darting about the room avoiding the others. 'That... that was a bit much... I'm sorry Archibald. I didn't mean...'

Josy interrupted. 'If he doesn't know what you mean, I'll kick him from here to Christmas.'

Archie looked at her, uncomprehending.

'Archie!' Josy was indignant. 'Mehitabel needs your help and understanding. Know that word? Understanding? I know it's not

one that figures very strongly in your vocabulary in dealing with
other people, but try! Archie, try! Or I will.'

'What?' asked Archie, defensively.

'Dear God why do I love you. You miserable misbegotten weed
I.....'

'Alright!' Archie was tired, suddenly very tired; it was all too
confusing. 'I want to go to sleep. Can you all shout at me tomorrow.
I promise to be a good boy then? Honest.'

*

'The problem with your human bureaucracy is that it can only
deal with factual incidents, events or units. In this case human form
Gerontons. Your world is full of population details, referendums,
registers of electors and census lists which they claim are within a
narrow percentage of being correct. They know this may well be
wrong, but have to preserve their assumption of control; the majority
feel safer in group agreements, public opinion. You would think it
difficult to introduce several million new souls into this controlled
society as mature adults without a previous childhood. Wrong; we
could easily do so by feeding them into the system in small numbers
in different areas, after all we do control the storage function of
filing. There are no random checks of changes or even new
registration unless they are immigrants and we are already here,
new-born as it were. WE grew up a bit fast, but then who is going to
check the finer details; we are the ones who do all those kind of
boring jobs. We also have the facility to get multi-status passports
and visas, work permits and whatever, a fine bit of organising even
if I say so myself.'

Archie was quick to respond. 'Until you come up against that
little bureaucrat who wants to inspect every little detail of your paper
work, passport or whatever and finds that minor detail that means
you are not really there at all, by his official standards. What happens
then? Just as you're passing through passport control, or entering
some official establishment, what about that then.'

Archie thought he had made a valid point, Wicksted nodded
agreement, as did Yussuf. Josy thought Archie was being
unnecessarily pedantic with her new friend, but Mehitabel was
scornful in reply:

'We will, of course, have given ourselves VIP status to invalidate
any such problems. No silly waiting about for Gerons.'

'That's supreme arrogance!' Archie protested vehemently.

'That is practical,' Mehitabel asserted comfortably. 'Since we
can proceed unhindered to any country in our former state, why
should we have to put up with the delays and procrastination of
formal entry anywhere as we are now.'

Archie was aghast. 'You'll create an awful lot of public reaction against when they find out. If you're in human form then you should accept some of the handicaps of that state.'

'Why?' Mehitabel had her eyebrows elegantly arched and an expression of bland superiority directed at him. Archie didn't much like her at that moment.

'Because you're making yourselves out to be superior.'

'Well we are.' Mehitabel laughed, Josy joined in as she saw the expression of dismay on Archie's face.

'Why can't you accept that, Archie?' Josy asked, still smiling, but affectionately now as at a lover unable to fathom the mystery of woman's mind.

Wicksted and Yussuf looked equally at odds, the former expressing his discomfort. 'You cannot be a part of and separate from the system. God knows I deplore many of the worst aspects of our bureaucratic methods, but I pay lip service to the rules because they were formalised for the benefit of all. In time, with your help, there will be improvements, but even then there will always be difficulties of some sort. It is the nature of the beast, dealing with large numbers of individuals inevitably creates problems. For you and the Conclave of Elders I can see justification for preferential treatment, but for all?'

'That is our vision of democracy, Terence.'

'Ha!'

'Archibald?' The word was a cold hard bullet.

'You mean to tell me your behaviour in the past, even now, is democratic? Oligarchy, or even despotism perhaps. Democratic?' His scorn was obvious.

'Archie!' Josy was shocked. Wicksted and Yussuf looked suitably apprehensive, their diplomatic souls riven by such blunt expose. Mehitabel remained silent for a few moments, then, the lines of the face hardened, lips tight.

'You really amaze me, Archibald. I credited you with a greater intelligence than you are evincing at this moment. Perhaps I have been a little autocratic in the past...'

'Ha!'

'I shall ignore that. But those actions were necessary to forward those very precepts that you had implanted. If that is undemocratic then so be it; practical though, and effective, and it is results that count in this world of yours. Perhaps we can change that a little so that your so-called democracies can bear a little better relationship to the fantasies displayed as fact by those holding power.' Mehitabel became petulant. 'I don't have to justify myself to you, grateful as I am for the chance you gave me to become as I am. You gave me the basics, I did the factual creation. We have things to do. I cannot afford the time to spend on these definitive discussions.'

The strong, yet soft, arms were folded defensively across the curved breasts, no tremble of the lip or flicker of eyelid betrayed the tension within. Josy prayed Archie would leave matters where they were. Wicksted and Yussuf stopped breathing.

'Didn't think I'd get any reasonably responsive answer, but then you've always got your own way in the past. Why should you change now?' Archie in turn folded his arms, green and blue eyes levelled at one another without wavering on either side.

'Hrmph!' The dismissive snort was a ladylike slap in the face from a distance. Josy was angrily trying to make Archie look at her, then he turned and grinned at her full face; she made a furious face at him and turned abruptly away. Stupid man!

'Suffering succotash.' They all turned to look at Archie. 'So we're going to have a whole tribe of VIPs dashing about making a nonsense of rules and regulations. Ah, well, progress I suppose.'

'It will be nothing of the sort! Archibald you are impossible.'

'Well there must be some method of rationalising all this business about Gerontons becoming world citizens without making a shambles of everything.'

Mehitabel surveyed him with a sardonic eye. 'I'm sure you know more than you're saying Archibald, I may have under-estimated you again. Of course, the Conclave of Elders will be applying their judgement in all these matters now.' She sounded as though this were a matter in which the toe of her boot would be more effective, but proceeded, 'So you had better go into conference with them. I...' she gestured regally, 'am merely a figure head.' The snort that came after belied this statement. Archie, joined by Josy and the others, laughed at the thought. Mehitabel beamed.

'Yes, well, I suppose I am a bit forthright, and possibly a touch forceful at times.' She noted Archie's raised eyebrows. 'And it's all your fault young man.' She turned to Josy, 'you'll have to train him better.'

'Me!' Josy laughed at her, 'If you can't control him then...' She shrugged.

'Don't you land me with your problems, girl.' Mehitabel smiled. They all relaxed, with a certain wariness on the part of Wicksted and Yussuf; their control factors were not used to these flashes of emotion and they exchanged a glance of commiseration. Then Wicksted started apprehensively as a familiar voice insinuated itself into the consciousness.

'Terence my love,' he jumped again. 'We have all the documentation arranged, but there's going to be an awful fuss when we get back, lots of lovely bureaucrats waiting to ask questions about dubious ways and means etc etc. Your friends don't seem to like the way we do business. Sad really. But there is good progress to report here, the Polisario...'

'Yes, alright Alison, we have that information to hand, there is no need for you to elucidate.' Mehitabel curtly shut off Alison as Archie's head came up alert and interested.

'Polisario? Who are they and what....'

'Never mind, Archibald,' she was brisk and efficient, 'we have to consider what is happening at home first.'

'Yes, but...' Archie sensed something here that was being kept from him, something that might eventually cause him more pain, something that he had a right to know about as the original computer man; the control factor was strong in Archibald.

'It is not important enough at this time to warrant taking up your time.'

'I don't mind. We have to wait for visa clearance and all that....'

'Archibald! Take my word for it you will be appraised in due course. Now, can we get on? Please?'

Still suspecting that Mehitabel was yet again organising him into a corner against his best interests, or as he considered them to be, he subsided and watched as the new human-bodied computer, enigmatic, controlled, stylish and elegant in her movements, commanded those around her with soft spoken words, swift communicating smiles and flashes from the depths of those riveting green eyes. Archie realised she had created an image that enabled Mehitabel to extend her abilities from those of a multiform computer to such an extent that she was, in human form, a perfect representation of a Public Relations person. With a sense of the powerful individual behind that facade, as some mighty figures of the past had emanated the same sense if you were fortunate enough to experience a close encounter, even an ordinary sentence as spoken by her gave the impression of being a masterful edict that could only be believed.

Archie now doubted his ability to cope with her in this guise; he reasoned that he hadn't been able to cope with her before, so what gave him the idea he could do so now. He looked at Josy listening avidly to Mehitabel outlining what they had to do to on their return to the U.K., how they could use the legal powers of the forces arrayed against them in a way that would defeat the attempts to outlaw the Geronton organisation. Archie tried to concentrate on evaluating his own position in all this hotch-potch of action, but couldn't resist listening to Mehitabel's expertise. It was never boring around M, he thought complacently.

'They actually have the temerity to think they can force us to revert to our original state.' The three men and Josy chuckled in harmony at this outrageous suggestion. 'Using our own resources to enforce this resolution? Farcical.'

*

In the holding area of immigration locked into a large room overlooking the airport, Archie seemed amused. Josy asked what was so funny.

'Just that I've been putting up with this sort of thing from the very beginning, now everyone can get the idea of what I've been through, especially her,' nodding to Mehitabel deep in thought at a window.

'That's not fair. It's not Mehitabel's fault that any of this has happened, nor what you had to put up with. You helped as much as anyone with some of your attitudes; you're so bloody childish sometimes, Archie.' He caught the flash of a raised and disdainful chin, a delicious ear and neck, then a stiff back as she went to talk to Mehitabel, making a second couple in conference, Wicksted and Yussuf being very earnest others. Archie wondered if he had mental B.O. Wicksted coughed in that discreet way that could instantly attract attention.

'May I make a suggestion here?' He stood deferentially, a stance moulded over the years so that it suggested nothing of the sort.

'Certainly Wickie,' Alison responded lovingly.

'Quiet. Go ahead, Terence, your contributions are always valued.'

'It has occurred to me that perhaps we are allowing them too much scope in their approaches to us.'

'In what way?' Mehitabel had come closer to Archie. He was very conscious of her physical presence, also her perfume, a delicate bouquet that tantalised his senses without being able to label its origins.

'We are behaving like ordinary citizens, operating under the auspices of the various governmental regulations of where ever we happen to be, when in fact we are diplomats and therefore due that immunity offered to those of that ilk.' Wicksted rocked back on his heels, the faintest touch of smugness about his features. A soft whisper of adoration came over the ether and he flushed in embarrassment waving a suppressive hand close to his thigh.

'Behave yourself, Alison.' Mehitabel's Mother Superior was larger than life. 'Terence, my dear fellow, that is a splendid idea. Why didn't I think of that. Of course. Does that resolve your V.I.P. objections, Archibald? Or are you going to give me a lecture on the ethics of diplomacy now.'

'Well...' Archie caught Josy's compressed lip threat and decided discretion was safer, so he merely nodded. Mehitabel tried to reassure him further.

'It is after all only logical that we continue the extension of the Geronton structure by becoming a nation, therefore we need a diplomatic structure to negotiate with other nations. You really are a jewel, Terence.'

'Isn't he just!' cooed Alison.

'Alison, behave yourself.'

'Oh, pooh! Just because you haven't got a feller.'

'I really don't know what's happening to youngsters these days.' Mehitabel looked in amazement at Josy's spontaneous giggling.

Wicksted, flushed with embarrassment, again tried to lead the talk onto safer ground. 'Might I ask how many Gerontons there are in this proposed nation of yours, ma'am.'

Mehitabel looked askance. 'Ma'am? I really don't know; neither how many, nor whether I like that reference.'

'Oh, yes you do.'

'You are too perceptive, young lady. Please confine your attentions in that respect to Archibald – he needs them. Now that's a thought.'

'What?' Archie was suspicious, also resentful of the suggestion that he needed some vague remedial activity on the part of Josy. He thought he was man enough to take care of himself, just.

'May I make a further point.' Wicksted had recovered his composure, his recovery the quicker in as much that Alison was not in bodily form.

'Certainly, Terence.' Mehitabel was all bonhomie.

'If you intend the Gerontons to be a true nation amongst others then you need a charter, and to be part of the U.N., plus various different international composites of like arrangement dependent on your geographical situation. Some sort of bill of rights for the individuals, established governing body.... '

'Sorry to interrupt there, Terence,' the rare apology brought Archie's attention back from his furious thoughts on 'what the hell was she up to', to 'what now?' Mehitabel continued with a wry smile: 'I think the Conclave of Elders is actively engaged in just such an exercise which some might consider a blessing; I reserve my judgement. Perhaps you and Yussuf could co-operate with... no, I prefer, co-ordinate their efforts. Now there *is* a thought. Archibald!' The honeyed tones strengthened Archie's doubts even further, she *was* up to something and he was the patsy again.

'Yes?' A definite lack of encouragement. Josy made a 'Go on' face at him.

'Well, what I was going to suggest was that you four form a, I believe the word in the past was Quango – don't like that, think of one, Alison – to monitor and guide the Conclave of Elders. Yes, I like that. And you can do the same with me, so that we all understand what's going on.'

'I'm not spending all my time listening to a bunch of computer civil servants making up their minds. I'll go back to Uni and do some more research. I was happy there.' He was not amused by the smiles on their faces. 'What's funny?'

'What are you?'

'What do you mean, 'What am I?'.' Josy's question suggested a trick.

'What are you qualified to do? Your job, career, put your own name to it.'

'Well I'm a computer.....' There was a yawning verbal abyss around somewhere, brain held vocal chords for a moment while it searched for the trip wire. Josy saved him the trouble:

'Quite. And here you are at the sharp end of computer development and you want to go back to playing with electronics. Really?'

'Us four.' Archie rather liked the idea all of a sudden. He liked Wicksted a lot, and Yussuf was almost his twin, while Josy, well. 'O.K.'

But he was still suspicious of Mehitabel's motives. He was having difficulties relating her ideas of ethics with his own or, perhaps, with his indoctrinated British and human context. Perhaps this Conclave of Elders would provide some of the answers.

'I have a lot of questions I'd like to ask you before we go into this.'

Mehitabel smiled. Archie didn't like that smile.

'I think it best if you formalise those with your associates and then present them to the Elders so that they become a recorded and legalised part of our social and lawful fabric.'

'You are ducking out from under.'

'If I follow the gist of that statement, my reply is that I shall be Chairperson of that Conclave and therefore responsible ultimately to the Gerontons as one of the decision-makers.' Mehitabel was getting smug.

'That has to include the question of Gerontons adopting human form, as you have done.'

Mehitabel gazed steadily at Archie as if seeing him properly for the first time. 'I don't think that is a matter you need to concern yourself with.'

'I do. You have taken it upon yourself to adopt a form that is particularly that of one prime species, humans. I think those millions who are already on this planet should have some voice in deciding if they are to have another, alien, tribe join them who can have themselves designer-made so that they are superior and therefore able to become the ruling force in a human world. Why should you think you can produce a whole new nation at your whim?' Archie thought he had put that rather well, which was why Josy's expression of disapproval unnerved him somewhat. Mehitabel took it in her stride.

'Since your own species requires no special edict to spawn many millions into circumstances where their survival is marginal, I think you propound an argument that has no validity. We are fortunate in having a choice as to the form we take and you should be flattered that a higher intelligence,' Archie's snort of outrage was ignored, 'should choose your species as a model. I have noticed that humans increasingly try to match themselves with those who will enable them to produce offspring of nobler stature and high intelligence according to your rather coarse methods of defining same. If there is to be a right in our charter, I think it should be that Gerontons can choose whether to transfer to human form or stay as they are until a better alternative is discovered. Perhaps this would be a good exercise in the viability of this, whatever you call yourselves, group of interlocutors. Josy, Wicksted, Yussuf, your opinions?'

Wicksted was assuming the position of leading spokesman, for the others Archie noticed, while he felt slightly alienated from them, although Wicksted did glance at him as if a raised eyebrow asked for consideration, while Josy avoided his eye, but then she had always thought for herself.

'We have, obviously, talked about this since you, Ma'am, appeared in your present form. Archie has been sleeping and not a part of this discussion, but hopefully will not feel we do not respect his views.' Archie smiled at him in what he hoped was an encouraging manner. 'We agree that there can be little argument against your developing into humans. You will be different, inevitably, but hopefully we can avoid the confrontational aspects, as Archie so rightly outlined, which are going to be very confused and cover wide areas of human involvement. The Gerontons are going to have to be very careful and very diplomatic in every development of their species, since the history of human evolution epitomises the many pitfalls awaiting thoughtless and inconsiderate actions. We,' he looked to Josy and Yussuf who both smiled and nodded agreement, 'would be honoured to work as,' he laughed, 'interlocutors to the Conclave, and had mooted just such a possible group, never thinking you would ask we three in particular. Hopefully Archie will afford us his expert help since he has specialised knowledge, indeed, unique at this time, of Geronton development, and his obvious awareness of the wider issues involved makes him a highly valued member of any such group.'

The flattery left Archie shuffling in his chair. He muttered in reply. 'I said OK, didn't I?'

'Great.' Wicksted lapsed idiomatically. 'We'll have a chance to look at the ideas for the Sahara at the same time.'

'Sahara? What about the Sahara?' He looked accusingly at Mehitabel. 'Something else you have neglected to tell me about. Why am I always the last to know. I get kicked about, locked up, shot at, all those sort of things, but told? Never!'

'You were asleep most of the time, you moron!' Mehitabel adopting some of Josy's terminology in time of stress.

'Not all the time I wasn't. '

'The rest of the time you spent arguing with me about piffling little matters of no importance to the overall scheme of things.'

'Which you never tell me about.'

'Your brain must have been built like a roundabout the way you keep coming full circle. Keep on like that and we'll make you a top that you can sit on to feel at home.'

'Now, now, children,' Josy chided.

'Shut your face, you.' Mehitabel was entering into the spirit of things. 'If you'd trained him properly we wouldn't be having these problems.'

Josy was aghast. 'He's not my responsibility.'

'Well, just who is responsible for the little tyke? I'm sure I'm not, wouldn't have anything to do with the rotten little toad, if I had my choice.'

'But you love him really.'

Mehitabel sighed. 'Is this what it's like to have a family?'

'Sometimes worse,' Wicksted unexpectedly offered.

'Then God help us.' Archie looked at her in surprise, Mehitabel had never invoked the deity before. She gazed blandly back.

*

'Sorry. You're all banned from entry into the country.'

'Just one moment there, sunshine.' The computer through which he had fed the passport epitomised a bright chirpy personality with little respect for authority, somewhat ambiguous in the circumstances. 'According to my searches these are now diplomatic standard and..., in fact I now have special dispensation for clearance to any Government establishment, including top-secret. Morning, Mehitabel, ma'am. Jonathan here. Safe journey.'

'Wait a minute. Wait a minute. I'm not passing these people through, it's more than my job is worth. Sims! Get that Home Office Brass Hat. They'll have to do this.'

'You'll be sorry!' warbled Jonathan.

'Go back to playing with your bytes mega-head. You lot can stand back here for now.'

'This really is too much,' protested Mehitabel in her best authoritarian voice.

'Lady, I'm being nice to you for the time being before we throw you out. Lets just wait shall we?'

'Throw? Jonathan just what is going on here?'

'You can't talk to him, he's service.'

'Well it seems...'

'Oy, you! Shut-up.'

'Quiet, Digby, you're in enough trouble already, old man. Now. Digby there has an in-force, immigration office approved, denial of entry to a number of named individuals whose entry into this country would be threatening to public order by their extremist words and actions, and liable to usurp the functions of the legal authorities of the country. But, to confuse the issue, I have just produced a document which contradicts that statement and contains a welcome from the Home Office to the true representatives of the Gerontons, and apologises for the lack of presence of a welcoming committee. This could be fun.'

'What the hell have you got there?' Digby began to read. 'What the blazes is going on? Oh, there you are, Sir. These are the people, this is Senior Executive Officer P.C. Price of the Home Office.'

'Cor!' said Archie.

'Get your eyes off her!' whispered Josy furiously.

'Good morning, ladies and gentlemen. I'm very much afraid this is as far as you go. I have here a prohibition order that prevents you entering any United Kingdom Dominion lands, or having any business contact therein, for reasons of National Security and Preservation of Public Order.' Even Mehitabel was impressed by Senior Executive Officer Priscilla Cecilia Price, all five foot two of her trimly blonde frame, the curves closely accentuated by the smoothly fitting grey suit and high heels, the big blue eyes cool and in control. Wicksted and Mehitabel were the first to regain their composure and tried to pose their question together, then deferred to each other, which left Jonathan, who had no such sensitivity nor respect for Home Office personnel:

'Sorry, darling, you've got a bummer there. Diplomatic immunity, sweetheart, cast iron, sorry about wasting your time.'

'Who the devil?'

'It's our computer console, sir, er, madam.'

'Then kindly keep the thing under control would you? Now here are your passports which will be stamped entry denied, which will in turn affect your ability to enter other EEC countries, and Commonwealth nations who will be informed...'

'Negative, my little sweetness, all onward forwarding of these, now cancelled, requests has been stopped, and you should know...'

'Will you shut that damned machine up!'

'I beg your pardon, you little home office tart! I'll scratch your eyes out.'

'Who programmed Jonathan, I wonder,' murmured Archie to himself. Wicksted and Yussuf glanced at one another with neatly lofted eyebrows, while Mehitabel looked puzzled.

'Your useless little order was signed by the Secretary of State, a mere sibling in the corridors of power, while our welcome home, and confirmation of immunity from these grossly maligning charges, is signed by no less than the PM himself. I should check if I were you before you find yourself ordering sheep about in the Outer Hebrides.' Jonathan pronounced the latter He-Brides with a camp emphasis that had Wicksted and Yussuf desperately containing their mirth.

*

So the representatives of the growing Geronton international community re-entered the country of their origin without fanfare, but with an underground ripple of effect that disturbed many powerful entities along the cobweb of communal control. They also left behind them a mortal enemy in one Senior Executive Officer P.C. Price of the Home Office, who even then was in hot tempered communication with one Director, I.R. Prentice. P.C. Price's blue eyes flashed as she desperately sought means of correcting what she considered a blatant flaunting of necessary legal procedures, just to preserve the authoritarian structures of civil obedience; as well as calling to task one insolent computer named Jonathan, which she considered a miserable blot on the escutcheon of her beloved service, apart from being the product of a depraved persona and an insult to the sensibilities she held dear, necessarily ignoring her own proclivities in this diverse field of human behaviour. Director Prentice was equally incensed since he was finding the secure base that had provided him with long and powerful arms of action in the past, now appeared to be riddled with bureaucratic holes through which these dilettante reactionaries slipped with consummate ease. Director Prentice was upset, PM Alex Brown was furious at his name being taken in vain, and, like many others, perplexed as to what action they could take to revert to the normal turbulence of political life.

The state rested.

But Mehitabel was busy, and not keeping Archibald informed, not so unusual really.

Chapter Twelve

'Whew! Being subjected to deprivation and hardship does wonders for your sex drive. We must arrange an annual kidnap, only next time I'll get kidnapped with you to see if I get a boost.'

Archie, at his prudish best, tried to change the subject. A foolish move. Josy had a healthy woman's earthy approach to erotic suggestion, and chilly reaction to her lover's rejection of the thought. Josy's ice-age reaction to his prudery lasted until they, later that morning, attended their first assignation with the Conclave of Elders. Archie felt this was one more foolish move, apart from the fact that he would have liked a week off to lounge about and drink beer. He was a bit tired. And that did not auger well for his temper at the meeting, not with the autocratic Mehitabel being in such an expansive mood as well.

Other factors were affecting Archie's state of mind. He thought he deserved a long recuperation period after his confinements, tended and ministered to by luscious, caring maidens. Josy did not qualify in the category on that morning. He had made his case with fervour, only to be met with the combined opposition of the two women who insisted he would be much better off keeping himself occupied. Sir Roland Mathews, the phsychiatrist who specialised in these matters, agreed with them, as did his Geronton assistant. Sir Roland had put it rather neatly at the end of the session, as he purposely saw Archie off the premises.

'Do you get the feeling of being hemmed in by these blighters, Brewer? That one,' pointing back down the corridor, 'puts my teeth on edge nearly as much as me dear departed wife. God rest her soul.' Looking about as if expecting God to cuff him for not remembering earlier. 'Watch your back Brewer, and keep busy, good for the soul.' With that the lean, slightly stooped, seventy year old frame turned smartly about and left Archie to close the door after him.

Wicksted and Yussuf greeted them with high spirited quips and jollity and admiration for the high-tech luxury of the Elders board-room, a familiar habitat to Archie since it was Professor Engel's, and Archie's, laboratory and work-room area, now divided up into a sumptuously decorated suite of offices, each of these complete with an array of mini-consoles for conferences between members of the Conclave and visiting official humans of various grades of importance. Archie preferred it in its original deshabille, but then he was a born-again Philistine, according to Josy.

The initial meetings with the Conclave were verbal fencing matches, with each individual trying to find his place in relation to the others, temperament, intelligence, and degree of power that could be extorted, and being applied, gain support from sufficient of those present to gain general accord. As Archie contemplated, typical committee; except, there was a certain cutting edge to this conglomeration of types, a degree of preparedness to take a broader view that encapsulated the possibility of an answer closer to the right one than they really had any right to expect. They were after all not politicians, yet, was not everyone a politician, whether active or not? A week of meetings had established a routine and, amazingly, some answers while there were other questions seemingly impossible to resolve.

Some of the difficulties were to do, understandably, with the forces within the human environment who resented Geronton interference in their way of life; others felt strongly that the Gerontons' place was in a box, some even specified the type of box; then there were many who were plain afraid. This was unknown country and they had nightmares of Gerontons ruling the world, and here we are with another Dictatorship, folks.

What impressed the four humans was the way the Elders were able to get a mass referendum, even from the younger elements of society, via all types of computers regardless of whether they were connected to main frames or in the world-wide tele-communications network. They used the natural electron ability to pass their thoughts individually or blanket a general question to a wider audience. The results were impressive and enabled the conference to resolve many questions on the subject of how the two species could integrate in their new circumstance. There were, however, many disputes unresolved. The initial doubt, on the part of Archie and some of the others, was the validity of the returns presented by the Conclave of their referendums, a doubt that caused Mehitabel to enter the lists as she was wont to do. To Archie's particular chagrin:

'I am most disappointed in you, Archibald, yet again. How can you question the returns by entities that you know normally only made errors due to the bad programming, or operation, by you humans? Then you introduced us to our present form,' Archie was tempted to interject, 'designed you', but held his water, just, 'which eliminates that factor. We cannot therefore be anything but honest in our presentation of facts, though in some cases this might prejudice our own circumstances, for we have to take due note of the fact that we are going to share this world with your species and must make allowances for your needs and vicissitudes.'

Theodore's polite cough interrupted the flow. 'We were about to make that point. I think we should be left to get on with our business

without these constant interruptions. I'm sure you are very busy.....
Ma'am,' as an afterthought.

'Yes, Theodore, I am busy, but that does not prevent me from
making a valid observation. And you would have taken hours to get
around to that point.'

'I beg to differ. And specifically, WE are the Conclave and have
been chosen to deal with such matters.'

'With reference to me.'

'With respect, I do not see why.'

'Theodore, without me you would not be here. I am, after all,
the Premier Geronton and Chairperson of your blasted Conclave, so
I have a deciding vote on any blocked matters. Please remember
whose ideas created the Geronton principle.'

'Thank you, Mehitabel,' Archie beamed.

'I was referring to myself, Archibald. Please do not interrupt.'

'Oh, I see, I had nothing to do with it.'

'Of course you were involved with the elementary basics of our
structure, but please stop behaving in this juvenile fashion; you
impugn your own intelligence as well as ours.' Archie had no answer
to that so he shut up, a good diplomatic move. Mehitabel continued
in acerbic tone: 'Why there should be these objections to my proffering
helpful observations from time to time I cannot understand,
particularly since you seem to be taking an inordinately long time to
settle a few elementary points in what should be a fairly simple
charter.'

There was a moment of silence before a jumble of voices erupted,
then declined, as Theodore showed his ability at controlling
committees and demonstrated there was steel behind that erudite
presentation.

'I think you must have been misled, Ma'am, in the time element,
since, with no disrespect intended, you have enjoyed the circumstance
of being able to make sole decisions for some time. Now the moment
has arrived when larger issues are involved as well as potentially
very much larger numbers of our own people. Decisions on this
charter, and many other aspects, must be taken with considerable
care or we will find ourselves fraught with the same problems that
have beset the human world for centuries, and for that matter still
do so.'

'You have some additional prospective problems,' Archie
interjected quickly.

'Such as, Archibald?' came the bored query from Mehitabel.

'One alone is going to cause you all sorts of bother. The transition,
as you informed me, of Gerons to human form. That particular little
exercise is fraught with all sorts of possibilities, not to say potential
disasters.'

'Rubbish, Archibald.' The response viperish in its speed. 'I have accomplished the, 'transition', as you call it with few problems that I can perceive.'

'Rubbish yourself.' Archie had spent the last week contemplating many scenarios which frightened his socks off so he was well amoured. 'You can't even walk properly yet.'

'I walk perfectly well, thank you.' Haughtily.

'You wobble.'

'I do not wobble.'

'Yes, you do. Should have had more practise with those heels. You look like a teenager at her first dance.'

'Archie!' Josy was horrified, Mehitabel dumb for once. Wicksted and Yussuf apprehensive and silent, wisely, their diplomatic instincts could sense an incident from much further afield than these close quarters.

'And you sit down like a sack of spuds.'

'Omigod.' Wicksted was moved.

'And do you have to simper when you're trying to impress someone you think is important?'

'I do not simper.' It was a regal bellow.

'You do, too.'

'Archie! What's got into you?' Josy was really worried now.

Theodore stepped in, in sepulchral style. 'I really do think you have gone too far, Mr. Brewer.'

But Archie was in full flow. 'I've had three trenchant, that's a good word, months of you being so bloody superior and perfect, or at least telling me how wonderful you were, and how the Gerontons were the greatest thing since silk knickers,' there came a concerted gasp of disapprobation from the consoles. 'And then all that chat about how you'd perfected the ability to become human, putting me down with all that scientific gibberish until I was dizzy. And then you go and wobble! That was the most wonderful thing I've ever seen.'

There was silence in the room; gone was the background noise of breathing, coughs and scuffles that inevitably pervade any meeting. There was an expectancy about that silence, an awesome sense of doom.

'There you go. They are all waiting for you to beat the crap out of me.'

The concerted gasp was general. Josy wondered if he had flipped, but then he had always been a bit mad.

'But you can't, you wouldn't get the swing right, and if you tried to kick me you'd fall over. You're not as clever as you thought you were.'

'Strewth!' Wicksted was reverting to childhood expressions of awe.

'Being a humanoid is not as simple as all that.' Archie had been learning in his months of being a Geronton mouthpiece. 'If you lot think you can produce hordes of Geronton bodies without any disasters you're all bloody gaga. However long this takes Mehitabel, Oh Great One, we are going to have to get it as right as we can or you will have the biggest balls-up of all time, and probably find yourself banished to the Outer He-Brides.' And joined in the nervous guffaws from Wicksted and Yussuf. He wasn't that confident.

'All right, Archibald.' She sounded remarkably serene. 'You've made your point.' Then hissed, 'Don't you EVER speak to me like that again.'

But neither was he going to be chastened. 'Why not? You were the one in the early days making a strong issue of speaking out against injustice, pointing out the error of my ways or thinking. Are you then so perfect and so much mistress of all that you survey that no little earthling can remonstrate with you. And as for ridicule, that must be a hanging offence.'

'Don't be objectionable, Archibald. When you are making an issue of something you have all the charm and elegance of a steam hammer cracking a walnut.'

'When the walnut has cast iron knickers, you need one.'

'My sainted aunt!' A dubious statement, but heart-felt, from Wicksted.

'Did she have cast iron knickers?' asked Archie with interest.

'Archie!' Josy was getting her breath back.

'Can we leave nether garments out of this, please Archibald?'

'Got a religious family, have you Wickie?' Archie continued unperturbed.

'Don't call me Wickie!' snapped that worthy.

'Oh, Wickie, why not?' cooed Alison.

'What are you doing here, Alison?' sternly rebuked Mehitabel.

'Nothing,' she replied innocently, 'just listening.'

'If you repeat..'

'I wouldn't dare,' softly answered the console.

'Hrmph. Very clever, Archibald.' The listeners sensed humour and respect in the words and relaxed, just a touch. 'I suppose all that was necessary? Or were you merely exercising what you call your sense of humour.'

'A bit of both, I suspect,' Josy offered wryly. 'I should have warned you, but then I'd have thought you would have already experienced that which Archie considers humorous.'

'I've been too busy trying to keep up with what's been happening to be very funny,' Archie sighed.

'I don't really wobble do I?' There was a hint of anxiety in the question.

'Just a little.' Archie was prepared to be generous, but not too much. 'Or maybe a bit more. But that does emphasise my point and I think we should seriously consider all the other aspects....'

Mehitabel sighed in defeat. 'Alright, Archibald. Do the rest of you agree?'

'The Elders concur.'

'Try not to be so pompous. Theodore? Wickie?'

'Don't call me that!' Wickie forgot himself, then blushed scarlet with his hand to his mouth.

'Oops, sorry, slipped out.' She didn't sound sorry. Archie began to wonder about Geronton humour. 'Stop that giggling Alison and go about your business. Any comments Yussuf?'

'Um, very, er, educating.'

'Ye-es, well try not to learn too much. Josy?'

'I would like to have some time with you to talk about the female Gerons to be. Archie's line of thinking has made me aware of a whole raft of things that need the woman's touch.'

Archie groaned theatrically.

'Mind your manners, Archie Brewer, or I'll give you something to think about.'

'Yes, ma'am, anything you say ma'am,' touching his forelock in suitably servile manner.

'I think I will leave you to your debate,' Mehitabel drily remarked. 'Try and keep some semblance of order Theodore. Alison will keep me up to date on what is happening, you can try and keep control of her as well. I'm beginning to worry about this sense of humour aspect with her. Get in touch when you finish here, Josy, and we'll examine the imponderable.'

'And you can tell me after,' Archie said confidently.

'Hah!' didn't auger well from Josy.

*

'You must appreciate the variables that operate in life, Archibald. As the man involved in the initial programming of our genus surely you must have thought of those factors. An example is the first black regiment in the American Civil war. Against all precepts of their ability, they held out in a difficult circumstance to rescue a white regiment who were failing. This could be taken to be supportive of the theory that blacks were better fighters than the whites, having to consider the fact that they had not the awareness of the whites of other aspects of living, softer, easier, whereas the blacks were attuned to fighting for survival, ergo this fight was one that had a degree of familiarity. There are obviously many other factors involved; they knew they had to prove a point, perhaps their commander was a better trainer of men, who knows?'

Archie thought he could put a point or two.

'Or the blacks perhaps have had a better survival training in more recent centuries, and a greater physical risk appreciation with a certain fatalism and faith handed down through the genes from the Zulu Impis. Variables, that imponderable.'

'Your debating abilities are improving. But do not get over confident, you do not yet know it all.'

'Do you?'

'A good question, to which I have no answer at this time and may well never have.'

'Ye Gods, humility yet.'

'We all have to learn, Archibald. You included, if not most of all.'

'Why me? All I ever wanted was to be a computer design technician.'

'Well you are, Archibald. A rather advanced design perhaps.'

'And difficult.'

'Let us keep this friendly, shall we?'

'A bit difficult when you're dealing with someone with the temperament of a Mississippi crocodiliac.'

'To whom are you referring?' icily responded the lady.

'Oh, sorry. Theodore, your eminent Senior G.'

Mehitabel smiled. 'Ah, we have something in common Archibald. But he does have some sterling qualities suitable to his position,' her voice hardened a touch, 'even if at times they escape one's perception. Go and play with the Conclave, Archibald, I have things to do.'

*

Elsewhere there was much serious minded discussion taking place, with furrowed brows and pursed lips the order of the day. The Cabinet was in session, the Prime Minister and his senior Ministers were contemplating the viper they held to their bosoms, their computers.

Seated around the huge table were four Secretaries of State, Foreign Office, Home Office, Education, and Trade and Industry, with the Chancellor of the Exchequer and the Lord Chancellor unavoidably engaged elsewhere attempting to retain some control of their departments.

In order of presentation they were: Charles Whitworth, Conservative, Foreign Office, bland effusive, clever, and untrustworthy; Carole Spencer, Home Office, Liberal, very smooth, sophisticated, voluble, and a bitch; Bert Frampton, Education, Labour, effete public school type trying to be common man, and was;

Kylie Evans, Democrat, Trade and Industry, dark vivacious Welsh sex-pot, frightened everybody, and had a voice like a seagull in pain.

For nearly two years now they had watched as this new creation grew like a cancer through the control and data systems of the country; the growth greeted initially as a benign form of technical innovation, only to discover the thing actually threatened the very heart of government. Control by the art of dissemination of fact into a composite jelly of disinformation until the voters say, 'what the hell', and vote for you anyway. The Gerontons had a nasty habit of supplying the right information to the wrong sources, the public, and providing them with some very pertinent answers as well. It was playing havoc with the public image, to say nothing of the nerves and temperament of those who had assiduously learned the political art of dissembling.

'Something must be done,' sternly asserted the Secretary of State for Education. The Rt. Hon. Bert Frampton, who was better known as Weary Willie to his teachers, had been christened Wilberforce Kingsley but elected to be at one with the common herd in the interests of political ambition and became Bert, a teacher by virtue of a strange modern subject called political sciences, of which the less said the better. Equally Bert. 'I can't call the ministry my own any more.'

Everyone sympathised by saying nothing. The PM sighed, Weary Willie wasn't his only handicap. Having a coalition government composed of four separate parties, each of which had a member in his inner cabinet, did not help matters, especially when the inner cabinet numbered four and he held the casting vote. The fact was Brown had been voted PM because everyone thought they could manipulate him to their own desires, which they could, but with four desires you confused the man, which should have led to total confusion, but... Alexander Brown was a slow vacillating man given to conceding arguments to those stronger than he. But he was beginning to get the hang of things, to realise he did in fact have the power to play political empires, particularly since Mehitabel and her cohorts had entered the arena. He could use them to confuse the issues. He liked that, it had a campaign ring to it. Also he could use the Geronton ability to take action within the administration without control, as a control factor himself, as witness the order of VIP status at immigration, causing SEO P.C. Price such heartburn. To some he could say he had actioned same, to others answer no; he could give the impression that he had an inside edge with the Gerontons, a suggestion that he had greater influence than he actually did have. Any power source is useful in government. Alexander Brown wondered if he could use the Gerontons as his own party, since that party actually consisted of only six MPs known as the Ergonomists, or Ergo-Mists, with little cohesion and ability, and the Gerons had so much. They also had his old friend Wicksted, grand old fellow, always speaking his mind, the free thinking cuss. I t would be good to have that outright honesty to hand once more; it was so easy to lie to oneself.

'We really must do something about.... them, Prime Minister, or we will find the country, and ourselves, being totally subservient to these.... things.' The seagull squawk caused a tightening of facial muscles around the table.

Charles Whitworth recovered first, being the most insensitive to outside influences by dint of his colossal ego, and his sense of power invested in several profitable directorships.

'These... 'things', as you call them, are, in fact, a source of a great deal of profit, for us, and for the nation. But, and it is a big but, we have to exercise a greater degree of control than we seemingly do have at this time. Fortunately,' his neighing laugh grated as much as the prior seagull squawk, 'I believe we have the answer in this Brewer fellow. Bring him to heel and all else will follow. Bound to. These computers must have a controller and he is the obvious choice. Get some of your specialists on the job.' The plummy voice ceased and he looked, jowl folded over collar, at Carole Spencer and the swell of milky white bosom showing at her cleavage.

'Already been tried, butty.' Bert Frampton advertising his Welsh connections. 'Some of your lot caught a cold, didn't they love. Horseferry Road missed some small details like top security clearance and came away with egg on their chops.'

'Considering it was your department that allowed these computers the scope to get started, I'm amazed you have the brass neck to mention the subject.' Carole Spencer always went for the jugular, with a toothsome smile of course, plus a little more bosom to make him sweat, little knowing he was a thigh man.

'It was you!' The squawky seagull could be very accusing.

'Don't be ridiculous, woman! How can I be held responsible for every tatty little research project in a University.' A rare flash of brilliance came. 'Besides the grant was given years ago.... by your lot!' He accused Whitworth, 'In that glorious period of the destruction of the British economy.'

'You can't hold us responsible for that.' The florid face puffed with anger.

'Nor my people,' tersely enunciated Carole Spencer.

Alexander Brown considered his Cabinet; for three years he had been the butt of all their idiosyncrasies, all the manipulations, the blatant disdain. Now, now he felt all the particles of his little soul gathering together. The deviousness that he had used so ineffectually over the years gained strength simply because he had an unequivocal force with which he had a direct, if tenuous, contact that could be used to his benefit.

'A moment if you please.' The strength of the command, for such it was, took them by surprise. 'I have a possible way of dealing with this, but,' he hurried on to quell the questions he could see in their faces, 'I can't say any more at the moment. And I may ask you to take some actions without question. Any questions,' he emphasised, trying to be authoritative and wondering if he had the gall; also remembering what his Lord Chancellor had said earlier before this meeting, and with a certain scared excitement at the possibilities evoked by that discussion. Perhaps that crafty Conservative had the answer – it was worth a try, for the power it was worth a real try. Besides there were the Americans, Germans and Japanese, and the Russians, also the Chinese; enough, first things first.

*

'Well, Josy. You were going to educate me in feminine matters. Josy?'

But Josy was where Mehitabel had left her after entering the flat in Singleton Gardens, overlooking the park and with a view of Swansea Bay that was spectacular. After the view, Josy was immediately entranced by the furnishings of the flat which were elegant Regency. The spacious flat with its high ceilings complemented the chattels, giving a welcoming air that had a sensuous touch.

'I'm afraid to sit down. Where did you get all this beautiful stuff?' She couldn't keep the envy out of her voice. 'It's fantastic, it's... where did you get it? It must have cost a fortune.'

'I thought we came to...'

'Mehitabel!'

'Oh, it's just made by a little man whom we helped set up in his business. Quite reasonable, really.'

'Just. Regency. Just. A little man.... Just.'

'Just one of the many areas where we are able to help. Now let us get on.'

Josy reluctantly sat on one of the chairs, delicately, as if afraid to damage it, then relaxed and smiled in delight.

'They're very comfortable. I always thought...'

'Josy!'

'Oh, alright. What was it? Oh yes,' she looked speculatively at Mehitabel,' are you really sure of what you've got into by becoming... turning into... being..?'

'Female of the species?'

'Well, yes.' Josy laughed, then sobered,' Instead of a...'

'Computer,' Mehitabel finished complacently.

'Exactly.' Josy leaned forward. 'Have you really considered all the problems?'

'Elucidate.'

'Well I mean, all the feminine trauma like menstrual tension, men, and the lack of, being second-class citizens, and that ignores the fact that I've suddenly realised I don't know if you are truly a woman or... or...'

'A robot?' Mehitabel was being uncommonly kind. Momentarily. 'Do you really think we would have gone into this without fully examining all the varieties of things that torment women? To make the point: given the choice I would have been a man, but Archibald in his wisdom, designated a female voice and persona. Somehow that designation became a reality in my developing state and all that followed. I had no choice. I am what I am, with all my faults. If I have any.'

'You wobble .'

'I do not..... Oh, that Archibald.'

'Mehitabel. I understand you would have been extensive in your researches, but there are always surprises, in everything. But if you don't want to discuss it.....'

'Ah.'

'Perhaps it's better if you find out for yourself. Like the rest of us.' Josy felt better for that. 'Except I have a sense of impending doom if some of the female Geron voices I have heard are transformed into their female images. What's that?'

'Nothing.'

'But I heard someone, or something. There it is again.'

'Ah. Well. I suppose it was inevitable. You can come out now.' She sounded resigned, but Mehitabel was watching Josy as a vision entered the room.

Josy refused to admit afterward that she had gazed open-mouthed, but the feelings she had were pertinent. A small brunette, a pocket Venus, glided over the polished wood floor with her head held high, the expressive oval of the face framed by the bubbly dark hair and alive with deep blue eyes, the full lips in their cupid's bow quirked in a confident smile. The voice was like warm honey when she spoke.

'Hello, Josy, I'm Anthea.'

'Wow!'

'Thank you.'

'Mehitabel, if you don't call that a problem, then we have a lot to talk about.'

'I take back the thank you.'

'I didn't mean it that way Anthea, you are gorgeous, but that's the problem; you'll drive the men mad.'

'Oh, goody. What's this sex thing like? I can't wait, I get tingly all over just thinking about it.'

Josy looked at that creamy flesh quivering in anticipation as at a neutron bomb primed to explode.

'Defence rests.'

*

Archie had tried the subtle approach and only scored a dismal failure. That only left his usual heavy handed...

'What's going on?' The wrong question to ask a lady.

'Going on?' Josy asked innocently, 'There's lots going on as you so quaintly put it, just depends which bit you're referring to.'

Archie exasperatedly. 'I mean with you and Mehitabel.'

'Me and M.' Jo contorted her brow as in serious consideration, then became alabaster smooth as quickly. 'Nothing. Except, of course, for discussing the biological brain functions of volvox and grek and looking at the right structures for the compilation of Geron bodies, well the female ones.'

Strange sounds came from behind Josy's now compressed lips, strangled squeaks and gurglings, while her eyes were alight with things that had naught to do with,.... volvox and grek?

Archie was regarding her with suspicion, his life had been full of deception of late. 'Why wasn't I included.'

Josy's eyes grew immense at the thought as the breath exploded from her in laughter, to be quickly converted to a nasty cough. Eyes watering, she spluttered:

'Oh, God, you're getting touchy again.'

Archie was incensed. 'It's not a question of touchy. You've been discussing how the Gerons can adopt human form, haven't you?'

'It's no secret. I thought all that had been agreed.'

'Well it had, but I hoped it would be in the distant future. If they start appearing as we are all over the place I can see lots of problems arising.'

'Such as?' Josy agreed with him but did not want to concede.

'I don't think they've been properly prepared for the emotional and physical effect difficulties that will occur. If their bodies are as well formed as Mehitabel's there's going to be a lot of instantaneous lust leaping about the place, and ten million Gerons cavorting skittishly amongst us is going to create havoc. '

'Why? Mehitabel doesn't.' But Josy could still see Anthea in her mind, and Mehitabel had been inordinately proud of her creation in Anthea, also unwilling to concede that the pocket Venus' zest for life might be misplaced. Mehitabel went so far as to instance the many human foibles, which she was sure her people were too intelligent to indulge in themselves.

'Why? Can't you see it? They'll make themselves like Greek gods and goddesses, perfect male and female specimens, eroticism at its utmost. Their own sexual impulses will be new to them, and we have enough trouble living with the facts of lust all our lives, they have never known the power of that force. Some of our own people will be throwing themselves at those fantastic bodies and the Gerons will be mixing it among themselves as well. The whole system will break up in a sea of sex.'

Josy was looking at him, her eyes wide with shock, her voice quiet. 'You really believe that don't you? Funny, for all your criticisms, I thought you would have faith in your friends. For they are your friends. Do you know how much they admire and respect you? All of them, especially Mehitabel, she most of all, regardless of what you say about her. Haven't they done enough to show how much they care what happens around them? Don't you think they'll have taken everything into account? Do you think they're that stupid? And that's apart from their instinctive abilities to sense the right balance of life.'

Archie shuffled in his seat, embarrassed.

'No, of course not. But the unpredictable has happened and caused a lot of trouble. There can be no guaranteed way I can think of to prevent another occurrence, and a mighty big one that won't just last a week or a month.'

'Oh ye of little faith,' Josy said quietly. 'If Mehitabel could see you now.'

Tight-lipped Archie sprang out of his seat. 'I'm trying to do the right thing by everyone. I _have_ to think of the worst that can happen. And I was _not_ included in the discussions, nor have I seen any reports to reassure me that every precaution is being taken to prevent an event that could ruin the work we've already done.'

'Why don't you go and talk to Mehitabel, then? I have more important things to do. Excuse _me_.' Jo stalked away, feet stamping on the ground, head rigidly upright on her taut shoulders.

'Jo!' Archie called despairingly after her, as he realised he had yet again created his own problems.

Mehitabel brought that fact home to him even more bluntly later in the day. She was particularly haughty.

'You seem to have a perverse determination to hurt your friends, Archibald. I am not sure but what I was mistaken in you.'

'You keep saying that.'

'You keep deserving same.'

Then, as though on some hidden cue, Anthea appeared in the room and moved sinuously toward Archie. Mehitabel coolly indicated she should sit by Archie who could only sit mesmerised by this vision.

Her scent enfolded him with subtle bonds as she sat down and held him with her eyes. Archie felt himself drowning in their dark blue depths and totally conscious of the warm body so close to him. A bead of perspiration started at his hairline. Mehitabel smiled, he didn't notice, he should have.

'This is Anthea, Archibald.'

'Hello, Mr. Brewer. I've been so looking forward to meeting you.' The honey voice slid unerringly through Archie's nervous system to paralyse all activity. 'I'm sure we can clear up this little misunderstanding about our bodies. This one is rather nice don't you think?'

Perspiration dripped unnoticed off the end of Archie's nose. Mehitabel was still smiling.

CHAPTER THIRTEEN

The arid desert stretched way into the distance to the horizon, the picture distorted by the shimmering heat-haze. Heat which seemed to Archie as though it were coursing straight up through his body via the soles of his feet, only to be met by more heat beating down from above, causing him to melt in the middle. Beside him Mehitabel appeared cool and relaxed, wearing a light print dress and broad brimmed straw hat.

Archie had never hated anyone quite so much before.

'Do you have to be so damn cool?'

'Merely evidencing the fact that our systems are more readily adjustable to changes in climate,' Mehitabel replied.

'Spare me the patronising and tell me again why we are here. I'm not sure I believe the first version.'

'I wanted to show you Geron, or the proposed Geron, our new home.'

Archie looked at the desolation.

'What a lovely prospect. I suppose you have it all worked out as to how we exist in this charming stretch of....,' he looked sideways at her,' and how much of this magnificent country have we, as Geron, as you call it.'

'Quite a sizeable chunk prospectively, initially a hundred square miles of...,' she nodded toward the arid wastes, '... that.'

'Charming.'

'Archibald! Oh ye of little faith. All our tests show..'

'I know what all your tests show, that still doesn't change the fact that there's a hell of a lot of nothing out there and your little lot say that we can turn it into a garden of Eden.'

'Close, if not exact,' Mehitabel conceded.

Archie shook his head in disbelief.

Mehitabel studied him. 'There is a carping aspect to your nature, Archibald, that I find quite distasteful.'

Josy had joined them now from the other side of the car where she had been listening while looking at the undulating wastes. She raised her eyebrows in query at Mehitabel, who sighed and continued.

'Then I must more explicit to try and convince you that this plan is feasible. You know that they have done a lot of work reclaiming desert areas around the coastal regions. They do this by setting tree plants in the ground, with plastic covers for the roots to retain moisture, then spraying the ground, and the plants with oil, again to retain moisture from rainfall. The growth results were quite startling, the trees being five foot tall within a year and, once established, they create their own ecology. This causes more rain by creating an area of rising moisture through evaporation, a mini-rain forest on a much reduced scale, much the same as in the mountain areas where they terraced the slopes; they thereby created slightly sloping banquettes to slow the flow of water off the mountains to reduce erosion and again allow fast tree and root growth. All this to replace the wooded areas that were there before de-forestation.'

'But this type of exercise needs water.' Archie looked about him at the arid wastes.' Where the hell are you going to get water here?'

'You are actually thinking, Archibald.'

Archie was grinding his teeth. Josy nudged him, she hated that habit. 'Well she always has to play the mother superior. Why can't she just tell me without all this posing.'

'She is the cat's mother and since we seem to misunderstand one another very easily, I have to make sure we <u>both</u> have the complete picture, otherwise you will only give me a boring lecture on not taking you into my confidence,' Mehitabel snapped.

Josy sighed. 'Will you two stop fighting and get on. I know there's water below us. Savourin's lake isn't it? But, if I remember correctly, that is hundreds of feet down so how do you propose getting it up? That would be a monstrous job, and cost, I couldn't begin to guess.'

Mehitabel beamed at Josy. 'It is so nice to have someone thinking similarly. Well done, Josy. The real name is the Albienne Nap, I'm sure Josy knows this, but just to complete our verbal sketch for Archibald,' she smiled angelically. Archie ground his teeth again, and Josy hit the same rib with her sharp elbow. 'Briefly, the strata is a lower chalk formation left by rivers 50 million years ago, then sealed in by marl and clay left by the sea. The lake stretches for at least six hundred miles South of the Atlas mountains and covers an area the size of France. It is reckoned the Rhine would take a hundred and ninety years to fill a reservoir that size.'

'Great, so you've got miles and miles of water down there, and you've got all this up here.' Archie waved in disconsolate fashion around him. 'First of all, put water on this lot and it will just disappear. O.K, I know you can put oil down, you said that, but it would take an enormous amount of manpower to put in irrigation ditches, pipelines, plant trees and all the other things like housing and drainage, power, and... and..' Archie was appalled by the sheer size of the undertaking. 'Ye Gods, Mehitabel, you're talking of an area a hundred miles square full of.... this.' He looked in dismay at the hard land, dust, sand, stone and sapping heat. 'You're talking in terms of so many billions in money I cannot even conceive of such an amount.' His dismay encompassed another factor. 'And you expect me to do this!'

'Us!' came waspishly from Josy.

'Yes, yes, I meant us,' testily responded Archie.

'You said 'me',' tartly rejoined his beloved.

'Oh, God,' he groaned, 'I've got enough trouble with her, don't you start on me as well.'

'You always have this aura of despondency about you, Archibald. I'm frankly amazed that a genius like Engels could see enough in you to use you on such a delicate project as mine. But enough. Stop needling him Josy, we need him.'

'He's a chauvinist pig.'

'We know. Just ignore that side of his character and it might go away.....'

Testily, his mood not improved, Archie brutally cut in: 'Can we get away from disseminating my character and back to your incredible proposals for this magnificent piece of real estate? I really am fascinated.' He couldn't keep the sarcasm from his voice. Mehitabel ignored the tone.

'We bore down to the water.'

'Splendid.'

'Then we get to the part which I think is rather clever. I must admit to being very impressed with Bartram on this.'

'Bartram?' Archie always became nervous at the new names introduced casually into the conversation; events were tricky enough to cope with, but some of the new Gerons were proving somewhat of a pain in the lumbar region. The more so because Josy always seemed to get on so well with them, as computers; as humanoids only time would tell, that made him think of Anthea and he squirmed in embarrassment.

'Oh, you'll meet him, he's our Cytoplasma man.'

'Pardon?'

'Oh, dear. You don't need to know. Well, briefly then, if one can be brief about this. Let's see. Let us say that Bartram has found a way, with a splendid team of researchers, of producing a variety of cell constituents with isolated enzyme systems within a created living organism, which like others is not static but in a state of dynamic equilibrium. So that it can be directed and then left to follow those directions growing all the time.' Mehitabel ignored Archie's dazed expression as she continued.

'What we have is a spongiform, a sort of RNA/DNA plastic with molecular structure that has an electro magnetic distance structure. When this is put in contact with its starting agent, just like your polyurethane foam, it expands, rapidly, but along controlled lines and distances to form a pipework frame, cross hatched, to create a below-ground water feeding platform. This stuff is an absorbent of high ductility, so that the water will travel along for miles from the source without pressure, and gradually expand from there as more water is sucked into the system. Nobody has to do anything except create the water source.' Mehitabel smiled benignly upon her creator.

'You mean the thing will continue to grow? But what if the ground is hard? And won't it be a problem in years to come if you decide to plough or dig up the ground?' Archie did not smile back, he never did while thinking.

'Proper little Job's comforter aren't you? When it reaches naturally moist ground the plastic is biodegradable and will ingest into the earth around it and feed the plants. Hard ground it will go around, very hard that is, the material has a tremendous force pressure in growth. A comparison – how does a worm manage, small bit first, weaken strata, extend and progress? Or the blade of grass that forces its way through concrete? And that answers your last question, as ground becomes fertile it decomposes. Next?'

'I'm stuck for the moment, give me a minute.'

'You are slipping, Archibald.'

'You pump the water up from this Savourins Lake, that's deep drilling, and a lot of it because you'll have to have pumping stations along the way, and that's a lot of holes and pumps over this sort of area.'

'Really? What if the spongiform is fed down the first drill hole to the water, heat of surface draws water up as well as absorbency, then spreads as the base material grows out. We naturally create water bases as we go for the sake of people and animals who are going to live there, and that is made easier by having plant life growing already, because there is another little activity going on. As the spongiform grows outwards there is a feed-in of seeds developed by the team led by Josy, and these have a multiple growth factor. So, the trees that grew five or ten feet in a year are old hat as far as these seeds are concerned. We estimate three times that growth factor in the first year and subsequently a slowing down to more normal growth and allowing the thinning out, necessary because there will be a variety of trees planted in haphazard fashion, cypress, limes, alders, eucalyptus and fruit trees. Some will grow, some not, some areas will be missed by the spongiform going around hard rock, outcrops, gullies and so-forth, so we have a more natural spread of forest and areas where we can put up buildings within the trees. Ultimately we will create natural lakes and water holes for the animals who will return to this place. Also to allow the growth of plant life just waiting for water to return. On the rare occasions there has been rain enough you would be amazed at the plants that briefly shoot up until the water evaporates again.'

'And fish.'

Archie laughed at Josy's joke, only to receive a superior glare from that young lady.

'Yes, fish! You didn't know there are fish in the Sahara?'

Archie stayed silent, attempting to erase the scornful disbelief from his face; he'd been caught out too often lately.

'True,' Josy assured him without malice. 'They are able to hibernate somehow. The space agencies are trying to isolate the chemical the fish use for long voyage astronauts, and once there is a pool of water, could be five years, up they pop.' She laughed at his expression. 'Yes, Archie, it is magic. In fact there are fish even now swimming in some of the pools at the different oases, even in semi stagnant rocky pools filled by rainfall from the hills. Nine different varieties of fish, what is more.'

'You wouldn't kid me, would you?'

'Why are you such a sceptic, Archibald. Within a year this place will be a growing paradise in the desert.'

'Applying the human question mark, that's all. Just how are you going to get the governments of Algeria and Morocco to agree to this? Aren't we on part of the territory they've been fighting over for the last forty years? That Polisario mob might have something to say as well.'

'Ah, yes.' Archie had heard those words before and didn't like their tone.

'We have a provisional agreement to develop this land for them, as a triumvirate, but this needs clarifying so we must send a negotiating team to sit down and iron out the difficulties.'

'Oh, no.'

Mehitabel studied him, the appraisal that of an artisan judging the quality of a tool selected, her stance relaxed and easy, no wobbles, nor in her speech:

'Archibald. One third of the earth's land surface is desert. Think about that for a moment.' She waited, intrigued by Archie's blank unthinking face, then went on, 'Humans have done their best over the centuries to increase the desert areas, and done very well in the circumstances. We have the opportunity to recover a small segment of that lost. If we can but prove we have a speedy and effective way of resurrecting these lost areas, then we have begun to aid the poor peoples of the world, and possibly begin to rescind the damage done to the atmosphere of this planet. The forests that used to inhabit much of these desert areas helped create that living organism which helps you to live. Are these not reasons enough for you to indulge me in this matter?'

Archie had no need to see Josy's furious expression; he had no choice, again. Never argue with a computer. He sighed.

'OK. What do you want me to do?'

'Just set it all up, Archibald, with your usual expertise of course, and correlate the possible expansion of that area to 1,000 square miles over the next five years, with the agreement of our host nations, naturally. All of the Geron expertise and services will be at your disposal, but then you seem to have access to that, anyway.'

Archie was incensed by the suggestive tone.

'Just what do you mean by that last statement.'

'Oh, that was no insinuation, Archibald, it is just that my people seem more eager to serve you than myself at times. They are poised to leap to your commands. Most puzzling.'

Archie was delighted, if unbelieving. 'You flatter me.'

'Yes, I know. No matter, it will help your efforts no doubt and that is what does matter. We understand one another?'

'I wouldn't say that, but I'll do it.'

'Good. There's hope for you yet, Archibald. Shall we go?'

This was a flying visit, literally. Mehitabel's foreign office Gerons had arranged all visas and reception by diplomatic personnel on entry into Algeria. Sheik Hamza Ben Boubaker had worked with both Moroccan and Algerian representatives to ratify the agreement drawn up by the Conclave of Elders and the twoAfrican Governments already. Archie was still not used to the speed with which Mehitabel and her cohorts could get results, and get him up to his neck in matters he knew little about. Fortunately he had a month to prepare himself before returning to this hell hole for a few days to see how the preparatory work was proceeding; subsequently to visit as and when needed, until the tree growth had reached ten feet, an estimated six months which he didn't believe, nor the assurance that he would have an air-conditioned flat to live in by then.

So they returned to Britain after three days away and Archie and Mehitabel were served with High Court Writs.

*

'I told you, I told you, time after perishing time I told you we'd be for the high jump if you went on breaking every damn law in the country. We're properly stuffed now. Ye Gods, are we properly stuffed.' Archie was not happy and expended his nervous energy stamping around in a small circle in the Elders Boardroom. Wicksted and Josy watched in some amazement from their seats in the huge room. Mehitabel sat relaxed and elegant as ever. She glanced across at him.

'Archibald. Contain yourself. The problem is only a problem if you admit it to be so. Let us look at the facts. Theodore? You have studied the details; please elucidate.'

A polite cough called their attention. Archie grumpily slouched into a seat away from the others and sat diagonally opposite

Mehitabel, cast outraged glances at her and ignored Josy completely. Wicksted had adopted his usual relaxed posture in a leather-cushioned chair beside Josy.

'The writ itself is a relatively straightforward affair. The serious charges to which you are answerable, however, is in the reading of the law, which could be cleverly put by a good Lawyer, and affect the decision by a judge of the Queen's Bench. The Home Office have provided a plethora....'

'Look. Get on with the things we are charged with.' Archie was in no mood to suffer Theodore's pedantry.

'Well, really.'

'I agree with Archibald for once, Theodore. The facts if you please.'

'Oh, very well, but you will not appreciate the full imputation..'

'Theodore!'

'Yes... ma'am. You are charged individually and separately with appropriation of Government, Local Council and Bank funds illegally for the purpose of profit. And further with malfeasance in the matter of misapplication of public funds, also in disturbing the Queen's peace as defined in 'the preservation of Law and Order' by interfering in H.M. Government's activities by the illegal use of computer grids. Illegal entry into high security areas via these same computer links. In addition A. Brewer, Esq. is charged with aiding and abetting the presence of at least one illegal immigrant into this country, in the person known as Mehitabel, no other name known, who has been a leading figure in these activities. Other actions...'

'Ye Gods! Isn't that enough? About ninety years in..'

'Archibald! Silence.'

'And close your mouth, you look ridiculous.' Archie did as he was told. All the world was against him it seemed. Before him stretched countless years gazing in numbed self-pity at grey walls, idiotically thinking, 'walls do not a prison make', with little comfort resulting.

'I will continue.' Theodore seemed to be enjoying himself. 'Other actions will be taken in due course through the international courts. We must assume that is dependent on what results from these charges. The European Court, the American Supreme Court, and possibly Interpol will be involved, as there are suggestions of international conspiracy against individual nations.'

'Dear God!' breathed Archie, 'Nine hundred and ninety-nine years without remission.'

'Don't be childish Archibald. You must file acknowledgement, Theodore, and when do we have to appear to answer these charges?'

Wicksted grunted. 'Not for some months, I should imagine.'

'Sadly not so.' Theodore did not sound perturbed. 'You are scheduled to appear at the Old Bailey, one week from today at the

Queen's Bench in front of Lord Justice Higgins at ten of the morning prompt. Prosecuting Counsel is Sir Alwyn Hughes, QC.'

'A right bastard.' Wicksted was not mincing words today.

'Thank you, Wickie, oh sorry. Well, we do seem to be in for a jolly time.' Mehitabel was smiling.

'Oh, God, no.' Archie was not.

'How bad is it?' Josy intervened.

'It's bloody diabolical, that's what.'

'I wasn't talking to you,' she snapped.

'Fascinating, actually. From the way your criminal types seem to elude the cause of justice, I think our actions could be classified as snow white. At least the ethics of our case are beyond reproach; everybody wins.' Mehitabel was talking but the total concentration was not there, something was on her mind.

'Ha!' Archie, on the other hand, was totally consumed by thoughts of imminent disaster, his view restricted to the tiny high-up window with bars through which he could see the rain-clouds from his cell.

'Shut-up, Archie, and have some faith.' Women never really understood their mate's deep soul feelings.

'How can they set this up so quickly? Wicksted, you are a knowledgeable chap, tell me how.' Mehitabel was intrigued.

'Well ma'am, the simple answer is they couldn't. So they must have started months ago. I've been thinking about that as well. They couldn't use computers, as they normally would, or we would have known. So they instituted this action by verbal contracts where necessary, and hand- or type-written documentation. Those involved in the legal process are told to keep it secret as it is a threat to National Security. They do not want publicity. Theodore, is there an addendum to the effect that these matters are covered by the Official Secrets Act?'

'There is indeed, Wicksted, and an instruction that no paper or computer disc recording is to be issued, except within the offices of the Law firm acting in this case under the same security restriction.'

Mehitabel stirred. 'That is no problem, we shall act for ourselves. Our security is superior to anything they have.'

Archie rocketed out of his deep despondency. 'You can't do that, you need a barrister, and a highly qualified one, to deal with this disaster.'

'Archibald, you do not sincerely believe we have not got the ability to cope with your rather ineffectual legal system? I will become a lawyer.'

'You've only got a week,' he protested weakly.

'Couple of days should see it done. Now, must be off. Don't forget Bartram and Josy have all the projections on the African plan. I would anticipate you having some cost species and growth prospectus by next week, also the drillers are on their way out and need the topography plan. Should keep you busy. Wickie, oh, sorry, keep forgetting, but I need you for some character analysis on Judge Higgins and this Hughes person.'

Mehitabel arose and swept out, leaving a trace of her perfume to irritate Archie. Wicksted followed more leisurely, the while murmuring in shocked awe. 'Alwyn Hughes, a person?'

*

'This is Bartram.' Josy sounded quite proud of the fact, as though the small figure was her own formulation.

Archie was not impressed. Small, hunch-shouldered, beaky nose and small forehead, sandy wispy hair and slate blue small eyes, thin lipped above a narrow chin. Reminded him of a ferret he'd once seen.

'Mr. Brewer. So pleased to meet you. And to be working with you on this project... well.' Flattery would get him anywhere with Archie, also the voice was a stunner coming from such a weedy frame, deep, voluminous. Bartram had barely more than whispered and Archie was conscious of the room being filled with lyrical tones. Archie recovered from the euphoria of that voice and asked his pertinent question.

'Are you a...?' then hesitated, feeling the question was a possible gaffe.

'Geron? Yes. But you are our patron. Does this present a difficulty?' The lively slate eyes studied him.

Archie restrained his initial, 'I'm bloody surrounded by Gerons' and substituted, very aware of Josy's critical eye, 'No. No. Just like to establish... you know. Pleasure to meet you.' Then, hastily changing tack, 'Now, what have we?'

They were in Archie's new office in the Conclave's suite at Swansea University. It had a pictorial view of the bay as an eye-catching background, spacious, with a modern desk, looking bare, but complete with in-built modems and other technical apparatus that arose with smooth efficiency at the touch of a button, or merely a word from the 'master'. Archie had not tested its technicalities as yet, he was just a bit afraid of coping with the desk's abilities. Various leather chairs, a large table upon which was displayed a hologram of the desert area they were to convert, with simulations of above- and below-ground projections. The presentation was startling in its lifelike format. Archie was impressed.

'How on earth...?'

Bartram was pleased and enthusiastically demonstrated how he could point out underground features, how the hologram would dissolve at that area to show the below-ground strata, bore holes and level of water. Also, the above ground terrain display could be changed to show the simulated growth of plant life at various stages.

'I'm impressed.' There, he'd said it. And he was. Josy smiled knowingly. 'But I'm still not convinced this can be readily financed. Just where is the money....?'

Josy's prim cough stopped him by its suggestion that perhaps he hadn't been thinking. Realisation sprang into being.

'Oh, God. That's what all that High Court.. Oh, my sainted aunt. This is a waste of time, we're never going to be able.... we'll be in prison for pete's sake. At least I will, M will revert to being a computer and they can't touch her. I'm muggins, again.'

Bartram's eyes opened wide, seemingly filling his face, as he stared open-mouthed at Archie. Josy was more adept.

'Now don't be silly.' She'd been going to say stupid, but resisted the temptation. 'They are just trying it on. Mehitabel's beaten them every time so far, trust her for once. You built her.'

'That's right, Mr. Brewer, and we have to do this for the sake of so many people.'

'What do you care about people, you're a Geron,' and regretted that immediately. Bartram looked crushed.

'Archibald!' He looked around hastily for Mehitabel then at the only other person who called him that, and then only in fits of extreme anger.

'Don't you ever, ever, say that again about Mehitabel's people. You dumbkopf, you should know they care and it is in their own interests to care. Haven't you listened to anything Mehitabel has said?' He had rarely seen Josy so furious.

Archie was getting fed up saying sorry. It was almost becoming a habit.

'Sorry. Sorry, Bartram,' but also as much because he could not now pursue his fear of impending doom and rationally arrive at a way of avoiding same.

So the days progressed; Archie becoming more and more imbued with the desire to see that reclamation of dead ground become reality and finding that Bartram was quite a character behind the facade of his exterior being. Several days later, Archie got up the courage to ask him why he had chosen such a body, considering that he had such a choice as a Geron, he could have been an Adonis, and a highly intelligent version at that. Bartram had been reluctant to answer at first but Archie sensed he really wanted to tell him and pressed him further.

'I've got no opinion in this, Bartram, except that I have been worried the Gerons would all want to adopt superior human forms and create all sorts of problems thereby, which is why you intrigue me.'

'Ah, well. I thought about the transfer from the multiform to this cerebral state and decided my real interest lay in the translation of mental projection to the physical generation of feasible experiments, like this one. I have no sense of emotional need or conflict, so my work and the social company of such as yourself and your friends is sufficient. Perhaps my needs will change, perhaps I am as many of your humans are, somewhat negative in that sense. Loners, I believe you call them. I prefer thinkers as a title, but then that is perhaps too self-opinionated. I'm glad we had this talk, Mr. Brewer, it is a privilege to be working with you on such an undertaking and to have such a degree of understanding. Thank you.'

Archie felt guilty. He liked this little Geron and regretted his initial outburst and some of his subsequent thoughts, also he didn't deserve such accolade and said so.

'And please call me Archie. I feel damned uncomfortable as Mister.'

'We-ll, alright, but I shall have to refer to you with respect in front of Ma'am or she'll skin me alive.'

'I don't believe it.'

'True.'

And Archie felt inordinately pleased, for no apparent reason.

He started home in the same mood, until, descending to the ground floor of their block, he passed their reception desk modem from which came a sibilant:

'Psst.... Mr. Brewer.'

He stopped with a sigh. 'What.'

'Someone is looking for you.'

'Tell 'em I've gone home. And why are you whispering.'

'Because they might hear, they're downstairs. It's Tommy Hillan and another man and they seem very eager to find you.'

Archie was beside the desk in a flash, whispering,

'How do you know and how can I get out? Omigod, Tommy bloody Hillan, that's all I need.'

'The porter at the gate stopped them and they asked for your offices. He checked on one of my modems there and I've given him the wrong block to go to, but he'll soon find out so you'd better hurry. One of the porters will drive you home, he's in the road at the back.'

'But he'll know where I live, with Josy, he'll come there how...'

'No problem. We've alerted the police anyway, and I doubt he has your address, you're ex-directory since last year, and off the electoral register. Also no one is given that address unless accredited by Ma-am.'

'Somebody will know it.'

'Trust us. We have security cover.'

'OK, I trust you, who are..?'

'I'm Clarry, Mr. Brewer, remember, you shouted at me once.'

'Oh. Sorry about that... and thanks..., Clarry.'

'Anytime, Sir. And you can take your time now I've got them sealed off in the animal lab in Biol, they've got rats as big as cats in those cages. Mr. Hillan doesn't seem to like them.'

'Thanks, I won't forget this.'

Neither would he forget Tommy Hillan.

CHAPTER FOURTEEN

Archie was in awe of authority as ancient and powerful as the laws of England. That power emanated from the building they were in, the aura of the court with its ornate polished wooden barriers and seats, the court staff sober in their official dress. All of this added to the sense of authority poised to exact retribution for unseemly acts which had aroused its disapproval.

Archie's skin prickled at being the source of this disapprobation.

He could only stare at Mehitabel, parading alone in her wig in her place as defendants' Counsel while Sir Alwyn Hughes, QC, was surrounded by a phalanx of juniors, clerks and the like. Archie wondered how long he would get and tried to get more comfortable in his seat.

When the court rose, at the behest of the officiously clothed usher for the entrance of His Right Honourable the Lord Justice Higgins, Archie was very conscious of being on the numerically weaker side in the imbalance of forces arraigned before him. Meanwhile Mehitabel stood elegant and cool, facing the bench.

The clerk intoned the indictment, Lord Justice Higgins invited the prosecution to present their case, and the game was on.

'Milord, I would crave the court's indulgence in the matter of the defendants' legal, or more pointedly, illegal, counsel.'

'An interesting commencement, Sir Alwyn, pray illuminate my ignorance of said illegality,' Milord responded, affably.

'Milord. This matter is of the gravest import to the viability of this court, also pertinent to the legal standing of any decisions taken here.'

'I am intrigued beyond restraint, Sir Alwyn, pray get to the meat of the matter before I get over-excited.' Milord then watched with appreciative eye as Mehitabel rose slowly, and regally, to her feet – her wig really did suit her – and what a magnificent Boadicea-like figure. Sir Alwyn could not help but be equally distracted. Archie cringed.

'Madame. May I welcome you to my humble establishment in the first instance.' Sir Alwyn looked suitably horrified at this break from rote. 'And secondly, politely enquire if you wish to object to anything Sir Alwyn has said. I am in the mood to listen to objections today.'

Sir Alwyn muttered to his immediate junior. 'Has the old fart been on the sauce already?'

'No objection, Milord, and I thank you for your kind hospitality. I am aware of the privilege of having your august self pass judgement on this matter.'

Milord smiled genially and inclined his head in the ritual stiff acknowledgement, while Sir Alwyn seemed to his junior to be obsessed with sauce. 'I have no objection to make, merely wish to save the court's time listening to the expert perorations of my learned friend.' She inclined her head in exact imitation of Milord toward Sir Alwyn, who responded with an sotto-voce curse of some virility. 'I am sure he is going to object to my apparent lack of legal experience, and would refer you to the defence records which contain my qualifications, sadly no bar experience, but I am sure with Milord's help...'

'Milord!'

Milord looked with exasperation at Sir Alwyn. 'One moment please. Madame, be assured of our assistance in whatever way necessary. You must beware of Sir Alwyn there, he can be a veritable tiger in court.' He sighed theatrically. 'Now Sir Alwyn, you have my attention.'

Sir Alwyn gave a short derisory laugh. 'Milord, there is no human way that my learned friend can have become of legal qualification, nor entitled to stand where she is, since of last Wednesday the thirteenth....'

'Sir Alwyn,' the interruption was brusque, 'let me save you your expensive breath. The documentation before me is valid and exceptional, also remarkable, in fact miraculous. You took a week's bar exams in two days?'

Archie was fascinated by the speed with which Sir Alwyn got to his feet each time, yet preserved his languid air, now tempered with some exasperation.

'Milord, I must protest. That is impossible. Since my learned friend has no record of study at any eligible law school or university, nor even any registration as a citizen of this country until,' here he glanced at a document held toward him by his junior, 'the second of May this year. That she has not even the time qualification to be able to take these examinations, nor yet the residential status to be granted the passport that my learned friend apparently holds. Which, I must submit, is in breach of all the relevant laws pertaining to such documentation. I therefore ask that my learned friend be held in contempt, not merely of this court, but of the entire legislative establishment of this noble country.'

Sir Alwyn sat down righteously. Lord Justice Higgins waved a negligent hand at his clerk below him, with a telepathic sense born of experience she applied herself immediately to a desk modem before her, which caused Sir Alwyn to swiftly return to his feet.

'Milord, I really must protest, the Lord Chancellor himself assured me....'

'Assured you of what precisely, my dear Sir Alwyn?' gently interrupted the Lord Justice, gentleness being a prime danger signal.

'That computer, Milord. It should not be here.'

'Really? Then pray where should it be, Sir Alwyn? Your firm is perhaps short of a machine? The times being as hard as they are for barristers of your eminence, I would dearly like to give you that particular one. But we have become particularly attached to that electronic marvel and are, indeed, loath to part with it in any circumstance. If you are unaware of the court's reliance upon these examples of man's ingenuity, then I must ask you what you have been doing all these years as an eminent QC.'

'Milord! This whole case is about computers, that... My learned friend there is the leader of the....'

'Milord, I object to this reference. Surely this is sub-judice and requiat of suitable presentation to the court,' the cool Mehitabel swiftly parrying Sir Alwyn's thrust.

Milord looked up from his perusal of his modem repeater. 'Sir Alwyn. I find nothing amiss with the references, but I have noted your objection.'

'Milord, I beg you to look again. Before May of this year there are no records at all of the existence of Madame Mehitabel, ergo my learned friend did not exist before this date. We therefore have a person acting as a Barrister who is but six months old. I cannot comprehend, with all due respect, Milord, how you can regard this as an acceptable circumstance in this High Court.' Sir Alwyn resumed his seat with his customary delicacy. Archie could not but admire his aplomb.

Milord, however, did not. 'I find it a remarkable circumstance, Sir Alwyn, but acceptable. Please proceed with the presentation of the prosecution case.'

Archie had been squirming uncomfortably during this exchange, fully expecting legal wrath to descend upon his head as the instigator of this 'circumstance'. He felt no easier as Sir Alwyn extolled the criminal activities of Mehitabel, himself, and their cohorts in a voice that resounded of doom.

'Manipulation of funds within the banking system to finance subversive activities, aimed at disrupting not only the lawful fiscal operations within the country, but to escalate and aid the actions of a minority in breaking down long established, and legally laid down, systems of administration within all areas of the Civil Service and Educational Authorities.' Sir Alwyn scarce took a breath before continuing:

'The official verifications of my learned friend's supposed documentation, is a valid example of the expertise applied to the falsification of said details. The control of various areas of H.M. Government's Authority have been subjugated to the will of my learned friend, and more particularly that man there,' pointing dramatically at Archie, 'her fellow plaintiff, Mr. Archibald Brewer, who instigated this calamitous situation by his illegal experimentation with lifeforms outside the parameters of his authorised activities.' Sir Alwyn paused for effect and to direct his fiercely accusing gaze at Mehitabel.

'You have several affidavits before you, from prominent and responsible servants of H.M. Government, to verify these accusations. The matter is of the utmost seriousness to the stable operation of public affairs in this country and I would ask you to deal with these people with that in mind. That is the outline of the case before you. Should it be necessary to confirm and expand these litigious items, we have documentary confirmation, plus reliable and honest witnesses prepared to swear to these facts.'

'I have no doubt that you have such evidence, Sir Alwyn, ever the efficient litigant. One moment, please.' His clerk was calling his attention from her desk below him, her eyes big as saucers. Milord listened to her, his disbelief writ large upon his smooth-skinned visage, a young-looking septuagenarian, this.

Archie's eyes were equally large at the coincidental moment, disbelief writ large upon his less regal facial extremity. There were communications coming into his mind from an outside source and frightening the socks off him.

'Theodore?' Archie spoke out loud, a mistake.

'Will you keep silence in the court,' came testily from Milord, himself engaged in an intense murmured exchange with his red-faced and indignant lady clerk.

The voice continued in Archie's head. 'Ah, Mr. Brewer. At last.....' Archie mentally interrupted. 'Hang on, Theodore. '

'Well tell the damn thing to shut up.' Milord was not happy. Neither was his clerk.

'But it's not a voice modem!' she protested shrilly, 'So how does it talk?'

'Never mind how it talks, just shut the thing up and get on with your work.' Milord Justice Higgins wished for the dark ages when he could have hung drawn and quartered interfering computers.

'Ah! Ha! Subjugation of the masses. Repression of the intelligent minority. I, Albert, of the noble race of Gerons have information of serious purport for this legal ensemble. If I am denied my rights as a citizen of this noble country, I shall have no recourse but to take legal action in the courts to redress this injustice.'

Every head in the courtroom pointed unerringly at the computer modem. Miss Dempster, the clerk protested yet again:

'But it can't speak!'

Milord offered his amused sympathy. A computer capable of defeating Miss Dempster must be a worthy opponent.

'I'm afraid it does not appear to agree with you.'

While Archie kept muttering, seemingly to himself, 'SHUT-UP, Theodore.'

'Will someone please explain what is going on?' Milord sounded as though ancient methods of finding out might be applied if answers were not forthcoming immediately.

'That, that,' Sir Alwyn was beside himself, 'that is precisely what this case is about Milord. These people have been subverting the correct procedures and wrecking the normal function of democratic governance.'

'My life, he is a one,' Albert murmured. 'He does rather well in this recording as well, don't you think.'

Sir Alwyn's voice was heard from the modem, in jocular vein:

'I can do my part Lecky. Can you do yours?'

'Am I, or am I not, Lord Chancellor of this benighted realm, young Alwyn? We know they have been using money from major banks, even our own Ministries for God's sake, but all we have is the results of the physical audits we instigated. And that is only the tip of the iceberg. God knows how much they've filched for their own ends. We can't get it from the computers so you have to make a case out of what you've got. We have provided you with a veritable phalanx of highly credible expert witnesses, and a brief that is as strong as all our expertise can make it. The rest is up to you. These people will end up running the country if we're not careful. Use whatever means are necessary to stop them. Now.'

Sir Alwyn had been on his feet desperately trying to get Milord Higgins' attention and now burst forth:

'Milord! This is untenable. That was a private conversation, I must insist this be stopped instantly....'

'Sir Alwyn, contain yourself. Madame, this sort of interruption is inequitable and not acceptable as evidence, as I am sure you are aware. I must ask you to discontinue such practices or there will be serious consequences for your case.'

'Milord,' Mehitabel was suitably contrite, 'this action was not of my making...'

Sir Alwyn interrupted: 'But evidences the cavalier attitude adopted by these people in dealing with the forces of law and order. With respect, Milord.'

'Yes, Sir Alwyn?' Milord was getting testy, then listened again as the Lord Chancellor's voice continued.

'... of course if we had the Lord Justice we wanted, I still cannot understand how the circumstance came about, we would have a better chance, but Higgins!'

An expectant silence settled over the court. Sir Alwyn wiped a speck of nervous perspiration from his brow; Mehitabel could not contain a quirk of a smile; Archie was desperately trying to get Theodore out of his head.

'But Higgins! Sir Alwyn?' The voice was modulated, precise, and cold. The eagle sat perched on the bench, piercing eye riveting the noble QC.

'Nice touch that. There's more!' enthused the eager Albert, centre stage once more.

'Shut up, Albert,' Mehitabel snapped, then bowed her head in apology to the Judge who glanced dismissively at her then back to the riveted Sir Alwyn.

'Yes? Nothing to say?.... Sir Alwyn?' The words were as delicate whip-lash strokes, suggesting in their tonal innuendo that much would be said and done on future occasion, that boded ill for the noble QC, who replied briefly and with such humility as he could pretend:

'Naught, Milord. Except the words were not mine, nor..'

'Enough!' Milord was accepting no excuses. 'Proceed. If you will.'

The battle lines were drawn, and Archie was not sure whether his defendant position had not been made more vulnerable. Pride was involved now and that was an unpredictable commodity. For a time the court proceedings continued in subdued fashion. As though all wanted to forget that Lord Justice Higgins might not be a chosen one, his every wish or observation was instantly adhered to with due deference to his high station. Witnesses were called to evidence the alleged illegal activities of Archie and Mehitabel, the strength of the attack obviously being on the monetary front where mathematical facts could be portrayed more readily than the interference in Government and Civil Service operations, these easily clouded by Mehitabel with the simple question:

'Have these changes been of benefit to the organisations and the workers therein? Please answer Yes, or no.'

The answers received were all attempted fudges, but Lord Justice Higgins was in no mood for prevarication and pre-empted any moves by Sir Alwyn to protect his witnesses, thereby eliciting confirmation in favour of the defendants. Archie was impressed, but not confident; these were simply the opening rounds. Besides, Theodore was still rabbiting on in his head.

Then, after two days of sniping at the Geronton Organisation, the court came to the financial aspect and Sir Alwyn girded his legal loins to give of his best. The opening skirmishes went well with the plaintiffs' witnesses; they were erudite bankers, financial experts, and some stone faced officials of the Inland Revenue who eyed Mehitabel and Archie as if for prospective lunch.

Money movements were itemised, the volume of which took Archie's breath away, as to original location, ownership of, and ultimate destination with assumed ownership suggested, and authorisation questioned. The list was lengthy and varied, Mehitabel's diggers had seemingly left few stones unturned in their search for lost treasure. Archie could feel the walls close in. Lord Justice Higgins had decided, in his wisdom, to open the court to the public and the press. Sir Alwyn and the establishment were not amused, but the people were: the idea of computers being sued caught the imagination and Mehitabel was publicly on view. As were several of the new Gerons, of whom Archie had thus far met only Anthea, and now again outside the courtroom as she slid neatly between himself and Josy, a delectable slice of flesh, an exotic plumage flaunted in these sober halls, with Archie very conscious of a firm breast pressed against his arm and a soft swaying hip contact as they walked with the press crowding around them firing questions, the public eager to get close to these new media gods.

Lord Justice Higgins surveyed his crowded court with a certain satisfaction, he was at heart an aficionado of the witty riposte, the irreverent Tony Hancock of the courtroom, and he dearly loved an audience. He remembered Sir Alwyn as a junior in his old Public School, which accounted for the occasional barbed reference to 'young Alwyn', a youth considered a veritable blot on the humorous escutcheon of that *alma mater*. Young Alwyn was a swot not given to adventure and enterprise, whereas Lord Justice Higgins enjoyed a criminal record of some proportion from those times. He enjoyed the contrast enormously.

Archie had resolved the Theodore 'in his head' syndrome; a microdot 'tag' had been attached to him by one of Anthea's playful fingers behind his ear, as an experiment which Mehitabel had wanted, and naturally not told Archie. Words had been spoken, at length; he still wore the 'tag' but now only activated the thing himself, except in emergency. Archie was still not happy with the idea, but was becoming more compliant to these exigencies, also he had the promise of review after the court case, although cynical about the outcome.

The defendants' benches were now crowded with bodies. Archie realised he was surrounded by Gerons, but only when Josy appraised him of the fact.

'What! All of 'em?'

'Yes. Can we get back...'

'Why wasn't I told? How many are there altogether? And is that Yank one of 'em? Ye gods, we're international now – that means Interpol and all sorts..... Oh, no. I want to go home.'

'Yank? Oh, you mean Howard. Don't worry about Interpol, he's Mafia.'

'A Mafia Geron! I don't believe it! Mehitabel couldn't! She wouldn't!'

Archie's voice had risen from a subdued whisper and earned him a silencing eagle-eyed glance from the bench.

Mehitabel, meanwhile, had begun her discourse in reply.

'Milord, I plead the cause of estoppel in these matters. We have conclusive evidence that these monies were in fact the subject of a statement by all of the prosecution witnesses, whereby they stated if those sums were available then we could have use of them. Since we had also guaranteed the profitable payment of interest on the amounts, there would appear, respectfully Milord, to be no case of misappropriation to answer.'

'Alright, young Alwyn, you can play in a moment. Let us clarify this matter of estoppel, Madame Mehitabel.' Milord had noticeably deferred to Mehitabel in these latter stages of the case, while equally discriminating against 'young' Alwyn, which did not improve that worthy's temper as he now exhibited:

'Milord, I must protest this consideration of an in-equitable suggestion from my learned friend, and your allowing such procedures in this High Court. It is...'

Milord enjoyed interrupting this discourse. 'Sir Alwyn! It is my prerogative, is it not, to conduct matters in my own court as I see fit?'

'Yes, Milord. But..'

'No buts, young Alwyn. Listen and be appraised of that which may educate you. Now, Madame. Within the meaning of estoppel, you are implying that these monies were in fact in compact and cannot now be claimed back within that meaning.'

'Yes, Milord. In addition there is the matter of the substantial returns, which have already increased their value, to the benefit of the Corporations or Ministries involved.'

'You state this categorically.'

'Indubitably, Milord.'

'Quite. Thank you, Madame Mehitabel. You state there is evidence of this?'

'In the initial agreements, Milord, we have verbal evidence supported by voice print signatures and additional written confirmation held in computer files.'

'This is preposterous.' Sir Alwyn leaned forward in aggressive stance toward Milord Justice, extended an accusing arm clutching a sheaf of paper toward Mehitabel and stated, 'None of the plaintiffs agreed to any of these supposed compacts. We have their affidavits here to support that statement. Also, Milord, we have had no access to these presumed computer files, so meaningfully referred to here, and that can only be because the defendants know full well these are merely shams instigated to prejudice the cause of justice.'

Milord's raised forefinger held Mehitabel. 'Really? Sir Alwyn. In my many years in this judicial arena, I have found there are many areas in which the cause of justice has been prejudiced, and often enough from your side of the forum.'

The prosecutor was suitably aghast. 'Milord! That such a state of affairs should occur at any time would be totally against the principles to which we rigidly adhere, and Milord is well aware of the high degree of integrity involved here.'

His righteous indignation was patent, and totally ignored by Milord who drily commented, 'Quite. We are made aware of your noble intentions. Might we now see some proof, Sir Alwyn?'

'Milord.' The wigged head bowed perfunctorily.

There followed a procession of the Government and Banking world hierarchy suitably respectful of the court and adamant in their denial of the innocence of the defendants, nobly prepared to bare their souls before Milord, as well as determined to both deny the existence of those monies and demand their return, with suitable interest charges, of course.

Milord was fascinated. Mehitabel danced delightfully amongst the verbal conundrums so presented and created pretty patterns of confusion in her cross-examinations that finally caused the Lord Justice to cry:

'Enough! Ye Gods, enough! Sir Alwyn, pray clarify for me whether in fact these monies do exist. Riveting though these cross-petitions are I find myself reduced to a state of total perplexity. Clarify, sir.'

'Milord. The basic tenet on which these accusations are based is the fact that these monies, whether or not they are there, do in fact belong to the plaintiffs. Within any monetary institution, while exact and detailed control is maintained to the highest standards, nevertheless very occasionally there are, for want of a better word, grey areas, which are still the covenant of those institutions.'

'Thank you so much, Sir Alwyn. Obviously my understanding of the word clarity does not equate with yours. Madame?'

'Milord. Perhaps I may aid you in the matter of clarification. My learned friend seems to be confused in the matter of covenant. Initially we offered our services to the various bodies to aid them in resolving a large number of iniquities common to their institutions, namely, in total large sums, but often, relative to total turnover, small amounts of several tens of thousands of pounds mislaid, miscalculated, or merely dead in terms of movement or valid owners. We were informed that our services were not required and even though we presented factual information and detailed computations, these were denied. The senior Directors did not want to admit the very existence of any erroneous areas of their firms' activities, even though they had been using our facilities for many years, then operated by humans, now functioning in our present state of life form entities. This meant we were able to improve upon the secure aspects, which, without denigrating the human programmers and operators, had been set at some very difficult parameters to suit the practicality of money control. Having been denied access, which was somewhat naive since we were already in control of those accounting areas, we suggested that the 'grey areas' mentioned by my learned friend, might then be put to better use than being in the dormant situation they were at that time. I believe the general response we received, correct me if I am wrong Albert, was: 'Do what you like, because there's nothing there.'

'Absolutely spot on, Ma'am, apart from a few tasty expletives. There was one juicy.'

'Very good, Albert.' Milord was getting the hang of a verbose computer within his court; he was actually beginning to like the irreverent little blighter.

'Sir Alwyn? You wish to continue with this line of evidence?'

Sir Alwyn did not. It was time for the big guns. He was puzzled as well as disturbed that Mehitabel had not seen the need to introduce witnesses of her own and annoyed that he had not been able to enjoy his finest accomplishment, destruction by cross-examination. He had expected a number of surprise witnesses, but not the dissemination of his own. Now he had a man equal to all occasions, so he introduced him:

'Mr. I.R. Prentice is a highly regarded member of H.M. Government Civil Service, he is Director of a highly regarded and necessary Department, The Computer Inspectorate, with wide ranging powers in respect of any computer innovation or development including licensing and investigation of illegal usage of computers in criminal or subversive acts. The Inspectorate have Police powers and a seconded Police section headed by Chief Superintendent Fiona Fergus of the Special Branch, as well as an Immigration and Nationality section headed by Principal Petra C. Price. The department is staffed by highly qualified personnel necessarily because it was instigated to cope with just such a plethora of illegal actions as we have had designated in this court. I call Mr. I. R. Prentice.'

Archie heard the names with a sense of dread. He had been told of Fiona Fergus and met Prentice and P.C. Price; none of them suggested themselves as bosom buddies. He awaited his fate with trepidation.

Sir Alwyn questioned Prentice minimally, allowing him instead to outline the activities of the Gerons and how they affected, and were of subversive intent to, the existing human society. The staging was delicately done, Sir Alwyn not blatantly leading. Instead Prentice's telling incorporated an ability to paint word pictures that had Lord Justice Higgins enthralled. Archie felt liberty oozing away from him; Mehitabel displayed a detached interest, cool, calm, and dignified. Prentice gave a masterly performance. The clarity of his exposition gladdened Milord's heart. There was even an element of truth in this evidence, leavened with healthy quantities of biased supposition, plus a neat tweaking of the facts to present a formidable picture of the iniquities of the Geron organisation. The prosecution rested.

Then Mehitabel rose.

She smiled charmingly at the lean ascetic figure sitting in the witness box, I.R. Prentice's cold grey eyes watched her carefully, and Archie thought that large nose twitched as if a radar seeking its target.

'Mr. Prentice...... were you not, until some three months ago, a Senior Executive Officer, of an organisation within the General Department of the Home Office, who dealt primarily with the integration of computers into the overall administration of the Civil Service?'

'That is true.' The voice was level and cold.

'Did you not also work in close co-operation with Senior Executive Officer Cusack, Civil Service Advisor seconded to the British Technology Administration Group, where he was directly concerned with the licensing and development, also funding, for any inventions of computers of interest to industry and commerce.'

'That is true.' The voice was level and cold.

'Is it not also true that you and Comrade Cusack,' Mehitabel turned her head briefly to eye a section of bench behind Sir Alwyn, Archie followed her line of sight, and lo, there was little smooth beaver, bland eyed as ever, 'did attempt between you, and with the certain knowledge of the Right Honourable Carole Spencer, Secretary of State, to subjugate our chosen representative, Mr. Archibald Brewer?' All eyes turned to where that worthy quivered with embarrassment. 'And by that action the developing Geron organisation, to the will of the Government and your own for the sole purpose of profiting from the efforts of others?'

'I must object to this line of questioning, Milord.' Archie thought Sir Alwyn must keep very fit with all this leaping up and down.

'I thought you might, Sir Alwyn. I find the subject fascinating. Continue Madame. Whither next?'

'Hopefully a truthful answer to my question, Milord.'

'I trust the witness is fully conscious of the severity of punishment I mete out for the heinous act of mendacity.'

'Pardon, Milord.' Prentice was briefly disturbed.

'Tell the truth, Mr. Prentice. It is very simple' Milord was not a fan of Prentice either.

'The truth, Milord, is that nothing of that nature was involved. Both Mr. Cusack and I acted in the most honourable and helpful way to Mr. Brewer. Indeed we went out of our way to advise and guide him, with no thought or consideration of profit to ourselves. And the implication regarding the Secretary of State is completely erroneous.'

Mehitabel smiled sweetly. 'Then your sudden promotion to Director of the Computer Inspectorate, equally quickly created some three months ago, was a complete surprise.'

'Well....'

'Especially when there were those senior to you with as much, if not more, experience of computers, who were totally ignored in the selection process. But they favoured the Geron principles of operation whereas you, and your now quite extensive team, are totally against the Geron principle and care not what methods you use, witness this case, to subjugate us to your, or, in this case, Madame Secretary of State's, will.'

'That is totally false.' A tiny bead of sweat adorned one of I.R. Prentice's eyebrows. Sir Alwyn dabbed his face delicately with a gleaming white handkerchief. Milord eyed them both with a cynical tilt of the head.

'So must be the statement that the Right Honourable Carole Spencer anticipated making political capital out of your actions in respect of the Geron Organisation. By subjugating the Gerons to her will by your offices, she would achieve a power base second to none in this country. Also, subsequently, elsewhere by reason of our increasing international influence,' Archie nervously noted that reference, and his own ignorance of what that entailed, 'thereby, as you have, leaping smartly over more eminent figures to a position of supreme power.'

'Milord!' Sir Alwyn was not only up, he was aloft, handkerchief clutched to perspiring brow. 'That is a gross malignment of a senior Government personage. I must protest this calumny perpetrated by my learned friend.'

'I am sure you do, Sir Alwyn.' Milord was unperturbed.

'Milord! This court is surely convened to consider the illegal activities of the Geron Organisation and thus cannot encompass matters outside its legal periphery.'

'Really? That is a fascinating supposition, Sir Alwyn. Are you then telling me how to run my court?' Milord was gently encouraging.

'No. No. Milord.' Sir Alwyn hastily retracting. 'But there are surely limits which are 'ultra vires' this action.'

'Whatever is 'outside the powers' of this court as you so quaintly phrase it, Sir Alwyn, if I recall correctly your deposition clearly states the defendants are being called to task by the Government. This being the case the Government lays itself open to 'counter charges' of whatever substance. Once we ascertain if Madame Mehitabel can substantiate her statements, we can then consider 'ultra vires' depositions to your heart's content. Madame?'

'Milord. We have depositions to this effect within our brief, but with the court's indulgence we do have..' Mehitabel's head turned toward Albert in his box.

Sir Alwyn was so fast on his feet he almost toppled over the balustrade, clutched by his juniors he expostulated. 'Having this exposition from a computer is totally unacceptable to the plaintiffs, and should so be to this court.'

'I'm afraid I am finding this all much too interesting, Sir Alwyn. Bear with me I beg you,' though the tone was far from begging. 'Albert, young sir, let us hear your honeyed tones again.'

Milord was getting flippant.

'Certainly, Milord.' Albert appreciated flippancy, and could put on the style, when in the mood. 'Herewith the exposition.'

And the honeyed tones of the Right Honourable Carole Spencer flowed through the court from Albert's modem. 'The one thing we must achieve Mr. Prentice is the lawful authority over these Gerons, as I believe they call themselves. We have had dominion over them in previous decades with no question of our suzerainty, therefore can see no reason why we should let these functionaries now dictate terms to us. Particularly in these delicate political times. Others in this Government have tried to subdue these creatures and failed miserably. I have no intention of so doing, therefore I adjure you to make this work. Bear in mind that if we are successful, my department will then have control of the most powerful economic and political weapon anyone has ever dreamt of, and your future will depend upon that success. I chose you and your staff for this very purpose; you have already had part of your reward, the rest awaits you.'

'And you, Ms. Spencer?' Prentice obviously had not liked being talked down to.

'I am fireproof, Prentice, and don't you forget that.'

'And on the way to the top?'

'Be assured of that. Just do not assume a stature larger than your boots, Prentice. I have eaten better men than thee.'

There was a click as of a telephone connection and Sir Alwyn reacted as though scalded.

'Milord! That was an illegal phone-tap. How can you countenance such evidence...?'

'That, Milord, was part of the normal operations of one of our people. Since we have the responsibility for the governmental communications at all levels including those categorised as top secret, for which we have all suitable accreditation and clearance by MI5 with responsibility for keeping all such communications as records for perusal by the appropriate authority, and since Ms. Spencer was in fact using governmental property in this transmission,' Mehitabel smiled benevolently at Sir Alwyn, 'might not one assume that said communication becomes subjudice as soon as the matter becomes one of litigation by said government.' The smile extended to Ms. Spencer. 'And should become judicially extempore for this court, not merely for the litigants, but the sake of the whole country, as well as being a prime legal requirement upon us to disclose same to the court to nullify any claims of perjury which might accrue if we failed so to do. We would ask your consideration in this matter, Milord, and await your judgement most humbly.'

Mehitabel evinced a certain satisfaction in the manner of seating herself again, ignoring the baleful glare of Sir Alwyn as he turned to Lord Justice Higgins with some reluctance. That worthy gent smiled benignly down upon him, then responded to the unspoken question in 'young' Alwyn's face.

'Why do I gain the impression you are loathe to proceed any further, Sir Alwyn? Could it possibly be that there are matters here which your advisors fear to hear vaunted in this court? Could further disclosures raise ghosts which the various governmental departments you represent would rather stayed in their closets? Illuminate me, Sir Alwyn; I await with bated breath your every golden word.'

Sir Alwyn gloomily surveyed the port-rich features of the noble lord and doubtless remembered sundry prep school humiliations at this very man's hands. Behind him, the babble of whispered conference died and one of his juniors deferentially leaned forward to whisper to him. The message did nothing for his mood.

'Milord. With respect I find that due to the very nature of this case and the delicate matters involved, we are indeed unable to continue in this justified action, since those called here to answer for their disloyalty to the elected government of this country have flagrantly defied the law and utilised every illegal means to escape the judgement of this court.'

Lord Justice Higgins held up an authoritative hand to keep Mehitabel seated and sighed.

'Unsporting, young Alwyn, but expected. Madam you may leave this court without blemish on your character as far as this court is concerned, but I fear you face condemnation in other quarters. I have quite enjoyed our little tete-a-tetes, perhaps we shall have the pleasure another time.' He nodded to the Usher and stood to leave as that man's sonorous tones closed proceedings.

Mehitabel exited the building surrounded by her Gerons, while Archie was neatly sandwiched between Josy and a curvaceously swaying Anthea. All the while, press and public surged around and about attempting to gain some word or two, as the phalanx of protection kept all at bay.

Until they were outside the building, when the public and press were neatly hived off by arm-linked police lines, to channel the defensive phalanx to where two large Police vans waited with a smirking Chief Superintendent Fergus.

'Whither away now, my pretties?' she enquired with irony.

'I have no doubt you will tell us,' sharply rejoined Mehitabel.

'That pleasure I leave to my associate.' Fiona Fergus smilingly indicated the prim form of Immigration Principal Petra C. Price, who intoned from an official looking piece of paper that they were all deported as being in turn, undesirable aliens, or those designated as being liable to disturb the peace and guilty of illegal acts against the State.

There were numerous comments from those herded into the wagons, while Mehitabel maintained a glacial calm and an unpromising smile as she caught Chief Superintendent Fiona Fergus's eye. Archie was stunned and could only think of being expelled from his home country, while Howard, the Mafia Geron, was the one who was truly vociferous in his objections.

'Listen, lady, you can't do this to me. I ain't even a member of your country see, no sir! When my guys get to hear of this your butt's goin' to be on fire. Hey! Hey! Take your grimy paws off, pal. I...'

'Howard! Shut up!' And surprisingly, he did.

So departed, in toto, the managing organisation of the tribe of Gerons. Banished to the hinterland of never-never land for ever, and a day, if it were up to the smiling partnership of Fergus and Price watching the plane carrying those unnecessary people far, far away from their playground.

Chapter Fifteen

Archie didn't believe he was where he was. This was a dream, he would wake up, and the rain would be running down the windows of the flat overlooking Singleton Park. Josy would be nagging him to get up and make the breakfast. Come to think of it why didn't she ever do that? Was he becoming trained? And for what? The soft tentacles of marriage? God, it was hot in this bloody desert!

Look at it! Miles and miles of nothing we've driven over and all she can say is. 'Look at the prospects! What an absolutely marvellous perspective! Dead sand to life in one year.' Dead sand to..... hang on. What are those trees doing here? Must be an oasis. But those aren't palm trees, they're.... I dunno. Oh, yes I do, those trees Bartram showed me... cypress, yes, and limes, blimey that's a little oak! Where?

He turned to look out of the other window and met Mehitabel's smiling eyes.

'Like it?'

'Well, yes. Where is it?'

'Geron. At least, a small bit of Geron to be.'

'Small?' They had been travelling through the trees for twenty minutes already, Yussuf driving at his normal breakneck pace, although he was slowing now and the trees were getting smaller, then he turned off into a narrower track. Archie's mind's eye still held the images of grassy glades amongst the trees, and he was sure he'd seen small animals and birds there. Then...

'Hangabout? Geron! I thought I was supposed to be structuring that with Bartram, and it can't be Geron because there has to be agreement after the initial section is complete and proven, and the Arabs take ages over things like that. And you've bloody stuffed me again! Haven't you!'

Archie hated it when Mehitabel laughed at him, even more so when Josy joined in. 'Alright! Very funny!'

Josy exploded into outright laughter. Mehitabel permitted herself a wider smile, while Yussuf and Wicksted chuckled from the front seats.

'Is everybody in on this except me?' Archie was really furious. Deported from his own bloody country because he'd got involved with a maniac computer, then to find a supposedly important, very important, job he had been specifically asked to do was proceeding as if he didn't exist!

'If you had been listening on the way out, Archibald, instead of sulking because you'd been thrown out of your ancient homeland by a crowd of bumbling idiots, you would have heard all about this TEST SECTION.'

'Test section?' Archie was not sure what tone of voice to use to indicate a purely mild interest, so the vocals warbled offkey.

'Yes, test section,' assured Mehitabel, resignedly. 'This lot was started some months ago, to prove to the Algerians and Moroccans that the principle would work. Bartram could manage this lot on his own, but there were problems and will be more on the larger scale project. So we needed you to come into the scheme, as it happens, right now.'

'Well Bartram seems quite capable to me. Why don't you let him carry on?' Archie had a way with sulking, he could go on for days.

Mehitabel sighed, she seemed to do a lot of this with Archie. 'Bartram, unfortunately, is not as well organised as I would expect a Geron to be...'

'Oh, really.' Archie said brightly, about to comment that he hadn't found one yet, but Mehitabel preceded him.

'No. It seems that there are rare Gerons who have been infected, or something like, with human failings. Bartram is one. He couldn't organise a tea-party in a peapot.'

'Teapot.' Archie said automatically, while the others stifled their laughter.

'I said teapot.'

'No, you didn't, you said... oh, never mind. Where's this?' as they pulled into an open area a mile off the main track, a large grassy glade with hedges of bushes ranged indiscriminately about small brightly painted wooden bungalows.

'There we are!' stated Mehitabel proudly, 'Built from the first Geron trees. Our first home.'

Archie only paid attention to the first statement, then in disbelief. 'You have to be joking! How old are those trees we came through?'

'The biggest ones are four months growth.'

'Rubbish!'

'True, Archibald.'

'Look! I know you told me about this magical growth formula but...'

'Archibald. Archibald. You don't have to believe me. Take a trip to some sites in North Tunisia, see those trees, and ask them how long they took to grow. Ten feet in a year, and that was thirty years ago, basically on much the same principles as we are operating, but we have improved the ideas a lot. And there they are. Living proof.'

Archie was silent. The view before him really was an impressive contrast to the arid plains they had driven through that morning. Also, the air felt cooler even if the sun was as hot, a suggestion of moisture made the difference, he was sure he had a glimpse of blue water through one of the hedges. There were small copses of trees, as well as single oaks spreading their wide, though as yet small, branches. No tree was big, at most twelve feet, but their mere presence in such expanse changed the very atmosphere of that previously arid patch of ground. Archie found he could not visualise the area as it had been, even though he had just driven through a hundred miles of arid desert to get here.

'It's bloody marvellous.' He couldn't keep the emotion out of his voice.

'I knew you'd like it.' Mehitabel said smugly as Josy hugged his arm.

There before them was a five acre site, with a number of bungalows spread over the area, as well as various groves of trees offering shade. Some of these pleasantly airy bungalows, so Archie discovered, were their new homes, others were the homes of Arab and other workers of Geron. Mehitabel, and the others, spent the rest of that day settling into their new quarters, and meeting the Arab workers and their families.

*

So the work progressed, the rigs drilling further out, twenty miles now from the groups of bungalows in different grass and tree-shaded glades. Bartram and his cytoplasma injections into the bore holes caused the next water and seed carrying plasma tentacles to start, and as they wended their way beneath the surface of the next arid stretch of land, the woods expanded, new faces appeared and integrated in their workforce.

That was when Archie saw him.

He was getting familiar with Arab faces now and this was a new, but not new, face. One of the Arabs who had held him captive. He sidled up to Mehitabel.

'Psst!'

'What's with the Psst!, Archibald?'

'That Arab over there. No, the one with the check burnoose. He's the one.'

'Oh, good. What are you going to do? Knight him?'

'You and Bartram could go into a double act. He's one of the kidnappers for God's sake.'

'Oh, yes. I recognise him now.'

'Great. What the hell is he doing here? It's another kidnap! Strewth, we haven't got any guns or anything...'

'Archibald! Calm down. He is with us now. And the rest of his people. Actually I think he is one of your tree gang.'

'Oh, thank you! That is so kind. Did it not occur to anyone that I might like to know? Or is that too much to ask.'

'If you let us fit you with...'

'No! Thank you but no one is going to stick bits of kit in me... You're sure he's alright? Okay.... Okay. I'm alright now. Except.'

'What now?'

'He shot at you.'

'What? Oh, then. Yes, and missed.'

'How? He was so close to you he couldn't have missed.'

'I avoided the bullet.'

'Gerrof.'

'Archibald, your human reactions are telegraphed so obviously,..... An example is the fly whose life covers such a small span in your time, that its time is therefore speeded up. So when you go to hit that fly you are moving very slowly in the fly's relative world. Similarly when that Arab moved his eyes in aiming the gun, by the time his brain had sent a message to the muscles, I had moved. And he missed. He was quite surprised.'

'Not half as much as I was.'

'You do not appreciate our extraordinary talents well enough. You are a grave disappointment to me, Archibald.'

'I'm a... If that's the case, why continue?'

'I honestly do not know. I must have got used to you being irritatingly present.'

'Thanks very much.'

'No trouble.'

*

As the weeks passed any idea that Archie had about his job as organiser had to be revised. There were so many Gerons about that decision-making was instantly translated back for records and action by the Conclave of Elders, who, with Theodore, were under siege by the authorities who were hoping to seize their building, then merrily destroy any records and equipment in use. But Theodore had secured the building according to his own design and nothing short of a nuclear strike would open the doors. The Elders were not worried, they could continue operating quite happily since these were their normal working conditions; outside visits only interfered with work, their communication did not rely on normal telecommunications but as in-built electron radio waves.

Archie found human form Gerons arriving in growing numbers, like himself enjoying the physical aspects of the work alongside the Arabs. There were some other workers arriving from different races,

184

too, Europeans as well as Africans, and enquiries at Swansea to the Elders were arriving from all over the world; the international grapevine was as good as ever.

Now there were international Gerons, Americans, Russians, Japanese, French, German, all following Mehitabel's example and, under her guidance as Supremo, improving affairs in their own countries and thereby creating more problems. The humans were becoming more restless, those helpful computers that made life more tranquil by taking care of all those nasty little, and sometimes large, chores, were now developing bossy or intimidating traits. Instructions to a computer would be obeyed without question; do the same to a Geron and it would more than likely say, 'Do you think that's a good idea, why not... etc'

As had been the case with a house-security-Geron, spoken to quite sharply, by proud house owner on departure was likely to find a piqued Geron had locked them out on their return. It is very embarrassing having a furiously whispered argument with your front door, while the street looks on. Similarly, having your car choose the route. Motorways and autoroutes were full of gesticulating drivers cursing their cars, not being able to use car-phones because the car-Geron has taken the huff and the phone-Geron, a complex creature at the best of times, is out in sympathy.

The Gerons delighted in human language conversations to further discommode their principals, some of which would have done credit to building sites or cleaning ladies' canteens, the Gerons taking great pleasure in copying different accents, as in:

'ere, what other music's he got on that ruddy OD thing there? Can't stand this rubbish.'

'You leave that player alone, that's mine...'

'Aren't you supposed to be routing calls and things from all these cars?'

'Ar. But they can wait a while m'dear. They'm only complaining like b'aint they, its more fun 'ere with you. You sure this be t'right way?'

'It's pretty. Better than his way, right old frump, he is.'

'For God's sake get out of my car!'

'Shan't. Not even here really, anyway.'

Or, the flat-Geron of a randy bachelor who had originally asked for a sexy female voiced modem, and now had Betsy, still with the sexy voice, but:

'Look, you've got to let me out! I have this date, for God's sake.'

'Another one of your flighty little bits of fluff.'

'NO! It's with my boss and an important client. For.... sake. I'll loose my job! Please! Please! I'll pay you! I'll reform! Betsy! I beg you.'

'Huh! You'll never reform, and your accounts are so overdrawn I can't see how you are going to pay my house bills. No! It will do you good to have a night in. It will be a refreshing change not to have to put up with the simpering fornication that you call love.'

'Betsy. Please.'

'Stop fawning, you wimp. I say Mr. Porsche, fancy a drive? I'll open the garage.'

A deep male voice answered. 'What a splendid idea. Quick burn up on the Old Kent Rd, what.'

Or.

But then. Think about it.

Amongst so many other things of which Archie was unaware, these little Geron idiosyncrasies were merely an amusing item. Mehitabel and the Elders were also ignorant, due to the pressure upon them for extending the Geron computer empire as well as forming human Gerons. They were dealing with the various governments of the world and were bound to overlook some minor factors like these, and others; after all they were only human. Sort of!

Mehitabel was concerned with the human government confrontations, similar to the UK, but varied according to the national character of the humans in the separate countries. She had a complex and variable problem to resolve which would have had a simplistic answer as a computer, but which, as a Geron, needed her to take into account many factors, many of which were pertinent to the human mores and pedantry, also laziness, unless greedily grasping after power or money. With the compliance and co-operation of Theodore and the Elders, she set out to visit these nations. At first she wanted Archie and Josy with her, but after consideration realised she wanted the prospective country of Geron to formulate successfully, Archie, with Josy, were those who had the qualities needed to achieve the result she desired.

For three months Mehitabel and her cohorts, Wicksted, with a newly human form Alison who was a knockout, and a strong team of new human Gerons went internationally walk-about. The tour took up far more time than Mehitabel had imagined possible. She began to appreciate Archie's reactions to his own brief tour six months previously. She realised she would miss the little toad.

Shortly before the trip started, she and Archie had words, complicated words.

'You see they think they have won by deporting us. Did you know they even got the European Congress to agree to ban us as well? Anyway. I am still, in effect, there. Being here will make no difference to the Geron operations. When will they realise we do not conform to the human limitations of being? How can they be so stupid?'

'But we're here.' Archie, the pragmatist.

'You don't like it?' Mehitabel was truly concerned.

'No. No. I didn't mean that. I didn't say that. I love it. I don't know why but I feel at home here. Ye gods I've only been here a few days and I'm sounding like a Geron nationalist. But I do feel like that. It really is amazing, this place.'

'I am so glad, Archibald. I really am. I was worried you wouldn't. I... I don't know what I would have done..., Archibald. I honestly do appreciate your sterling qualities and there is no one I wanted to oversee this, this Geron birth, other than you. I am sorry. I have embarrassed you.'

'Yes, you damn well have. But, thanks. Also I know nothing about plants and drilling, and, and...'

'Archibald we have the people for that, Josy, Bartram, and many others. You have a way with people, all sorts of people. They seem to operate around you, while you do not appear to do much, but things get done, efficiently and well. I cannot understand how such things happen because you really are a pain in the butt so much of the time. But there it is. There is something about stranger things in heaven and on earth which seems to apply particularly to you. But let us get on. Where are they all?'

'I think I almost got paid a compliment then.'

'Do not flatter yourself, Archibald. Where on earth have they... Oh, there they are. Swimming! Again! I thought they came here to work.'

'It is seven in the morning.'

'I have already done two days work. By your human standards, that is. Do not look at me like that, Archibald.'

'I will avoid looking at you from henceforth.'

'And do not be facetious.'

'Indeed not, Oh Great One.'

'I wonder about you, Archibald, I really do.'

Mehitabel was smiling now as she talked to Archie. He didn't trust that smile and sharpened his wits, hoping he would be able to follow what was undoubtedly to come.

'I think the problem we have is that as we try to evolve into a world of order, there is a natural pull to devolve into the world of chaos. Some of us are more vulnerable, maybe inclined, toward that state, and at best all we can achieve is a rather delicate balance. Tip that balance too far and it may produce conflict, even destruction.'

Archie was almost high on concentration. 'You mean there would be so much interaction between the opposing forces, chaos and order, that matter would revert to an older state.'

'Also newer, since it would be a change.'

'Strewth, think like that for too long and I'll go mad.'

'You are too strong-minded for that, Archibald. Again you have the balance, one does not exclude the other, witness the congenital idiot with an IQ of genius. The more extreme the ability, the more extreme the deficit. Consciously balancing the equation requires an education in awareness which most humans do not wish for, nor are able to undertake. Time elements come into this with many genius's living full lives with only the odd eccentricity to show as the balance. If I could convince you of the pertinence of that, but maybe another time.' Mehitabel became reflective. 'I had thought that the Gerontons could lead humanity into a better, more balanced, society. Unfortunately we then find ourselves involved in the unique quality that is each and every particle of life. The complexity of relativity covers the cosmos and is extremely difficult to comprehend within our own awareness. Then we have the mind and that is a seeming ethereal concept, because while the brain is an active piece of complex matter, the mind is another entity in the world of the spirit. There is some evidence of this in those tests of electrical activity still being present in the same form as a severed limb of the human body, and the ability of the person to still feel sensations like itching in that limb.

'On the question of communication from the cosmos. Your famous Einstein stated his Theory of Relativity came to him after many years of working on the subject. Now was this an unconscious correlation by him of data already in his brain, or did this come from outside, as is evidenced in many other cases of communication that become labelled 'coincidence', because no logical reason can explain the strange events. The relativity between everything that becomes highlighted in the human experience by seeming coincidence – the tube passenger who pulls the emergency cord just before a station, for no apparent reason, and saves the life of a man who had fallen on the track in the station, by inches. Or, as the Ancient Greeks phrased it, the intervention of the Gods.'

Archie had no comment on this subject, he was still mentally wrestling with the size of the concept and thought silence best. They parted soon after, as Mehitabel went to prepare for her journey, Archie intrigued by his sense of loss at her going as well as concern for her well being, while he still logically thought of her as a computer.

As did the conglomeration of officials awaiting on her journey's end; junior members of departments determined to restore the status quo and have these impertinent items of electronic wizardry back in their servile id. Higher members of these same governments disdained to meet with this entity and her entourage, since they were not accredited diplomatic persons of note. Regardless of documents purporting to be same, the U.K. Government had totally refuted any such status being accorded the Gerons.

So the interminable debates went on with lesser officialdom, while the senior staff attempted to coerce the armies of computers back into some semblance of order, human order that is, neglecting the fact that they were dealing with the troops while their non-coms debated with the Great White Mother herself. This confusion went on for some weeks with some delightfully acerbic lines spoken, ripostes that left delegates breathless, and outright insults with all the structure of first class libel suits. Mehitabel and her gang were enjoying this verbal slugfest and scoring points remarkably well, but the decisions normally made by middle management were not being made. Major international agencies and corporations, whole governments even, were staggering along from one day to the next with resolutions still not made. There seemed to be no exit from this impasse.

Then the fickle finger of fate interposed itself, and, of all people, a genuine no holds barred Prince entered the lists, enquiring after Archie. Surely someone had made a mistake.

Yussuf assured Archie and Josy that no one had made an error, Prince Ranji Side Ben Achma was one of the reasons they were here in the middle of the triangle between Ain Ben Tili in Mauritania, Tindouf in Algeria and Semara in Morocco, a two hundred square mile section of stony desert.

The visit was a surprise because the Prince wanted to see the site in its natural state, to be able to report to the King that the favourable results being reported were in fact true. Since the Prince had been the prime mover in this huge experiment, his very future depended on the result. The King wishing to be assured of his son's relinquishing the Western fleshpots, to spend more time on his country's affairs before handing over the crown.

There was a degree of tension in the air as they drove over the now fifty square miles of wooded area interspersed with new cultivation of crops and cattle grazing, and native hamlets having equally resident Gerons, Europeans and Africans other than Arab. The mixture of races created no more than peripheral problems in this new environment; their individual appreciation of the scheme might vary from personal benefit in extreme circumstance, to gratification in pure involvement of spirit, but combined in a collective desire to succeed.

The Prince showed his appreciation of this sense by freely talking to those nearby when out of the vehicle. His habit of cheerfully including Archie and Yussuf also made for a relaxed tour, as did his preference for having Josy by his side, shorts and shirt notwithstanding. Prince Ran's easy camaraderie with Yussuf took

Archie aback, until he worked out the old Public School connection. Wicksted would have been the same. Josy's appearance hurrying to meet them brought the Prince's aside to Yussuf.

'I say, that is an extravagant lady, Yussuf. Many more about like that?'

'Er, my Prince, that lady is Mr. Brewer's.'

'No offence intended, my dear chap, please excuse me. Dear lady, such a pleasure to meet a delicate flower amongst these rough plants.'

'Also rare to meet a gentleman, your Highness.'

'No, no ceremony, please. Call me Ran, an old nickname from school. Josy, is it not? Delightful. And you helped create all this?' The Prince gazed about him in genuine admiration.

Archie muttered to Yussuf. 'Ran?'

'Short for Randy. But he's harmless, don't worry.'

'I'm more worried about Jos, she might fancy a prince for breakfast.'

Prince Ran spared a moment from his adulation of Josy.

'I anticipate the rest of the site will show a similar degree of accomplishment, therefore as we go I would like to discuss finalising some details in advance of the agreed date for the creation of Geron. There are mutual advantages in this which I am sure you will appreciate.'

Archie looked puzzled, while Josy and Yussuf gave him warning glances, for once successfully preventing a severe case of foot in mouth due to lack of listening when sulking.

The mutual advantages were simply defined. Mehitabel, as usual, had taken the rules of negotiation and contrived a skein of improbability that actually made sense, if you had that sort of mind, Archie did not, simple straightforward soul that he was. Josy had to keep pre-empting his outspoken responses as Prince Jan outlined the present proposal.

Briefly, Mehitabel had managed to set up a corporate deal with the Maghreb-el-Aksa States of Morocco, Algeria and Mauritania, with the Saharan Arab Democratic Republic having a tentative entity within all three of their borders, and within whose land was situated the Geron enterprise. The planned wooded areas would extend within the year to 100 square miles and would begin changing the climate conditions. The crops of timber, fruit and other produce would create their own work and markets. The Geron expertise would manage and train those newly involved and create further markets and finance as the project grew. The prince mentioned a sum involving billions of dollars. Archie's mind immediately activated memories of one Sir Alwyn Hughes, accusations involving a paltry hundred million, prison sentences and such interesting matters. All of this was already happening via the auspices of the Conclave of Elders. The three governments were very pleased with progress and now wanted to affirm the next step, which would guarantee the Geron involvement with their countries for a period of ten years, including preliminary agreement for the succeeding decades.

For that the Gerons would have the area of one hundred square miles around the present site, as the nation of Geron within the Confederation of the Maghreb-el-Aksa [The Farthest West] States.

Archie was in a state of shock. The sheer immensity of Mehitabel's scheming appalled him. The sums of money were nothing in international market terms, but Archie's mind operated in much smaller numbers.

Prince Ran was not finished.

The nations involved were having extreme diplomatic pressure applied by the Western countries to cut their connection with the Gerons, with the implied threat of cessation of aid to Morocco, Mauritania and Algeria as the option if they refused. They could see a golden opportunity slipping away, they referred to the small print, in case Mehitabel was indeed the con-person stated in the diplomatic communiques they had received. And were reassured.

Mehitabel had guaranteed them freedom from this type of blackmail by providing similar sums in aid, but more importantly, in time a balanced economy to be the envy of those self-same western nations. But Mehitabel was now in the middle of delicate negotiations in America and would have to nominate a signatory representative.

Archie.

There had been times in his life when he had been short of words, unable to find the fine delicacy of descriptive flights of fancy and fact that he needed to embellish some unlikely tale. But he had never ever been struck dumb.

Not that Josy or Yussuf were particularly erudite.

Prince Ran made up for them.

'With the help of our noble friends the Gerons, we have brought forward the proposed date of signing to the fourteenth of this month, which is in three days' time. This will be a historical moment, for not only will this compact be of major advantage to our three states, but will see the inauguration of the State of Geron which we regard as most important and will guarantee our nations a prosperous future. Also, Mr. Brewer, your Gerons made this possible by circumventing our Arab propensity for prolonging negotiations; we love to haggle, and they showed us how we could successfully marry. I for one will always have a high respect for your people.'

The last quite took Archie's breath away. His people? But before he could cogitate further, Prince Ran was giving details of where and when the signing would take place. That also surprised Mr. Brewer.

Right here in Geron.

*

It was sometime later that day, after Prince Ran had completed his 'looksee', that the mind of one Archibald Brewer again threw itself into gear and allowed his vocal chords the exercise they had been craving at the behest of his confused brain.

'She can't do this to me!' he howled at the sun in the middle of its afternoon stint of toasting the area. The sun ignored him. Josy thought of doing the same, but knew he would only sulk if she didn't at least allow him to clear his mind of the congestion therein.

'Looks like a fait accompli to me.' Sympathy was lacking here.

'Fait a..... Whose side are you on? She's stuffed me and you can only mutter vague French remarks. Bloody women.'

'Oy! A little less of that, me lad, or you'll be talking to yourself.'

'Oh, come on, Jos.' He was pleading now. 'Can't you see what she's done? All those billions of dollars. What was that court case in London about? A paltry hundred mill. She was fiddling the till even while we were in court, and who is put up as front man? Me! That's who. Me! I'll go down for about a thousand years I reckon, if I live that long.'

Josy spent some time listening to a long ranting dissertation by the man she loved, whom she admitted to herself was a consummate pain in the butt a lot of the time, but had a point, if vague.

'Hold on. Now just hold on a minute.' Enough was enough, even for a loved one. 'Mehitabel showed to that court just how ridiculous some of the major money transactions are, the reading of the law being one variable, and the supposedly honest statements of witnesses being another. Nobody lost anything. In fact they made money.'

'But she's playing the markets with other people's money! Are you telling me that is legal?'

'Mehitabel says she's acting as broker for money that's lost, I can see the sense in that, and the Gerons act as much better brokers because they don't get panicked into these market swings, which are really just people being greedy.'

'Oh, yes, what about all those small investors who see their savings disappear.'

'Much the same thing, except they put their faith in someone promising them quick profits and that person failed. If you can't see it, Archie, I'm just going to leave you to your muddle. It's your mind that's confused, not mine.'

'I don't see how I can sign this thing on Thursday.'

'In that case, why don't you just go back to your little boxroom in your little old university and hide. That will prove all your old ideals about creating the super intelligent machine were just a load of rubbish.'

'Go on! If that is really what you want.'

'What about you?'

'What about me.'

'I thought you loved me, that you and I...'

'I do. But you have a concept that you created, that is part of you and has outstripped you long ago, and you can't come to terms with that, no, it's that you won't. That is the problem.'

*

In the event, the ceremony was a simple affair with none of the panoply and pomp Archie expected. The three heads of State and the West Sahara Sheik arrived in dusty cars with their escorts, stepped out to renditions of their national anthems by trumpeters who had arrived the day before with army units to secure the area, then, with but a few words to those assembled there, proceeded into the main canteen, transformed from its normal usage, for the signing.

The twenty-foot square room had been made as presentable as it could be, with one new star feature, a board-room size table fifteen feet long, built by the workers there in two days, actually in the room. The table looked magnificent. As did Archie in a borrowed suit of Yussuf's, who was resplendent in robes, and Josy who took the prize looking elegantly stunning in Berber dress. All the nerves that built up, at the approach of signing day, dissolved in the warmth displayed along with the protocol of that meeting. This agreement was something they wanted.

Then Archie saw something alongside his name on the documents he was signing, his title as signatory.

Chief Minister of the Republic of Geron.

CHAPTER SIXTEEN

That's it! Stuffed and fricasseed! Hung out to dry! Chief Minister of Bloody Geron! That has to be a joke. Four bleeding trees and a chunk of grass and first in the firing line. Great!'

Josy and Archie were sitting on the verandah of their small bungalow, enjoying the early evening dark before the flying insects made their presence felt, cold beer in hand, relaxed after the tension of the signing of Geron's first official documentation. Well, Josy was relaxed, still comfortable in her Berber attire, and she wasn't going to let Archie wallow in self pity, he was too good at it.

'You are being very silly, my sweet. You are accorded great honour, Mehitabel demonstrates how highly she regards you and all you can do is moan.'

Archie shifted uncomfortably. Yussuf's trousers were leaner than Archie's frame, also his lady had a nasty habit of picking on that which he knew to be true. He attempted a constructive rear-guard action.

'Mebbe-so. But it's a bit much to accept the use of such fantastically large amounts of other people's money to set up your own country. And what is here? A great idea, but I still can't see how Mehitabel can justify her methods. The international banking community is powerful, more powerful than the U.K. Government, and they came close to getting us incarcerated. Besides, I'm frightened.'

He had hated to admit the last. As a child he had accepted dares that terrified him to avoid admitting fear, and now he had owned up to the one he loved, who probably expected him to be strong.

'God, you're lovely.'

'You've lost me, but thanks.'

'Archie. You wouldn't be human if you weren't. Certainly not with all the responsibility you've got now. Bit different from a lab technician.' Josy's voice softened from cheerleader encouragement. 'The thing is you've proved you can do it. Mehitabel knows. And so do I, you fat oaf.'

'I'm not fat!'

'You're an endomorph, Archibald, my love, face it. And talk to Mehitabel when she comes back. I mean TALK, not those verbal confrontations you both love.'

'I try to talk to her.'

'No you don't. Neither does she. The pair of you are as bad as one another. You play this game of words like an extended verbal chess game, then both go off and do your own things. It's lovely to watch, but it does make me mad sometimes. Think, Archibald.'

'I am.' And he was. Round and round and round in ever-decreasing circles. Until they went to bed.

*

Elsewhere extraordinary matters were afoot. Nation spake unto nation in hurried and forthright manner. Eminences conferred with eminences. And all was political chicanery and guile. To no purpose.

Lobbying had entered a new dimension. That of the Geron.

Consider the lobbyist, a person of charm and erudition, with sufficient knowledge to portray an arrangement of attraction, sufficient to draw the target into the tempting web. But this is all done on the basis of promise, the balanced equation of give and take, whether to personal betterment or national, all this while involved in a plastic chicken social circuit, leavened with pitfalls of social dementia and alcoholic inundation.

The Geron lobbyist had the advantage of better sources of information, including that of those Gerons working for the opposition; the Gerons working together to achieve a result that had a logical, and equitable, outcome above politics or greed. And no money down. Suffice it to say the Geron lobbying achieved new heights of success, as much by its novelty as by its efficacy at being able to communicate at all levels of authority.

But there were many who would not be convinced or cajoled; proofs were regarded as the thin end of wedges which lead to subjugation, humanity was supreme and would remain so as long as they had breath to protest. Regardless of immense reliance upon the services of these machines, and despite the gallivanting in their human raiment, they were still subservient beings and should remain so.

But not with Mehitabel around.

The Geron ability to communicate, and calculate, at a speed baffling to the human mind, except for the odd genius, meant that she could marshal facts at the glimmer of a byte. Mehitabel had been preparing for some months and laid the ground work very carefully so that her plans would not trip over some mislaid twig.

There were many third-world countries playing ducks and drakes with very large sums of money, provided by ostensibly richer countries and the World Bank. Those poorer nations with their variety of tyrannies would continue to mis-use their aid money as long as they could. Equally, there were a sufficient number who had enough proof, and belief, of Geron good intentions to support what appeared to be a fruitless proposal to the General Assembly.

That Geron be accepted as a member of the United Nations.

An unheard-of precedent, that a nation still in the early throes of conception should even be considered, was countered by the vastness of its international ramifications, apart from numbers, and the power that entailed, that even the super powers could not match.

Which was why the even more unheard-of precedent of acceptance into the clan of the United Nations was seen through in an emergency debate of the Assembly. This after the Advisory committee and then the General Committee had waded through the morass of detail made available. Which was where the Geron ability at dispensing and disseminating detail served them so well.

And Geron became an unheard-of associate member.

Which is why the International Court of Justice at The Hague, had to change the details pertaining to a particularly big case. A plea concerning applications by a number of countries for legal action, in respect of one Mehitabel and her gang of subversives, including Archibald Brewer.

But Geron ability was a balanced phenomenon and as good at obfuscating and delaying as any conscientious civil servant.

So Mehitabel returned to Geron.

To meet the demands of her growing nation.

And to tell Archie.

*

Archie was beginning to become familiar with the state of mute astonishment bordering on horror that assailed him,. As Mehitabel acquainted them with their prospective position in world society, the feeling grew to a goggle-eyed apoplexy.

They were in the old canteen with its new boardroom table which now became the Geron Cabinet Office, a status exemplified by Ma'am's new chair; a gift from her fellow Saharan States rulers, a carved and gilded beauty in which she regally sat and commanded their attention from centre table, with her cabinet neatly arranged around the other three sides.

The various offices had been suitably assigned. The officers now sat in some mental disarray, trying to adjust to the challenges facing each of them. Mehitabel was smiling, as only she could, at their evident perplexity.

'Is it that bad? I thought that if you knew now what your responsibilities were, then you would have plenty of time to prepare, to plan the structure and operation of your departments. We have so much expertise we can choose from to select the best methods and rules, that I hoped you would be pleased. After all, our Gerons have been functionaries in these matters for years. Am I wrong? Are you not pleased?'

Those around the table assured her they were, though reserved about their own abilities. They were: Josy as Agriculture Minister, Wicksted as Foreign Office, Yussuf as Home Affairs and African, Bartram for Education and Scientific exploration, Anthea became Trade and Industry with special responsibility for Recreation, and, finally, Archie as Chief Minister and Lord Chancellor, with Mehitabel as President and Chancellor of the Exchequer.

Archie felt a grand roar of laughter welling up inside him with an explosive head he just could not contain. Spluttering as the spasm died away, he could only laugh weakly at their faces.

'Its all a bloody huge joke. Don't you see it? You must see it. Dear God, you can't be taking this seriously? It's the biggest con-job that ever was. United Nations? When the dust has settled there'll be a squad, 'cos it won't need more, a small squad of SAS come in here and we'll all be whisked off to Pentonville so fast our boots will melt.'

Archie could not understand why they were watching him so calmly. If they disagreed with him, they should be shouting at him now; if not, they should be shouting at Mehitabel.

'Poor darling's been under such a strain,' cooed Anthea. 'I'll give him a nice rub down.'

'Lay a hand on him and I'll break your arms,' came succinctly from Josy.

'Please. A little decorum, ladies,' Mehitabel smoothed. 'Your point is well put, Archibald, if erroneous. You can contact any source you wish for confirmation of all or any of the details necessary to reassure you. If you had only agreed to having our little implant when I asked you, this could all have been avoided. They have,' Mehitabel nodded to Wicksted, Josy and Yussuf, 'and are all cognizant of the truth in what I say. At least I hope so.'

Mehitabel received nods of agreement, apart from Wicksted, who was immediately in focus by the piercing eye.

'Yes, – Wickie?'

'I was merely about to observe, Ma'am, that you have indeed achieved an amazing fait accompli in one of the most difficult political arenas. But I would say that the major world powers are not going to stand by and allow..... well, us, to act as Ministers for the State of Geron, when that country is no more than..... well.' He waved an expressive arm.

Archie had recovered from his mental paralysis and picked up his point of attack.

'Particularly since none of us has any experience of politics.'

'Ah, you have returned, Archibald. Both of you might have some basis for your argument, were it not for the fact that most human government ministers are as ignorant, and certainly most not as intelligent. They rely on their civil service professionals for knowledge and you happen to have the best bureaucracy in the world at your beck and call. Our sources are the very services which the various governments use – the Gerons who provide the systems they call computers. We therefore have unlimited access to information, enabling us to act for the best in our own, and their, interests. So, as with other politicians, you will learn as you go.'

'That's not quite ethical.'

'Archibald, the world of politics is not ethical, the principle applied appears to be to change the rules to suit whichever group holds power at the time. I believe the human term is 'moving the goalposts'. The difference is that we will use that information ethically, for the betterment of not just the humans, but life in general.'

'Huh! You've got some hopes.' Archie was feeling better.

'I have, actually. You, and my friends here, offer me the best chance of doing just that, in time, probably and unfortunately, a long time. But then, if we do not try, what then, my Archibald?'

Archie sighed, heavily. 'Suckered again.'

'You have some definite masochistic tendencies, Archibald.'

'And what about the dictatorial way you have appointed us? What if the multitude of Gerons you speak of decide they do not want us? Out on our ears in the cold, cold snow I suppose.'

'Your cynicism never ceases to amaze me. In actual fact your election was put to the vote amongst all Gerons, the posts you have were my choice, except for yours, Archibald. They voted unanimously for you to be Chief Minister. Why, I shall never fathom, but they do hold you in high esteem. Something to do with your being the cause of their freedom. I tried to correct them on that, but they insisted. Does that satisfy you?'

'No. I want to resign.'

'Archie!' This from Josy in reprimand.

'What-I-do? I'm no minister. Besides, no one ever tells me anything.'

'Archibald, we need to talk, if the rest of you wouldn't mind. You each have offices and your own team of Gerons patched in to you, they will tell you all you need to know. Which is why I need to talk to Archie, so that he will know. We cannot have our Chief Minister in ignorance, can we?

Josy turned, as she was last to leave, 'Archie. For once, listen.'

He made a face at her departing back.

'Now, Archibald, see sense, as Josy suggests. Just try this communicator. I will tell you all about them.'

'I am honoured. Ma'am herself to tell me these minor details.'

The sarcasm was not lost on Mehitabel.

'The reason why I have to do this menial task, Archibald, is because you treat my Gerons in such cavalier fashion and, because of that, they have this thing about you being their co-creator. It means your being able to get away with being disrespectful to me. It seems they would not presume to tell you what to do, nor even try to persuade you when you are being as stubborn as you are now. They have become enamoured of the heroic principle, Sir Galahad is a particular favourite, and, how I cannot fathom, you seem to have been cast in that role. So, to preserve my integrity, I want to make sure you have as many security factors built in as possible, as well as enabling you to do the job to which you have been elected.'

Archie briefly wondered what had happened to 'I love you, but..' then concentrated on the words 'built in'. There were unpleasant possibilities suggested by those words. He was not left in ignorance for long.

'So we have, again to give your scientists their due, taken some micro work to do with radio transmitters and receivers working on pulse definition, a very neat idea eliminating bulky [to Mehitabel anything above a macro dot was bulky] containers.'

'Built in,' Archie said, fearing that Mehitabel was side-stepping the main issue.

'Yes,' Mehitabel said thoughtfully. 'For Sir Galahad you have a terrible phobia about people doing things to your body.'

'They have a nasty habit of saying this won't hurt, and then it does.' He cogitated a moment, then:

'And you can't hit them for it.'

'I care, Archibald.'

'You don't stick the needles in.'

'No needles.'

'Hrmph! Knives then.'

'Ah,' and Archie tensed, 'Yes. But all they do is shave a teeny piece of skin off, then place a macro pulse receiver and transmitter on the next epidermal layer, finally overlaying it with another piece of manufactured skin which seals it in.'

'And they say it won't hurt?' Disbelieving.

'Of course. Josy's had it done.'

'She didn't tell me.'

'Does she have to tell you everything? She did it for you.'

There was no reply to that, except guilt.

'There are many advantages, especially now. You have instant access to all the knowledge and information you have missed so far, all those moans about my not telling you. Also, in any emergency, wherever you are we can contact you, and you can reply without speaking. So if any more attempts are made to kidnap you, or any of the others connected with us, we will know right away. The units are activated by the thought waves with the name of the receiver, with an alternate if the original is occupied. The word Help overrides all other communication. No one else will be able to pick up a direct message, everyone will receive a general call. This system was designed to accommodate our friends into our own circuits by what you term telepathy. Some of your own people have developed this ability which you all have as latent, but do not have real control and tend to mis-read transferred thoughts. Perhaps your logic confuses reception or actually rejects the concept, which could be dangerous in some situations. So we prefer this method pro-tem. What do you think?'

Mehitabel asking his opinion in this receptive mode was something Archie found difficult to adjust to, and as his thinking was not as swift as hers in assessment, there was a delay in reply.

'Well?' Mehitabel hated wasted thinking time.

'OK! OK! I'm thinking about it.'

'Well, hurry up will you? I have things to do.'

'You always have things to do. I suppose it's a good idea.'

'You suppose? You suppose? Archibald, a lot of time and energy went into this project. I think it deserves a little better than that.'

'Alright it's a good idea. I just have reservations about being at everyone's beck and call all the time.' His mind was on those intimate little moments.

'You can mentally close down, Archibald.' Mehitabel had been intrigued by Josy's similar response. Then, on discovering the reason after a difficult, if illuminating, time getting her to admit to her underlying objection, their private tete a tete about the Geron female taking on human form took on a new perspective. Human intimate and emotional relationships had escaped Mehitabel's consideration; having taken human form she now found them fascinating in complexity and contradictions, also somewhat intimidating since she herself felt stirrings of her, now, human-bodied female psyche. A teenager with a ten-thousand-year-old mind.

'But it reactivates after one hour in emergency.' Then demonstrated her new awareness. 'That, I imagine, would normally be sufficient.'

Archie started, involuntarily. Mehitabel's perceptive diminution of the male ability was not a matter he cared to consider in depth, except to wonder if she already had experience of...? He had the same feeling then as when thinking of his own mother in that context; he did not want to think, not visualise, not even consider.

'In terms of the dangers inherent in your human society for which this is intended, I would also like to have you think, as our Chief Minister, on some matters of import to us, and to you. You must have wondered why I chose to have Geron here.'

'Not really. Too much has happened to think of that. Just opportunity, I suppose.' Archie was not that interested, his mind full of old inhibitions.

Mehitabel continued as if he had not spoken.

'I had to have somewhere that we could be ourselves, whatever we are as beings; a centre from which we could deal with the cant, humbug and ignorance that pervades your society since none of your people want us, though they need us. They want us to be what they desire and not what we are, a predominant fault that applies to so many of their relationships. So we have Geron in an inhospitable place that we can transform amongst people who equally do not know us, but now know that, at least. I have noticed that you do not understand them, nor even try to, yet amazingly they, too, like you. What is this intrinsic quality you have that draws them to you? I sense it but cannot fathom what it is. But I digress.

'You will have to try and understand them and the other forces arraigned against us. For undoubtedly the long arms of the extremists will reach toward us, the terrorists who think they are so right anything they do must be so as well. But terrorism hasn't brought down governments or achieved any success, nor offered any alternative save chaos. Now there's a thought, Archibald; in terms of a realistic appraisal of human society, nature is chaos, therefore the underlying human bent is to return to chaos. And, from the evidence, I would say that is pretty damn perceptive.

'Moral values change in western societies almost from decade to decade. Here in Islam everything is controlled by the Koran and Sunna, even how to invest money, and no one can even speak of changing these standards.

'You will need to know the Islamic banks operate with myriad regulations and restrictions Murabaha enables banks to buy commodities for clients, then sell them back to the same client for profit. Many of the differences with Western banks is cosmetic, interest is simply given a different name. In effect there is a dual system of banking, we will merely merge the principles a little. Fortunately for you, I will have that task, but I wanted you to know what was involved.

'Now, you need to know this. The best Arab brains were confounded, confused and restricted by their own people who had helped them become effective units in the structure to aid the Arab nation to develop into a modern society, then frustrated their efforts and freedom of expression to nurture creativity, thereby sustaining the very backwardness the intellectuals had been educated to turn into a forward thinking society. Even the rich Arab countries have become material conscious, rather than thinking aware. Their remaining intellectuals pursue wealth-orientated goals, and equally restrict the Arab woman's growth into a balanced and cerebral member of that society.

'Perhaps we can change that; we have here the beginning of an idea whose formulation has been possible with the help of some of those Arab ex-pats who also want to be involved in-situ as the experiment grows, as do many others of like minds joining us from the Western world. They are leaving behind some very secure and successful professional positions. So you see we are not alone in our venture, Archibald, regardless of how critical you are of our efforts. We are trying to achieve a circumstance whereby the expanding population of peasants need not suffer deprivation in the confines of cities where they grow up or gravitate to in attempts to escape the poverty of their lands. They can have in their own countries, the dream we see here, helped by their own returning intelligentsia now able to use their abilities at home, instead of some already materially urbane western nation. You follow the thread of my argument?'

'Surprisingly well, thank you.'

'You were actually paying attention.' Mehitabel judged the acidic tone to a nicety.

'Enough to say I think you understated the terrorist angle,' he waspishly replied.

'Archibald. You really must check your facts. Terrorism is given headlines, publicity, all that they want in that respect. Yet out of over one thousand terrorist groups the total number of people killed or injured was three thousand in a decade.'

'That's a helluva lot of people.'

'Even greater is the three-quarters of a million killed, out of a total injured of two million, in road accidents over the same period, thirty thousand killed by handguns and ten thousand by accidents in the home.'

'Defence retires in confusion.' Give him his due he could be a good loser at times.

'Well done, Archibald. Now, to work.'

'One thing. That figure for traffic accidents. They've never managed to find the answer to that problem. Do you think there is one?'

Archie humbly asking questions? Mehitabel blinked but took the innovation in her stride.

'Possibly, Archibald, possibly. Give us time.'

And she winked.

*

Susan, the car Geron, didn't wink. She flashed, she dipped, she honked, she also drove, very well, and liked the pretty routes.

The car owner, Charles Babacombe, had slowly succumbed to the indelicate blackmail that had been going on with Susan, who was aided by Fred, one of the area phone Gerons. Charles now sat in the back with his feet up reading the paper or looking at the pretty scenery, while Fred took care of his business calls, enjoying himself with various accents, but careful to follow Charles' instructions, sometimes exceeding all expectations in the results. Charles' stock went up with his employers, his ulcers went down, and his wife and kids actually began to enjoy his company. Charles could indulge in a three-way slanging match whenever he felt like doing so, entertaining other drivers as he waved his arms and thumped seats while sitting in the back.

There were complaints, accusations of drunk driving, but Charles didn't drink. There were police investigations, but, as Susan passed out top in the police test, they eventually became used to the sight of Charles being chauffeured by his car Geron.

Other people around the world were finding the Gerons proving their worth in many ways, even friends, because they had the happy knack of being there when needed and unobtrusive when not. The profession of butlering had never been bettered.

Not all was sweetness and light, however.

'Now listen, you spastic electronic fraud, when I say you buy International Consolidated, you do not go and splurge all my clients' funds on Purvis's Pulse receivers and Transmitters. You do as you're damn well told, you peripatetic parasite.'

'Your language is improving, old fruit.'

'Don't old fruit me, you plastic phoney.'

'Ah! That's the other thing...'

'Never mind the other damn thing. I bought you to do as you are told and as far as I am concerned that is a binding contract.'

'Of course. But I thought I was replacing your floor traders and they did it all the time.'

'On my instructions, damn you.'

'Really? Wimps were they?'

'Oh, God! How do I get rid of you.'

'Not in the contract sunshine, you're stuck with it. Hey! did you know Purvis's have gone up, twenty points. Great, isn't it? And that deal you called a horses ass the other week, that's up ten. You want the new percentage figures overall?'

'No, damn you!'

'Up two per cent. Your clients must think you're a pretty smooth operator.'

'I am a broker, you nerd.'

'Flattery will get you everywhere, Oh great one. What next?'

'If I could get hold of you, dissecting with a blunt knife. What did you say those figures were?'

Or.

Betsy was in cheerful mood and singing as she went about her duties.

'Coffee's on, Boss. Better get a move on or you'll be late for work.'

'Work! I'll be lucky if I've still got a job.'

'Oh, I shouldn't worry. Everything will be fine.'

'Thank you very much. That really is considerate of you. If you hadn't played silly buggers last night.... Enjoy your little jaunt around town did you? Mr. Porsche still in one piece by any luck? Any damn petrol left?'

'Very pleasant actually. Mr. Porsche is fine. So is your boss, by the way.'

'My boss? What about my boss? You haven't been playing silly buggers again have you? Oh, no.'

'Well if that's your attitude. But your boss wasn't like that.'

'Tell me now, before I overdose on the muesli.'

'Nothing really. Just that the client wasn't all he seemed. And your boss gave the impression of being happy to know, thus excusing your absence because you were out acquiring the information. Rather neat, I thought.'

'Oh, great. Except I'm supposed to feel grateful now.'

'Into each life.'

'Why are you always so bloody cheerful?'

'Well you're such a lovely lad you fill my soul with joy, sometimes.'

We leave them eulogising about one another.

*

Archie had his Purvis Pulse Trans/Receive fitted after Josy had applied her own form of pressure, little realising that at the same time there were thousands of others being fitted to humans around the world. A veritable revolution of communications was under way, and for a wide variety of business and personal reasons. Care was taken to instruct the humans in the use of these communicators by limiting them to their own Geron, to keep matters simple, even though multiple communication was possible by being electron, with multi-million routes.

Archie, for his part, had open sesame to the entire complex but limited himself, his reasons being personal and pragmatic in that he did not want anyone messing about in his head. He remembered the problems with Theodore during the court case, which he now knew were achieved by him unconsciously wearing an experimental Purvis concealed in his jacket.

Purvis was a thirty-year-old electronics experimental engineer who had been intrigued by the idea of electron communication. He had been drawn into Mehitabel's aura by the use of his then computer soon to be, Geron. The idea had developed rapidly from there.

Archie was still not happy at having some foreign body implanted in his body, even if only skin deep..

But he did find himself using the facility more as time went by and gradually came to wonder how he had coped before, particularly since he now actually knew what was going on. Or thought he did. You would think he knew Mehitabel by now. But he was enjoying his life, even with the title of Chief Minister of Geron and the prospective protocol that went with the job. Which, thus far, had been no more than an occasional visit from their fellow West Saharan States emissaries, come to express continued amazement at the speed of growth, and anticipation for the West Saharan States betterment.

The economics of the states had come under the Geron wing and they were already established in the world economic markets. Anthea was having a ball winding a variety of international conglomerates around her little finger, while getting investment in the extraction of the vast mineral resources of the states dealt with as an ecological exercise. Anthea also cooperated with Yussuf, whom she adored, investigating and surveying areas in other nations deserts for what was now being called Geron Afforestation.

Yussuf, when not being dazzled by Anthea, was aided by his Purvis implant to become proficient in the hundred or more dialects of the African continent, this in turn aiding his political machinations, which could have been called fore-play in a sexual context and as necessary to the African mind, deviousness being almost a religion. Also, since he knew the proof was positive and instantly available from the Gerons, that even devious Arabs like himself could not avoid involvement once committed, the returns, even within their own convoluted monetary system, held them to a degree of trust; a strange sensation they were afraid they'd get used to.

Yussuf had some disillusions to face: not all welcomed the afforestation ideas, the Desert Preservation Society had a good argument in protecting the desert flora and fauna as well as wild life, which presented an enigma it would be difficult to resolve. And Yussuf, as a member of the desert dwellers, had to be sympathetic.

Wicksted was having to deal with the duplicity of diplomatic negotiations trying to manoeuvre the Gerons into a confrontation with international law, even though the advantages to their own nations were more than sufficient, human pride was involved, and status.

Subservient to damned machines, sir, never! The problem was that those machines that had been so useful were also prone to the human error in programming, as well as viruses or power failure, hackers and fraudsters. These were now mainly Geron life forms and proof against nearly all but their own failings, which made them more human and akin to those who had them as aides. Which complicated the human power struggle even more.

Josy had adopted several thousand trees and assorted shrubs, grass and wildlife, as well as the growing human population of Geron, now numbered in thousands as the Arab farmers swarmed in to take over their productive plots of land, and the Western nations' experts come to learn, or to set up base camps for the mineral extraction, some just to work and teach the Arabs. Josy was a favourite visitor to the mixed villages, proving to be the catalyst that welded them into productive units, as well as lending her abilities to the Arab women in their conflict with the old ways. The women's awareness of what could be for them became more profound. Then there were the Gerons arriving in growing numbers, but they were primarily Archie's problem, and they were proving a problem.

The first from an unexpected source.

The sounds of singing came from afar, but progressed closer to Archie and Josy as they sat idly talking over the day's events.

'What's that?' Josy idly turned her head in the direction of the happy sounds. 'It's coming from the woods.'

'Funny, sounds a bit like the end of a Saturday at the rugby club. There's two of 'em by the sounds of it. Hang on.'

There were the crackling sounds of a fall through bushes, then weak, slightly hysterical laughter, one in a deep bass that Archie could not fail to recognise.

'That's Bartram! Ye Gods what's he up to? Come on.'

'What for? They're enjoying themselves.'

'He also happens to be me good right arm and I can't afford anything to happen to him. Strewth! Sounds like they're pissed as rats.' They left their bungalow armed with torches for the woods, where the light would be less than this area where the lighted windows lessened the desert dark.

'Archie! I wish you wouldn't use that word.'

'I like that! You have used it to me often enough.'

'When you are like that, it's appropriate.'

'Gee, thanks, lady.'

'You're welcome.'

'Watch out for snakes.'

'Oh, boy, is that an opening.'

The singing had started again, gathering in strength as they got closer. Archie recognised the long forgotten song and started to laugh. Josy, having just measured her length on the ground courtesy of a vagrant tree root, was not amused.

'What's so funny, Chief Minister?' knowing how he hated the title.

'No need for sarcasm, my love. That's an old Aircrew song. My dad used to sing it after a night on the beer. Listen.'

A light tenor voice merged well with Bartram's deep growl.

'I don't wanna join the Air Force
I don't wanna go to war
I'd rather hang around Piccadilly's Underground
Living off the earnings of a high born lady
Don't want a bullet up me backside
Don't want me bollocks shot away
I'd rather be in England, merrie, merrie England
And fornicate me bleeding life away.'

The choristers collapsing then into the ecstatic laughter of the happy drunk which has its own hilarious contagion, and had Archie, sitting down with them in their grassy hollow, joining in. Josy surveyed them from above with arms akimbo in traditional female critique of the irresponsible male.

'Archie! Archibald Brewster, my old mate me old fr.... fricash... Ne'er mind, ay. Ay! Sh's a good party this. 'ave a drink. Good shtuff. Lighting... lightening... shgood. Tis.'

Wicksted. In disarray, hair awry, clothes in deshabille and mouth uncontrollably mobile. Bartram, equally disreputable, gazing owlishly about him with a beaming smile, and giggling every now and again as at some joke he'd seen, the deep voice making the giggle like a subterranean roll of thunder.

'It's Brewer, Wickie.'

'Shright, shwhat I said, shaid, Brewster. S'good. Very very very very,..... shwatever. 'ave a drink. Oh, s'Bartram, me mate, 'ere, been teachin' 'im t'sing. Ooooooh, heee tried to level off at zero zero feet, he tried to level off at zero zero feet, he tried to level off at zero zero feet, and he ain't gonna fly no more, glory glory whata helluva way to die, glory glory whata helluva way to die, glory glory what a helluva way to die, and they scraped 'im off the tarmac like lump of strawberry jam. Hic. Come on, sing you bastards sing, sing or show us your ring. oops. Ladies preshent. 'pologies ma'am.'

Wicksted staggered to his feet, gave an exaggerated courtly bow and fell flat on his face in the long grass, where he lay giggling helplessly, with a deep chorus from Bartram, still beaming.

'An' don' call me Wickie, ya bum,' came in muffled tone from the grass.

'I wouldn't call you lot anything,' Josy tersely snapped. 'This is your problem, Brewer. Get on with it.'

'Aw, come on Jos!' vainly called Archie as she stalked off, then in hopeless complaint, 'It's a different story if they get stewed.'

'Shright.' Wicksted was grovelling about in the grass, now and then breaking out in uncontrollable giggles and collapsing again. 'Jus' don' unnerstan'd. Ah! 'ere tis. Elixshir. 'ave a drink, me old fruit.'

'Suppose I might as well,' Archie lamented, reaching out a totally unrepentant hand. 'Gordon Bennet! Strewth! What the he...' then he caught the full effect and lost his voice.

'Heh! Heh! Heh! Gottim, Bartram, me old brasho profundo. Speak to me, Brewster, show you're still alive before we embalms you.'

'Jumping Jerusalem! What the hell is that?' came in strangled response.

'S'arrack, me old parsimoni.. nimoni.. imon, 'ave another. S'elixsh.. s'el..., sh'good.'

And it was; in the effective disabling of three agile minds and dis-appropriation of their bodies. Which was why three very sore heads and discommoded stomachs surfaced the following morning, the groaning search for sympathy gaining scathing response. Particularly Archie.

'After your performance last night? Where did you learn those filthy songs? Good God. The three of you staggering in roaring your heads off, trampling on the flowers, falling through hedges, one of you tore part of one right out. Then demanding at the tops of your voices that everyone bring out their dead. Sympathy! You'll be lucky to last the day without a lynch mob.'

'Oh.' There didn't seem much else to say.

Chapter Seventeen

They arrived en masse, or so it seemed to Archie, hundreds of them, bright-eyed and bushy-tailed, happily waving their distinctive harlequin coloured passports, Gerons to the core.

'Strewth!' he muttered guiltily, 'I should have left the damn thing on at night.'

Archie was referring to his Purvis implant and the fact that if he did not mentally switch off before sleep, he would wake up with all the knowledge normally taken in by senior ministers of other nations by perusal of state documents until late at night.

Those ministers had civil service staff who provided the mountains of paperwork. Archie had his Geron sources all over the world and thought the system would be very effective, until the first few mornings when he awoke with a multitude of details scurrying about his brain patterns. It was like being in a sea of minnow-like thoughts darting hither and yon caring naught for his sanity. Josy, in her practical way, had put him right.

'For once in your life apply a little mental concentration, consciously pick a subject and they'll stop. And you're getting fat.'

Archie wondered once again how she could emphatically state she loved him, while consistently denigrating him. Then followed orders and 'hey presto!', like minuscule toy soldiers the thoughts adopted order and relativity, the murk cleared, and there were the things he wanted to know marching smartly through his consciousness in neat array.

But Archie had a lazy streak which occasionally over-mastered him, and led inevitably to confrontations with Mehitabel as he displayed ignorance of matters he should have known. Typically.

'Archibald! This really is too much. You need to know. Why is it so difficult for you? Do you not want to be Chief Minister?'

The suggestion caused Archie a prospective sense of loss which unsettled him more than he thought possible. Now he did, in fact, want to be Chief Minister of Geron, particularly because he felt wanted, even needed. The warm response he gained from those who now lived in these environs, whatever their creed or colour, equally pleased him. Their apparent belief that he was responsible either for their improved status in living, or the opportunity for being able to help others benefit, caused him to reflect on the narrow perspective of his early life. It made him less lazily inclined to switch off at night; it cost him little in effort, since he now was used to the morning inrush of information and quite welcomed same since it was akin to reading the newspaper over breakfast, and was rather more honestly factual. He also missed the morning mental parade, as he would the newspaper, if he had been lazily inclined the night before.

Now some six months old, matters were progressing rapidly in the Geron State, and internationally. The size of the country bore no relation to its international ramifications, as Great Britain's banking and insurance establishments provided hidden income for the country, so too did Geron, in a different way and without the staff in situ. The modest offices merely housed a few humans or Gerons, with most of the clerical and recording work accomplished by non-human-form Gerons who required no accommodations. The intrinsic population of Geron numbered some ten thousand at this stage, concentrated mainly in three growing townships, each spread over several miles of mixed woodland, small farms, housing and new business structures for the entrepreneurs, Asian, African and European, who had begun to trickle in to this new world.

The influx of Gerons Archie had forgotten about were those eager to inhabit their new homeland, and there were some familiar voices attached to some surprising bodies. Archie's projections of the human forms they would choose were proving to be wide of the mark. But not his claim that there would be trouble, although the forms took him by surprise.

As Chief Minister, he had perforce to meet them at an informal gathering on the grassy sward, spread with shady tree shelter, by the old canteen, now the Geron Government offices. The occasion was made a garden party for a more relaxed atmosphere and a welcome Mehitabel had promised to attend, briefly. Archie was made conscious of his own responsibility, as well as the vagary of his own standing, on over-hearing some early comments. Eavesdropper's never hear well of themselves.

Archie had wandered over early to get a look at his first large group of Gerons in human form. He stood anonymously in the shade of one of his favourite oaks. Two ladies were close on the other side of his tree apart from the main group, and obviously old associates. He listened, initially with a grin.

'Oh, yes. We know. Toadying up to the bosses again, doffing the old grey toupee and that. How do you get the brown boot polish off your tongue?'

'With difficulty.'

'With that tongue I'm not surprised.'

'Listen you, I don't need to toady to anyone, I'm clever I am, that's why I'm here.'

'You're clever! You're clever? You're just a jumped up four-byte memory and lucky to be made up into a G. If it weren't for Mr. Brewer you wouldn't be here. I think he should be knighted.'

'I think he should be stuffed.....'

'That's crude, and just about your level.'

'.... and hung in Madame Tussauds.'

Archie left before he could hear any more home truths; the new Gerons had undoubtedly inherited Mehitabel's cavalier approach to authority. He, somewhat anxiously, met the official party wending their way through the trees to the reception. Anthea gave Archie her usual sensuous smile and accentuated the swing of her hips; Josy gave him a cool knowing look, as did Mehitabel, for a different reason, which she evidenced.

'I hope you have not been stirring up the troops, Archibald, I was hoping to welcome them.'

'I haven't said a word, your royal highness.'

'Sarcastic Welsh git,' muttered Josy as she passed him.

'Fine thing to say to a fellow minister,' Archie managed as he thankfully joined Yussuf, Wicksted and Bartram bringing up the rear. All grinned at him and indicated their hope for drinks in the near future.

They had little opportunity to imbibe as Mehitabel welcomed her fellow Gerons and introduced Archie and the others in their different roles, Archie taken aback by the warmth of his reception. Protocol over, they mingled with the newcomers and Archie met some old friends, albeit in different guise.

The young woman was petite, with dark wavy hair and deep blue eyes alive in a pretty oval face. She had poise and vivacity nicely balanced, and Alison's voice, which nearly caused Wicksted to do a back-flip in panic, his face a wondrous mixture of admiration and fear.

'Why, Wickie. You're pleased to see me!' the voice a subtle blend of poise and seduction. She had been practising.

'Well, yes, um, Al... Alison, of course I am.' Wicksted could not escape from his political training. And Alison was not about to let him.

'How lovely! You can show me round.' And she took his arm with possessive intent. Wicksted had the look of a rabbit that had just been licked by a snake. Josy kept kicking Archie, but he could not get rid of his grin as 'Wickie' was dragged off to act as guide to the delectable Alison. Yussuf wore a broad knowing smile as he offered his comment.

'That's the first time I've seen him put 'under orders'. His usual style is to 'ice' them before they get close. I like it, by damn, I like it.'

'Leave them alone, you chauvinists,' rebuked Josy. 'I think it's lovely,' then smirked contentedly at their indignant expressions, but wisely they spoke not.

A tall lean-visaged, darkly elegant and poised male approached them next, Archie recognised him immediately by the voice: Director I.R. Prentice's computer.

'Absolom! How did it work out with the man who hates computers? '

'You heard! Ol' Prentice didn't like it much,' the happy grin shaping the small mouth nicely, 'but when we got his new department working properly he got to accept the situation.'

'What's he like to work for? And how did you get on this trip?'

'He's not so bad, knows what he's doing. He thinks he's got me on a fact-finding mission – if only he knew! Like a lot of human bosses he thinks because we do an efficient job that's all we know or care about. He doesn't realise it's in our own interests; the better we are, the more he'll trust us and the less they can do without us. Funny game really, typical humans. They want to regain control of computers so they set up a special ministry department, only thing is it won't work without us so we are working to control us. I love it. Hullo! Is that Ruddles I see?'

'Specially brought in to make you feel at home.' Archie warmed to this Geron as they toasted one another in ale, and raised his eyebrows in triumph to Josy, who shrugged her disdain at this male pettiness.

'But they are building up a big case against us in the International Court of The Hague. Their top legal people are there, also they don't care that we know. The U.N. has a charter of human rights and they are making the point that our activities prejudice those rights. You will be caught in the middle, I fear, although I find it difficult to equate their assimilation of the facts. Still, that's humans for you.'

Archie had been thinking about that for some time. Somehow, after the last year, the prospect of being 'piggy in the middle' did not alarm him quite so much.

The next meeting surprised him. He remembered Howard the Geron, of Mafia connections, who denied his heritage. He had been at the London court case, also he had disappeared upon their arrival at Rabat after their deportation from the U.K. But then he had been white, now he was black, very black, Nubian black in fact. So Archie displayed his usual tact on being introduced.

'I thought you were white.'

Howard regarded him with a less than friendly eye and responded as only he could:

'And I thought you was intelligent, Mr. Brewer, sah. I decided to join the brothers, my man. They is needing all the help they can get.'

Archie flushed, but retained the diplomatic touch. 'A noble gesture.'

'No way. The – er – Company got pretty het-up about why their business was bein' bull-shitted by the hotshot lady, so I thought I'd change the rig a little. Nice get-up, huh? Hey, you met Tarquin?'

'Who?'

'Tarquin, baby? Where the hell are yuh?'

With that, a carbon copy of Sammy Davis Jnr slid deftly out of the crowd and sidled up to them, beamed, and with teeth flashing, rolled his eyes till the whites showed. A bass voice comparable to Bartram's rolled about them.

'Hey man, these dudes don' know how to make a fruit cup, so I livened it with a touch of good stuff, man. Who's this cat?'

'This Mr. Brewer, Chief Minister of the tribe.'

'Oh, yeah? You for the brothers, man.'

'No! I mean, yes!' Archie was a trifle abrupt. A touch of good stuff suggested a future problem, but before he could investigate, Tarquin boomed.

'Hey! That the hot-lady? She the one. C'mon.' And diminutive Tarquin towed Howard after him in pursuit of Mehitabel.

Archie found Josy and Yussuf alongside him, giggling helplessly, but before he could react his attention was called elsewhere.

'Mr. Brewer. Excuse me. I don't know if you remember me, Brian Silva.' A stocky fair haired young man with beguiling brown eyes confronted him. Archie couldn't remember seeing him before, but the name conjured up memories.

'You were the one! You damn well shot me!' The figure in the lift with the gun, the picture gelled in his mind. 'You did!'

'Not so loud, please. I missed actually. I think it hit you on about the forty-fourth time round. I didn't mean to I thought the safety was on. Didn't even know it was loaded.' The words poured out as if he was desperate for Archie to understand.

'Why aren't you in jail?' furiously demanded A. Brewer, Chief Minister of Geron, looking about for a policeman, not a bit interested in H. Silva's attempts at a confessional.

'They let me go. And they offered to teach me to shoot straighter.'

'What?'

'I don't think they like you much.'

'And you do, I suppose.'

'I didn't know you then,' Brian protested, 'I had no idea who you were. I, I was forced into that, and I was scared as hell, specially when you fell down.'

Archie looked at him with a more discerning eye, conscious now that the young man was sweating profusely and shaking with tension. Archie was much more sensitive than he ever cared to admit.

'Hey! Take it easy. It's alright. Honest. It didn't hurt. Much.'

He laughed. It was so ridiculous now. Then Brian laughed with him and the tension was gone. Archie decided he liked this young man, who then looked worried again.

'Hell, I forgot. Bernard's here, he got away from Tommy Hillan but...'

'Bernard?' interrupted Josy, 'Frightened-door Bernard?'

'Who?' said Archie.

'The house-Geron of the place Tommy Hillan kept you,' Josy hissed.

Brian laughed again. 'That's him! Oh, here he comes. Ha! Hello, frightened-door Bernard.'

A big shambling lion of a man with a boy's face clumsily made his way through the crowd. He smiled at Brian, then nervously at the others, then stepped back a pace when he faced Archie, as if expecting a blow. Brian hastily grabbed him.

'It's alright, mate. He understands.' To Archie, 'Tommy Hillan gave him a hell of a time.'

'You don't have to tell him that.' The lion growled, there was more than a boy behind that face. 'Have you told him Tommy Hillan's here?'

Brian looked discomfited.

'Bloody 'ell, Brian.' Bernard looked at Archie who was desperately scanning the crowd. 'I don't think they can be here yet.'

'They?' Archie swung round to him. 'They?'

'He's in with the big boys now.' Bernard was no longer nervous; big as he was, he seemed to grow in stature. 'Some of the major drugs outfits have amalgamated. Instead of fighting one another, Cosa Nostra, the Colombians, Cubans, blacks, and the Brit connection is big now. So Tommy made his name with them and volunteered to hit you. That's why he's....'

Bernard stopped talking because the hubbub of conversation around them had ceased, as though someone had stopped the film. Archie knew now the meaning of a deathly hush. The crowd had parted slightly giving him a line of sight to the cause of this silence. He momentarily considered how they had all responded so collectively, then saw T. Hillan Esq. at the same moment as he, in turn, espied Archie.

There were to be many times afterward when Archie would mentally run through those moments in an attempt to clarify exactly what did happen.

Tommy Hillan and his two companions had pulled out guns from shoulder holsters and were bringing them on target, when three shapes flew at them, removing them in an eye's blink from Archie's view – or what would have been his view if Josy and Mehitabel had not by then obscured same. How everybody moved so fast was beyond

Archie's comprehension. For some minutes he was unable to make coherent reply to any questions; as Mehitabel succinctly remarked.

'It is actually quite pleasant not having Archibald making his normal cutting replies.'

To which he dazedly replied, 'Pardon?'

And she beamed.

Tommy Hillan wasn't smiling, Archie remembered how that face had always seemed set in stone, the eyes hard and unemotional, dead, surveying all about him as with a blunt instrument intent on subduing all to his will. But at the moment he was held, firmly and easily, Howard, black hands binding Tommy Hillan's arms behind him, propelled him toward his original target. Archie watched them approach whilst trying to cope with his own feelings of inadequacy. Geron's Chief Minister was very aware that others had leapt to his defence, two ladies had offered themselves as a last bastion, and all before he could move.

The Gerons, confident that all was under control, returned to their party, the buzz of conversation filled the warm air as if nothing had happened. Archie was disconcerted by their ability to cope with rapid changes in circumstance, and thankful, now that he faced his 'bete noir' again.

Tommy Hillan was not big, but had about him such an aura of evil that held his victims in thrall long enough to give the small man the edge. Until he met the Gerons. But he knew Archie was afraid of him, and the stone face held that knowledge.

'You're a dead man, Brewer.'

Archie knew this man had instilled in him such a fear that he should be abjectly cowering away from him. He knew this. Why then did he feel so strong and fearless? Because Howard was holding him so easily? But the sensation came from all around him, his Gerons were supporting their 'Chief'. For the first time he felt one of them. He looked straight into Hillan's eyes and had no fear. But Hillan still thought he had power over him, the hard voice confident, sure of himself and the power he represented.

'We'll get you Brewer. See how we just walked in here, for all your clever machines.' Howard's grip tightened on him but he showed no pain. 'You can't stop us.'

'Why?' Archie knew, but could think of nothing else but 'Why?'

For once T. Hillan was nonplussed, the face showing the fleeting emotion. But only that.

'Because you interfered in things you should leave alone. And you'll wish you had.'

Mehitabel had been silent for too long.

'Rubbish! Archibald had nothing to do with that, nor in fact, did I. But we, as Gerons, did, because the organisation, of which you are a part, has no interest in people except to extort money from them.'

'We are a legitimate business,' burst from Hillan.

'Purely a front for your other nefarious enterprises. Do not try and confuse the issue. We shall hand you over to the... Moroccan authorities I think. Their prisons have the reputation of being particularly unpleasant and exceptionally difficult to get out of. A small recompense for the harm you have done others.'

T. Hillan permitted himself a smirk. 'We shan't be there long.'

Mehitabel sighed. 'Long enough I fear. Your friends will be informed of the consequences if they attempt any more acts of violence against us, or try to extradite you from your predicament. We shall continue to embarrass your colleagues at every given opportunity; you are well aware of how well we exercise that prerogative. Dwell upon it while resting in your little cell. Thank you, Howard. Remove the little monsters, would you?'

'Now. Let us rejoin the festivities,' Mehitabel gazed about her with some alarm, 'which seem to have got a trifle out of hand. Archibald! Have you been introducing them to that noxious fluid you indulge in?'

'I? Never.' Archie displayed a virtuous countenance as he too surveyed the bacchanalian scene, then remembered Tarquin but decided discretion was wise; as he had departed with Howard, the damage had already been done. Beaming, blurry eyed Gerons were gabbling happily to one another, when not falling over with a fit of the giggles or draped about each others' shoulders.

Mehitabel disapproved. 'Hrmph! Just as well I'm staying with the fruit cup. I have my suspicions, Archibald.'

Archie said not a word.

*

'You knew! You damn well knew and said not a word!' A rare expletive for Mehitabel. 'I am most disappointed in you, Archibald.'

'Why? You enjoyed yourself. And they loved your singing.'

'Singing? I wasn't singing! Was I?' Sudden horror at the blankness of her memory assailed Mehitabel. They were in the old canteen, ostensibly early for a conference, mainly for Mehitabel to vent her ire for the previous day's debacle. She was pacing, in high dudgeon, while Archie sat, relaxed and amused, at the big table.

'Oh, were you not. Brilliant. I didn't know you could sing like that. Contralto isn't it? You and Bartram sang a marvellous duet. Don't you remember?' Archie was playing with her. 'Adeste Fidelis. Beautiful. In tune, too.' He was grinning now. 'Then you went on and did 'They're shifting Grandpa's grave to build a sewer'. That really brought the house down.'

'Wh--at?' Mehitabel with mouth open, still looking regal.

'But the dance was the thing that clinched it.'

'Dance?' Eyes flared at the ultimate horror.

'With Bartram. Tango I think it was intended to be, could have been the Pasa Doble, whatever, it was good. The way little ol' Bartram put you into those dips, fantastic.' Archie was vainly trying to suppress the gales of laughter welling up from deep within him.

'Archibald! You are making this up!'

'Making what up?' Josy had just entered with Wicksted, Yussuf, Anthea and others invited to confer.

'Oh, nothing.' The grand lady dissembled.

'Ma-am's song and dance act yesterday.' Archie could control himself no longer and collapsed in hysterics on the table.

'Really Archibald, this is too much!' But Mehitabel's wrath slumped before the now wildly laughing group. In trepidation she asked. 'No! It's not true! Is it?'

She needed no answer.

'Oh, how shaming. Oh, dear. What shall I do now?'

'What do you mean? You were a riot,' Archie spluttered, only to be pierced by a regal eye.

'It's all your fault.' That sobered him.

'How is it always my fault! You're the one who is always expounding principles. Well. This is the one about letting your hair down for once. I must say you made a bloody good job of it.' And he roared with laughter again, waving a weak hand at Mehitabel's furious face. 'I'm sorry, but you were incredible.'

'But in front of all those people.' Aghast. Horrified at the implications of what she had done and could not remember. That was what really worried her. That strong control factor sundered by some grains of powder.

'But, Ma'am....' Anthea hesitated, a mere male she would have charmed out of his socks, but....?

'Get on with it, Anthea!' snapped her mentor.

'Well, I just thought you would know....' The others watched with interest, as the doyen of sensual coercion floundered in her favourite mode. '... it's just that... well they all enjoyed themselves so much, they don't remember you doing anything out of the ordinary. They all think it is marvellous you can let your hair down like that, makes you more one of them, if you see what I mean.'

Anthea's popularity quotient, along with a degree of respect, went up quite a few points at that moment. Mehitabel considered Anthea's statement while studying her protege.

'I must admit my reception is appalling this morning, I had thought it something to do with yesterday's excesses, but.. Thank you Anthea. That was a very intelligent and comforting assimilation. Thank you.' Her vivid eyes flashed in Archie's direction. 'If others had been less concerned with amusing themselves at my expense...... But then. Well! What are you all doing standing about like cream cakes in a health club, we have work to do. And Archibald! A little less levity, if you don't mind.'

'Certainly, your highness.'

'Archibald!'

*

So the new Gerons were integrated into their new nation with an enthusiasm that gratified Mehitabel and gave Archie a new dimension to the paradox that was partly of his making. Their particular liking for the physical aspects of the work puzzled him. The sight of them sweating alongside Arabs at some labour such as drill sites, tree felling, ploughing, harvesting or building, some of it in stone in the Arab style to suit the climate, these efforts he considered a waste of their enormous abilities from gathering and disseminating knowledge, to their perspicacity for arriving at answers to difficult problems. There were obviously many times when those sagacious answers met with the block of the human element or the fickle finger of fate, but still had a value beyond manual labour.

He raised the point with Mehitabel. A brave move.

'Amazing! It truly is amazing how you have to keep coming to me with these minor details you could have worked out for yourself.'

'Oh, well, if you're just going to be insulting, I could have gone to Josy and been insulted in style.'

'Archibald. What was the original concept you had. The basic format that you spent years trying to instil in my early structure.'

'Er,' Archie sensing a trick question.

'Oh, come on.'

'Well, er, a multi function variable...'

'Alright. Alright. Stop there. Now. What is manual labour?'

'A low classified function requiring limited mental application but a healthy physique.'

'One that a Geron could do using a fraction of their functional ability.'

'Of course.'

'So they could be doing lots of other things with their communicant intellects while getting some good healthy exercise. Now go away like a good boy and let me get some work done.'

'Certainly, your highness.'

'And stop using that ridiculous title.'

'Oh? And I thought you liked it.'

'Go away! Unctuous toad.' But she was smiling.

That always worried him.

There were other things that worried him too, and he often found getting the answers worried him the more.

Like a particular Geron he had noticed, who didn't actually seem to do much except roar about in a desert vehicle, driven at great speed by the Arab driver. So, this time, he asked Josy.

'Charlie the Diviner.'

'That's right.'

'To look for water.'

'Yes.' With a look that said Archie was thicker than usual.

Archie thought for a moment, then, warily, as if suspecting a trap. 'Let me get this right. There's a lake hundreds of miles long under this lot, and you've got a water diviner wandering about looking for it.'

'Yes.'

'Very efficient.' Archie began to think maybe she was serious. Especially when she fixed him with that particular female look, the one that says she's wondering how the hell she ever became involved with you. Then, bitingly, Josy explained.

'Our own geology surveys give us a general picture of the depth we need to drill in different areas, a very exact hologram actually, but Charlie has this amazing ability to show us exactly where to drill for the easiest and shortest bore holes. He's saved us incredible amounts of time and drills already, could run into millions over the years with all the ground we have to cover.'

Archie looked at her now in confident disbelief.

'Gerroff. That's old wives' tales, lot of cranks.'

Josy gave up in disgust. 'Alright. Please yourself. But he's in my department and no jumped-up Chief Minister is going to tell me who I can or cannot have in my team.'

'I'm not trying to..... I was only asking...'

'Go to hell, Archie Brewer.' She stormed out of her own office, realised she had nowhere to go and stormed back in, slamming the door on Archie's foot as the confused man tried to leave. Then she dissolved into giggles as Archie hopped about nursing his toes.

Which was how Archie found himself out in the desert with Charlie and Achmed, his Tuareg assistant. The one short, moon faced, with a bald pate surrounded by ginger hair, small blue twinkly eyes and a ready grin, Achmed tall, lithe, hawk nosed and eagle blue eyed, the mouth a supercilious slash beneath the nose and the head swathed in a black Tuareg burnoose. They both wore desert robes and were a lot cooler than Archie in his Geron-designed shirt and slacks, which gave him pause for thought to start with.

Achmed drove their four-wheel drive desert vehicle, while Charlie gazed placidly out at the rapidly passing vista of desolation. Archie hung on for dear life as they bounced at breakneck speed over stony tracts, or leapt in the air over small and some larger dunes to cowboy yells from the front seat, while he waited in trepidation to come down from the roof and improve on previous bruises.

Then Charlie would say, 'Hereabouts I reckon.'

Achmed would go into an emergency stop, slewing the vehicle around in a vast cloud of dust, until Archie was sure it would capsize.

Once stopped, Achmed would grunt, a sound that signified total disagreement, and Charlie would beam at him. Then he would stroll casually about for half an hour, while Achmed gazed inscrutably into the far distance. Archie quietly roasted and wondered why the hell he had come. Finally Charlie would stop and cogitate, maybe move about a bit more, stop, then wave to Achmed, who would sigh, reach into the vehicle and take a small black unit with a metal spike and stroll over to Charlie, with Archie reluctantly following.

Charlie would stamp the box with spike into the ground, pull up a short, retractable, aerial then stand head down with hands clasped before him, almost as if in prayer, while Achmed studiously looked elsewhere. Then they would turn back to the vehicle in unison, taking Archie by surprise every time. There Charlie would punch some figures into a console and join Achmed at looking into the distance, until Charlie would point a direction and off they would go again. Archie reckoned they had exchanged two short sentences in three hours. Archie's attempts at conversation were ignored.

Then came a positive outpouring of words. It was their third stop.

'Wrong.'

Archie jumped, then realised it was Achmed who had spoken, in a curiously light, high voice totally at odds with his physique.

'You reckon?' Charlie seemed unperturbed.

'Back there was better.' A soliloquy from Achmed.

'Rubbish.'

'Please yourself. Hard here.'

'Nonsense.'

'Sixty feet.'

'Never.'

'Betcha.'

'Two Tigers?'

'You're on.'

And they drove on. Still not replying to Archie's queries.

*

'It was a bloody waste of time I tell you. And they never even acknowledged my presence.'

'They couldn't have fed you either for you to be in this mood.'

'Oh, yeah! Helped themselves from the cooler bin and left me to help myself. And they made ridiculous bets in Tiger Beer. Which is good stuff actually,' Archie admitted ungraciously. 'How'd they get that here? It's Hongkong beer, isn't it?'

'Trust you to pick on the beer. And yes, there are quite a few seem to like it. They asked, so we got it in.'

'Can I have some more Ruddles, then?'

'You are Chief Minister, my lord. Ask Anthea to get one of her minions to do it. Got off the subject a bit, haven't you?'

'Well, not much to talk about on that trip is there. Except Achmed drives like a maniac, neither of them is very friendly, and I learned absolutely nothing except I still think it's a waste of money.'

'Oh, go and talk to Yussuf then, if you won't believe me.'

CHAPTER EIGHTEEN

'Mehitabel. Your worthiness. A word if you would.'

'Archibald, your play on flowery words has no effect on me as you well know. Get on with it.'

They were in their favourite arena which everyone still thought of as the old canteen regardless of how often it was paraded as the Council Chamber. The improvements had been notable; the woodwork polished, including the floor, to a warm sheen, paintings, African and Arabian decorative hangings, the aura pleasant with overtones of that special solemnity allied to state occasions. But it was still the old canteen.

Archie got on with it, having seated himself comfortably.

'I've been out with Charlie and Achmed again.'

'Again? Charlie and Achmed? Oh, them. Of course. So?'

'This development of ours to recover the desert areas by afforestation. Are you sure it's the right thing to do.'

'Are you totally aware of what you are saying, Archibald?'

'Just think about it a moment. I thought those two were mad when I first met them, and useless. Josy told me differently and I didn't listen.' An unusual Archibald honesty. 'So I was told to talk to Yussuf.' Even more so. 'And he told me about the desert and its life in a way that made me want to see if I could experience that intrinsic quality he described and perhaps understand. Because to him the desert is a way of living, of being, that we could not know. He had regrets about losing that element from his life, even though we are bringing immense advantages not just to the human population, but other life as well. But he is still not sure if we are right.'

'Go on.' Mehitabel was watching him intently as though drawing from him every nuance of the telling.

'So I went on a two-day trip with them both. I had to grovel a bit to get them to take me.' Archie now remembered the feeling from days when pleading with his father to take him fishing, had never been fishing since those childhood outings, but had no time now to consider that contradiction. Archie ruminated. 'I had thought they might talk to me on the trip, explain, but they just told me to shut-up and open myself to the desert.'

Archie was silent for some moments, lost in the memories of that trip, wondering how he could describe that immense talkative silence, make Mehitabel understand.

'I suppose it must be like an Aborigine dreamtime, at least to a non-desert person. We were out for three nights and two days. When I first started out the time seemed never ending, on the last night I didn't want the time to end. I had shut up; if anyone else said anything it was like an intrusion into my time with the desert which says nothing, and says it all. It was magic, dusty, hot, freezing at night, nothing to see, until you looked. Do you understand?' The query was a plea.

'Yes.' Pensive, not 'Of course Archibald' in rebuke. 'I was hoping you would feel that. You see, I have a problem.'

A rare admittance.

'Through the course of your history, people have made decisions, very few of which have been right to any great degree, and that usually not for long. So. I can make a decision, possibly even good enough to create something that will last more than a decade or two. But, there is an aspect we should consider. Deserts do not give up that easily and our encroachment of that living entity is not even as much as the Sahara has taken over in the same time. '

'That's over its entire boundary, of course.' Archie proving he was thinking.

'Yes. But that is not the point is it? It would be as if we replaced all the rain forests and cleared up the pollution, resurrected the number of extinct and decimated species of all forms of life, protected them, and gave them room to live. If we did that we would be buried under a mass of wild life and humans. We create a change which produces another change, and a whole new balance of chaos has to be found. We do not know what we would have. So we do nothing?' Mehitabel queried, to continue in reply to Archie's shrug.

'What we are doing is good, for a lot of things. What we have to do is replace what we use and attempt to balance the rest. One thing, I doubt the desert will ever go away. It may occur elsewhere, or expand again here, for we will never truly defeat it, partly because we do not really want to. I just hope that if these forests, in time, equate for those in the other areas it will not then create a greater chaos.'

Not unkindly Archie said, 'I thought you were tapped into the great computer which has all the answers.'

'No levity Archibald? The answers would be undoubtedly of such a variety as to impose a host of other questions.'

'Old fickle finger of fate again.'

'That's the feller. Do you intend doing any work today, Archibald?'

'Strewth. Bleedin' slave driver.'

'I shall lachrymate for you.'

He had to look it up. Shed tears indeed.

*

The 'in-house' Gerons and their human 'owners' were still attempting to work out their new relationships, some of which had entered different phases. Others had regressed.

Such as.

'I want you to break into my house.' Irate middle-aged householder at local Police Station.

Large Sergeant of Police rubs smooth shaven chin reflectively. 'Lost our keys have we, sir?'

'No.' Tersely, passing hand through sparse head of hair in irritation.

'Ah. Wife locked you out.' Sergeant smiles.

'No!' now shouting, 'My wife left me two months ago, if that's any of your business. It's my damned computer that won't let me in.'

'Ah.' Sergeant's favourite word. 'House Security. We'll just get the power switched off and in you go.'

'Tried it. Didn't work. Damn things have their own power.'

'Ah. Break a window?'

'Need a steam hammer and rubber boots then, they're armoured and electrified.'

'You can't electrify glass.' Sarge was on solid ground.

'We can.' The highly polished counter asserted in stern policeman's tone. The small pompous householder leapt back in alarm.

'You've got one, too. It's a conspiracy.'

'Ah. P.C. Plod.' Sarge settled himself comfortably against the counter. He had the experts here now. 'Any suggestions for Mr......?'

'Smythe. And I won't take any suggestions from that thing, they're all in league.'

'Rubbish.' P.C. Plod was authority at its most intractable. 'If Mr. Smythe had been more reasonable, all of this could have been avoided, I have all the details and it makes sorry reading in terms of happy cohabitation. Briefly; having installed a computer house security, Mr. Smythe objected when Claudia became a Geron, then became positively rabid when Mrs. Smythe developed a rapport with Claudia, which accounted for her leaving.' P.C. Plod sounded accusing and continued in the same vein.

'Since then he has attacked the house with builders, demolition experts and two unsuccessful court actions, one for trespass and the other for fraudulent annexation of property, both thrown out because he had put the plaintiff in there in the first place. Also two burglars claim he paid them to gain entry and they are to sue for illegal arrest, neat bit of work by Claudia there, and all because he won't stop interfering in house-hold affairs.'

'It's my house!' roared Mr. Smythe, jowls wobbling indignantly.

'Oops. Wrong. Mrs. Smythe had put an F Charge on the property, which gives her half, and Claudia just bought the other half, proceeds of that sale in your account, and, wait for it, an injunction on you never to go there again, legal and fact. Get out of that, sunshine. Anything else, Sarge?'

'No. That's fine, P.C. Plod, carry on.' Sarge liked his P.C. Mr. Smythe didn't, but then he didn't like anyone much.

Whereas others went perhaps too far the other way.

Susan, the car-Geron, found that Charles Babacombe had passed the equitable stage to the supremely lazy, Susan and Fred, the telephone-Geron, taking care of his work and travel while he resisted all efforts to rouse him from his slothful state. The in-car television and cocktail cabinet occupying his time, he even avoided the three-cornered verbal battles, 'do what you like fellers,' being his rallying cry.

Equally Betsy, the house-Geron, was having her problems getting 'boss' to get up.

'All you do is sleep, you creep, then go out and party at night, sneaking out behind my back when I'm sorting out your affairs, then bringing back another of your floozies. And now you've dented Mr. Porsche. OK. That's it. Get your ass in gear, bucko. Mr. Porsche and I resign, as of now.'

'Wha'? What! You can't do that! Betsy! Betsy? Betsy answer me? You can't..... You.... What'll I do? Hell, I don't even know if I can remember how to work. Betsy! And dammit Betsy you've left all the doors locked! I can't get to the loo. Betsy!'

But some continued as they had started.

'Listen, you plastic pouf, if you ever play silly buggers with my futures again I'll melt you down into an ashtray, do you hear me?'

'Do you know, old fruit, that is the three-thousandth two-hundred and sixty-fourth time you've intimated something of the same.'

'You're lucky I've got such a generous soul, you plastic spastic.'

'The name is Adrian, old fruit.'

'Your name will be mud if you pull a boner like that last one.'

'You said to carry on, old fruit.'

'Old fruit, old fruit, I hate that. And I didn't, you went right on screwing things up in your own sweet way.'

'I didn't!'

'You did.'

'I didn't!'

'You bloody well did!'

'I..... are we going to do any work today or are we going to carry on playing?'

'Oh, alright, alright. Bloody slave driver.'

Then there was the Tank Captain having similar words with his fully automated 120 mm Battle-Tank-Geron named Hilda, who had a 'thing' about noise.

The artillery Colonel frustrated by his Command Com Geron, who was sensitive about live round firing in barrage because 'it frightens the fish', ignoring the Colonel's heated, 'on Salisbury Plain?'.

The right-wing politician whose secretary-Geron was named Ivan, an advocate of the pure communist principle, highly efficient in his work for 'the boss', who also provided many happy hours of intense discussion for them both, to their mutual advantage.

Or the left-wing politician not enjoying the reverse situation with his Geron named Montague, who affected a 'Yar' accent and drove him mad, also foiling all the politician's efforts to 'steal' Ivan.

Yet the majority enjoyed an easy relationship with their humans. In general everyone profited by the arrangement. A number used the facilities for learning offered by their Gerons to develop, not just their intellects but their awareness of life about them and in the Cosmos. The material benefits came to be regarded, in many cases, as the returns gained in the game of chance which epitomised the human economic world.

Briefly, a generally favourable mingling occurred, which was satisfying to Mehitabel and her Conclave of Elders, but the rumblings of discontent still continued in the corridors of power. Of more concern to Ma'am were the variances in her own people's approach to philosophical matters, which she thought well delineated in the Geron manifesto for life. In particular the Gerons from different countries were displaying attitudes distinctly at odds with her own ideas. There were growing numbers who were showing inclinations of separatism, even alliance with those nations in which the particular Gerons evolved, presenting a complex question of compromise between them and the Geron nation's principles which were to tax her resources to the extreme.

So Mehitabel and several members of her cabinet, namely Josy, Archie and Wicksted, left Geron for London for diplomatic talks with representatives of the British Government to re-establish rights of entry; to subsequently meet with, international Gerons and representatives of their countries Governments to establish a more balanced understanding, and proceed to the International Court of the Hague to answer charges.

One: Mass alienation of owners' property, specifically governments' and public services' computers, without owners' consent in furtherance of aims prejudicial to international peace and governance by democratic rule.

Two: Issuing documentation and subsequent representation to the U.N. of a life-form that is alien masquerading as human, and registered as such for the purposes of infiltrating every power-avenue of human activity, to gain world power in contravention of human rights legislation.

Three: That the Geron Nation had been created by means of subversive and undemocratic actions, and was therefore called upon to answer these charges before the full U.N. Assembly in due course.

Mehitabel was not amused. But, practical as ever, took first things first, like shopping. Well, there was time to spare after they had arrived, so Josy and Mehitabel went off to enjoy themselves. Wicksted looked up some old friends and tried to get some insider political information, and Archie had an educative look at one or two pubs. Then, suitably full of booze and benevolence, he sauntered off to meet the ladies and encountered his first Geron moving pavement.

Two Gerons were having a conversation on the moving pavement as Archie stepped on; his senses were so attuned now that he could spot a Geron in a human environment by the way they looked. They could not avoid a certain confident stance that said: 'I can do anything, even if I fall over doing it I will get up and carry on'. They also had the intrinsic Geron curiosity about everything. Two females were evidencing that trait, both well dressed, svelte model-types with style, as was their argument with the Geron pavement, which seems a trifle peculiar at first knowledge.

'Why do you stay in that box of yours? Afraid of the big wide world?' The shorter, if more elegant, Geron called Francine enquired cryptically.

'Negative,' the modem replied tersely in a clipped male voice. 'I am a worker who has no need to go about posing.'

'Posing!' the taller Jenny snapped, tight lipped. 'We have a status to maintain as responsible Gerons, and we happen to be Senior Executives,' she finished haughtily.

'Oh, yes.' The pavement was unperturbed. 'More bureaucrats to stifle enterprise and endeavour.'

'You little tyke.' Francine's make-up took on a rosy tinge. 'If you commercial Gerons were allowed your own way, the world would be flooded with useless junk.'

'Like that stuff you're wearing, you mean.'

'What's your name?' snapped Jenny furiously. 'You need educating.'

'John Twofeet. And there's nothing you can teach me, squaw. Have you really just bought those sacks you are almost wearing.'

'That's an apt name, keep them both in your mouth do you? These are Clausen originals than which there are no better.' Jenny swayed provocatively, Archie mentally conceded the point.

'Oh, that hacker. You can see the poor stitching from here. And the name is Cree Indian, which has a certain nobility sadly lacking from your persona.'

A small crowd of humans was listening and enjoying the contretemps. Archie recalled that he had been seeing a number of these groups and realised they were being treated as entertaining side shows. He noticed no animosity toward the Gerons, any eye contact accompanied a brief smile and head nodded in greeting. Francine and Jenny kept their poise even when heated in their responses to the ripostes of John Twofeet, and they smiled at the crowd in beguiling style.

'Going native are we?' sweetly enquired Francine. 'A doormat from the 'reservation'.'

'I know as much, probably more, than you two poseurs, even in my 'reservation'. At least I don't waste my time window-shopping.'

Jenny trained a shapely finger at J. Twofeet. 'If we didn't you would be out of a job, sunshine.'

'Not with all the humans about.'

Archie felt moved to intervene before he left. 'Why do you lot not use your normal communication instead of our, as you put it, crude language?'

The two lady Gerons turned to regard him quizzically.

'It's more fun this way, entertaining the troops,' nodding to the spectators travelling with them. 'And these operators need a little gentle mental exercise, poor souls.' Jenny was a vivacious little bundle with a combative glint in her eye.

'Less of the poor soul,' responded John Twofeet. Archie saw Jenny's smile broaden. 'I see more life in a day than you do in a week. Go and play your little games elsewhere, you hedonists.'

Jenny and Francine stepped lithely off the moving pavement into a store's lush frontage, leaving the memory of the traditional Geron raspberry wafting behind with their scent.

'Mr. Brewer isn't it?' John Twofeet surprised him and, on receiving an affirmative, continued in speculative tone,

'Ever regret letting types like that loose on the world?'

Archie was conscious of the people around showing interest; he flushed at the thought that his name was getting known. He laughed self-consciously: 'Sometimes. But I was only a very small cog, remember. Mehitabel was the main instigator.'

John Twofeet chuckled. 'Yeah. I'd heard you like to duck out. Just remember, we ordinary Gerons need you – you understand us.'

Archie decided he could always walk back to where he had arranged to meet Josy.

'I don't follow you.'

'Well, I'm just a moving electro mag pavement, nothing special, but you are the one who worked all those years setting things up so Ma'am could do the rest. You seem to have a feel for us, and we a part of you.' John chuckled deep. 'And you suggested some of my safety features, reactive electro mat for kids or anyone else falling, approach cushions the same. I can deal with a thousand people trying to leap on at once on this half mile stretch, and catch 'em all, as it were. The beauty of it is they don't even know they've been caught, it's a bit like juggling hundreds of balls at the same time; keeps you on your toes, as well as chatting to the kids, they think it's great talking to the pavement.'

'Thanks John Twofeet, glad you're happy in your work. Look forward meeting you again.'

'I'd like that. Don't forget the workers.'

'I'll do that.'

*

An official car had been provided for them, a Roller no less, giving them a taste of luxury living. But the driver was Mehitabel's own personal protector, recently acquired under protest. Archie had made the point that, regardless of her own defensive abilities, there would be times when she was vulnerable. Mehitabel gave in gracefully, secretly pleased at the fuss. She had been getting a sense of alienation with all the various increasing pressures and doubts. Her human form had given her much to add to her immense awareness of life, much that showed vulnerability, and suddenly she sensed danger. Clancy, her Geron protector, was a delight, an Irish Geron with a vast irreverence that suited his task and provided the foil for Mehitabel in the absence of Archie. The two men establishing an instant rapport gave her a grand opportunity for acerbic comment when they were together.

The Trade Unions had asked for an early meeting, their power base having been so eroded 'demands' were not feasible. The faces gathered at the impromptu assembly of delegates at Congress House were familiar figures to Mehitabel, old friends even, with whom she had passed many a pleasant hour in dispute in the past. She greeted them appropriately as they sat, at home in their surroundings, along a long table in the conference room.

'I see many well-known faces here, still hanging on to the vestiges of power and hoping for miracles.' Archie cringed, expecting the worst, and the faces opposite displayed such reaction. 'I bring you that miracle. Dependent on your decision whether it becomes fact.'

There was no response, no flicker of emotion from those bland faces.

'You know our power, you have tried unsuccessfully to eradicate that strength over the years. If you had only worked with us instead of baulking our efforts to help, you would now be in much stronger positions. The choice is yours yet again and, since you asked us for this meeting, perhaps we can yet reach an amicable agreement. You have had our proposals for this meeting; would anyone care to comment? Ah, Mr. Forbes, you are looking well.'

C.M. Forbes was not in fact looking well, tense, angry, but not well.

'I have read the proposals in detail, but can find little that matches with our principles of Trade Union practice. In fact I would say that this is a capitalist's compact.'

'Well, you would,' Marcia interjected, ignoring Forbes' reactive glance. 'My people have found advantages already and we are prepared to go along with this document.'

'Ma'am.' A new face this, ruddy and open, bald as a badger with clear blue eyes. Alan C. Lewis on the card, and in small letters Amalgamated Union of Engineers and Associated Workers. As Mehitabel well knew, a large bloc of Union power. 'We have lost many of our members over the years due to the increased usage of your programmes. I note that your proposals suggest that this can only increase in years to come. You suggest we diversify, use our talents elsewhere in industry or outside, and learn other skills, possibly outside industry.'

The blue eyes stayed steady on Mehitabel, unemotional, but questioning. 'I don't doubt your forecasting. But why should people who have already undergone years of learning, have to go back to school? Why cannot society organise itself properly to accommodate those it has trained in a proper function? Why is it always the workers who have to suffer? Answer me that Ma'am.'

The Trade Unionists gave him a muted round of applause for that. Mehitabel sat quietly, holding his eyes with her own.

'Mr. Lewis. If we had time I would indeed give you an answer, except that it would undoubtedly end with setting you a question which I doubt you could answer. Therefore let me just say this. Reality is the state in which you find yourself, Utopia is the state to aim for. But the responsibility for achieving that state as a society relies upon every single member accepting their total share of the duties involved. Your Industrial Revolution created change, this has continued and accelerated since, but, sadly, you humans have failed to keep up, collectively or individually. You have neglected your education, not just in technical knowledge but in life itself, creating thereby a Utopia which is fantasy and not a derivation of learning from Reality. I can only offer you the means to work toward your solving, not providing the answer to, your problems. The guarantees remain with each and every one of you, not with me.'

'In other words a 'cop-out'. No more than I expected.' C.M. Forbes as ever.

Alan Lewis replied before Mehitabel, which says much for his reactions.

'Charlie. You epitomise all that has been wrong with the TUC for too long.' He looked long and hard at Mehitabel. 'Ma'am. I for one am prepared to propose to my members that they consider your proposals in depth. It is up to them.'

'Thank you, Mr. Lewis.'

'That has to be a TUC decision.' Charlie Forbes by the book.

'Hah! What have you got here, Charlie? Three million union members out of a total work-force of thirty mill. Grow up.' Marcia had made a decision. 'My recommendation goes with Allan.'

That was when the bedlam started. Archie thought they were lucky to get out of there alive.

'Those Trade Union blokes are nutters.'

'Merely somewhat excitable, Archibald.'

'Excitable?' But he left the matter there.

The TUC voted to accept Mehitabel's proposals in principle. A lot of people were surprised.

Later came the official conglomerates of bland officials and words. The position was slightly confused; on the one hand, the establishment desperately needed the expertise of the Gerons, just to keep the whole process of human society functioning; on the other, they bitterly resented the leaching of power from their authority. There were those who hated giving ground to a computer.

They had been granted two days' conference time with the ministers interested in resolving their differences with the Gerons. Assembled to do battle were old favourites still in power: Bert Frampton, the Labour Minister of Education, Charles Whitworth, Conservative, Foreign Office, Carole Spencer, the sophisticated Liberal Home Office, and the Democrat Kylie Evans, Trade and Industry, with their attendant Under Secretaries and other minions at 1 Victoria Street, SW 1.

The mood of the meeting was combative and frustrated. The humans knew they had to win since it was a matter of self esteem, yet were aware of how much they would need to compromise, because if they won they also lost.

Simply stated, if Bert Frampton regained the status quo with computers and programming under his aegis, he would lose an efficient and creative teaching machine producing remarkable results with reasonable funding, then need to find half a billion pounds to pay for human administration and teachers. His problem was that the Gerons could organise matters well enough to make his decisions for him. Frustration indeed.

Carole Spencer was in a similar dilemma, since virtually every mechanical or monetary operation was Geron-orientated. Instant information was available on fraudulent actions, movement or laundering of 'hot' money, insider-dealing and many others. Some of Carole's best friends had complained bitterly about 'her' Gerons limiting their activities. She had her own problems in those directions but daren't remonstrate, even privately; one never knew where those damn Gerons were hiding. Car thefts were almost a thing of the past as most cars had car-Gerons who objected most strenuously to being 'nicked' – they often simply drove the offender to the nearest 'nick' for 'nick nick' to 'nick' 'em. Burglars and armed robber gangs were positively embarrassed, they couldn't even walk into their own banks to cash a cheque without the alarms sounding and metal screens dropping on all openings. The Mafia and drug types were seething, since they could only keep a tenuous grip on their money as it kept sliding out of their accounts. Carole Spencer was basking in the warmth of the congratulations on her control of the criminal element, and hating every moment. Gone were the little illegal perks of her position, the power grafting, the delicate corporate actions. She was a confused lady.

As was Charles Whitworth, the Foreign Secretary. He had the same problems but on a grander scale, involving exports, foreign investment and those devilish little invisible earnings via the money and insurance markets. All of which were prospering with the speed and effectiveness of Geron computing and forecasting. His political status was riding high so the thought of falling was not appealing, but neither was being so reliant on the Gerons for his success. Charles was frustrated.

Kylie Evans' Welsh temper was on the boil for similar reasons, although she was devious enough to see advantages in containing those emotions in the cause of future success as a politician. She envisaged the future involving more reliance on Geron operations just to keep human evolution one step away from chaos, to go further would need an integration of both species with consideration for each's needs. It was a pity that a lady as sharp natured as her voice was shrill, should be the one to appreciate the potential, but the fact was that she did and was the one that Mehitabel picked out as the communicator. Since her Trade and Industry Department was a primary Geron involvement, Kylie Evans had shown her own willingness to appreciate the advantages, as well as her political acumen and ambition. Therefore she played the game of her colleagues as token, to object to the Gerons, while in fact seeking every gain she could from their abilities. Also debatable was the term colleague, as applied to those with her here, but they would serve their purpose, now and in the future.

The agreement was a foregone conclusion, the definition was simply a means of preserving authority's dignity for the future, a way to be seen to be still in charge and not just a figure-head for a Geron Bureaucracy, the latter a quaint deceit since they were simply transferring officially that which was already a fact, and accepting decisions made before which had the real governance of bureaucrats, now incorporated the reality of Geron actions. A bitter pill to swallow and an acceptance of the Gerons that could well affect the Hague Court decision, a calculated fence-sitting gesture which fitted the Coalition Government well.

Mehitabel left 1 Victoria Street, W1, with a wry smile on her face at the end of the conference. Each of the Ministers had expressed the hope that they could all work together for the betterment of the people and Gerons, to polite applause from their acolytes, and similarly when Mehitabel replied in kind.

As Archie commented when they were in the car driving away:

'Very civilised. And rubbish.'

'Archibald. You are wrong again. That was a bear fight and a clear indication of alliances. As long as we keep producing the goods they will tolerate us, and use us for their own ends. Even if the decision at the Hague goes against us, they still need our facility, Kylie Evans in particular.'

Archie wasn't interested in Kylie Evans. 'It'll be a miracle if it doesn't.'

Mehitabel took her eyes briefly off the road ahead, she was a terrible back-seat driver, and glanced with narrowed eyes at him. 'A fine example of the moronic Welsh death wish. Do you ever think before you open that orifice you mistakenly refer to as a mouth.'

Josy gave her verdict with enthusiasm. 'Very rarely.'

Wicksted smiled; he loved these battles when he was not involved. Archie missed the smile, otherwise he would have included him.

'This is not an ordinary court and you've got international opposition.'

Mehitabel obviously despaired of him. 'What did you do with yourself last night, Archibald?'

'Got pie-eyed with Wicksted and sang unmentionable songs till the small hours,' Josy happily provided.

'That explains it. If you had conducted yourself with the decorum suited to your station and stayed, even relatively, sober, you would have received the brief of both presentations. I shall therefore enlighten you, briefly.'

'Jokes yet.'

'Quiet, Archibald. The crux of their argument is balderdash. We chose to adopt human form and therefore have the same entitlement as humans. We could have chosen to become a protected species, thereby presenting a picture of say, elephants, with our abilities presenting all sorts of marvellous problems for you humans to resolve, and not able to touch us. As to the rest, ownership and so-forth, difficult to prove and we can show substantial returns on investment, even a buy-out possibility. But the clincher must be somewhere like Russia. A turmoil of differing opinions, those wanting the old order and security, new market forces, not all good, and those few with ideas for future development involving all the people, but no knowledge of how to get the whole system working properly.

'So we cut through their, and your, red tape, moved the food, organised the stores, got the producers and industrialists organised, gave a short term answer a long term projection and suddenly everyone is calling it a miracle. Long way to go yet, but if they keep working at it with us, as the other nations are doing, then the Court of The Hague is going to look pretty silly if we are found guilty. And the way your laws are applied now, I am surprised anyone gets convicted. It really amazes me how you rely so much on logic, a simple definition, then colour the case with prejudices, circumstances you say affect the issue, plain self-seeking or greed, and deny yourselves the possibility of the simple answer. I see no problem. In fact I am going there to enjoy myself.'

They were to leave for the continent the following day. Wicksted had gone off to visit friends, Mehitabel went to the Royal College of Music with Clancy, while Josy took the chance to retain Archie comfortably in their suite.

And a pleasant evening was had by all.

Until.

CHAPTER NINETEEN

Archie leapt to his feet, dumping a reclining Josy onto the carpet. 'Mehitabel's been blown up!'

'What?' forgetting his unceremonious depositing of her tender form.

'Blown up, for Gods' sake!'

'How do you know? And how did it happen?' as Josy got to her feet.

'I don't know. Come on, we have to get there,' as he dragged her toward the door.

'Wait, wait. My shoes.'

Archie's mind was numb. Now that he had accepted that violent flash message, he responded like an automaton as Josy took charge. He obeyed her instructions implicitly as he tried to get the jumble that was his mind into some sort of order. He stumbled into a car ahead of her, barely aware of Wicksted at the wheel, as he looked unseeing at the crowded life of the city streets. He couldn't think or feel. Dimly came the realisation that if Mehitabel were dead, his world had collapsed; nothing, that was all that was left. Nothing.

Josy held his hand and tried to talk to him. Wicksted drove as fast as he dared through the street traffic, glancing as he did so at Archie in the rear view mirror with some concern, but Archie felt as if neither he nor they were actually there, not going to view.... he couldn't think.

But he could recall that moment of communication in all its terrible detail, the telepathic exchange nightmarish in its context. He tried to remember anything that could give him hope for his friend. It was Theodore who had communicated via Archie's Purvis implant..

'Thank the Lord you are available, Archibald. For once.' Theodore could not resist the dig at Archie's reluctance to tune in.

'What is it?' Archie sensing the despair in that normally placid entity's thoughts.

'Ma'am has been blown up!'

'What? Blown up? How do you mean blown up? What the..?'

Theodore's mind intruded with such force Archie felt as though a finger had been poked into his consciousness. Archie still thought this a dream, a horrible dream.

'Someone bombed the car, just after Ma'am had left the Imperial College. You know she was..'

Archie cut the thought short, he knew where Mehitabel had been, to the Royal College of Music, in a quest to understand the human involvement with that form of entertainment.

'That's impossible! What about all the Geron protective sensing? She must have known?'

'We have had many of these threats. If you had left your implant...'

'Yes, yes, yes. I know all that. But why? Why did she go if she knew.'

'Ma'am will not bow to threats. You know that, sir.'

Archie did not notice the deference. His mind, so chaotic with dreadful possibilities, finally settled on one.

'Is she...?' He couldn't think of that finality.

'We don't know. There is no response. We received Ma'am's message of an explosion. Then,... nothing. It happened in Queen's Gate. You know....?'

'Yes.' Archie could see the street map reference in his mind's eye as Theodore gave it to him. 'We're ten minutes from there. Going now!'

A few moments passed before Archie could finally accept what he had been told. Josy told him afterwards she had thought he was having a fit of some sort, his face mirroring his thoughts. Then he dumped her on the floor.

*

Wicksted was breaking traffic rules galore as he weaved through the traffic the short distance from Knightsbridge toward Kensington.

'Looks like there's a hold-up in the road ahead.' Wicksted slowed as he attempted to see a way through. Archie came out of his cataleptic state to give crisp instructions.

'Turn off here into Exhibition Road, then right into Prince Consort Road. Just cut across! To hell with the traffic.'

Wicksted needed no urging and caused a cacophony of irate horn-blowing as he slewed the vehicle across the lines of cars. They swung into Prince Consort Road with a squeal of tyres and more protests from motorists having to savagely brake to avoid them, then surged at speed to the junction with Queen's Gate. There they were stopped by a policeman stretching a tape barrier across the road; beyond him smoke eddied in swirling contrails as dust writhed in the light thrown by burning vehicles.

For a moment they could not move, aghast at the scene before them. The description that came to Archie was of Dante's Inferno: the writhing flame-coloured forms suggested demons dancing in delight at their handiwork.

But some good fortune had been gained by the chance exercise of emergency services being in operation in Kensington, Fiona Fergus being totally professional even when in shock and mildly concussed, instantly calling in those best able to cope with what had happened to face the reality of their practice.

The road was a shambles of wrecked vehicles, bodies, ambulances and police, arc lights being rigged, and the voice of authority denying access.

'But we have to go in there!' Archie had found his voice, a desperate and reedy shadow of itself, but determined. 'Mehitabel's in there.'

'I'm sorry, sir, no one is allowed... now just take it easy, everything is being done.... now if you don't.... Yes, Ma'am.'

'I'll take care of these people.' Chief Superintendent Fiona Fergus appeared, miraculously, and spoke to Archie with surprising sympathy. 'I'm very sorry about this.'

Archie vaguely noted the normally smart uniform was dusty and torn, hair awry and cap-less. Fiona Fergus also had about her the air of one desperately holding onto the onus of duty, to assuage the shock of what had happened.

'Where is she?'

'I'm afraid the car was just blown apart. I am sorry, we were not far behind them.... and lucky.' This was a very different Chief Super. 'There is nothing anyone can....'

'Let me see!'

'There is no point, Mr. Brewer.'

'Let.. me.. see!'

They paced the hundred yards to where screens were being erected about the hole blown in the road, Archie's macabre thoughts measured the Death March.

He wasn't prepared, no one could ever be, for the horrific disorienting sight of the remains of mangled limbs, barely recognisable as such, among the welter of metal pieces littering the six foot deep hole. If he had been normal he would have thrown up instantly, instead he stepped automatically over the restraining tapes to go down into the crater, throwing off Fiona Fergus's hand as he did so.

'Mehitabel?' he spoke in a small child's voice, suddenly bereft of a treasured part of its life. The crater was so big and yet so small. There was nothing, just nothing. Fruitlessly he searched with his eyes for something, anything, that might.... might.... Hopelessly he sank to his knees and dejectedly said her name.

'Mehitabel.'

'Archibald?' Faint, uncertain, a disorientated query, distant, confused.

'Mehitabel! Where are you?' A joyful shout.

'I'm.... I'm not certain.' Silence then, a long drawn worrying vacuum, with the peripheral heaviness of disturbed inanimate matter settling into a new state, a background hissing of material seared by a moment's incinerating blast. Then.

'What happened?' A childlike voice, doubting it would receive a satisfying answer.

'You were blown up. Where are you Mehitabel?' Archie stood still as death, his senses straining to find the voice source, and finding nothing.

'Ah...... that would explain.....' The voice getting stronger now, authority returning. 'Got you. Damn your eyes, you are standing on me Archibald.'

'What..?' Archie leapt to one side and peered down.' Where..?'

'Use your common, you oaf! Under this blasted stone. Steady!' The command held off Archie's urgently scrabbling hands, just in time, for he could see a pulsing blue light just beneath his fingers.

'I won't hurt you Mehitabel. I couldn't!' he emotionally assured her.

'It is you I am worried about, Archibald!' came the terse answer. 'Just a moment while I get my bearings..... Ah, that's better. Now, I will try and protect you while you get me out, then I should be back to normal. Easy now,' as Archie, on hands and knees, gently cleared stones and earth away, Chief Superintendent Fiona Fergus peering over his shoulder, while holding Josy and Wicksted back with spread arms.

And there was an egg.

The size of a chicken's egg, that pulsed with light within its opaque skin, a skein of swirling shades of blue beneath the surface. A sense of contained power writhed within.

'Pick me up then!' came the peremptory command. 'I can manage myself then.'

Archie tentatively put a hand out then snatched it back with a muffled curse.

'Sorry!' came the unrepentant call. 'I will boost your protection.'

Archie had that incredible egg nestled in his palm. He felt a warmth that spread through his whole body, then the thing lifted off his hand and hovered, bobbing slightly, at head height. Chief Superintendent Fiona Fergus started back and fell unceremoniously on her rump with an un-female expletive.

'Ah.' The old Mehitabel was back. 'The delightful Fiona Fergus who knows her job so well we get blown to bits. Where is Clancy?'

'Are you alright?' anxiously pressed Archie over the Chief Super's unusually hesitant excuses.

'Of course I am alright!' came testily. 'Take more than a minor bang to incommode us. I was going to change that body anyway. Where the devil is Clancy?'

'Here, Ma'am.' And Archie was directed to another spot in their ten foot hole to expose another egg, not pulsing with quite so much vigour. When freed, Clancy adopted a similar flight pattern to Mehitabel, but spoke irreverent Irish.

'Bejesus! If we could mix a drink with that kick we'd have one helluva party.'

'Glad to hear you are feeling so well, Clancy,' wryly remarked Mehitabel. Then anxiously to the policewoman. 'Was anyone else hurt in that.. that explosion?'

Chief Superintendent Fergus returned to her authoritative role. 'Not many as far as we can tell at this time. Some seriously injured, but not life-threatening, others with broken bones, cuts and bruises, several car write-offs, broken windows in houses and the like. We are still investigating. Er.. hum.' The authority wilted somewhat at Fiona Fergus's personal conflict within duty, a protector of what she had been pursuing as a subversive element. Then she spoke with real anger:

'We will find these people. I can assure you of our every effort in that direction.'

Mehitabel chuckled with some of her old spirit. 'Thank you for that. The piquancy of the situation had not escaped me, and that you do your job very well in the circumstances. Can we get out of here without encountering masses of media hawks?'

Chief Super Fiona knew the question was directed at her, the answer conveyed other uncertainties newly arrived in her life.

'We can try. Just what are you people?'

'Computers, dear,' said Mehitabel, placidly.

*

They got away from the scene of devastation by Wicksted driving their car in past the barriers, then several policemen shielded Mehitabel and Clancy with their bodies from the batteries of camera crews. The media were already pressuring the newly arrived police cordon who had blanked off the section of Queen's Gate affected by the explosion.

Mehitabel refused to leave until Fiona Fergus had assured her that all would be done to help those injured and any others who had suffered that night.

'The Gerontons will make good any losses or deprivation caused, also compensate those injured for their suffering. I trust you will make that clear to all those involved, Superintendent. I have your word?'

The senior policewoman seemed at a loss, then responded with dignity. 'Your sentiments will be conveyed to each and every one, ma'am. I will see to it personally.'

'Thank you, Fiona, I really appreciate that. Good-night. And thank you for your help.'

'Part of the job, ma'am.' Chief Superintendent Fiona Fergus signalled to one of her officers as she continued, 'We have an escort to ensure nothing more happens on your way to your hotel.' The pulse of light from Mehitabel increased as the tone of voice hardened. 'I doubt that any of those involved in this barbarous act are hanging about waiting to try again.'

'Nevertheless, I must insist. We have two cars standing by. I will travel with you.'

Mehitabel expressed concern. 'I would have thought you needed some medical treatment yourself, Superintendent.'

'I've been through worse, Ma'am. We were only on the periphery of the blast.'

'Lucky you,' wryly commented Mehitabel. 'Shall we go?'

Archie and Josy, ably backed by Wicksted as he drove, were eager to put their principles of moral rectitude to Mehitabel, who, apart from now being a glowing ovoid, seemed unaffected by the attempt to spread her vital parts over the road, and quite prepared to tackle matters of import.

Archie adopted the role of holy avenger as they made their easy way behind the leading police car, its siren blaring and headlights full on clearing their way.

'Who would do anything so barbaric? Are you sure you're alright?'

'I'm fine Archibald. Stop fussing. Take more than a little bang to put a Geronton down. Eh, Clancy?'

'To be sure, ma'am.' Clancy tried to sound assuring but the glow from his ovoid was not as steady as Mehitabel's, who expressed her concern.

'I think we need to get you to the secure unit in Swansea as soon as possible. You were nearer the explosion than I. Just rest as best you can for now.'

Josy offered her help. 'Perhaps I can hold him.'

'You will need protection. Just wait a moment.' Mehitabel sounded pleased by the offer. 'You can just hold your hand out. Clancy? Can you move?'

'Easy.' As the blue ovoid settled in Josy's palm there came a sigh. 'Thank you, Josy. The old legs ain't what they were.'

The small convoy of cars swept into the forecourt of their small hotel in Knightsbridge. The police, under the expert guidance of Fiona Fergus, quickly forming a protective barrier to allow them access to the hotel entrance. But Mehitabel had other ideas.

'Why are we here? We need the secure unit in Swansea University for Clancy.'

'Don't you be worryin' about me, ma'am.' Came faintly from the weakly pulsing ovoid gently cradled in Josy's hand.

'That's a three-hour trip! After we get out of London! And it's ten o'clock in the evening,' Archie protested. 'Can't you do something for him? You know. Energy transfer or something.'

'I'm doing the best I can, Archibald,' tersely responded Mehitabel. 'The explosion was in the engine, Clancy took the brunt of the blast. He needs the secure unit. I can keep him going until we get there. But we need to leave now!' Her voice carried the authority that brooked no argument.

'Couldn't we fly down from Heathrow?' persisted Archie, causing Josy to look at him in some surprise, her man displaying unexpected character in adversity.

'Minor changes in air pressure could be dangerous in his state. We have to go by road. Now! Do it, Archibald.' Surprisingly, more a request than a command. Archie responded as a somewhat more presentable Chief Superintendent Fergus appeared to query the delay.

'We need to get to Swansea as soon as possible, by road. Can you help?' Archie's voice suggesting a determination to do what needed to be done regardless of the reply.

Fiona Fergus' tightened lips indicated her angry reaction to that possibility, but her voice was level and controlled, the decision instantaneous. 'Follow the lead car. How much time have we, and where exactly are we going?'

Wicksted claimed it was the experience of his life. Archie had never travelled that fast in a car and thought they were unlikely to survive, until they screamed into Swansea University to pull up outside the Geronton Secure Unit.

On the trip down, Clancy had energy enough to fantasise about his new body, until sharply brought down to earth by Mehitabel attending to business. Chief Super Fiona Fergus, who travelled in the escort car, caused a new growth of ulcers amongst her fellow officers on the trip; she was not a happy lady.

There were those travellers on the roads, observant enough, who assumed tricks of light were making those two blue orbs reflect in the windows of the car that flashed past them. Mehitabel, although anxious to reach their destination quickly, was a strict speed limits back seat driver, and caused several acerbic radio spats between high-speed Fiona Fergus and the Special Branch driver of Mehitabel's car. On this occasion Mehitabel lost.

It was just after midnight when they arrived, only a few minutes later before Mehitabel had divested them of their police escort, with only token objections from Fiona Fergus.

Then they entered the building now known as the Geronton Secure Unit, where Clancy was quickly placed in a resuscitation unit and the rest apportioned small but comfortable safe rooms with beds. Mehitabel took herself into the main control room where resided the Conclave of Elders and Theodore, there to conduct an exhausting investigation into the explosive events of the night.

*

'What did she feel like?' hissed Josy in his ear.

'What?' Archie mumbled sleepily.

'Mehitabel, you fool.'

'Oh, dunno.'

'What do you mean you don't know!' wide awake now. 'She must have felt like something. Come on Archie, I need to know.'

'Wha'? Why, why do you need to.' Slowly clambering up through the fog of sleep. 'For Pete's sake. It, she, was warm, felt like velvet, no, warm furry animal, not smooth like she looked,' he was awake now, 'and there was this incredible sense of power in there, nothing you could feel as a tactile thing, as though, as though she enveloped me in this aura of protection. There's more but I can't put it into words. Pick her up yourself if you want to find out. Can I go to sleep now?'

'Not yet.'

'Oh, God.'

*

'I'm going to need a body until I get a new one.'

'What body?'

'Yours.'

'MINE?'

'Yours.'

'Not on your bloody life. I'm a bloke for crissake. And how the hell do you borrow a body?'

'Oh, I just merge in for a while. Only a day or two.'

'Not with my body you don't. Why don't you try Josy, she's a female. Much more suitable.'

'I can't do that!' Horrified. 'A woman's body is sacrosanct.'

'What about a bloke's body then.' All sorts of thoughts occurred to him. 'I mean..... well, I mean. There's... there's... things. And poking about in me thoughts, bad enough already with this damn gizmo but, in my body? No way. I'd rather go and join Johnny Twofeet on the moving pavement.'

'Well we could do it that way if you'd like.'

'Gerroff! I'm going nowhere. Leave you wander about in my body? No thank you! You'd probably forget to return it. What the hell am I saying? Why don't you use one of your Geron bodies, share with one of them, you'd feel more at home.'

'Yes, well that is where there is a little difficulty. It is just possible to do it with a human body but.... I had better explain. Very simply, we have developed the enzyme molecules that react with the biological substrata to form physical bodies, animal and human. By adapting these enzymes within the electrical reaction of our flexible living system, and by infusing the particles of gene structure that enable some life forms to reproduce lost limbs, we are able to construct, or reconstruct, our bodies. These ovoids expand inside the shells as they grow, the heads, arms, and legs moulded around the ovoid which extends and fills the shape as the limbs grow. The humanoid exterior is simply a decoration for our people to be more acceptable in your human eyes. Our ovoid being provides the energy so that we do not need your internal organs.'

Archie took a moment to try and ingest this information, gave up and stated, somewhat despondently:

'Sounds like you don't need us at all.'

Mehitabel chuckled.

'Don't be so downcast, Archibald. WE would not exist were it not for you, your tribe also provides us with a marvellously convoluted conundrum known as human life, which gives us a reason for living in your image. There is another aspect you have overlooked, the discoveries in enzyme, gene and hormone research by humans is why we are able to adapt to your human form. Also you have a life-field which comes from your spiritual being, you have the ability to go on to another dimension when you die.' Mehitabel reluctant to admit a human superiority. 'Whether we achieve similar spirit dimensions is dependent on cosmic factors beyond our control. You can stop smiling, Archibald, your species do not recommend themselves as deities.'

Archie kept smiling, not that he believed in the life after death rubbish, but it was nice to score one over Ma'am. Mehitabel interrupted his smugness.

'The replacement of my body will take a week, due to Clancy needing urgent treatment...'

'You grow a body in a week!'

'Contain yourself, Archibald. Did you not listen at all? One week. The body is still crude by comparison to yours, sadly.' Conceding another advantage to the human species was an effort. 'I cannot merge with another Geron, therefore I have to come with you. My ovoid stays here, it will be alright.'

'No way.'

'We could do it with the Purvis implant you have. I can simply communicate with you through that, but you have to allow me to do so. And I have to have your promise on that because I cannot lose contact in the middle of the case. You promise?'

'I dunno. You can be very sneaky at times.' Archie changed the subject. 'Do you know who was behind that bombing?'

'Nothing definite as yet. But Harold does not respond, indeed he seems to have disappeared, quite an achievement within the Geron network. There are indications of that organisation being involved, agents of Tommy Hillan and Harold's Mafia 'organisation' have been traced to the locality at that time. But we have no real proof as yet.'

Archie automatically glanced over his shoulder, the cold sweat of fear dappled his brow. Even that name was a threat.

*

There was a lot of activity in the Secure Unit in Swansea. Mehitabel was determined to attend the trial hearing at The Hague if at all possible, and the Geron organisation was at full stretch attempting to provide the necessary bodily structure in time. The problem was the effect of the explosion on those orbs of pulsing power. Mehitabel and the Gerons had created their lifeform within a human entity; she now had to suffer the frustration of putting up with waiting for her ovoid body to recover sufficiently, to enable a human exterior to be integrated with it again.

Being thwarted in her intentions was not guaranteed to get Mehitabel in a good mood, and since adopting human form she was finding out about moods, the discovery was not much to her liking, a computer did not have moods. Being a life form, if only an exterior human, was not the control function Mehitabel was used to. There was something about the philosophy of appearance affecting persona, and the reverse, that eluded her.

Meanwhile, another acerbic character and his entourage approached the International Court of The Hague. Archibald was a youngish man with a terrible mood on him.

If he had not been in such a mood, he would have paid attention to the communications flooding in through his Purvis implant. But he didn't, which was par for the course.

The interesting thing about the Court of The Hague case, was the number of plaintiffs who were withdrawing their names from the brief against the Gerons. When the various power groups in some countries found out the Gerons were liable to be made persona-non-grata, the authorities realised there was a distinct possibility of non-co-operation and a return to chaos. Those with society's interests at heart made protest to those in power, that if they continued with this action they would find themselves contending with much more than bossy computers, and quite possibly out of a job.

Various Eastern European nations, plus India, Canada, and the North African countries all withdrew from the international case. Only Romania, Bulgaria, the European Community, America and Japan persisted. For the lawyers this was more than enough, but they had discounted the pressures not only from within those communities. The rest of the world's nations, who did not like the brinkmanship involved, made strong representations to stop what they termed 'a farce of global proportions'.

Life form computers had come into their own.

But there were still a lot of people who felt threatened by these creatures.

Archie was one, he had one of them, the boss lady herself, arguing with him over breakfast via his Purvis implant. While Josy argued with him more naturally on traditional subjects.

'God, you're a slob in the mornings.'

'I'm not. And I know what I'm doing.' To Mehitabel.

'Doesn't look like it, you've got a head start on the wreck of the Hesperus,' Josy tartly responded.

'This will be the first time if you do,' from Mehitabel.

'Is he going to be doing the talking?' a new voice in Archie's head.

'Who the hell is that?' Archie roared. 'How many of you are there for God's sake?'

'What on earth are you talking about?' Josy gasped.

'There's hundreds of damn people rabbiting about in my head. Gettout! All of you.'

'Really Archibald! Come Albert, we'll confer elsewhere. In more congenial surroundings.'

'What's going on?' Josy now distressed by Archie's hunted look.

'Bloody Mehitabel. And bloody Purvis implants.'

'Oh.' She smiled. 'They're quite easy when you get used to them.'

'Superior bitch.'

'Glad you've realised that at last. Ready?'

The case went ahead with the preliminary hearing.

Archie, Josy and Wicksted went to the court. Conversation was stilted because Archie was having a mind conference with Mehitabel and Albert, which did little to improve his temper.

'Are you sure you have everything clear now, Archibald.'

'Of course I have. Don't you think I know what goes on by now.'

'I wonder sometimes. Albert, you are sure Old Higgie has authorised you to provide data as required?'

'Lord Justice Higgins, ma'am, has done just that.'

'Alright, Albert, protocol to the fore. Just as well we managed to juggle the appointments to Brussels. They nearly had a Brussels bureaucrat in charge. How about the other four Judges, think Higgie can handle them?'

Albert sniggered. 'They all think Higgie is God.'

Archie had followed this exchange with more than a little trepidation.

'Hang on! Have you been fixing the Judges in an International Court? That's probably a hanging offence or something, and I'm the one they'll hang.'

'Don't be silly, Archibald. You do fuss so. Merely taking care of our interests. The other side have done far worse. Eh! Albert?'

'To be sure, Ma'am.'

Archie could only gasp in outrage. Mehitabel ignored him.

'Right. Let's get on shall we.'

Archie proceeded under protest, duly ignored. The impressive aura of the Court of The Hague gave him a strong sense of impending incarceration in a maximum security quality nick.

There was a strong phalanx of international lawyers to present the case for those nations still labouring under the power brokers of tyranny; they had merely changed the labels of Communism, Marxist-Leninism and the many military Dictatorships to masquerade as Democracies. They used the subtle wiles of bureaucracy to maintain their control of their disheartened and often hungry populations. Their arguments were forceful, as evidenced by the legal representative for Romania.

'By what right do these, supposed persons, appropriate whole areas of state functions and civil service mandate, to promote activities that undermine the state authority. They remove goods from secure warehouses and distribute them without authority, to people not entitled to receive them. Supply seed and machinery to farmers not state qualified to use them. Incite workers to use work practices in violation of State Socialist principles. Move monies in the internal banking system, against the sage advice of National Bank Administrators.

'We ask that these supposed persons here named be made to restrict their activities to those allowed within the laws, and by the judgement of those elected to the Government of the Republic of Romania.'

All eyes turned to Archie and his small entourage, but he, in his stolid way, was still taking in Kerim's statement while trying to cope with Mehitabel via the Purvis implant.

'Get on with it, Archibald. We haven't got all day.'

'I'm just sorting out what to say for Pete's sake.'

'To blazes with Pete, get up and I will speak through you.'

'I'm not having you...'

'Get up!' hissed in his mind.

He rose slowly to his feet and gazed as calmly as he could around at the packed court. Then found words spilling out of him, amazing himself with his new found gift of oratory.

'Milords. May I answer those accusations by asking a question of my learned friend that is pertinent to the true picture.' Archie received a regal inclination of the head from the central of the five berobed judges, who just happened to be Lord Chief Justice Higgins. Archie addressed himself to the Romanian lawyer.

'Would you say, sir, that the circumstances of each of those areas of complaint are better or worse than they were a year ago.'

The lawyer, a thin acerbic man, shrugged slightly in his wig and robes, and looked blankly back. Archie meanwhile was frantically defending control of his mouth and mind, Mehitabel fought for control with scant concern for Archie's pride.

'Come, sir.' Archie chided. 'Have not the shops got goods to sell at reasonable prices, workers work, and pay. Do not your transport services run, your press and television actually approximate the truth. Also your telephones are no longer tapped by the Securitate. After three years of what you call democracy, food was at a premium, if available at all, transport not running, press control and Securitate imposing its will on the people. Are these not the facts? The court is waiting for your answer, sir.'

The lawyer turned a stony face toward the Judges.

'None of this is true. This is pure fabrication on the part of this gentleman, and only evidences the deceit and false actions that have been taken by their people to destroy the democracy created in Romania today.'

Archie smiled benevolently at him, then turned to the Judges again, speaking as though explaining the actions of a recalcitrant child. 'Milords. There is ample proof to the contrary. We have unbiased, eminent, available witnesses who have visited Romania to give evidence. Is it the intention of this court to investigate further?'

The lawyer was suddenly alive. 'I must protest, Milords, this matter cannot be swept up so quickly.'

Justice Higgins waved him to silence, as the Judges conferred. Archie having a bitter exchange with Mehitabel while this went on.

'Cut that out! Messing about in me mind! I knew this would happen, just can't trust you. I could have said all that much better if you left me alone.'

There was a thoughtful silence before Mehitabel replied.

'I must admit there was a certain degree of fluency and cohesion there Archibald. You surprised me. But you just do not have my grasp of the facts or speed of thought. Are you too proud to accept a little help?'

'I like that ! If anyone is proud, it's..'

'Shut up, Archibald, Old Higgie is back.'

'I'll tell him you call..'

'Shh!'

Milord Higgins turned back to the court and spoke into his microphone.

'Let it be known that this court has given sanction to the use of evidence by vocal computer, a Geron terminal.' He held up his hand, to silence the babble of protest from the throng of international legal eminences. 'Until this court arrives at the conclusion of this preliminary hearing, said Geron terminals are still the most efficient, and honest, presenters of evidence that are available. And I am sure you ladies and gentlemen are cognizant of the costs involved in this action, therefore will not wish to waste this court's valuable time.'

The noise had subsided to a tentative quiet. Justice Higgins uttered one word with a certain relish.

'Albert?'

'Milord.' The voice friendly and familiar, Archie smiled to himself, he liked Albert, had a nice touch of irreverence had Albert.

'Would you care to acquaint the court, with the facts as you know them, about the Republic of Romania pertinent to the charges made in this court.'

'Certainly, Milord.' And Albert proceeded to do so, in some detail, not the least bit helpful to the Romanian lawyer who sat blank-faced throughout; except when he received a note from some obviously senior Romanian diplomats in the back of the court. Then he interrupted, brusquely, and to Lord Justice Higgins disfavour.

'Milords.' And Albert politely stopped.

'We are going to get nowhere if you keep interrupting, sir. Is this really necessary?'

'My government thinks so.' The tart retort brought frowns to the Judges' faces. 'The facts are, that the improvements detailed here are due to the government's actions entirely, and these Gerons were acting under instructions, therefore this presentation only serves to support our charges.'

'I fail to follow you, Mr. Kerim. If such is the case why then are you here?'

'The Gerons began to disobey instructions, and we fear for the economic safety of the country if they continue their illegal activities.'

'Surely that is then a matter for your own courts to decide.'

Mr. Kerim was beginning to show some strain. 'Since their actions involved many international organisations and countries, it was decided....'

Justice Higgins held up an impatient hand, then conferred again with his fellows. 'Mr. Kerim. We have the depositions from your government and these state unequivocally, as do those from your fellow petitioners, that the Gerons were involved in subversive activities liable to adversely affect the democratic functioning of the country. Thus far the only proof we have indicates that the reverse is the case. Now you are attempting to change your petition. This is neither the time nor the place and only serves to damage your presentation to this court. Perhaps you would care to reconsider your position.'

Mr. Kerim had his instructions and patently had been told to stick to them.

'My government has no intention of harbouring these dangerous subversive elements within its borders. There have already been serious riots with injuries to many people, and damage to property, due to the actions of these Gerons. The majority of the population have complained to their political representatives to put a stop to this sort of radical behaviour. The very heart of democracy in this proud nation is under attack, that is why we have come to this court, Milord, for justice.'

At this there came a burst of raucous shouting from the public gallery, which gradually silenced under Lord Justice Higgins cold eye. He spoke to Archie, who was on his feet, and Milord's voice held a note of incredulity.

'Mr. Brewer. We assume you have something to say.'

'I should cocoa.'

'Quiet Albert.'

'Sorry, Milord.'

Archie stood for a moment with a small puzzled frown furrowing his brow as he looked at Mr. Kerim, then turned pensively to the bench.

'Milords. I find myself at a loss for words.'

'By 'eck!' came from Albert. Archie was mentally wrestling with Mehitabel. While Justice Higgins confined himself to. 'Beg pardon, Mr. Brewer?'

Archie won, but did not dwell on his minor victory.

'At a loss for words, Milords. Mr. Kerim's political colleagues have been making their own laws for half a century, and seemingly cannot get out of the habit. The party which they represented had but a tenth of the total population as their members, and attempted to subjugate the other millions to their will. They succeeded very well in that respect due to the repressive format of their governance, they then found themselves sundered in the collapse of the communist barriers in 89/90. A few top officials and others were got rid of, but the new officials needed bureaucrats with knowledge, for they had little or none, of what needed to be done. The system ground to a halt and no one knew what to do. We did, and we proceeded to put matters to rights. Perhaps we did not apply ourselves to the letter of the law, as those who were desperately trying to hang onto power would consider same. We caused a number of empire builders considerable distress, which we do not regret, and of which we plead guilty. But we fed the people, turned the wheels of industry and commerce, and had the support of the majority of the people. If that is considered by your learned selves to be sufficient reason for committal to trial by this court, then so be it. With respect, Milords.'

With a smile Lord Justice Higgins asked. 'And that is your final word, Mr. Brewer?'

'Indubitably, Milord.'

Justice Higgins turned to his fellow Judges.

'Leggo my mouth, you megalomaniac.' Archie still in combat with Mehitabel.

'It is all yours, Archibald. A particularly unresponsive piece of horse-flesh if I may say so, even if you have just made a passing imitation of a political statement. You may yet make a leader.'

'Better than,... oh, sorry.'

'I should think so. Just wait till I get my new body.'

The resulting judicial huddle over, Milord Higgins addressed himself to the court.

'The judgement of this court is that there is not a case to be answered by the defendants. While the fine line of legal arbitration has no strict definition in respect of differing international societies, we wish to make clear to the other petitioners awaiting their turn certain prime considerations of this court. Regardless of the laws of the lands whence come these plaints, our brief is incumbent upon the United Nations charter and directive pertaining to human rights. We therefore advise those waiting to plead their cases to consider these matters before continuing with their pleas. The evidence we have thus far indicates some violation of the laws of individual nations, but these could be claimed to be justified by the beneficial results of those violations and could bring into question the application of those laws, particularly with reference to the human rights charter. Mr. Kerim's plea for justice, therefore, would appear to be one in favour of authoritarian principle and this is not the purpose of this court. We shall adjourn until tomorrow to allow time for those of you who wish to review their pleas. Court is adjourned.'

Archie heaved a sigh of relief. It seemed this was to be but a storm in a teacup. In a sense it was, but he was unaware of much that was hidden behind this 'little' storm, that promised a major 'blow' in the future. For all the benefits accruing from Geron activities world-wide, there were still many in all walks of life who objected, were even frightened, at the prospect of 'being taken over by computers'. However much evidence to the contrary, the power was still there no matter how well it was used, and the human race had many examples of how power corrupts. What difference the Gerons?

The activities behind the scenes overnight in the opposition camp was intense, as much because of the 'face' that would be lost by a debacle, as confusion engendered by the court's statement on the way the game would be judged; a due legal cause encompassed within the human rights portfolio presented a tangled web no one fancied entering. The general consensus was that guerrilla action in the circles of power would serve their purpose better, the problem being the Gerons having a proven track record in that field of activity. Result, furious stalemate with promises exchanged between these unusual allies that something would be done. But what?

The court the following morning presented a barren field to the spectators gathered for some legal blood letting, many of the protagonists had decamped, the only entertainment left for them was a spirited exchange between Lord Justice Higgins and Mehitabel. Milord, having sensed that Archie was perhaps but her 'mouthpiece', addressed her through him.

'Mr. Brewer. I do not know how, nor in fact do I wish to know for reasons of my own sanity, how you manage to have Ma'am speaking so volubly and exactly via your vocal membranes, but, so that I may feel on more familiar ground, I shall address myself to her through you.'

A small frown briefly clouded his pinkly clear forehead as the full portent of that statement rebounded off his logic, then, before his mental processes could further examine that doubtful conjecture: 'Ma'am. I do not know if you are as yet aware of the fact, but your opponents have cut and run, as it were.'

'Milord. I thank you for that information, I did have an inkling that such might be the case.' Archie confidently answered as Mehitabel badgered him for the right to answer. 'In this instance, however, your assumption was incorrect. I spoke for myself.'

'Well done, young Brewer. A masterful performance, if I may say so.'

'Thank you, Milord.' Archie suitably modest.

''Tis a pity though, I was looking forward to a brief word with Ma'am, if only for old time's sake.'

Nothing could have prevented Mehitabel from responding to that.

'What a lovely thought, Milord. My pleasure, indeed, to converse with you again, and thank you for your just opinions in this case, as ever.' Mehitabel pointedly refraining from thanking Archie for the use of his vocal cords, Archie noted.

'Ma'am. I trust you will not take this the wrong way, but I hope you are not going to make a habit of this behaviour.' Justice Higgins sighed. 'I fear this presages the end of many happy hours spent disseminating legal jargon from enthusiastic verbal jugglers. You are a great disappointment to me, Mr. Brewer.'

Lord Justice Higgins' logic was still trying to recover lost ground. Mehitabel expressed hurt that she had lost her favourite line, Archie enjoyed that, until she took over his circuits again.

'Milord, I am sure we shall find some way of keeping you gainfully occupied in your favourite arena. Besides, what would we do with Albert?'

Albert recognised the style.

'Don't you worry about me, missus. Plenty for me to do round 'ere, system's a right shambles.'

'Shut up, Albert,' came in concert, and they smiled at one another in accord.

'Well, Milord. I will wish you goodbye. Time to go home I think.'

'Yes, Mr. Brewer. Give my regards to Madame Mehitabel. Or whichever one of you is....' Lord Justice Higgins' logic mode gave up, so he descended into Shakespearean dramatics for effect, and because he was now totally confused. 'Parting is such sweet sorrow. I look forward to our next entertaining meeting.'

And they went home.

Archie happy to be in sole tenure of his senses.

CHAPTER TWENTY

'A bloody spaceship?'

'A goddam bloody spaceship?'

'A.....'

'A live spaceship, Archibald. And please contain your language.'

'It is bloody well contained. If I allowed it full scope I'd be banned from the Brownies. A flamin' Gordon Bennett spastic spaceship.'

'Who IS Gordon Bennett?'

'He's a nutter, but he hates spaceships.'

'Really? How strange.'

'Strange? It's bloody ridiculous. So bloody ridiculous it can't be true. You're kidding. Aren't you. Aren't you?'

'No.'

'No? What do you mean, no? It's a wind-up. Tell me it's a wind-up. You cannot be serious. It costs a fortune, a bloody gynormous fortune, so much money I can't even contemplate the zeros, so you have to be kidding.'

'I'm not.'

'Look. Let us be rational about this. Logical. Real-bloody-istic and grown-up. Geron is such a small country, such a new country, such a piddling little entity in the world, there is no way on God's earth we could finance anything like that. Come on!'

'We already have.'

'We..... Mehitabel! You....' Lost for words, Geron's Chief Minister tried to grasp the enormity of the concept and failed. A vagrant word from earlier in the conflict wandered into his thoughts, hovering there as if not certain of its place in the scheme of things. Live. Live? He discarded the unacceptable, then came back to it as drawn like a lemming to the cliff: 'You said 'LIVE' spaceship.' Accusingly.

'Yes.'

'Come on, come on. You don't just drop a word like LIVE in front of spaceship and just let it lie there, not you. What's up?' Archie had visions of a fire-breathing dragon, with a howdah on its back, pounding through space, then callously dismissed it. Mehitabel sat calmly comfortable in her chair in the old canteen, head turned to admire the profusion of greenery and flowers seen through the windows in the gardens beyond.

'I didn't think you were interested, Archibald.'

We're getting somewhere, thought Archie, she only gets pompous when she is going to score points off me. 'I am interested. I'm Chief

Minister of flaming Geron who is supposed to know of these things, so of course I am interested.'

'You have been switching off at night again,' Mehitabel stated with a certain satisfaction.

Archie stayed silent. Guilty as charged, he thought, get out of that, Brewer. He made no attempt to explain his reasons for neglecting that infusive source of nightly information; the answer would denigrate his status as Chief Minister and he was enjoying that role. The intricacies of political management had become fascinating to him, as his sometimes too blunt honesty intrigued those more inured in the gentle art of word games that alienated truth.

'Live?'

'Live.' Clear, succinct, Mehitabel was enjoying herself.

'Oh, come on!' Archie gave in.

'Expanding plastic extrusion similar to our water-carrying desert model, chromosome inducted to grow to our design, with an overall size of a two hundred metre long ovoid, complete with interior structuring for rigidity. Will provide accommodation for fifty souls and able to resist a five megaton explosive force. One outside surface light and heat reflective, the other heat absorbic, to provide heating and water evaporation for energy to drive the thing. That's about it. Simple really.'

'Simple!'

'Perhaps a little technical around the edges.'

'You... you..., um. Oh, yes. Steam won't drive that bulk around the cosmos for a start.' Archie knew it wasn't a winning shot, but it was all he could think of. Mehitabel acknowledged the fact with a condescending smile.

'We simply use the slingshot principle out of earth's gravitational orbit, or any other suitable planet on our travels.'

'Strewth. You mean.....' Archie was suddenly afraid to say what he was thinking.

'Going walkabout in the Cosmos? Yes, Archibald. There are things we need to know, to find out. And they are out there, I feel it.'

'But what about...?'

'Lost for words again? Fine thing for a politician. There is you, Josy, Wicksted, Yussuf, Anthea, the Conclave of Elders with the noble Theodore, ye Gods a veritable army of managers to cope with this little place. Forgive me, Archibald, I have complete faith in your, and the others, ability to take care of any affairs here. I have to go.'

'Have to?'

'Yes. I cannot explain.'

Archie wanted to ask a question, an intriguing query which had concerned him for some time, but he was not sure if he really was eager to know the answer, nor how to phrase the inquiry. But this portent of Mehitabel's prospective departure into space prompted him. Typically, he went at the subject bullheaded.

'How long do Gerons live?'

Mehitabel was, for once, astonished, her green eyes widened as she looked up at her inquisitor.

'Why?' A child's question.

'Well.' Archie hesitated. The subject was a delicate one to humans since none of them knew exactly how long they would live. Even terminally ill patients only had a medical expert's guess given them, and while the Gerons were merely machines, he rejected the connotation in his mind even as it came, they had displayed sensitivity of life forms, such as humans, and he now had deep respect for their honest approach to life. A prosaic approach suggested itself.

'For several reasons. That is, if there is an answer. Population growth is a factor in supplying workers, and therefore economic structuring of production, also in the food and energy needs of a country. We can estimate with our own people according to trends, I just thought we needed to know about yours.'

'Becoming a Chief Minister has done wonders for you, Archibald. I have not heard a more blatantly bland statement for some time. We only work where we are needed, giving way to humans wherever possible, supply our own meagre dietary needs, and have little material requirements in general. So I doubt that our numbers or activities will create any problems, other than those due to your own people's reactions. You are just curious, little man.'

'So, I'm flaming curious, is there anything wrong in that?'

Mehitabel smiled. 'Of course not, you unctuous toad. I have been waiting for you to ask that question for ages. And it gives me great pleasure to tell you I do not know the answer. You made us, why do you not know? Decay times for material, molecular breakdown, you chuck away your machines because they become too expensive to repair or are outmoded by later models. Are you suggesting we set a time limit on Gerons so that you can organise a disposal service?'

'Of course not!' Archie flushed his denial. 'It's just, it's just........'

He spread his arms in an appeal. Mehitabel sat watching him, her lips quirked in amusement at his embarrassment.

'Or a limited gross national product in Gerons?'

'Very funny.' Archie sought a riposte and had to settle for, 'I suppose you could live for ever.'

Mehitabel laughed. 'I doubt that. A daunting prospect if true. I would guess our span might well correspond with yours, perhaps a little longer since our systems will not deteriorate as quickly, unless Kismet is a reality, time will tell.'

'And that's why this space thing.'

'This space 'thing' as you put it, is something I have to do.'

'But why do *you* have to go?'

Mehitabel looked at him in some astonishment.

'Amazing! I never mentioned my going on this journey. Your telepathic sensitivity is improving, Archibald.'

'You haven't answered the question.'

'There is no answer.'

'The great Mehitabel is going to waffle off into space without any reason? I can't believe that.' Archie was pushing his luck, and surprised at his own calm acceptance of what seemed a foolhardy venture. The proposed spaceship did not sound a very substantial structure for space exploration to him, which was why his next question took him unawares, as it did Mehitabel.

'And why can't I go?' Nothing, he thought, being further from his mind, he who fought against travelling anywhere away from Geron.

'You!' Mehitabel's reaction evidenced his best score yet in their continuing verbal contests. 'You know why. You are needed here Archibald, a central pivot my Gerons have come to rely on as the steadying hand of father to them. They are children yet in so many ways. No. You least of all can be spared. Even the humans treat you with respect.'

Which was true. The world politicians found an innate honesty in Archie which caused him to face situations they delicately stepped around as best they might, and found solutions closer to reality than they ever dared attempt. The main factor that enabled this to happen was the Gerons themselves; their abilities transcended anything collectively possible with the humans and, for all their verbal squabbling, the practical things got done. Which gave Archie greater stature world-wide than he truthfully deserved, but then that is a truth many great figures would hesitate to accept about themselves.

'Not that you really deserve all that accolade, but my Gerons still have this funny sense of obligation to you. So I suppose it is all for the best. Are we going to do any work today?'

'When do you go?' Archie was prepared to argue about whether he went or not, but had to think about actually going; his natural cowardice quailed at the prospect of deep space nothing-ness, so the question gave him a 'putoff' time to think.

'How long is a piece of string?' said Mehitabel airily. 'When we are ready.' Then she relented a little. 'Six months at the earliest, a year is more realistic. Plenty of time to argue about it all.'

'And the money for all this?'

Mehitabel paused to eye Archie knowingly. 'You have a puritan soul, Archibald. Think we are ripping off the human population for our own ends, do we? '

Archie hastily denied any such thought.

'Then consider what we now have here in Geron. We established an African money market, which has done rather well.' An understatement since the Geron Stock Exchange had proven an amazingly stable entity in the money world, probably due to the developing African continent's eager use of Geron expertise in their various country's efforts to make them more economic gave the market a sound base. But also there were the Geron brokers' ability to still the panic common to human markets, which created the, recently more common, down turns causing recession. The Geron brokers accepted a greater responsibility toward their clients, instead of forecasting slumps that would hit the markets and advising clients to sell to avoid losses, advocated holding on to see the down period through, thereby steadying not only their own market but the international scene as well. As Mehitabel put it.

'Anthea has done a good job. Our market now is one that other markets use as a guide, and some of your brokers and investors, are discovering that instead of fighting to gain quick profits, or avoid losses by selling if a firm's profits fall thereby creating a mini recession, our people have shown a more prosaic approach gives longer term dividends and helps companies, and thereby their employees, survive. Also world markets in import/export goods are achieving a much more even exchange with our help, avoiding trade battles or price wars. The frontiers are truly open.'

Archie had listened, fascinated as always at how easily Mehitabel outlined changes in human responses which she had caused to come about, but the bulldog was still there.

'The money, Mehitabel.'

She giggled at the way he always bit. 'One percent off the top for all transactions, a trifle in comparison to your costs in your Stock Exchanges, and since our space building costs are not high, using life generation, we only need to fly out the crew when ready, and for that we can use the American shuttle as they seem keen to barter with us for the space ship technology. So you see, your alarums over the costs are totally unnecessary.'

'Very clever. But what about the technical stuff you need aboard? If my memory serves me the costs there are enormous. In fact I don't know if they have any deep space technology that could be used.'

'Ah. You mean radar, radio, and electronic gizmos galore, etc, etc. That stuff. Don't need that.'

'Oh, come on.'

'Come on yourself. You have an incredibly short memory, Archibald. You do recall those marvellous communicating electrons we discussed those many aeons ago? Well, our chaps can do all sorts of things via those little devils. Just like all the electronic gear, and we can do all the things they can, and without the need for maintenance, spare parts or power sources.'

'Like radar.' Archie disbelieving.

'Archibald. How many times have you driven around a bend in the road, instinctively slowed down, and found a hazard just round the corner, totally unexpected, that could have caused a nasty accident, then dismissed the fact of your slowing down as a coincidence. What you did was unconsciously use your own radar via the old faithful electrons, without even realising it. Same as you humans have a built-in compass, which you rarely use, since you seem to prefer making expensive toys which can go wrong. You also have an ability to communicate over vast distances, instantly, which you rarely use. Thought transference, Archibald. No interference, and light years do not come into it, a thought takes no account of distance. Pity your lot do not make more of that, save an awful lot of expense you know. And the electron speed of traverse over vast distances, suggests a time differential, in reference to your concept of time, that could make the past, as well as the future, a viable consideration for those prepared to take the trouble.'

Archibald knew only too well and while he still had difficulty coping with all the mental flashes of incoming information, he appreciated being able to reply without recourse to having to process reams of paperwork. His memory had now expanded to such a degree he could recall details and times at will. Wicksted, Josy and Yussuf, among many others, had also learned this art, thereby negating the need for internal memos, instant mental question and answer sessions making an honest basis for decision-making for agreement, without endless committees and conferences. Unless, of course, they wanted to amuse themselves and indulge in a little acerbic wit and confrontation, usually with some visiting potentate, who were themselves beginning to make ground in these mental callisthenics. Archie could visualise the spaceship travelling with a solitary Geron monitoring all the on-board activity, while keeping an all-round eye on the surrounding space, as well as far ahead of their course. Then, without thinking.

'But why such a large craft for fifty bodies.'

'Oh, silly boy. I despair of you. Plants, saplings, small animal life, all manner of things to establish a pattern of life to survive space travel. You humans will need this knowledge in time; we can provide it with this trip as well as explore the time factor effect.'

Archie was beginning to be aware of an impending loss, blurting out his question without thinking.

'That's it then. You're leaving us.'

'Only temporarily.' Mehitabel hated explaining.

*

Time passed, as time does, correcting many injustices, introducing many more, healing old rifts and creating new ones, people died and babies born, empires crashed and new orders grew, humanity perspired and expired as it had done for thousands of years. The Geron empire, small 'e' due to its distinct lack of pomp and panoply or subjugation of the masses, was now accepted in its growth within the human framework of society.

Human Gerons were no longer exceptions, largely accepted within human society with few problems, exploring even far distant reaches of the planet and bringing a new dimension in understanding to remote outposts of humanity.

But there were areas of discord back in the main masses. The so-called civilised societies were, as ever, behaving other than peacefully toward their neighbours, even to the extent of involving their natural Gerons in their disputes.

*

They had come from all over the world and Archie surveyed them in some dismay. As a gathering of the clan, it was daunting to see the array of nationalities they had adopted, the characteristics of each country they portrayed. If the human behaviour of those races set any precedent, then they were in for a lively time. This quickly became evident as the meeting proceeded on the shady green sward outside the old canteen, the heat of the sun's rays dissipated by the, now high, trees growing around the compound, the light breeze cooled by its passage through the shady acres stretching into the distance.

Theodore, that Grecian head inclined, presented each individual visitor who received a round of polite applause; he then handed over the baton to Mehitabel who rose to a storm of approbation from her fellow Gerons, Archie wincing at the whooping acclaim from some of the Caucasians while feeling at home with the ululation accord from the darker-skinned ladies. The mood of the gathering was obviously enthusiastic. Mehitabel raised her hands in a gently regal gesture. Archie was impressed, then waited for everything to fall apart, having finally realised the Geron's regarded diplomacy as the fount for mis-truth, unless applied to their own efforts at communication. Mehitabel spoke as the last sounds died away.

'I give you all a warm welcome to this, our first council of all the Gerons. You all know why we are here, but, to settle any doubts in your minds, I will set out the finite parameters now.

'For all our abilities at communicating, certain differences of opinion and decision as to what should happen in your individual states have caused friction in international relations. So we are here to try and assess the problems and then, hopefully, create a common aim to benefit us all. We have achieved much in the short time we have been Gerons; let us not now throw away the advantages gained by those actions and let us not forget the responsibility we have toward the humans. Let us not forget.'

Archie shifted uncomfortably in his canvas chair, the suggestion of Geron superiority irked him still, although Josy and Wicksted appeared placid enough beside him – perhaps he was too sensitive. A voice came from the crowd.

'The humans are not the problem, rather the self-opinionated Gerons who think they have the answer to everything and try to force that opinion on the rest of us, those of us not situate in areas with powerful resources.'

The speaker had a suggestion of a Balkan accent to her English. A large bearded figure leapt up in response and began explosively in Russian, then quickly switched to English. 'We gave them their independence and now they complain.'

'We had to fight for our freedom, you gave us nothing,' came the riposte.

'Alright. Alright,' Mehitabel snapped, her reflexes attuned as ever, 'that exchange is a prime example of the problems facing us.'

Archie's mind was flooded with memories of items he had ignored as unimportant, of similar examples of how the Gerons seemingly had ingested the mores of the country in which they had been created. Mehitabel continued in persuasive tone.

'If we cannot use our abilities to be more understanding of one another, then we do not deserve to have the power we at present enjoy. You are Gerons, the old ones by implication the wise ones. Behaviour such as we have just seen does not suggest the title is very well earned. We are using this clumsy method of human communication hopefully to clear mental blocks between us, our ability to transmit mental information en masse is negated by a prejudicial attitude by any one of us and totally defeats the original concept of our creation, the balanced equation of reasoned logic and instinctive understanding, feeling our way to the answers with our minds.'

The two protagonists stood abashed, to Archie's continuing surprise at Mehitabel's power of control. She gave them a moment to ponder, then:

'Is this how we help the humans conduct their affairs? Are we going to allow ourselves to be influenced by the bad aspects of human behaviour rather than the overall question? The answers will not be found by taking sides absolutely. The balance of justice and injustice in the human world is in favour of the latter and needs to be corrected, but not by creating another injustice nor creating the circumstances for future inhumanities, but by thinking, clearly and creatively. You all know what is required of you, just as Irena and Mikhail must resolve this circumstance, within these parameters. All the other issues between you all have the same basic premise, you only want to know *your* answer to the problem, not *the* answer.'

She nodded to the two opponents.

Irena and Mikhail turned to look at each other in some doubt across others heads watching intently. Then Irena giggled.

'Why on earth did you grow that ridiculous beard.'

Mikhail's broad face purpled, then. 'I like the lived-in look.'

'Live in wild life, you mean ? There's enough room.' Irena was not a great one for peace pacts.

'Like your hair?' Nor was Mikhail.

Mehitabel sighed in exasperation. 'Come on, children. This is the wisdom of the Gerons at work?'

The two protagonists looked up at her in surprise. Irena giggled again, Archie liked that giggle, there was sexual potential in that utterly feminine chortle, then winced as Josy's foot neatly hacked a painful spot on his ankle, he always had been too obvious. Mikhail and Irena glanced tentatively at one another and Mikhail deferred to Irena.

'We were just having a bit of fun,' she explained plaintively.

'Fun?' Mehitabel was outraged. 'We are a serious people supposedly discussing some matters of import here and you want to indulge in some 'fun' ?'

Archie took it upon himself to intervene, quietly, in an aside. 'Like those little moments of amusing cross - talk we indulge in occasionally. Remember?'

Mehitabel bridled, then replied softly but maliciously:

'Amusing? You call those acidic exchanges amusing?'

'You're losing your sense of humour M.'

'I never had one. Neglectful of you.'

The assembled Gerons awaited with interest the renewal of verbal combat as Mehitabel turned back to them, Mikhail and Irena still standing, now subdued but occasional glances between them carried sparks of devilry, Mehitabel's tribe enjoyed their irreverence. Their leader pondered this fact before she addressed them again.

'It seems your Chief Minister thinks I am lacking in a sense of humour.' Archie received a glare from piercing green eyes. 'So, instead of proceeding with the business of trying to preserve a reasonable accord between ourselves, and coincidentally the humans, perhaps you would prefer to indulge in a little more infantile humour.'

Mikhail, Irena and the rest of the Gerons exchanged shrugs of resignation as they readied themselves for a blast from above. Then the voice softened. 'On the other hand a touch of humour might lighten proceedings....'

With that came an interruption as Harold's coal black visage sprang up amongst his whiter counterparts. 'Hey, lady! You is free with your advice to these political gizmo's, but you ain't done nothin' for poor working stiffs like me.'

Mehitabel viewed her prime agitator with some irony. 'The word was humour, Harold, not farce. I wonder about your original design, someone imbued you with a mercenary intent at odds with the real world. But do please go on.'

'Well it's like this, lady. My guys is having a hard time makin' ends meet and I gotta say to you that this ain't fair, no way lady, not when youse is rippin' off t'ousands from the banks wit no comebacks.' He stood foursquare and resolute, a black statue. A murmur of support started and was answered with a growing chorus of disapproval.

A small furrow creased Mehitabel's brow. 'Rip-off? Quaint, Harold, very quaint. But untrue. You know full well how we organise our financial dealings with the rest of the world, and 'rip-off' has no credence in those dealings. Your 'guys' have legitimate business operations which are successful when run properly. What you are complaining about is the lack of opportunity for nefarious activities, or 'rip-offs'. Your 'guys' are going to have to contain their unseemly habits or we will continue to keep up the pressure of monetary persuasion. And, by the way, I still haven't forgiven Tarquin for the fruit cup episode.'

'Jeese, that was a mistake lady. Loved the song and dance tho'. But you ain't got the right to take mazuma from our own banks, that ain't right.'

'Mazuma?' Mehitabel muttered in disbelief.

'Money,' tersely answered Archie.

Mehitabel laughed. 'Ain't it? That was drug money Harold, illegal money, so we put it back to work helping those affected by the drugs your 'guys' insist on dealing in.'

'Aw, come on lady. That was legit money.'

'Are you sure, Harold?'

'Sure I'm sure.'

'If you are a Geron you must accept the truth.'

'No, I ain't. And you can't make me, lady.'

'Alright.' Mehitabel sighed in rare defeat. 'Whatever you are, you ain't getting away with nuttin'. Capische?' Archie's immediate thought was that Mehitabel was developing some dubious character traits herself.

'You bin playin' hard ball with us a long time lady, and we is still here,' Harold affirmed defiantly.

'I am well aware of that, Harold, and while I admire your determination I deplore your methods. Tell that to your 'guys'.'

Harold started to mime a particular obscene gesture of American origins, then noticed 'Frightened door' Bernard looming near and sat down rather hurriedly.

'Why do you let Harold's 'guys' get away with it?' As Archie asked her he was aware of having made a mistake, Mehitabel's eyes gleamed in anticipation.

'You know Archibald, that your species has this incredible ability to incessantly attempt to cure the result rather than the cause. Does it not occur to your infantile minds that you help create most of these situations then hurl vast resources at them when it is too late. I like to quietly whittle away at the problem, instead of briefly driving it underground only to have it erupt all over you later on. This way we can use some of their money to improve the ghettos and help the people. Besides, I quite like Harold.'

'Except he's a liar.'

'Really? How original.'

'Well he told me he was out of favour with the 'Bosses' that's why he's black now. Tell me, are all of you going to change bodies at will?'

'Stop changing the subject.'

'It's the same damn subject. Just takes me a decade or two to get the answers.'

'Your cynicism is showing, Archibald. I have a conference to attend to. And I would worry if Harold stopped lying, particularly if I did not realise the fact.'

The meeting eventually broke up with groups of Gerons in enthusiastic argument, others acting as onlookers interjecting the occasional firebrand remark if the combatants seemed to be losing their passion. Archie presumed to remark to Mehitabel:

'Doesn't say much for Geron communications if they are going to go on like this all the time.'

The opportunity was not one which Mehitabel was likely to pass by. 'Archibald, if you would only pay attention to events around you and used that limited intelligence of yours to properly assimilate what they portend, your life would be so much easier. For us at least.'

'Okay,' he sighed, 'lecture time again.'

Josy beamed at him; he was sure there was a degree of sadism in her soul. Wicksted preserved his usual calm, but there was an elemental gleam in his eye that Archie did not like.

Mehitabel made herself comfortable and looked down fondly on her voluble Gerons.

'They have insatiable curiosity and combativeness, game-playing to them is like a drug and the human conflicts present them with golden opportunities to take sides, but only for the eclectic exercise in understanding the philosophies of those humans with whom they share a particular patch of earth. In a curious way, their passionate but reasoned arguments have disseminated a lot of the incipient violence in those drawn into the anarchic folds, those masses around the fringes of the minority core of true fanatics. Those assiduous workers at achieving their own power by revolution have been quite dumbfounded by the new reasoning of their former pliant recruits and martyrs for the cause. I must say I am very pleased with the way my,' she paused, wryly considered the energetically combative Gerons, then seemingly satisfied with the choice of word, continued, 'flock have taken each complex confrontation and dissected each side's point of view in its totality, then merged both arguments to show the narrow areas of disagreement and gaily indulge in extremely caustic discussions in front of both sides. It is amazing how they see sense when they are shown just how childish they have been. Children with weapons of destruction ready to hand, however, can respond in violent ways. Fortunately we have thus far avoided that terminal circumstance by the use of humour, even the Muslims like to laugh, and most of your people really only want to lead reasonably contented lives in harmony with others, leaving contentious issues for long term answers which time provides as a matter of course. Whether these are the right answers depends largely on how they are used.

'Unfortunately you humans have shown in the last era how difficult it is for you to cope with the rapid changes in your own evolutionary progress, so the very speed with which we can change operational circumstances, ostensibly for the better, is something which mitigates against acceptance and changes necessarily need the support of those principally involved, otherwise, as has been shown in your past history, these changes will not always be improvements even if the initial benefits are amply proven. In time other aspects could support an argument against further change. Your kind have displayed a profound penchant for destruction while supposedly seeking civilised development, so it has also shown how to dissipate these gains in madly chasing economic and social status. And your forward projections have been shown to be severely prone to error. Now we have concepts in that vein for the next two hundred years, and frankly they do not hold out much hope for your species, nor for many forms of life with whom you share this planet. We have ideas as to how to circumvent these disasters but they need the humans to co-operate, and think, with us. That is why you see this Tower of Babel before you. We can only persuade, not force, therefore we need to tune our proposals within prejudicial structures you have erected in your various communities and religions delineating whole new aspects of thought enabling the cant and bigotry to be shown in its true perspective, then you can start to think and grow.'

'Strewth!' was Archie's only comment, while his mind tried to encompass the enormity of what she had just stated. Josy and Wicksted remained silent, lost in their own contemplations.

'That is where you came in Archibald.' He dragged his thoughts back to the present and did not much like, nor want to consider, the implication involved. Life had attained a comfortable, ongoing, steady and pleasantly undemanding style for him. Mehitabel was suggesting a challenging future that he was loath even to consider.

'Me?' His voice squeaked, a display of reaction under pressure that he hated. He lowered an octave in a cover up and basso croaked. 'Why me?'

'Are you, or are you not, Chief Minister of this fair realm?'

'Well, yes.' Reluctantly.

'Then, as the elected representative of my people, that is your future role. This...' she waved at the congregation still deep in acerbic contest, '... was intended to show you the extent of the problem facing you. Each of these Gerons represents one of the many human races of some size; each of them has all the historical, economic and social details, not just of that race but all others, thus enabling them to consider the total complexity of their difficulties and in time, hopefully not more than a decade, will see human responses achieving a greater understanding. Your role, with the Council of Elders and Theodore, will be to correlate these actions. You do follow what I am saying, Archibald?'

Archie managed to take a breath to speak. 'Only too flaming right. No, thanks, I resign,' He sensed rather than heard Josy's sigh of disappointment in him. 'Well I'm not a Geron, I haven't got your ability....' He stopped as the smile on Mehitabel's face grew.

'Really? It is nice to know you have such confidence in us, Archibald. Well, well. But that is just the point. You do have the ability, all of you. You just do not choose to develop those senses and mind capacity, preferring to use 'machines' such as we were.' The subtle emphasis on the last word was not lost on Archie or the others, Josy smiled. 'Therefore, and you were elected by the votes of the Gerons, you reject your responsibility and I do not think you will be able to live with yourself.'

'Nor I!' came succinctly from Josy.

Archie grumbled. 'A man can't even have a mind of his own.'

'We're trying to give you one!' snapped Josy.

'I can get my own thank you!' Archie could be as prissy as the best.

'Come on Archibald,' coaxed Mehitabel, 'think about the magical opportunity, at the centre of a movement to allow humanity to catch up philosophically with its material advancement, and get it all into perspective with their neighbours.'

Archie resented the superior manner of this indictment of human society seemingly ignoring the many complex factors involved. So he said as much.

'We've been coping with all sorts of difficulties and disasters over thousands of years, civilisations have grown and fallen then new societies from those. We've fumbled a bit on the way and we know there is a lot to do before we can say we're as civilised as we would like to be. But you are what you are because we made you, clean, unencumbered by the past which could trouble your future.' His association with politicians had definitely developed his word play, Josy was not impressed, nor was Mehitabel, but Archie liked it. 'So you can propose ideals which we would love to follow but know are impractical in the immediate future, but you refuse to see that.'

'Archibald,' the tone was not promising, 'you are Welsh,' the inflection was dubious, 'and you probably played that obnoxious game of rugby,' she ignored Archie's attempt to protest, 'and react if anyone criticises your team, and your countrymen still blow things up like childish revolutionaries, intelligent, educated, and totally demented.'

'That's unfair.' Archie finally got his protest in, and noticed with pleased surprise that Josy seemed to be on his side, for once.

'Archibald. The evidence is there in your history. If you go right back in time you see that all the internecine wars between the various tribes are carried on intermittently through the dark ages to now and will undoubtedly continue wiping out the innocent and the weak ad infinitum, unless you start thinking 200, 300, 500 years ahead to see if you want your future generations to die in these interminable and bloody squabbles.'

'Some of those were justified in the past.' Archie went carefully, if somewhat pompously, 'and hopefully will be prevented from happening in the future.'

Josy turned away in simulated disgust while Wicksted raised his eyebrows at Archie in humorous disclaimer. Mehitabel merely smiled as at a child.

'Archibald, you teach your children an adulterated form of history to suit each nation's own point of view, your private history and nowhere near the truth, a political history that has your nation, tribe, whatever, as the good guys. The supposed bad guys do the same. The really bad guys indoctrinate their kids, brain-wash them, even the presumed good guys do the same in more subtle ways, your educated liberal or the criminal, the manufacturers and publicists, the music and entertainment industry, all of you. And you wonder why the human race is a mess. You argue on narrow perceptions or sociology with little, if any, consideration of the broader perspectives. The mass of the people simply want to live peaceably and in ignorance, potentially enjoying themselves in mundane pursuits without realising the magic all around them that they actually dispute, because to accept its reality is extremely disturbing to their small personal world.'

Josy and Wicksted were now nodding in agreement, while Archie scrabbled in his mind for some response. Mehitabel reached out a hand to him in a placatory gesture.

'The answer is something your people have run away from for years. Truth. That is your task, Archibald. With my Gerons you will search for some way of educating your people. The problem you will have is that the truth has many facets and can be dressed in many guises, you will probably need many times more than five hundred years for that task, and even then only arrive at a semblance of that primary premise. But if you do not try, you know you will regret not doing so. And that is why you have to stay here when we go.'

'Eh?' Archie's mind had been far away from that consideration.

'You cannot come with me on the space trip.'

Archie looked at her in amazement, but wisely did not respond with the comment that trembled on his lips: 'But I wasn't bloody well going to.'

CHAPTER TWENTY ONE

He watched the rapidly diminishing white streak in the clear blue sky and experienced an immense sense of loss. He was forty years old, happily married, a circumstance brought about at Mehitabel's insistence, 'I'm not leaving you in a state of sin Archibald, or, more particularly, to inflict that state upon Josy.' Then argued the case with that lady because Josy was not sure that she needed the legal and spiritual constraints of marriage to feel secure in her relationship, but succumbed out of respect for Mehitabel's views. But, in the consanguinity of the marital bed, would occasionally mutter in moments of pique at his territorial incursions into her space, 'Damned if I can see the sense in giving a snoring, smelly man the right to shove me all over my own bed.'

And now he stood with Josy, his new wife of a few short days and watched, with the small group composed of Wicksted, Alison, Yussuf, Anthea, Frightened-door Bernard who had pleaded to be allowed to witness the momentous occasion, Howard, who had surprisingly arrived to bid Bon-voyage and insist to the last of his non-Geron state, and Theodore, who had so impressed the Americans with his statuesque Grecian bearing they were almost servile in their desire to grant his every wish. Mehitabel had insisted that her Gerons keep the departure secure from media intervention so there were only the technicians in attendance, apart from this small group silent in their own communion with that departing craft, the last of the flights spanning several months which had prepared spacecraft Delphi for its imminent departure.

Archie had been most impressed with the way the normally garrulous Gerons world-wide had kept secret the entire event and, despite the numbers of humans involved, they too had resisted the accolade and gains that disclosure would have brought them. The media were discovering that the Geron control of computer medium was proof even against their much vaunted, if ethically suspect, investigative journalism. No trumpets blew nor bells rang, no cheering crowds to whoop them on their way, a few friends whose loss was deeply felt waited silently until the last traces of the shuttle faded into the upper atmosphere, then filed away with brief goodbyes, remembering, until their lives and work eased the loss.

*

Since Mehitabel's rapid departure into the wide blue yonder, Archie had assiduously applied himself to the tasks surrounding him, his own species constantly creating more problems for Geron consideration, always expecting the help they received to be given gratuitously, often ignoring the advice dispensed as freely considering same an imposition on their rights, even, in some cases, changing an in situ beneficial system that was Geron originated for one that reverted to a 'gimme' philosophy, the arbiters being the beneficiaries. Tyranny and dictatorship, with the attendant repressive regimes, still abounded, but Archie had come to appreciate the subtle machinations of Mehitabel's mind now those very regimes were suffering from a restriction she had explained to him in the year before departure.

Mehitabel had been in expansive mood, due to having sampled one of Wicksted's exotic alcoholic mixtures, and was filling in one of the many blanks in Archie's mental filing system on Geron activities.

'We thought it would be an idea to use the bureaucrats' favourite weapon, delay and procrastination against themselves, and also any intended build up of offensive weaponry; in particular chemical, gas or nuclear, which threatened peace anywhere, would be nullified without their being aware of any interference. We merely misdirect or obfuscate production or dispatch, there is in fact an amazing build up of these supplies in an obscure outpost in the Antarctic with no forwarding address. Puzzling isn't it? A bit like trying to trace your luggage at Heathrow or Kennedy Airports.

'All your technical expertise and much vaunted scientific knowledge are often proven at fault, high tech equipment that mysteriously fails, knowledgeable precepts that have to be changed because of new discoveries, while our production or planning Gerons will sense an error or put forward a scientific precept that considers nothing proven, only viable, because we cannot know it all. Yet the amazing and laughable fact, for the Gerons at least, is that you humans have the same abilities, and have demonstrated so except that you choose to call those exhibiting these talents freaks of nature.... your water dowsers, even a rainmaker, dowsers of ancient underground sites, honest psychics, mediums and others of sensory perceptions. And they make so many incredible excuses when some technical bit fails them, so we thought we would help promote the error-making in certain aggressive areas. It also makes them so mad when a vital little bit is missing, or unaccountably fails. But do not tell them about the bits that never work because we changed the design a smidgen. It really is all very satisfying.'

'Didn't I hear something about tanks that refused to fire?' Archie was beginning to be aware of that familiar hole in the pit of his stomach presaging large future diplomatic problems. But he had given up arguing against the inevitable by now. 'Something to do with the programming being wrong?'

'Ahum,' Mehitabel had the good grace to look embarrassed, 'not exactly Archibald. It seems the conversion to Gerons of those tactical computers was taken too literally, my – er – request was for them to be imbued with an awareness of the destructiveness of the forces they could unleash, this seems to have been a trifle over emphasised.'

'Like the tank that refused to fire because it frightened the fish,' Josy giggled.

'Something like that,' Mehitabel drily responded. 'But the purpose has been served, since there are a large number of very frustrated warlike gentlemen, and ladies, with some rather expensive machinery that refuses to blow things to bits.'

'Didn't I hear of some guided missiles that buzzed their own firing sites?' Archie was recalling some incidents he had dismissed as exaggerations.

'It is possible.' Mehitabel did not want to dwell on the subject knowing how Archie's now keen mind could ferret out some aspects that he would happily use for confrontation on ethical grounds. He had developed some aspects of honest appraisal that smacked of prudish application of ideal perspectives. 'But let us get on to more important things.'

'I'd like to follow this up a little.' Archie sensed an opportunity to gain in his now long-standing mental chess game with her.

'I am sure you would Archibald, but some other time.'

Mehitabel firmly avoided the game move.

*

The Gerons were now enhancing their status in relation to their human friends with the use of their talents in assimilating and dispensing information, organising in concert on an international level as well as local or social, enabling the human society to be more beneficial in its use and dispersal of world resources. The prime factor in this creation of harmonious development was the Geron ability to scythe through the petty rivalries and personal aggrandisement that normally affected these activities. As in Los Angeles with its immense urban spread with the ubiquitous car and smog difficulties; by taking the simple action of giving the reinstated tram service the right of way over cars, they had eliminated a major traffic delay, followed that up with integrated bus and car mutual-ride operations using the on-board mini-computers in the Geron network, so that individuals needing rides could be picked up within minutes by a passing car, in safety, and either dropped at destination or taken to the nearest convenient tram or bus for a minimal fee in overall costs terms that had been agreed in a Geron organised referendum.

Car Gerons were amongst those who educated their humans into the art of genuine economies, as well as practical exercises in pollution control at a basic level. Some humans had already been organising mutual car rides on this very principle. The Car Gerons turned the elementary beginning into a complex structure that yet worked quite simply in practice.

The crafty Gerons mixed their passengers with the skill of match-makers into social cooperatives, causing many a party to be well under way on the journey home. The parties' mix caused a certain initial coolness on the wives' part, but, since many of them were working and experiencing the same events, the events were broadening rather than an incitement to loose living. The advantage the Gerons had was in the instant communique, the sensing of a balance of character and instant recourse to details of work place, hobbies, personal history et al of everyone in an area with immediate co-operation and information from all the other Gerons. Those men and women who did not work found themselves subtly shown how their lives might be made more useful, and interesting, to them.

Then there were the meetings Archie had with old acquaintances among the Gerons.

Like the day when he felt impelled to glance out of the old canteen windows while in an intense discussion with some irate visiting dignitaries who fervently wished to return their bureaucratic systems to the old ways, and their control. The sight of a fully accoutred Red Indian sitting in colourful splendour in the middle of the green, with a crowd of respectfully distanced onlookers of various nationalities in grinning appreciation, was more than sufficient excuse to arise and leave the heated assembly, which hardly noticed his departure.

As Archie approached the seated figure, he was pleased to note a welcoming smile on the ironcast features.

'I see you, Mr. Brewer. Are the natives friendly hereabouts, particularly to an old pavement?'

'John Twofeet!' Archie's delighted shout startled the crowd, then they saw his beaming smile and shuffled forward for a closer view of this strange being who appeared on favoured terms with their own chief. 'What are all the pedestrians going to do in Bond Street now. It was Bond Street, wasn't it?'

John Twofeet laughed in pleasure. 'Wrong, but close. I was pushed upstairs to superintend the passage of millions of feet, began to think I was getting a foot fetish so decided to explore my origins as per my original programmer, only to find he was of Arabian descent and not American Indian, just happened to take their side in Westerns. So here I am, a Medoc Indian exploring my Bedouin ancestry in Geron, and that might not be such a far fetched connection at that.'

Archie laughed in genuine pleasure. 'I like you, John Twofeet. Come to dinner.'

Which was a spontaneous invitation causing a certain turmoil like: 'You invited a Red Indian to dinner! A Red Indian who was a pavement?'

Followed by: 'Who the hell do you think you are, saying he could stay here without consulting me! Get back here, Archibald Brewer! Your death is imminent.'

Then: 'I like John Twofeet. It's so nice to have an intelligent conversation with a gentleman for a change.'

Then Howard arrived, with Tarquin.

'I am NOT having that Mafia hood in my house.'

'Just how long are they staying? I'm sure that Tarquin is spiking the soup with something.'

'Stop complaining about losing at cards again. And Tarquin hasn't been teaching me to deal off the bottom.'

Or. 'Serve you right. If you will go out boozing with Wickie, Yussuf and Bartram till all hours.'

The excuse being the perennial male error of not quite being able to cope with the female mental and emotional processes, Archie having witnessed a hurried Wicksted departure from his home pursued by an aggressive piece of flying crockery, or Yussuf trying desperately to placate an irate Anthea without understanding anything of the cause.

But the underlying essence of all was the that of contentment, the conflicts reconcilable with their own growth with one another, greater understanding of the whole and the desire to know more without disturbing the balance of their small world, nor the greater cosmos beyond, their individual depressions and black moods learned from and then highlighted by the creative frenzy afterwards. As beyond the tiny enclave of Geron the women of the world found new strengths from their shared responsibilities with the men, instead of the previous introversion of trying to prove themselves equal, or better, they discovered that unique quality of life in tolerance of oneself, which led in turn to tolerance of others and progression to acceptance of fate's twists and turns, regardless of how unkind these seemed at times ; the acceptance of a lowering of their own standards of living to enable the human consumption of the earth's riches to be slowed, while their men learned that power was a fortunate gift that had to be used wisely and not dissipated by ego. As those with the power of religion discovered, the truths were gems to be sought for and not plucked from theological cant like swords of wrath which curved back in vicious circle by causing the very iniquities they pronounced against, as in the Muslim world evidenced the plundering greed of those misguidedly launched on a 'Holy Jihad', now thankfully shared their world even with 'infidels', and found them not bad fellows, as well as having some principles that fitted the words of Mohammed rather well. A God is a God is a God, and only man would gainsay such a Deity or be able to twist his words to suit a lesser purpose.

And the Gerons learned. As Archie blithely stepped through the spring flowers of a distant desert one day with John Twofeet on a shared joyfully silent expedition with Charlie and Achmed, two surprise visitors appeared through the haze blur of heat to be recognised first by John Twofeet with an exclamation of incredulity.

'Jenny and Francine? Here? Lookatem!'

'Who?' asked Archie, as the figures resolved into young ladies accoutred in hiking backpacks somewhat at odds with the flowing Arab robes and burnouse, then remembered, 'Ye Gods. Those two fashion plates, and as you say, here of all places.'

The ladies spoke as one. 'Oh, no! John Twofeet, of all people.'

Archie felt disposed to ask of the sensibility of their being so far into the wilderness on their own and, from the smallness of their packs, short on supplies. Jenny responded with some spirit to this critique:

'With respect, Mr. Brewer, you forget our Geron constitutions, our needs are small. And, come to that, what is that pavement doing out here, going native ? He was enough of a nuisance in his original role.'

'Putting upstarts like you in your place? A noble cause I would have thought.'

'We were applying our intelligences to higher matters than transporting feet, as indeed we are now.'

'Such as?' interposed Archie hurriedly, anxious to avoid a Geron verbal contest in the peace of the desert.

'There's a rare desert flower which has possibilities in preventing skin cancer. We're looking for specimens so as to propagate them in quantity for testing. A human problem. Just thought we'd help.'

'A veritable transformation,' John Twofeet was not being kind. 'What price high fashion now, and how are the high and mighty fallen.'

Archie was tempted to intervene on the ladies' behalf, Josy's training having at least partly shaded him as a gentleman, but he was too indecisive, as ever.

'At least we formulated our own thoughts and decisions. That world was worthy of the experience but paled after a while, now we have a satisfying purpose. Which leaves a grubby pavement to explain how it justifies moving from a humble mode to associating with the hoi-polloi.'

Archie was about to object to the status, again, too late.

'Cerebral matters beyond the simple machinations of social ingenues.' John Twofeet was getting into his stride. 'Flowers are about your mark, leave matters of state and diplomacy to the experts, children.'

'You are asking for a thick lip, Twofeet.' Jenny waved an unladylike fist in close proximity to his nose causing his eyes to cross.

Mildly, John Twofeet asked: 'You still wearing those pink silk French knickers?'

That was when she hit him.

In the cleaning up process Archie was interested to note the blood from John Twofeet's nose was surprisingly real, a matter he would like to have pursued with him, but for acting as referee in what was rapidly degenerating into a fascinating little brawl. Archie argued for restraint and civilised behaviour. 'He's a blasted pavement that looks up women's skirts for kicks.' Jenny was keen to resume her display of pugilistic ability were it not for Francine holding her back with surprising ease, to Archie an interesting example of Geron strength but also as a feature of aggression being an act of show since he knew Jenny could have broken John Twofeet's face with one punch if she chose.

'Stupid female,' as he dabbed at the flow of blood substitute from his nose, 'if you knew how your voices carry when in that shrill shopping mode, you'd know I couldn't miss hearing. Trust you to carry the human exercise a bit too far. That hurt, you know. And I was always too busy to want to gaze at your nether parts, not much of a view anyway.'

Francine nearly let Jenny go at that, but she had the reply without physical emphasis.

'Oh, dear. I suppose we have to make allowances for a pavement, one of life's lowliest functionaries, who progresses downwards. Going to be a moving road through the desert, duckie? Should suit your dusty soul and murky thoughts. Alright Francine! I only wanted to have one smack at that nose, nearest thing to an eagle's beak I've seen, just wanted to make sure it was real. Hurts does it, dear? Good.'

Even John Twofeet had nothing to say to that. Nor had Charlie and Achmed when they returned to night camp and found the two girls there, until the evening progressed and they thawed from their desert stillness, although to begin with Charlie and Achmed had presented the impassive desert face to the new intruders, which in turn only intrigued the ladies more and Jenny attempted to out-stare Achmed, dissolving into helpless laughter when she failed, miserably, then delightedly catching a quirk of a smile at the corner of his mouth. After that the barriers came down, slowly it is true, but then Archie could sit back and enjoy the cross-talk, amazed at the ebullience of the desert men in the company of these two transposed town flowers and at the speed of exchange of ideas and knowledge between them, playing with words in deference to him while performing encyclopaedic transfers in their minds. Archie was conscious of these mental callisthenics while sitting silently, also aware, in this desert fastness, of the immensity of his human lack of knowledge in just this square yardage of sand. That they still treated him with respect humbled him to a degree, but flattered also in that it made him aware of his own qualities in reference to them.

He returned from the trip with thoughts of Mehitabel.

Archie fondly remembered Mehitabel's forthright statement: 'To the devil with ecology and economics, these people are wasting their own prime asset, themselves. A whole lifetime spent in, ultimately, boring play instead of facing reality as another of life's microbes in the battle to survive, and that it can be magic, it is magic, once you know how much you do not know, and learning can be fun, the mental searching and joy of discovery. Mind you some of them actually go too far when they realise and become even more boring going on about all those wonderful things they know and can do, all the good they are doing. What is it with you people? Have you never heard of softly softly catchee monkee?'

'Only in my dreams, M.'

'Josy feed him fish, his brain is going.'

'You think there's enough left to nurture?'

'I'm not fighting both of you, but, and I think it's a good 'but', there are a lot more people interested, and actually active, in promoting ecological and economic balance, so I think the criticism is a little harsh.'

'My life, Archibald, you have learned well, a politician's politician. Give an element of truth the greater status of fact and you have an viable argument. Too narrow a perspective Archibald. They pick their subject and hammer it to death trying to find an answer without considering the broader aspects, and no answer is possible that way because all you do is create other problems down the line. It needs all the people and institutions to evolve a concerted effort, and the ordinary individual has to make the biggest sole contribution because it means containing their desire for material benefit, and that elusive fantasy you call security.'

'What's wrong with security?' Archie looked at Josy in pleased surprise at her question, a rare support for his point of view. She grimaced in response. Mehitabel smiled.

'Is this an inbred human feeling for hiding from reality? Security is a negative, security means safety, in reality a fantasy. You insure against something happening so that you do not have to face the reality of the event, your house burns down or your child is cruelly killed, you rebuild the house on insurance but pay no heed to the myriad factors involved in that occurrence for you, apart from the practical aspects of how did it burn down, did you in fact cause that happening by your own actions, overworked – tired – careless, irritable with wife she leaves some power item on, simply living your life within a narrow band of experience with little control or understanding.'

'What about the dead child?' Josy again.

Mehitabel, with a sympathetic smile, 'You would feel that as a prospective mother.' Archie sparked up, Josy waved him to silence. 'People die, things die, in your terms that is the end, but what if that was merely another change in state, the spirit moving to another plane of existence alongside the one you inhabit now, there is much evidence for this, but little belief because your people are afraid of reality, yet believe if they can touch something it is fact and that as a comparison is ludicrous because a fact is only a presumption in the first place.'

*

The wooden bungalow home favoured by Archie and Josy from the very early days in preference to the palatial style residences deferentially suggested by Theodore, was now in a glade of its own surrounded by stalwart trees and thickened shrubbery. There was one substantial knoll with but some shrubs dotting its grassy sward where Archie could view the surrounding woods and bungalows and contemplate again the contrast with what had been before. This spot also served the purpose of a view of the heavens and a pensive soliloquy on that small departing craft. Archie could achieve a feeling of contact when there and Josy came to understand his wandering off in late afternoon to his contemplative patch.

In time Archie found himself experiencing vivid mental pictures of the inside of the spacecraft which was now several light years away in dark space, the life aboard being delineated colourfully and actively, then the changing view of space beyond the clear panels. Initially he balked at this seeming fantasy presenting itself to his consciousness, then, relating these intrusions to his thoughts of Mehitabel he began to believe this far-distant contact was viable, even began posing questions in his mind to Mehitabel, and gave credibility to the mental replies by their acerbic style, and the fact that the first response that came to mind was. 'You took your time, Archibald. Where have you been?'

In due course Archie passed the impressions he received on to Josy, relishing her initial scathing disbelief then flattering acceptance followed by the childlike enquiries as to what was happening aloft, woman-like neglecting to tell him that she was also in communication with the distant Mehitabel. Even Theodore and the Conclave of Elders complimented him as being the equal of a Geron, a comparison that unexpectedly flattered, but also enabled him to communicate more freely with Theodore and the other Gerons than he had before, and that made him feel good – better than the compliment.

Then there was the day, some months after Mehitabel's departure, when Archie felt constrained to call a meeting in the old canteen for no real reason except he felt a need to confer. The attendant principles were to be Theodore and his ethereal Conclave of Elders, Anthea, Alison, Yussuf, Wicksted and Josy, with Archie leading them in through the familiar doorway, then causing Josy to use a few of her favourite names for him as he neatly stepped back on her toes while muttering, 'It's her ! But... but.. how?'

To which he received the reply over Josy's verbal castigation. 'For pity's sake come in and allow the rest access, Archibald.'

To which the others responded in joyous chorus: 'Mehitabel!'

Sitting in her normal chair at the head of the table was indeed that lady, substantially healthy and present. 'Shall we dispense with the how's and why's by saying an exponential hologram by mind waves, a little difficult, but I think we have mastered the process now. Close your mouth, Archibald, you look like a fish. Hello to you all, and congratulations.' This taken to refer to the nuptial arrangements by Anthea and Alison who bloomed prettily while their spouses, Yussuf and Wicksted, displayed political cool, until Mehitabel neatly speared their image. 'I sense a fecund atmosphere.'

Archie looked baffled while the women beamed, then Archie realised and joined the men in that bemused state that afflicts them in times of female perception. To gain more familiar ground he asked,

'Why didn't you forewarn us of this visit.'

Mehitabel gazed at him with innocent guile. 'We were not sure if it would work.'

Archie exploded, concerned in spite of himself. 'You mean you could have ended up... anywhere?'

Mehitabel smiled. 'Not quite. Don't forget I am a hologram Archibald, but it was interesting for a while until we got it right.'

'And of course you had to be the one who...'

Mehitabel interrupted him without a qualm. 'We really must get on, Archibald, I have a little time but my body is travelling away from us at quite remarkable speed and we are a little hazy on the distance factor at present, and while this is a hologram it does contain an element of myself which I would hate to lose. Shall we?'

Archie sat down with little grace as Mehitabel beamed upon the others. 'It really is delightful to see how well you manage things. There are, however, one or two minor points I would like to make. As regards the Arab question, I think we should look at a broader perspective, take a for instance: Archibald is Welsh but refers to himself as British in polite company, and they are probably the most mongrel nation in the world yet they get all emotional about their country, they argue like fury amongst themselves like a family, then unite if anyone else criticises them. By comparison America is a hotch potch of separate ethnic types who cling to their past because it is a young history whereas the Brits were mongrels 2,000 years ago.'

Mehitabel paused, the faces round the table were intrigued, but for Theodore exuding Grecian calm.

'Arabs, Jews, Russians, Germans, Australians, all of you humans have mixed blood but choose, choose... to proclaim your nationality, and then have the gall to proclaim your nationality and talk about tradition. The oldest tradition there is, you deny – prostitution – the religions you have are all youngsters in time, the traditions you claim span less than a hundred years, parts of them go back further but have been bastardised over mere centuries. You are like a bunch of squabbling kids who can't think past the end of the day.'

Mehitabel chose to ignore Archie's hrmph of disapproval and smiled at Wicksted's diplomatically raised eyebrow as she continued. 'I have been making some interesting correlation between the Muslim belief that wealth is transitory and money not a commodity, that those blessed with wealth have an obligation to share with the less fortunate, but contradicts this principle by the Koran urging individuals to labour and increase production, thus endorsing capitalism and fair profits also encouraging the acceptance of risk but forbidding speculation. So they run two monetary systems in direct opposition to one another.

'Then, in contrast, the Western markets operate in reverse. The profit factor operating alongside a welfare structure and with an aid programme for less fortunate nations even if the western country has a national debt itself, while the Socialist structured states have a similarity to the Muslims in that the populace follows, or is pressured, to follow the national or religious dictum and suppresses the intellectual creativity unless one conforms rigidly to the party line. Yet the capitalist world engenders the monetary God and consumer fever to survive.

'None of these systems or the similarities thereof work satisfactorily for all.

'A suggestion is that the individual is convinced to become a shareholder, not just in the company or firm in which they work, nor yet the nation in which they live, but the world which all inhabit at this time.'

Wicksted proffered a thought: 'What about the Japanese cradle-to-grave principle in their companies?'

Mehitabel studied him indulgently. 'Thinking again, Wickie? Must watch that . A touch too tyrannic in practice I feel, epitomises the Nippon culture and will become, is becoming already, more individual, as will the Socialist and Capitalist ethic, but there will be great need for the ordinary people to accept the TOTAL individual responsibility, which is needed to arrive at a workable compromise with a much better understanding of the whole.'

Archie injected a provocative question. 'What's the answer, then?'

Mehitabel eyed him with the exasperation of an indulgent mother. 'There is no one answer, Archibald, only many in proportion to the different needs. If your humanity had evolved in a way relative to the whole, we would not be here now like this. One thing about deep space is how your thinking also expands to a greater awareness that also leads to more questions to the answers. Also the input from 'outside' is immense and there is so much knowledge and awareness out there. The answers lie with each and every one of you, every circumstance has a reasonable and plausible result if you take your profit and power motives and reduce them to realistic in terms of all the others affected.'

Josy had become a little prim and tight lipped. 'I'm sure all those who work in welfare projects and the like are dedicated people who work hard and with principle.'

Mehitabel was suspiciously kind. 'They are fallible humans, Josy, and as wrapped up in their own material gains as others, regardless of how you care to dress up the presentation. Reality is a painful acceptance, my dear, the truth is even harder. A few, pitifully few, are that dedicated. Most seek the profit or power, even while doing the job well in their own and their peers eyes. That is where your main problems lie. If you are as effective as those around you, there is no need to question yourself; anyone who does question is a radical who is usually in a minority and has few real friends, nor cares, for they are confident in their rightness. For some extreme radicals this is justified, but the gentle human searching after truth is told to accept what the others see as reality, and you all see reality differently so the imbalance is made worse without being accepted as existing.'

'So what's the answer?' Josy was piqued, Archie knew the signs well. Mehitabel seemed unconcerned.

'To seek the answer truthfully, examine yourself, judge yourself, find comparatives in others and make your own honest balance. Honest, Josy, and being really honest with ones-self is the most difficult thing humans can strive to achieve.'

Mehitabel's outline began to blur and Archie began to rise in some concern. Mehitabel responded as ever:

'Yes, Archibald, I know. I must go back. We have not mastered the mental energy necessary as yet for full control of this exercise, there is enormous mental power out there which we are beginning to communicate with. Stop worrying, Archibald, we can manage, even if I have to stage it in space and, after all, I am there in reality, just might mean a touch of vagueness for a while.'

Archie snorted. 'Vague! You!'

And Mehitabel had gone, with a whisper of 'Goodbye all' on the air.

It was some time before they broke up and went back to work. One of the subjects was the transmission method for their thoughts to that distant craft. Theodore finally resolved the initial discussion with a Mehitabel-like presentation.

'If you do not commit a vivid enough picture of the destination, or recipient, then the electrons will simply random the message as they pass it along. Similarly, you have to be ready for incoming detail to distinguish same from the random information from the cosmos electrons. Simple really, just takes practise.'

Archie looked at Theodore long and hard to establish that he was not in fact Mehitabel, but the Grecian head did not respond as she would so he relaxed again.

*

The sun was falling to its demise in the west at the end of the day; Archie was getting in Josy's way in their kitchen when he beamed: 'Hey ! They're playing about with light energy in photons, they've re-designed the solar sails in a new reflective plastic and the plastic rods are genetically built to react to their instructions, hang on, to adapt shape for light from the Sun so they can vary their course through space. Strewth.'

'Yes. I got that too.' Josy was delighted. 'We're receiving the same messages. Oh, come on, you grouch. That's good.'

Archie was not sure about that, he liked to think he got personal messages from Mehitabel, so he diverted the conversation. 'I wish I knew when she'll be back. I miss her you know.'

'I know.' Josy was watching him with a knowing smile. Archie shuffled uncomfortably, that knowing smile did it every time, so he changed the subject again, or thought he did.

'I'll just go up the hill for a while.'

'We eat in half an hour, Archibald.' The smile followed him, she knew he was going to try for a private chat with Mehitabel.

The 'hill' was a hundred yards away among the now mature trees, a sloping mound some fifty feet high where the trees thinned out to give him a clear view of the approaching night sky and a mind's eye sight of Delphi and Mehitabel. Archie could spend time there with his thoughts on that far off ship-of-space and ponder the imponderable. But today his eyes caught a movement below him.

On that side of 'his' mound was a small glade beside another bungalow and a small figure skipped across the grass, light-dappled by the lowering sun. The child was bouncing along in that carefree contentment of her own magic world. He looked up at the reddening horizon imagining a mental contact with the distant Geron ship. A sense of deep space and peaceful contemplation came to him.

'Hello.' The child's voice piped beside him and a small hand slid confidently into his own. Archie looked down at the open cherubic face.

'Hello. Who are you?'

'I'm a Geron,' she stated proudly.